Belinda Jones
Café Tropicana

arrow books

Published by Arrow Books in 2006

5 7 9 10 8 6

First published in the United Kingdom in 2006 by Arrow

Arrow Books
Random House UK Ltd
20 Vauxhall Bridge Road, London, SW1V 2SA

Random House Australia (Pty) Limited
20 Alfred Street, Milsons Point, Sydney, New South Wales 2061, Australia

Random House New Zealand Limited
18 Poland Road, Glenfield
Auckland 10, New Zealand

Random House South Africa (Pty) Limited
Isle of Houghton, Corner of Boundary Road & Carse O'Gowrie,
Houghton 2198, South Africa

The Random House Group Limited Reg. No. 954009

www.rbooks.co.uk

A CIP catalogue record for this book is avilable from the British Library

The Random House Group Limited supports The Forest Stewardship
Council (FSC), the leading international forest certification organisation. All
our titles that are printed on Greenpeace approved FSC certified paper carry
the FSC logo. Our paper procurement policy can be found at
www.rbooks.co.uk/environment.

ISBN 9780099489870

Typeset by SX Composing DTP, Rayleigh, Essex
Printed and bound in Great Britain by
CPI Bookmarque Ltd, Croydon, Surrey

Café Tropicana

Belinda Jones's first paid job was on cult kiddy comic *Postman Pat*. Since then she has written for a multitude of magazines and newspapers including *Sunday*, *Daily Express*, *Empire*, *FHM*, *heat*, *New Woman* and *more!* magazine where she was a staff writer for four years. Belinda's widely acclaimed first novel, *Divas Las Vegas*, was voted No. 2 in the *New Woman* Bloody Good Reads Awards in 2001 and *On the Road to Mr Right* – a non-fiction travelogue love quest was a *Sunday Times* top ten bestseller. *Café Tropicana* is her fifth novel.

Praise for *The Paradise Room*

'You won't want to put this feel-good read down'
Company

Praise for *On the Road to Mr Right*

'This is definitely worth cramming in your suitcase'
Cosmopolitan

Praise for *The California Club*

'A riotous page-turner, full of witty observations about life and love'
She

Praise for *I Love Capri*

'With more twists than a bowl of fusilli and more laughs than a night out with the girls, *I Love Capri* is as essential as your SPF 15'
New Woman

Praise for *Divas Las Vegas*

'Great characters . . . hilariously written . . . buy it!'
New Woman

Also by Belinda Jones

Fiction
Divas Las Vegas
I Love Capri
The California Club
The Paradise Room

Non Fiction
On the Road to Mr Right

To embark on more fabulous journeys with Belinda Jones,
visit her website: www.belindajones.com

For Ty Simmons

(and everyone with jungle fever)

Acknowledgements

Unlimited gracias to James Breeds, the ultimate travel companion. (I'll treasure our Costa Rican adventures forever.) Kudos to my genius brother, G, for the exquisite map design. Golden beans a go-go to Ivan at www.ivantours.com, Lauren at Punta Islita and Jimmy & Derek at the Mawamba Lodge.

Complimentary biscotti to Gilly for the coffee tour of Bath and Uncle D and Suzanne Jones for toasty hospitality. Samantha Pengelly, you are a big-hearted starlet. Cheers to Claire Wallerstein – brilliant author of *Culture Shock! Costa Rica*, belated gratitude to Teddy for his insightful wisdom, monkey hug to Charles Thom for being such a loving, supportive delight and to my eagle-eyed mother and her amazing proof-reading skills! Also to handsome pragmatist Olly (with a y!) Richards and the newly-engaged J & S – congratulations!

Whole latte love to Kate Elton, Justine (ta for the waterfall inspiration!), Emma, Emily, Claire, Louisa, Robs N & W and all at Random House for your stellar dedication, patience and enthusiasm! Frothiest cappuccinos to Eugenie, Alicia, Dorian and Alice at William Morris Associates.

Finally to my father for squeezing my hands and

telling me 'I know you'll do the right thing!' at just the right time! Thank you!

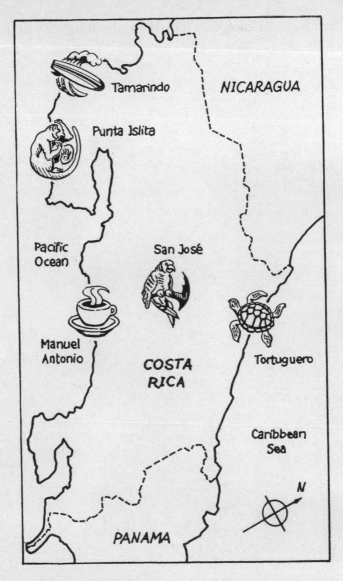

Tamarindo

NICARAGUA

Punta Islita

Pacific
Ocean

San José

Manuel
Antonio

COSTA
RICA

Tortuguero

Caribbean
Sea

N

PANAMA

© Gareth Jones

1

Yesterday my father married a woman I've never met. Today he tells me he wants us to meet. Why now? I want to ask. My approval is hardly mandatory or he would've introduced us before he made a big firework display of his feelings. (I mean really, just how heinous must she be if he only dare unveil her as a fait accompli?)

Of course divorced parents marry people their children despise all the time, but generally offspring are given the opportunity to become consumed with resentment and loathing before the grown-ups say 'I do'. That's just basic etiquette.

I can only assume Papa Langston and his ladylove became so deeply engrossed in each other that the outside world misted to a hazy irrelevance. Only now that everything is official, and thus a little more grounded in reality, is it dawning upon them that they may have overlooked a key element or two . . .

'Didn't you say you had a daughter?' I see a

quizzical look playing upon the brow of the new bride as the couple – now with matching surnames as well as bathrobes – breakfast on some sublime private balcony.

'Why yes, I do!' I imagine my father's initial startlement, softening to a smile of recollection as he nods, 'That's right, her name is Ava.'

'I'd like to meet her sometime,' my stepmother chimes as the sunlight turns her spoonful of marmalade to glowing amber.

'Really?'

'Well, she is your flesh and blood!' Here she leans in to flick a flake of smoked kipper from his chin. 'The way I see it, that's just more of you to love.'

'By golly, you're right!' he toots, throwing down his monogrammed napkin. 'I'll get on it this very moment!'

'No rush,' she shrugs, already disenchanted with the topic and ready to move on to more pertinent issues. Like where's the top-up on her Buck's Fizz?

But my father is already on a mission: 'On the contrary, my love – I consider it my duty to summon whatever your heart desires with the utmost expedience!'

And so it was, in my mind at least, that he reached for the phone and dialled my number. Never mind that it was 5 a.m. UK time. At first I thought I was dreaming, what he was saying seemed too absurd, but then I realised that only in my dreams is my dad considerate of my feelings. Here he was announcing that he'd married a stranger and demanding I drop everything to jet off to Costa Rica for cocktails and awkward small talk. Yup, I was most definitely awake.

'Couldn't you have waited until I got there to marry—' I stalled. 'What was her name again?'

'Kiki.'

Sick. Surely that's a name for a chihuahua not a human. 'Well, couldn't you?'

'It was a very spontaneous ceremony,' he said, his low tone smacking of a sexual urgency that made me shudder. 'But it's not too late to get acquainted,' he continued in earnest.

'Well, I'm afraid it's just not possible at the moment,' I brisked, sounding as businesslike as I could while splayed beneath my duvet in Betty Boop pyjamas. 'I'm in the midst of a property deal.'

'Then I really am your father!' he teased, inappropriate as ever.

My dad is in real estate. For years he's been goading me to grab a rung on the property ladder but, almost to be contrary, I've resisted. Even now it's just a year-long lease I'm bidding for but if I had the money I'd go the whole hog – this is a project I am so besotted with I can't wait to do the deeds.

'Why don't you give me the details and I'll see if I can't speed things up a bit?'

'Dad—'

3

'Who are you dealing with? Hamptons? Humberts? Hobbs?'

It's like the bloody mafia with him and estate agents.

'If it's Giles & Sons they owe me a favour—'

'Stop!' I yowled, taunted by the digital redness of my alarm clock. 'Firstly, I'm handling this. Secondly, even if you could speed things up that would just mean I'm all the more committed to staying here. As soon as the property is in my name I'll be overseeing the refurbishing and equipment installation, finalising the branding and marketing strategy, a million things!'

'So you're opening a business?'

I couldn't believe I'd let the cat out of the bag like that! I so wanted this to be all mine, no outside interference. Even conceding the word 'Yes' made me feel uneasy, as if I was giving too much away.

'What kind?'

I fidgeted within my bedsocks. Just how ambiguous could I be without being noticeably rude?

'A café,' I told him in a tiny voice, half hoping he wouldn't hear.

'A café, that's great! So what's the USP?'

There was no way I was going to give away my Unique Selling Point to someone I barely knew so I simply said I was aiming to supply a divine caffeine fix without the £3 shafting offered at more established chains.

'Interesting,' he mused. 'And you don't think this fabulous new career could wait even for a weekend?'

I took a Lord-give-me-patience breath and calmly reminded him that it would take me the entire weekend just to fly there and back, as well he knew.

'It's only a two-hour hop from Miami,' he reasoned, without in any way being reasonable.

'But I don't live in Miami, Dad, I live in Bath. Remember – jolly old England?'

'But Kiki really wants to meet you.'

I rolled my eyes. Of course. It's all about her. Or, more specifically, about him looking good in her eyes. My sigh came with a hint of a snarl. For someone who travels so much it's funny that it's never yet dawned on him that planes fly both ways.

'Tell you what, if it matters that much, bring her to me,' I challenged.

'Well, you know I would, darling, but . . .'

Oh here we go, I thought, the usual barrage of excuses – another day, another deal. A fine excuse when it's his money, but this time instead of him bandying around words like conveyancing and completion I hear 'honeymoon'.

I shouldn't have been surprised. It is, of course, the natural follow-up to a wedding, yet somehow I'm offended that Dad has deemed Kiki worthy of his personal time when he never extended that courtesy to me.

As he talked I thumped my head on the pillow, jolting the stack of questions racking up in my brain: where did you meet? Where's she from? How long have you known her? Are you sure she's not just after your money? Are there any other aspects to your midlife crisis I should know about?

'Listen, Dad, I've got to get some sleep,' I cut in, deciding that the less I knew, the less I'd be troubled. 'Why don't you call me later?' I put down the phone and roll over.

Married. My dad just got married without telling me! It's not like I needed to be consulted – his life and my life overlap so little these days – but it would have been nice to at least have been invited to the ceremony. Sometimes I wonder if he does these things deliberately to ram home just how insignificant I am to him. If Kiki (urgh!) hadn't expressed an interest in meeting me then would he have bothered calling at all? Maybe a year from now he would have referenced his wife in passing and I would have realised he didn't mean my mother and then it would have all come out.

'Didn't I tell you? Oh yeah she's terrific. Right little firecracker in the boudoir. In fact, you've got a little sister on the way.'

I sit up in bed. *She might already have children!* I might have just acquired stepbrothers and sisters without even realising it – whole new dimensions to what I laughingly call my family. I try to call him

6

back to find out more but the only number I have for him is out of service.

As usual, just when I need him most, he's utterly unreachable.

The next morning he calls to beg some more and each day he dangles bigger and glitzier incentives. On Tuesday he offers to fly me business class. On Wednesday he offers to pay for a friend to come too. No. And no again.

'Come on, Ava, if the estate agent calls you can dash straight back but you know these things can drag on for weeks.'

'It's too important to me, Dad. I want to be here.'

I find it infuriating that he's so dismissive of my commitment. This is the biggest thing I've ever done, I'm on the verge of a dream fulfilled, and to him it's just a glitch that's stopping him from getting what he wants. He doesn't have the first clue about the planning and the passion that has gone into this.

After years of fiddle-faddling with different careers, thinking I had to have a title like 'accountant', 'office manager', 'beekeeper' etc. (and ending up as a combination of the first two at a local architects' firm), I realised that the highlight of my day was my afternoon java. I loved the ritual of it, the sense of stepping into a haven where, for thirty minutes or so, I couldn't be got at. Not that I think the world is out to get me, but there's some kind of alchemy that goes on in a coffee shop that soothes the soul and revives the spirit. In that moment all you really have to worry about is foam preference and fluid ounces. I was never once too dull or too single or too chunky of thigh to inhale the fragrant wafts of French Vanilla. On the contrary, the warmth from the china in my palms transfused throughout my body giving me a cosy-calm centring sensation. Like liquid meditation.

'I wonder if they'd let you rent out one of these tables as your desk?' my best friend and co-worker Ollie pondered one day as we sat in the Bridge, a dinky, duck-your-head café set within the blond stone arches that wade across the River Avon in an achingly picturesque fashion. 'You are so Zen in here.'

'Are you inferring that I am a tad manic in the office?'

'A tad? Noo,' he shook his head.

'More than a tad?' I raised my brows at him.

He smiled benevolently. 'I just sometimes think you might be happier with a can of squirting cream than a marker pen.'

I grimaced, thinking of that morning's presentation, then looked over at the girl behind the counter – seventeen if she was a day – and all the treats and nifty gadgets she had at her fingertips: the cake tongs, the cinnamon shaker, the mushroom-shaped tamper to pack down the espresso powder, the ching-chinging till – and it reminded me of playing shop and hosting tea parties as a child. 'Can you imagine owning a place like this?' I mused, hugging my mug to my chin.

Ollie cocked his head to one side.

'What?'

'I don't know, it's funny, I've always thought older people owned places like this. Other people . . .'

And then his eyes met mine and we had the same thought. The thought that it could happen to me. I was old enough. I had savings. I'd seen FOR LEASE signs. Suddenly my breathing became exaggerated and my eyes flicked around trying to process the rush of possibility. We scrabbled for paper and scribbled feverishly, trying to keep up with all the ideas springing from our lips.

'Maybe it should be themed?' Ollie's eyes took on a crazed glint. 'So many tourists come to see the Roman baths – what about centurions instead of waitresses?'

Already I was talking over him. 'I know there's a tea room serving Mrs Bennet's lemon drizzle cake at the Jane Austen Centre but we could hire our very own Mr Darcy in a white shirt!'

'And the hundredth customer every day could get to throw a glass of spa water on him!'

I snorted delight then rattled onward: 'What's that Austen quote? "Who can ever be tired of Bath?"'

9

What about recliners and foot masseurs for sore-soled sightseers?'

'Or you could literally go the bath route – have claw-footed tubs instead of sofas, toilets as seats!'

'Rolls of loo paper instead of napkins!'

'That's such a terrible idea!'

'I know!' I screeched. This was a hoot!

I didn't do a jot of work that afternoon, every time my boss's back was turned I was scanning commercial properties and ceramic wholesalers online. Then night and day my thoughts were consumed with visions of me hostessing the cutest café in town: I'd wake up in the morning and my first thought was which speciality roast best suited the day ahead. As I percolated in my dinky kitchenette, I toyed with the idea of becoming a local eccentric known for serving my pre-10 a.m. customers in my pyjamas with bed-hair and sleep-gunked eyes. I'd open the dishwasher and wonder if I could give discounts or self-service refills to regulars who came with their own mug? Over break-fast I'd chew on what side-of-the-saucer delicacy I might offer instead of teeth-shattering biscotti.

Each day I'd leave the house early and visit (aka spy on) a different café, assessing their strengths and weaknesses. I loved the stencilled wall quotes at the Metropolitan Café but decided I'd prefer lyric-free music so as to not to direct people's thoughts. I salivated at the menu at Bar Chocolat – opting for

10

the white chocolate and cinnamon milkshake – and, despite feeling a bit sick, wondered if I might also offer smoothies. I envied the fact that Sally Lunn's had laid claim to the oldest house in Bath and wondered what I could do to create the newest must-visit establishment.

I timed service, tipped the smiliest staff and read *The Complete Idiot's Guide to Owning and Running Your Own Coffee Shop*, learning that, in terms of picking a location, having competition nearby is actually a good thing – that way you know the area can support your kind of business. So that's why Caffè Nero and Starbucks were comfortable with being separated only by a toff's clothing store on Old Bond Street. Interesting.

Though these places were always chock-a-block with customers, I decided that the decor in the popular chains was too masculine/laid-back gentlemen's club for my taste. I didn't want tea-shoppe chintz but I had to come up with an alternative to leather chairs, dark mahogany tables and bare floorboards. I started window-shopping at furniture stores instead of boutiques on the way to work. And I couldn't wait for my lunchtime powwows with Ollie.

'What about internet access?' he enquired the day we reviewed Carwardines at the Podium shopping centre. 'Little cybernooks. High-speed servers – and by that I don't just mean waitresses that move really fast.'

I giggled and then shook my head. 'Nope.'

'Nope? How can you be so dismissive? It's the way of the future.'

'I'm sure it is, but people who go to internet cafés go there to check their emails which essentially means checking out. They're not interested in their surroundings. I want people to be present so that they savour the company they're keeping and the drink they're supping.'

'Fair enough.' He reached for his own beverage then choked halfway through his sip. 'I've been meaning to tell you all day – last night on TV I saw this guy whose mission in life is to visit every single Starbucks in the world!'

'What?' I was aptly incredulous. 'There's got to be thousands!'

'Over nine thousand at the latest count!' Ollie confirmed. 'Aside from America, he's already been to branches in Spain, France, Japan . . . They're actually making a documentary about him called *Starbucking!*'

'Starbucking? I love it!' I enthused, then frowned. 'But it's never going to end, is it? They're forever spawning – *Coming soon to your cupboard under the stairs!*'

'I know, but I can't help envying him. He said: "Every time I reach a Starbucks I feel I've accomplished something, when really I've accomplished nothing."'

'I know just how he feels!' I collude.

'Speaking of an utter lack of accomplishment – work?' Ollie helps me to my feet.

'I never want to be that big,' I informed him as we strolled back to the office. 'I want to keep it personal.'

'Just one signature store?'

'Well. I wouldn't mind secretly owning a few, but all different. Obviously I'm going to have to start boxy and tucked away, but one day I'd like a place with a terrace or a balcony or a view . . .'

'A Brew With A View! Hey! What about that for a name?'

'That's a keeper!' I acknowledge. 'I'll copyright it for when I find a place that isn't opposite a dry-cleaner's.'

'I can't believe how hard it is to find a decent venue.' Ollie gave a sigh loaded with sympathy.

'Well, I'm seeing two more tonight so fingers crossed.'

'Names . . . names . . .' Ollie mused as we backed against a wall to allow a swarm of OAP tourists to pass. 'What about Oliver Macchiato?' he turned his head to mine.

'What, because you're so macho?' I scoffed at the lovable bear of a man beside me.

'Nooo! As in Oi'l hava macchiato. Oliver Macchiato!'

'Oh good Lord!' I clunked my forehead with my hand as we continued on.

'I've got more!'

13

'One!' I granted him as we loitered outside the office door.

'Whole Latte Love! Like the Led Zep song—' He broke into the chorus of 'Whole Lotta Love' complete with de-nuh-na-nuh-na guitar impression.

'I get it!' I held up my hand to make him stop. 'It's cute. If entirely inappropriate.'

Ollie grimaced as he held the door open for me. 'You're still hurting, aren't you?'

If by hurting he meant I was still beating myself up over my last relationship failure – Nick, thirty-three, cocky recruitment consultant with a chin dimple – the answer was yes but instead I shrugged and said, 'You know what? I'm fine. This project is an excellent distraction. I'm just impatient now to get it up and running.'

It was very nearly the truth. Besides, Ollie had been such a rock during the aftermath of the break-up, I didn't want him to feel his listening ear hadn't helped. (It was one thing having my girlfriends commiserate with me but I found his manly pragmatism bolstering in a whole new way, possibly because here was a guy, albeit a gay one, being so nice to me in the wake of one so mean.)

That said, it was actually me who did the dumping. But only because I felt I was being broken up with in less direct ways – I couldn't bear the slow-burn rejection.

My girlfriends said, 'Good riddance to bad

14

rubbish!' But is it ever that simple? Though abrasively brash at times, Nick was still a human being. Someone I slept next to night after night. And someone who ultimately increased my fear of being alone.

And, while he was at it, my fear of being with anyone else. Ever again.

I think it's fair to say that I'm actually ashamed of the person I become in a relationship.

The minute I start going out with a guy, I feel his feelings first and mine second. I always want to be available to him so I'm loath to schedule any arrangements until I know his plans for the week just in case we'd end up not seeing each other for a run of four days and then that would send him the message that he's not my priority and then he'll leave me for someone who makes him feel special and I'll be alone and riddled with regret. But by waiting on him to show his hand I get resentful that he gets to decree how the week is going to shape up and I get annoyed with myself for sitting with my hands demurely folded in my lap and not having the courage of my convictions to state, 'I'm going to yoga with Danielle on Monday and on Friday a group of us girls are going out dancing.' I'd be afraid of what that would start – he'd think I was out having fun without him so he'd plan some get-back night out with the boys and then where would that lead? Better I just keep a low profile socially so I can

15

always offer him a perpetually open door and a warm bed.

One of the symptoms of all my energy going into becoming the girl of his dreams, is that my personal ambitions dwindle. With Sean, the guy before Nick, I turned down a job that required me to work three evenings a week thinking that would be detrimental to our relationship, only to have him accept a transfer to Edinburgh within the month. I don't want to be that girl any more – the one who becomes compulsively self-sacrificing and feels paralysed until she receives his permission to move. But I have to be realistic – I can't trust myself to meet my own needs when I'm with a guy so the smartest thing for me to do is to stay away from them.

Especially now that I've finally found something that really matters to me.

The only person I would consider sharing the café experience with is Ollie – despite all this recent talk of weddings, I'd take his friendship over a romance any day.

2

At 6 p.m. as promised, my estate agent – aka mump-faced Mo – took me to see two new options. The first was a dank no-no, but the second was It. Perfection. Or, at the very least, Promise.

As soon as Mo led me down the narrow city-centre arcade known as The Corridor, I got chills. The other shops might seem curious neighbours – a skateboard retailer, a studenty record store, a laser hair-removal surgery – but the overall design with its high, greenhouse-style roof, wrought-iron twiddlings and gold-painted lion-head accessories spoke to me of Regency flamboyance.

The store itself was glass-fronted with a picture-frame trim. Inside, an interior balcony offered an intriguing split-level effect. I loved the potential for having two looks within one. As I climbed the spiral staircase, visions of dainty porcelain demitasses danced before my eyes, fronting a chorus line of cupcakes. How fitting to serve high tea upstairs!

17

High tea . . . As the words registered I started wondering how I could link that to the downstairs area – High Tea & Low Coffee? What's another word for low . . .? I gnawed my lip. Well, it's the ground floor . . . Oh my god! High Tea & Ground Coffee! I spun around in a tizzy of excitement! It was all I could do not to run out into the street and shout the name of my café at every passing pedestrian! I was on to something; I could feel it. Upstairs I'd have ornate mirrors and candelabra and chaises longues in plum velvet. Downstairs would be golds and ivories and a lovely warm fireside vibe. Cosy decadence – I'd found my theme!

'I'll take it!' My voice was a trembly shrill.

'Well, it's not quite as simple as that – the next step is to submit an application to the landlord—'

'Yes, yes. Tell me exactly what you need and I'll get it for you. I have to have it, Mo. I love it. *I love it!*'

He beamed a great, puffy-cheekcd smile, and I mirrored it right back at him.

Then I skipped – *actually skipped* – all the way home.

It was exactly one week later that my dad rang and dropped the bombshell about his wedding. At the time the only calls I was interested in receiving were from Mo or the assorted suppliers I was priming with my needs so, aside from the shock factor, a lot

18

of what he said was just blah-blah-blah to me. I got that he wanted me to visit him and Kiki in Costa Rica but he was deluding himself if he thought I'd leave now. After months of 'too poky', 'unworkable floor space', and 'would have to hire an armed guard every time I opened the till', I had hit the jackpot and I wasn't going anywhere.

Now it's Thursday. Having already deflected Dad's daily enticement, I'm not expecting any more international calls but nevertheless I check the caller display when the phone rings at noon.

Oh joy! Oh heart tremor! It's Mo! He's got news, I can sense it.

'Hello!' I squeak, barely holding back my celebratory squeal.

'Ava, I'm so sorry—'

My heart dips violently. Oh no. Oh no. 'What is it?'

'They got a better offer.'

'What?' I'm stunned. 'What do you mean? I agreed to their rate—'

'They were offered 20 per cent more. I'd counter but I know that would put you way over your budget.'

I open my mouth to protest but I can't argue with that. I was already at my limit.

'So that's it? It's gone?' I can't believe it. I've given my notice in at work, taken my overdue holiday and made myself free to fully devote myself to a café that doesn't now exist.

'I really am sorry.' Mo sounds equally gutted.

I put down the phone and sit motionless, unable to even cry. It seems incomprehensible to me that I could lose something that felt so mine. There must surely be some mistake? This can't be real. And no amount of 'it obviously wasn't meant to be/something better will come along' platitudes can placate me. I know for a fact that this was it. My one shot.

I think of all my research, the measurements, the custom-made purchases, the orders poised for submission . . . none of that counts now. I have nothing. No café. No coffee. No customers. No career. The disappointment is unbearable.

With every hour that passes I become more wretched. And weak. All my recent failures seem to pile on top of me, muffling my very breath.

I'm almost glad when my dad does call again so I can lash out at him, my bad-luck charm.

'They'll be others,' he begins.

'No there won't!' I spit, instantly scornful. 'Have you looked at the property trends here lately? Do you have any idea how expensive Bath is? That was it. The perfect place. The only place.'

'If you knew how many times I felt that when I was starting out—'

'Dad. Please. It's not comforting to have you say these things. It's just irritating.'

I wait for him to chirpily announce that I can now visit him in Costa Rica since there's nothing to keep me in Bath, ready to argue that I intend to descend into a deep and all-pervasive depression that would make my mother look as smiley as Sandra Bullock, but he doesn't go there. Maybe Kiki has gone off the idea of meeting me.

'Oh, Dean,' I can hear her tutting. 'Ava is so last week. What I really want now is a pony with gold-painted hooves.'

I hate everything and everyone. Especially my stepmother.

'You know, I have to confess your talk of coffee shops got me thinking,' he takes a new tack. 'It's still very much a developing market here in Costa Rica. And a booming one too, especially with all the American tourists who like their coffee a very specific way. I really think there could be an opportunity for you right here in Tamarindo.'

'That's a really long commute,' I grizzle.

'What if you came out and helped me set up for a month or two?' He tiptoes around my claws.

'What do you mean?' I didn't see this coming.

'I want to tap into your expertise. No doubt you've given this a lot of thought—'

'I have, but all my plans relate to Bath. I don't know anything about the market there,' I object.

'But I do,' he counters. 'At least I know the property market. You know the coffee business, and getting some hands-on experience in a country that produces its own beans . . . Well, that could only

21

benefit you, surely?' He pauses before adding, 'You'd be doing me a huge favour.'

He so nearly had me.

'Think about it,' he persists. 'My business savvy, your coffee consciousness, Kiki's people skills . . .'

'Kiki?' Oh here we go.

'Well, it would be a nice little project for her after you've gone back.'

I sputter and shake my head. There was I thinking he was doing this for me when really he's just using me to indulge his spoilt brat of a wife. I can just picture how this all began:

'*Chérie*, I'm so sorry – Ava can't come because she's opening a café.'

'A café? Oh that sounds adorable, can I have one?'

'Of course, darling! I'll get right on it – what size do you want – tall, grande or venti?'

Oh how they must have laughed.

It's just so unfair. I've spent the past six months working on every last detail of my dream only to have it taken away from me. Kiki mentions it on a whim and she'll no doubt be frothing cappuccinos before the week is out.

I shake my head in despair – if they think they're going to benefit from all my research and sales forecasting and creative brainstorming, they are sorely mistaken. Wake up and smell the coffee, people! Nothing and no one could persuade me to return to Costa Rica.

3

Fifteen years have passed since my last trip to Costa Rica. I hear a lot has changed. It has certainly become more fashionable as a destination. Previously, when I said my dad lived there people would look a little confused and wait for me to explain that it's the small Central American country between Nicaragua and Panama, famously resplendent with nature. (Did you know there is more flora and fauna per square foot in Costa Rica than any other country in the world? – 850 species of bird, 10 per cent of the world's butterflies, 9,000 plants including 1,500 species of orchid, all in a country about the size of Wales!) Previously I just had to say the word 'biodiversity' and my friends would swiftly change the subject. Now I get, 'Oh you're so lucky to have a relative out there! Haven't they just opened a new Four Seasons in Guanacaste?'

The deluxe turn-down service was definitely absent from my teenage experience. Dad had only just moved into his first property there and had yet to furnish it so we slept in a pair of matching hammocks, lullabied by the rattle'n'whirr of a plug-in fan. I remember my scaremongering mum convincing me (down the phone from the UK) that I was going to get 'banana-spine disease' if I spent eight hours a night in a crocheted curve but frankly that was the least of my worries. I, like any normal child, had a horrible fear of all things reptilian and there were far too many scaly-skinned, gnarly-nailed creatures skitting across the terrace tiles for my liking. The last thing I wanted to do was to go visit them in *their* home, but running out of ways to amuse me while he was wheeling and dealing in his office, Dad got his native assistant, Chepy, to take me on a nature trek though the rainforest one afternoon.

We'd barely snapped one twig underfoot when I freaked out at the sight of a gargantuan iguana – easily three times the size of Dad's 'pets' – with pimply-bobbly armour-plating, a horrible scraggy neckflap, a crest of rubbery prongs and a long, thrashing alligator tail. It was all too *Jurassic Park* for me – I stumbled backwards, tripped on a root, reached out to steady myself and gashed my hand on a rogue nail sticking out of the wooden bridge we were about to cross. That's when the really freaky thing happened – and I swear to god this is true: Chepy picked up a giant leafcutter ant, had it bite my wound closed, and then pulled off its body so its jaws would remain clamped like a stitch until we could get medical attention. Naturally I fainted, somewhat impeding my transportation back to civilisation. (Ticos, as the Costa Rican people are known, are predominantly a petite, lean people and my puppy fat was no match for Chepy's dainty physique.)

Ultimately I was returned to my mum's care scarred, splotched with sunburn, riddled with diarrhoea and having nightmares about headless beasties for weeks.

My mother forbade me to ever visit my dad in Costa Rica again and I was grateful. When she went to court demanding full custody neither myself nor the judge argued with her. What kind of father lets his daughter get burnt and bitten and just laughs and says, 'It's character-building!' Little did I know then that watching over my freshly divorced mother would be far more painful than any animal incisors.

Every day I'd see her fall apart a little bit more and it made me all the more determined to stick myself together with superglue. She let her grey grow in, I dyed my hair a brighter shade of red; she stopped wearing make-up knowing it would be sluiced off with her tears within the hour, I went to the No. 7 counter and asked them to recommend a stay-fast new look. She wore only tracksuit bottoms and pyjamas, I found that structured jackets and tailored skirts made me feel together and in charge. (And I wonder why I ended up with an office job. Even at uni I looked like a visiting auditor.) I don't know whether I was doing it for both of us or to distance us, to make sure everyone could differentiate between us – the mum might be in pieces but look how great the daughter is doing, she's really got it together!

As long as I looked smart on the outside, no one questioned what was going on inside.

At the time, what was going on inside was basically a lot of trepidation, especially with regard to dating. I offered a unique combination of clingy and one-foot-out-the-door when it came to relationships. It was tough living with a cautionary tale – 'Look what happens when your man leaves you!' my mother's whole being screamed. 'This is the fate that awaits you if you give yourself fully to a man. They'll wreck you. They'll take your soul. And your will to pluck.'

I used to wonder if I might tweeze her eyebrows when she was sleeping. Maybe smooth on some face cream and flush some blush on her cheeks. But it wouldn't have made any difference. It's almost impossible to look pretty when you're bitter on the inside.

She wasn't always this way. She used to be radiant, playful, known for her throaty laugh and flirty eyes, but Dad leaving knocked all the stuffing out of her and she never recovered. It's spectacularly depressing to see her with no hope, no self-esteem, just a pair of shadowy eyes and a snipey tone of voice. There's not a thing I can say to convince her that she doesn't have to live out the rest of her days wishing him harm and hurting only herself. Worse still, whereas her situation torments her daily, he's never looked back. Doesn't give a fig. I don't believe he ever even said the words, 'I'm sorry.' Just, 'I'm leaving.' Or rather, 'I've left. Please feel free to slash all my shirts.'

She seems to have made a home at rock bottom and I wonder how much bare-handed burrowing into granite she would do if she knew her ex-husband had remarried.

'Well, obviously she won't be breaking out the Babycham but that's no reason to turn down his offer!' Ollie reasons when I meet him for lunch at a juice bar (because right now I can't even be around the aroma of coffee).

'You don't think she'd find it a tad disloyal if I set up shop with Mrs Langston Number 2?' I cock a brow.

Ollie shrugs. 'If you want to protect her, don't tell her. It's that simple.'

'Well, I've no intention of telling her about the wedding but you're not suggesting—'

'You hardly see her these days,' Ollie cuts me off. 'She probably wouldn't even notice you're gone.'

'Dad's talking about a month or two, not a week's vacation!' I protest.

'So tell her – she won't hear you anyway.'

He's got a point. Her own misery seems to drown out all other voices.

'Anyway,' I continue with my resistance, 'my mum's reaction is only one aspect of me not wanting to go.'

'Come on, let's hear it!' Ollie sits back in his chair.

I snuffle a sigh. Ollie and I normally get along so harmoniously, but today I feel like he's deliberately baiting me. 'Okay,' I begin. 'Why on earth would I want to fly five thousand miles to put on a pinny and serve lattes at Costa Kiki or Kiki Rica or whatever absurd name my father has planned for this café? Why should I let him exploit my expertise and then let her take all the credit and have him boost his bank account when for the past fifteen years he's barely—'

'AVA!' Ollie lunges at me, gripping my upper arms. 'Can you take off your dad-hating blinkers for a minute and see what's in this for you?'

I gape back at him, shocked and embarrassed. My dad always brings out the pouty child in me. I'm not sure I know how else to be when it comes to him.

'You want me to see what's in it for me?' I repeat in a small voice, trying to win back Ollie's approval.

He releases my arms. 'Let's try it this way – what exactly do you gain by staying?'

I open my mouth but nothing comes out.

Encouraged, he smiles at me. 'Well obviously you'd continue to have the pleasure of my company if you stayed, but I can assure you I'll be here when you get back. Nothing ever changes with me, so how could you be missing anything?' He takes my hand. 'I might even visit you out there.'

'Really?' I brighten for a second but he's already moved on.

'As for your so-called expertise . . . not wanting to sound harsh, but none of that is practical or proven at this point. Can't you see this for what it is: an amazing opportunity to test-run all your ideas at your father's expense – he's paying for the flight, the accommodation, all the café bills, it won't cost you a bean, pardon the pun.' Ollie's just getting started. 'It makes me think that maybe you were supposed to lose High Tea & Ground Coffee so you would go out there and discover some fabulous hidden gem of a plantation and make all the personal contacts that'll give you an amazing deal for when you do return and open the café that you were destined to run.'

'Have you ever thought of switching to sales?' I risk a little cheek.

Ollie gives me a playful clip. 'Your problem is that you're too charged with emotion right now, you can't see the wood for the trees.'

'And you think going to a rainforest would help?'

29

I mock. 'That's nothing but wood and trees. And bugs. And reptiles with fluorescent fangs and monkeys that pummel you with their own poo if you look at them the wrong way.'

Ollie bursts out laughing. 'You know, there is one other aspect we haven't addressed.'

'And what's that?' I drain the last of my carrot and ginger concoction.

'The possibility of a holiday romance.'

I let my head thunk on to the table. 'No way.'

'Ava. It's been a year—'

'Ollie—' My exasperation returns full force.

He carries on regardless. 'I totally get why you don't want to start up something here, but over there you can be free to do what you want with whoever you want. There's no chance of being seen out with your hot Latin lover or any of the sordid details doing the rounds. It's such a great opportunity to get you back in the saddle again.'

''You're a fine one to talk! When was the last time you had a date?'

'Well maybe if you were out of town I'd actually get around to it.'

He's got a point. I know at least three chaps who'd like to rifle through his record collection but I never urged him to pursue them because I suppose I liked our exclusive little set-up. Perhaps I'd be doing him a favour by giving him some space?

I sigh. 'You really think I should go, don't you?'

He nods. 'You know why? Because I have your best interests at heart.'

I shuffle forward in my chair and lay my hand over his chest. 'And it's such a good heart,' I say, my eyes welling up as I look up into his. Though I'm resisting like crazy, I can't help but respect the fact that he's not afraid to give me a push when he knows that all I want is to be pulled into a 'poor baby' hug.

A smile creeps over his face. 'You're going to go, aren't you?'

'What makes you say that?' I frown.

He leans over and wipes a baby tear from the corner of my eye. 'Because you're missing me already.'

4

Ollie insists I call my dad directly with the good news, who in turn tells me that he's arranged £250 credit for me at the local Adventure Outfitters.

'Now there's a man who's used to getting his own way!' Ollie coos, so impressed by my dad's presumption that he extends his lunch break to watch me stock up on combat couture and Kendal mint cake.

'You know it's ironic that I'm going to be dressed head to toe in army green in a country that has no army,' I muse as I flick through the rack of multipocketed, excessively zippered, Velcro-strippered clothing.

'Costa Rica has no army?' Ollie baulks. 'I thought they bumped borders with Nicaragua?'

'They do,' I acknowledge. 'But the government decided to put the money into education instead. As a result they've got the highest literacy rate in Latin America.'

'Gosh.' Ollie gives due kudos as he holds a moss-coloured kagoule under my chin. 'Why do you need so much khaki, anyway?'

'It's rainforest policy: they don't want you scaring away the animals.'

'I would have thought that would be a plus for you.'

'Damn – you're right!' I say, swapping a sludgy knit for a cerise fleece.

'Oh, you've got to get a pair of these trousers that unzip above the knee!' Ollie enthuses. 'These ones actually have an SPF 30, can you believe it? And what about these hiker hot-pants?'

I take a moment to study the stitching. 'The thing is, when you've got spiky foliage lashing your thighs and beasties eager to chomp at your calves, the last thing you want is bare legs.'

'Ah. Good point. I suppose the same goes for arms? Less of the Lara Croft vests?'

I nod. 'Though I'm sure Kiki sports nothing but.'

Ollie tuts. 'There are you presuming she's this hot little Pussycat Doll when she could be Camilla Parker Bowles.'

'Oh I wish.'

He raises his eyebrows at me. 'Now that's not something you hear every day.'

'I really don't know what to expect of her,' I sigh. 'Dad's told me so little – every time I broach the subject I get gushy raptures but no real details.'

'Well, you'll know soon enough – they're going to meet you at the airport, aren't they?'

'Yup. I'll step off the plane all grimy and jet-lagged, legs throbbing with deep vein thrombosis, and there she'll be all fresh and polished—'

'All right, Audrey!' That's what Ollie says every time I get too negative – a poke at how I'm going to turn into my mum. Works a treat.

'Okay,' I give a falsely bright smile. 'Shoes.'

We make our way through the torture-chamberesque collection of home gym equipment, bypass the skipping-rope section (renamed 'jump' ropes and 'speed' ropes for the male consumer) and turn left at the Barbie fishing rods.

'This one ticks all your boxes.' Ollie holds up a trainer/hiking boot hybrid. 'Anti-microbial lining, compression moulded footframe and the colour of mud.'

'Well, I understand at least one of the descriptors. Since when did nature get so hi-tech?' I've found myself distracted by the snorkelling kits – one thing I didn't get around to on my last trip. 'Look at this mask – it has a silicone facial skirt!'

Ollie snorts as he reads the packaging over my shoulder. 'Alternatively you can go for the "reliance purge" model.'

We get giggly to the point of hysteria as we start to read the small print on everything we touch, going over budget as we add a frisbee that flashes bluc as it travels through the air (brilliantly named the Disc-o!), a small klaxon (ideal for all sporting events!) and a water bottle-cum-rucksack that feeds a constant supply of fluid from the backpack to your mouth by some ER-style tubing.

'All I need now is the bottle of vodka!' I joke as we hit the till.

As we emerge, we're both a little hyper. Apparently even making bad decisions can be quite a thrill if you do it boldly enough.

'I'm going to Costa Rica!' I announce, still somewhat dazed by my commitment.

'Yes you are, and your flight leaves at 9.45 a.m. so you'd better get home and get packing,' Ollie instructs as he loads me up with my assorted packages. 'In the meantime, I've got to get back to work and start acting like I'm coming down with flu so I can take you to the airport.'

'Are you serious?' I whoop.

Ollie gives his best sneezy-wheezy cough in lieu of a response.

Once he's gone I reshuffle my bags so that I'm better balanced for the walk home, then pause a moment to decide upon the least congested stretch of pavement. I think I'll cut through Queen Square—

'What are you doing?'

I freeze at the sound of my mother's voice. My

first instinct is to cast the bags in the gutter and grab some passing woman's M&S fare.

'What?' I try to use blankness to buy time but she's already nosing inside.

'What's all this gear for?' she asks, pulling out a torch.

'Scotland,' I blurt. 'I'm going with Ollie. To visit his parents.' (Who actually live twenty-five miles away in Little Somerford but I doubt she'll remember that.)

'You're taking a mosquito net to Scotland?' She holds up the offending article.

'Well, we're going to the Highlands, you can never be too prepared.' I am so rubbish at lying.

Her eyes narrow. 'You're going to see your father, aren't you?'

My shoulders slump in submission.

'I suppose he's paid for all this?' she challenges. Suddenly I feel shamefully bought. I've always been so adamant about standing on my own two feet. Have I just taken the first step back to being beholden? As I hang my head, I feel a spattering of water on my brow and for a moment I believe that my mother has perfected projectile crying. But when I look up I see it is in fact the sky spitting at me.

'Come on, let's get a cuppa,' I try to sidestep her into the nearest bakery for a 35p bun and an over-stewed brew but she defiantly redirects us to the

Pump Room. I know she's doing this to make a point. The Pump Room is for special occasions and entertaining visitors, not for rain-sodden recriminations. It's really pouring now yet my mother makes no attempt to shield herself from the deluge. In some small way I'm grateful for the weather – with everyone's hair in drippy rats' tails we won't stand out so much.

'Table for two.' My mother sticks her nose in the air like a grande dame despite the fact that she's wearing baggy-kneed leggings and what I suspect are her slippers, as opposed to the empire-line dress and white gloves that would really fit the room.

We're seated beside a trio of musicians playing a medley from *My Fair Lady*, which I know my mother will take as a personal taunt seeing as life is so patently *un*-fair.

All I want is a cup of Lady Grey, so while my mother is perusing the menu my eyes roam the fading grandeur of the room – the long coral drapes, the sparkling chandelier, the slender grandfather clock. I look at the old dears in their knitted suits and brooches, the tourists filing around the cordoned-off edge of the room and the brave folk queueing up for a taste of the sulphurous spa water. I'd swap with any of them right now to avoid having the scheduled conversation with my mum.

'We'll have Afternoon Tea for two,' my mother addresses the waitress.

'Mum—' I go to explain that I've not long had lunch but she dismisses my objections saying, 'Don't worry, I'm paying.'

This makes me feel worse. I know she's broke and that tomorrow as she's reusing a pre-dunked teabag she'll regret this extravagance, but what more can I do? Over and again I've offered her money, but to accept it and make use of it would ruin her suffering. It's like the more she suffers, the more wrong she makes my dad. For her to move on would be like saying that what he did is okay. And it's never going to be okay with her.

'So,' she says, staring pointedly, disappointedly, at me. 'Why now?'

I'm amazed to find I actually have a valid response. 'Well, I didn't get the chance to tell you yet but the lease on the shop I fell in love with fell through.' I pause to allow a sympathetic coo of 'My poor darling!' but none is forthcoming. 'Um, then by coincidence, Dad called to say he's opening a café in Costa Rica and so he asked me to go out there and do the initial setting up.'

'And that's what you want?'

'Not exactly. But the alternative is to stay here, jobless—'

'What do you mean "jobless"?'

'I told you, I quit because I thought the lease at The Corridor was a sure thing and—'

'No you didn't.'

I purse my lips. This happens all the time. Fortunately our waitress has returned to present us with a selection of dainty, cress-frilled sandwiches and large, trollopy cream cakes, serving as sufficient distraction for me to move the conversation on.

'So anyway, I can either stay here twiddling my thumbs on the off-chance that another fantasy property will show up, or be out there actually doing—'

Again she interrupts me. 'You know he has an ulterior motive? He won't be doing you a good turn just to be fatherly.'

The truth of this stings a little, but I can't let on so I give a breezy shrug and say, 'Well, that may be so but I'm just grateful for the chance to get working on a café – I'm so geared up for it, I don't want to lose my momentum . . .'

I'm actually starting to believe this is a good idea.

Mum sighs and shakily transports the teacup to her lips. 'After what happened last time,' she winces, 'I don't know how you can even consider going back.'

'Dad assures me that Costa Rica now offers one of the best healthcare services in the world; besides, I'm an adult now, I can look after myself.' I sound assertive but my finger involuntarily traces the faint scar on my palm.

'I just worry that when he lets you down again – *and he will* – I won't be there to pick up the pieces.'

I want to laugh. She's never picked up a piece in

39

her life. All she ever does is smash things further with her braying 'Told you so's'. Knowing she's about to hark back to when he abandoned me during 'my impressionable teenage years' I decide to appeal to my mum's Achilles heel – her broken heart. 'The thing is, Mum, ever since I broke up with Nick I've felt so jittery and constantly on the verge of tears. Only working on the café has eased that – it's been great to have a project to focus on – and the thought of going back to feeling so lost and—'

'You only went out with him for a year!' she snorts. 'Twenty years I was with your father. Twenty years of memories and promises, twenty years of sacrifices and support, twenty years . . .'

On and on she goes.

I reach for the plumpest, squidgiest cake and ram it in my mouth to stop the screaming. Then I tune out her vicious lamentations in favour of the yearning hum of the violin. As I do so my heart does its first little leap of anticipation.

There may be worse horrors awaiting me in Costa Rica but tomorrow, for at least ten hours, I shall be suspended in mid-air high above the tug-of-warring with no one telling me what I should and shouldn't be doing, no one goading or guilt-tripping me. The only words I will be obliged to respond to are: 'Is your seat belt fastened?' and 'Would you like wine with your meal?'

Bliss.

5

'Good evening, ladies and gentlemen, this is your captain speaking. Due to dense fog conditions we are unable to land in San José at this time.'

A collective groan of displeasure from the passengers.

'In fact, no plane has been able to land for the past three hours.'

Followed by an 'Oooh' of concern.

'We have enough fuel to remain in a holding pattern for the next two hours, but if the fog persists we will be forced to relocate to Liberia airport in the north of the country, refuel, and then return and try our luck again.'

Several hundred hearts sink into their boots. I see their frustration – so near and yet so far! If they had a parachute I suspect they'd take their chances. Me, I'm keeping shtum, feeling partly to blame as ever since I changed planes in Miami I've been dreading touchdown. I had secret fantasies that I'd boarded the wrong plane and would continue going south until I got to Rio or Argentina where I would become a carnival queen or a polo champion and live happily ever after, never having met my dad's new wife.

Not that she's really the problem – that would be my dad. Sometimes I even question calling him that. Personally, I think father status should be revoked if the man in question can't meet some basic parental criteria. At least my mother has some sense of closure in being able to call him her *ex*-husband. In many ways he feels like my *ex*-dad, so it bugs me that he gets that title for life no matter how he behaves. Not that he's a monster by any means. If you met him you'd find him a charming and generous host, for the duration of dinner. He only seems to fully engage in the presence of food and booze. Without a goblet in his hand and a drumstick between his teeth he becomes a distant phantom, mind whirring on other matters, predominantly business.

He wasn't a full-blown workaholic when he first met my mother. And I don't want to insinuate that he became one just to get away from her because in the beginning they were great together. (I remember many wonderful pictures of the two of them laughing and nuzzling at some glitzy social event, though these images are now banished to the loft.) My theory is that, as his property business grew, he started working longer hours and in turn started

missing dinners. You see where this is going . . .
Often he wouldn't get home until ten or eleven at
night and, having ordered takeaway at his desk, the
attention he paid my mother was reduced to the
duration of a late-night snack or whisky nightcap.
Technically she should have been the one having
the affair – she was the most neglected. (With me
coming a close second. Not that I really knew any
better as a child. He was just that big man in a suit I
saw from time to time.) But she was so proud of his
successes and wanted to see him reach his potential
– and besides, she had me to keep her occupied.

Things improved for a while when she bought a
home fondue kit but then he started purchasing
properties overseas, mostly holiday condos, first in
Spain then in Florida, and he was obliged to make
frequent trips abroad. And as a result he started
eating out. A lot.

Despite subsequent affairs with a sushi chef, a
donut glazer, a chick with a bullet belt of tequila
shots, a salsa sample hander-outer and a chance
meeting with his long-standing crush Jilly Goolden,
he actually left my mum for a flight attendant. At first
I didn't see the connection, but then I flew long-haul
business class for the first time and I realised these
women with their pencil skirts and movie-premiere
up-dos stop by every few minutes with champagne,
pretzels, hors d'oeuvres, a three-course meal, movie-
time ice-cream then (following a few hours' kip) a

wakey-wakey Buck's Fizz, cooked breakfast, Danish pastries and finally the mint to suck to prevent ear poppage. He didn't stand a chance.

I was surprised to learn that Kiki is an estate agent. But I'll bet you anything she can cook.

Having packed everything in my bag in preparation for landing, I decide to retrieve my book and in doing so pull out Ollie's parting gift to me: a paper coffee cup.

'It's empty,' I had frowned, peering down the mouthpiece.

'Well, if that were true it wouldn't be much of a gift, would it?' he huffed as he popped the lid and pulled out a scrolled computer printout.

'*Café Britt Coffee Tour*,' I read the banner headline.

'It's a couple of hours at a coffee farm and roasting factory just outside the capital,' he explained. 'I thought it might give you a heads-up on the native beans.'

'Gosh! That's amazing, how—?'

'Last night on the internet. I looked it up, paid with my card, printed out the receipt . . . It's the modern way, Ava. Even in Costa Rica.'

It was a timely reminder – half of me was imagining I'd be serving coffee roadside from a giant flask, tsking at the squirrel monkeys for queue-jumping.

'What's this?' I said rustling a second package.

'Well, much as you want to dismiss the chance of any romance . . .' he smirked as I tore back a corner of the wrapping to reveal some naughty-looking lace, '. . . I'm not giving up hope!'

'Oh Ollie!' I embarrassedly stuffed the undies back in the package.

'What?' he laughed. 'Having a frilly bottom is not an arrestable offence!' He pulled me into a strong-man hug as he lowered his voice to a gentle whisper. 'You'd better be going, babe.' I looked up at him plaintively. 'I know you don't know quite what lies ahead but I'm going to be reading up on Costa Rica on my now lonely lunch breaks, and I hereby give you permission to call me at inappropriate times of the night, should you need to discuss flavoured syrups, or any other dilemmas.'

'Don't make me go!' I whimpered, burrowing into his shoulder.

'If you won't,' he said gently prising me from him, 'I will.' And with that he turned and walked away, breaking into the Morecombe and Wise hand-to-head exit skip just in time to turn my tears to laughter.

Even looking at his handwriting now makes me feel sentimental. There's something to be said for having a good man in your life, even if it's not a boyfriend or a father. Swapping someone as supportive and attentive as Ollie for my dad is just going to further highlight his flaws.

'What are his crimes, exactly?' I remember Ollie enquiring the first time I pulled a face at the mention of my father. 'Aside from his absence.'

'And his infidelities?' I chipped in.

'Well, that's really between him and your mum.'

I thought long and hard and the best I could come up with was that He's Just Not That Into Me. I am not a priority in his life, more of an occasional aside. He'll come and visit if he's in town on other business, but never make a special effort just to see me. It's as if a time-and-motion expert did a study and advised him to always be multitasking when I'm around, because any hours spent exclusively with me are wasted. Even if we're talking on the phone after a six-month gap he'll be updating his diary or replying to emails or showing a house. It's like now – he finally wants me to visit because I serve a purpose: getting the coffee shop up and running, and indulging his wife. (Though anyone who thinks that introducing stepchildren into the equation is a good idea obviously has a very rose-tinted view of life.)

I suppose what galls me the most is that he has no interest in finding out who I am as a person *today*. I'm not the teenager who watched *Ghost* ad infinitum and then took up pottery to give him misshapen mugs and ashtrays to ridicule and it bugs me that I'm still referred to as such. I've tried to 'update his system', but our conversations are so superficial – just a few tried and tested topics on rotation. As far as my career goes he only ever asks about pay rises and promotions, never job satisfaction or colleague camaraderie. Admittedly I've always been primarily involved with computer figures and desk-bound paperwork but it's not like I work in a vacuum. I'm perfectly capable of having personality clashes with the folk in neighbouring cubicles. In fact, when I was having a nightmare with my boss before last I was so despairing I actually asked his advice (he's employed hundreds of staff over the years, I thought he might offer some insight), but he just said, 'I'm sure you'll make the right decision,' and changed the subject. He may as well have just said, 'Not my problem.' Even when it's something good that I want to share – like when Ollie joined the firm, and I wanted to rave about this great new friend who made my working day bearable – a couple of sentences in he'll start making 'round it up' noises. It's like I'm rushing my Oscar acceptance speech, trying to show him who I am before the music swells and drowns me out.

I know he's not alone in this and that, to a degree, it's just a man thing. But I hate feeling like the left-to-last chore. What would it take to have him stop what he's doing, look me in the eye and pay me some attention?

He seems to think that as long as he keeps the money coming, he's doing his bit. He doesn't get that I'd take a card with an in-joke cartoon over a bank statement informing me that a transfer has been made into my account. Whenever he misses my birthday he sends me double the usual amount. When I was younger I considered sending it back saying, 'You don't know me at all if you think this is going to make it all better.' But then I read that phrase about taking lemons and making lemonade and decided instead to open a savings account and fill it with his guilt money. My intention was to do something life-changing with it, as if one day I'd have enough to buy myself a nice new dad. After I broke up with Nick I thought of spending it on therapy (appropriate that my dad should fund that seeing as he'd no doubt be getting the blame for inspiring my dud relationship choices). But then came the idea for the café and the thought of creating something tangible that I could be proud of really appealed. I liked to think that if I did a good enough job it would cancel out all the disappointment.

I suppose that's what I'm still hoping for now. He's not the only one with an ulterior motive. Maybe we're not so different after all – I certainly wouldn't be coming all this way just to hang out with him.

I'm just getting into the chapter on how best to lay out your coffee shop stockroom, when the fog magically lifts and we're cleared for landing. My heart does a nervous loop-the-loop and I quickly practise my fake smile for Kiki, and my cheery rendition of the word 'Dad!', before placing my tray table in the upright position.

At least it's late. Nine now, maybe ten by the time I'm through customs and have collected my suitcase. Just enough time to say hello, exchange pleasantries on the ride to his house, and then bid each other goodnight. Oh for the sound of my door clicking shut . . .

I wonder if there are any other people on the plane having misgivings about their travel plans? I saw one woman at the airport repeatedly turning back to wave at her beloved, showing him ever more pink eyes and a snot-bubbling nose. Why do we do this to ourselves? All these hellos and goodbyes, it's just so disruptive. I certainly don't take after my father in his desire to charge from country to country. What's he looking for? I wonder.

When I do finally emerge into an unkempt throng of duelling trolleys and pushy taxi drivers, I can't see anyone that resembles him at all. For starters, he's six foot three with silver-grey hair and everyone around me is at eye level and dark. And then I see myself, or at least a sign bearing the words AVA LANGSTON.

Very swish and self-important, yet it doesn't really compare to having a father standing there who actually knows your identity.

Having said that, even if he did come to meet me it would probably be wise for me to be holding up a sign, or at the very least a name badge. It's been a while. My hair is longer and redder than it ever has been. I'm sporting jeans instead of my usual executive two-piece, and my usually matt face is uncharacteristically glossy due to the ultra-balmy night.

'Er, hello.' I approach the petite, nattily dressed chap holding the sign.

'When you are Ava, I am Wilbeth,' he introduces himself in his own special way.

I want to ask who he is when I'm not Ava, but decide instead to shake his hand. As I step closer I see that his young, slim face is bejewelled with beads of perspiration. It concerns me that even the locals sweat so profusely, but I suppose heat = sweat wherever your place of birth.

Handing me an envelope he announces, 'Your father is inside.'

What I actually find is a typed paragraph. The content presumably explains my dad's where-abouts, but I can't be sure because the words are in Spanish. Did he get confused and think Penélope Cruz was coming in my place?

'I'm sorry, could you possibly translate this for

me?' I turn a pair of pleading eyes towards Wilbeth.

'You want I read?'

'*Si*,' I encourage, instantly exhausting my Spanish vocabulary.

'Welcome to Costa Rica!' he begins enthusiastically then looks up, seemingly awaiting my response.

'Oh! Thank you.'

'We decide it makes um, *more logic* for you to come to us in Tamarindo rather than we three travel to you—'

I hold up my hand requesting a pause. 'Did you say three?'

'*Tres. Si.* Three.'

Who is the third person? Dad, Kiki and . . . I try to fill in the blank but come up wanting. I do know she doesn't have any kids; I already did a step-sibling check. Maybe she insists on a travelling hairdresser to combat jungle frizz. Or, better yet, a marriage guidance counsellor as their vows are already in crisis!

'Is okay?' The messenger reminds me that I'm getting distracted from the real point – two people, three people, the numbers don't matter – not one of them is here to meet me.

'So what's the plan?' I try to pull myself together.

'Well, two options are present,' he says pointing to two bullet points on the page. 'One I drive you to Tamarindo now.'

'How far is that?'

51

'In hours, about four.'

'Four hours' drive?' Despite excessive travel fatigue my eyebrows climb high on my forehead.

He nods confirmation.

I look at my watch calculating we'd arrive at 2 a.m. I really need a bed sooner than that. Besides which, I'd no doubt be greeted by a second minion with a second note, probably written in Hungarian, just for kicks.

'Or?'

'He has made a reservation for you at a local hotel and tomorrow you can fly to Tamarindo.'

Another flight? I sigh and ask, 'How long does that take?'

'Forty minutes.'

'Oh, that's not so bad!' I brighten.

'But the flight does not leave until three in the afternoon.'

There's always a catch, isn't there? In the moment I take to deliberate which has the edge, a good night's sleep versus awaking in the destination, I remember Ollie's gift of the Café Britt tour. I take out the printout and show Wilbeth.

'Do you know this place?'

'*Si, si*. Is in Heredia. Very close to hotel.'

'Really? Well, I don't want to go there now,' I assure him. 'But maybe tomorrow, before the flight?'

'Of course. We can arrange.'

'Really? Then I'll stay.'

I know I've made the right decision when I step aboard the minibus assigned to transport all one of me, and discover that the seats have equal spring and comfort to an ironing board. Fine if the roads were ice-rink smooth, but this is a country so renowned for potholes that locals joke you get a free massage with every road trip. Four hours slammed repeatedly against these seats would practically constitute abuse. Even on the half-hour journey to the hotel, I'm wondering if my fortune might in fact be made substituting car seats for beanbags.

I look out the window. The night is so black. And not a little sinister. I read that 60 per cent of the population of Costa Rica live in this central valley and yet just a few miles out of town we're bumping along roads that Wilbeth seems to be making up as he goes along, crowded by wild hedgerows and only occasionally passing civilisation in the form of the odd scrappy bungalow with a corrugated-iron roof and bars on the window. This looks like kidnap country to me. I study the back of the head of the strange man who is driving the car. I'm pretty sure I could have Wilbeth – he's so slight – but if he had a knife or a gun or five friends . . .

'So,' I scoot forward hoping to reassure myself that he's legit. 'You work for my father?'

'Si.'

I need more. 'This hotel you are taking me to, is it a favourite of his?'

'No.'

'No?' I fret.

'No. We go to Finca Rosa Blanca. This is Kiki's favourite.'

I breathe a sigh of relief. Never did I think her name would act as a magic password but right now it works a treat.

'Your father he prefers to stay at the White House,' Wilbeth continues.

I smile knowingly. I see his delusions of grandeur remain intact. I noticed that hotel in the deluxe section of my guidebook – the only one with its own helipad. It also mentioned that the women's loos are labelled 'First Ladies', a fact that amused me greatly.

'Now we arrive.'

I use my last scrap of energy to grind back the minibus door, eager to see how Kiki's taste compares. This property is also painted white, but instead of stately Doric columns and Southern plantation-style balconies it has a free-form, almost Gaudi-esque curvature to it.

'Everyone sleeps,' Wilbeth whispers as he opens the *Alice in Wonderland*-esque like door and guides me through the shadows, making no attempt to find a light switch as he levers my suitcase up the stairs. I feel like I've snuck into an artist's hideaway as opposed to a hotel – in the moonlight I can make out a two-storey atrium with tapestries slung over the whitewashed balcony, hand-painted murals climbing the narrow pillars and earthenware ceramics nestled in assorted window-sill nooks.

Wilbeth opens the door to my room and steps aside. 'Tonight you tiptoe in the dark. Tomorrow all will be revealed.'

'Where's the bed?' I ask, seeing only the outline of a wicker desk set and a pair of matching sofas.

'In the sky.' He points to a unique 'woodland' take on the spiral staircase – stepping stones made out of varnished slices of tree trunk. Apparently the action-adventure portion of my trip has already begun – I actually have to use my hands as well as my feet to make my ascent. As soon as I see a four-poster awaiting me, all thoughts of nighties and toothbrushes desert me. I flump down, delighted to be able to stretch out in every direction and wrap myself in the duvet. Within seconds I'm asleep, dreaming of awaking to my first authentic cup of Costa Rican coffee.

6

What I actually wake up to is the feeling that I've tangled my hand in one of those old-fashioned string mops. For a second I wonder if I've sleep-walked into the cleaning cupboard but then I open my eyes and see that my four poster bed is strung with macramé braiding. As I raise myself up and lean back on the scalloped wicker headboard I understand why it's so darn bright in here – I am entirely surrounded by floor-to-ceiling arched windows. It's almost as if I'm in a glass birdcage.

A balcony trims the perimeter and when I step out on to it I discover I am in fact in some kind of fairy-tale turret. Acres of rumply apple-green foliage sprawl below, the sky is baby blue and in the distance I can hear the plantation pickers singing. Wow. This is a good morning.

I take a deep breath and there it is – that most alluring of aromas: coffee. The breakfast patio beckons to me, making me wish they'd installed a fireman's pole directly to it as opposed to my suite's precarious staircase, tricky even on the descent.

Now that it's daylight the lower tier of my room reveals its very own terrace (from which I can admire the watercolour wash of the distant mountains) and a bathroom overlooking a collection of trees that resemble those mesh pom-pom bath sponges. I feel like a cartoon woodland creature as I bathe in a rock garden tub surrounded by forest muralling

The artistry of the Finca Rosa Blanca has me totally beguiled. If Kiki has in mind a café version of this place we might work in harmony after all.

'French toast with coconut syrup,' a friendly face serves me a breakfast that has me nearly cross-eyed with pleasure. The only downside is that Ollie is not here to share it with me – he's the only person I know who actually likes the taste of starfruit and it seems a terrible waste not to be able to fork my slices on to his plate. As I accept a top-up for my coffee cup I take out my mobile to call him, but find I have absolutely no signal. I feel a little slump of aloneness but then the waiter calls to me: 'Miss Langston? We have a phone call for you.'

I scurry inside – could he have tracked me down? I make an optimistic leap. But no. The man on the other end of the phone is my father.

I mean to be a little surly on account of him

57

standing me up last night, but my environment is so inspiring I can't quite pull it together.

'Good morning!' I sing-song down the phone.

'Did you sleep well?'

'Like a princess,' I chirrup, recalling my all-white turret.

'Kiki thought you'd like that bed. The pair of us barely leave it when we stay there.'

Great. Now I feel like I need another shower.

'So, Dad.' I try to force the image of them playing Rapunzel & Suitor from my mind. 'In your note – which by the way was in *Spanish*—'

'Oh I forget you don't speaka da lingo.' He gives a verbal shrug. 'It's second nature to me now.'

'Well, anyway, you made some reference to the *three* of you?'

'That's right,' he confirms.

'Well?'

'Well what? No OJ for me.'

Is he talking to a waiter? I feel like I'm going to have click my fingers to regain his attention. 'Dad?'

'Yes?'

'Who is the mystery person?'

'No mystery, it's Santiago,' he says, infuriatingly matter-of-fact.

'No mystery to *you*,' I coax him.

'You didn't meet him on your last trip?'

'I haven't visited for fifteen years!' I splutter.

'Oh, well then, that would explain it, he's only

58

been working for me the last five.'

'So he's an employee?' I continue to nudge him, wondering why he never went into politics since he's so expert at withholding information.

'Oh, he's so much more than that.' The pride, the boastfulness, the appreciation in his voice turns my stomach – I am instantly envious. 'You'll see,' he continues. 'He's a very special young man.'

For a split second I wonder if my dad is intending to set me up with him but then I realise I'm being absurd – he has a blatantly high opinion of this fellow so if he was going to play Cupid, the girl would have to be equally special, at least in his eyes.

'Anyway, I just wanted to let you know that Wilbeth will be with you in an hour,' Dad concludes. 'I suggested he show you the sights in San José before your coffee tour.'

'Okay.' I certainly don't have any better ideas.

'And then we'll see you later this afternoon – I'll send a car to pick you up at the airport so you don't have to worry about a taxi.'

'Couldn't you pick me up yourself?' I dare myself to ask for what I want, though I'm not thrilled about how plaintive and needy I sound.

'Well, we usually have cocktails at five and I don't like to drink and drive . . .'

Oh my god! He won't even reschedule his booze for me! I feel a kick of indignation that makes me persist: 'See if you can make an exception this once.'

'We'll see,' is his best offer.

Though my breakfast is unfinished, I find my appetite gone and head instead up the fig-lined footpath for some privacy. A lone tear streaks my cheek. He always makes me feel like this. I hate it. I will have taken three flights to see him, and he won't even trundle ten minutes down the road for me. I shake my head – I have to accept that he's not going to change; it's up to me to change my attitude to him, but how?

I turn a corner and find myself beside a view-skimming swimming pool and an amorphous stucco pool house showcasing more bold and vibrant murals. If Frida Kahlo had painted coffee planta-tions they would have looked like this. I love how all the windows are weird blob-shaped cut-outs and that the changing-room doors are pinned with life-saver rings – I almost believe that a 1920s starlet might appear at any time. In a bid to connect to the sublime design and let my dad-angst go, I slip off my flip-flops and swoosh along the shallow slope of the pool.

I am going to have to work on being stronger, more resilient. I don't want to continue with this crying, it's just too much work to have to pull myself up again. I sit down on the edge of the pool and swill my hands, creating gentle ripples. I so wish I had Ollie's level disposition – he's so pragmatic. I swear, in my next life, I'm going to be so unemotional I'll barely have facial expressions. It'll be like I've been Botoxed on the inside.

I'd happily while away the rest of the day here but along comes Wilbeth, eager to serve. 'I am here to carry you into town!' he announces.

I look at his twiglet legs and check, 'You do have the minibus with you, don't you?'

'Of course!' he exclaims.

I get back to my feet, shake off the chlorinated drips and place a hand on his bony shoulder. 'I'll get my case.'

I can't help but wonder at my dad's motive for suggesting I mooch around San José town, though I certainly get why he recommended I go with Wilbeth. Personally I'd prefer to have been assigned someone ten stone beefier carrying samurai swords, but I guess he knows the lie of the land. He's certainly emphatic about me keeping my handbag clasped to me at all times – the streets are crushed and chaotic and every few paces we seem to enter another pickpocket hot spot. On the way in we passed a lot of tatty buildings in pretty peely pinks and turquoises that put me in mind of Havana, but the overriding colour of the centre appears to be grey. It doesn't help that the sky has clouded over. I look up and Wilbeth mistakes my concern for rain as admiration of a multi-storey bank.

'That's our tallest building – nineteen floors. The second highest is the Holiday Inn.'

For a moment the place seems almost quaint, but then I get roughly jostled and Wilbeth warns me again to keep a tight grip on my bag. Jeez! I feel like I'm walking down the street clutching loose bank-notes to my chest. While the locals are hustling and hurrying in their stride, I notice my fellow tourists look a little bewildered. This could have something to do with the fact that addresses are not given in the conventional '120 Elm St' fashion but described as '400m from the old church'. Charming but flummoxing if you don't know the relevant starting points or landmarks – some of which no longer exist, Wilbeth casually informs me. (Never was a GPS system more valid.)

'You want to see the market?'

I nod and we step into an even more claustro-phobic environment. Each section seems to be elbowing and overlapping with its neighbour – there are innumerable rucksack knock-offs dangling like lanterns, a hundred variations on the traditional *chorreador* coffee strainer (what looks like a sock dangling from a miniature gallows) and every form of rainforest memorabilia vying with giant prongs of real aloe vera at the 'pharmacy' stand. I myself am a source of fascination to the locals hunched up in the tiny café. Try as I might to fit in, I just can't wipe the perturbed, uptight look off my face. I clearly did not have an enquiring mind as a fifteen-year-old because I haven't got a clue about Costa Rican customs and trends, and decide that I have some serious homework to do before I make any blunders with my café clientele.

Perhaps sensing my concern, Wilbeth relocates me ten minutes down the road to a rustic tourist-friendly restaurant called Nuestra Tierra with bouquets of onions and peppers dangling from the ceiling and waiters in folkloric costume. From our window seat he points across to a former prison (now museum) and tells me that Costa Rica has the peculiar honour of having two former presidents in jail. I try to imagine the same thing happening back home and get so distracted by an image of John Major and Maggie Thatcher sharing a cell that I agree to try the Tican alternative to coffee – *agua dulce* (cane sugar with hot milk) – and a *tres leches* pudding for my elevenses. When I'm done I feel I know the true meaning of the words 'lactose intolerant'. Sugar milk, condensed milk, evaporated milk and cream – that's way too much sickly-sweet dairy in one sitting.

Afraid I'm going to throw up into one of the decorative vegetable crates, I tell Wilbeth I'm going to step outside to gasp a little fresh air but find I may as well be sucking directly on the exhaust pipes of the grimy, packed buses. Apparently only a small percentage of Ticans own their own cars. I think

63

how lucky I am to walk to work in Bath, but then I realise I don't have a job any more. It's hard to believe that this is my bright, shining future. Suddenly I get an uneasy feeling that this entire trip is going to be a grind – and I don't just mean the coffee beans. This is just too hard. I'm too different. An overwhelming sense of defeat and homesickness causes my body to slacken and in the split second that I loosen my white-knuckle grip on my bag, it's gone.

'What the—' I've just been mugged! I can't believe it!

Before I can even manage a time-delay 'Hey!' Wilbeth is by my side holding up my passport and my purse.

'I removed them while you were in the restroom,' he explains. 'I had a bad feeling.'

You and me both, I want to mutter. 'Can we go?' I quaver, afraid that if I stand still any longer a thieving hand will reach in and grab my kidneys.

Again I blame my father. This was his stupid idea: 'I know what'll be fun, Kiki – let's stand her up at the airport, make her feel all abandoned, but then put her in a wonderful hotel so she thinks everything's going to be all right and then, while she's still a good'n'staggery from the jet lag, frighten the bejesus out of her with a little inner-city crime!'

'Oh, Dean, you're such a prankster!' she'd pet

64

him. 'Now I was thinking of either Mojitos or Cuba Libres for tonight, what would you prefer, my love?'

I just want to get back in the minibus and lock the doors but Wilbeth insists we go via the 'Catedral Metropolitana'. Having seen one too many shops selling cheap, gaudy tat, the hallowed grandeur proves a welcome respite, though the reverent hush typically found in places of worship is polluted by the sound of trucks juddering by outside and the street-corner lottery-ticket salesmen working their pitch. There's also a noise I can't quite place – it's only when we exit into the town square that I notice the trees are a-squabble with bright emerald plumage.

'Parrots!' I exclaim. I saw plenty of birds on my last visit – snowy egrets and tiger herons and turkey vultures – but that was in their natural habitat, not flying over concrete and harried shoppers. Besides, they were whites and blacks and taupes, not the jewel-bright hues I'm blinking at right now.

'It is good to meet your smile!' Wilbeth tells me.

Poor guy. He certainly drew the short soda straw having to escort me. I decide to make a concerted effort to brighten up. And as I do so, the sun re-emerges.

Things get perkier still at Café Britt – as soon as I arrive I'm handed the perfect cup of coffee: piping hot and freshly brewed from shade-grown organic beans. Better yet, it's free.

We're told we have twenty minutes to mooch around the gift shop before the tour begins and having stroked the furry monkeys, tried on the embroidered baseball cap and chuckled over a chocolate bar called Mr Big, I notice the complimentary Internet access – time is limited to five minutes but that's all I need to let Ollie know that I'm making use of his going-away present already.

Three new emails – one from Ollie, one from a company offering me a pill that claims to flatten your stomach while plumpening your boobs (must come with its own DIY liposuction and breast-enhancement kit) and one from mump-faced Mo. For a second I feel queasy – what if The Corridor has come back to me? I quickly click on his message but he is merely wafting a new property under my nose. Hmmm. I did once see a café next to a butcher's in Camden but it's not my idea of a dream location – I'm not a big fan of the smell of sawdust and carcass intermingling with one's freshly baked cookies. I wonder if I should tell him that I've left the country? Actually I think I'll keep an eye on upcoming properties, and if anything promising arises then Ollie can check it out for me. Which brings me to his email . . .

'Hola Ava! Is your phone not working there? I thought you had triband . . . I need to be assured that you didn't bail in Miami. Please tell me that you made it to your final destination, as opposed to

66

taking up with the vice squad or meeting some man on rollerblades with a pastel condo.'

I type back, 'Don't worry, I'm not with the Vice Squad or the rollerblader – but I'm having a lovely time kipping on the sofa of the Golden Girls!'

Then I press send, just in case he's online.

Before I can even compose my next missive one pops up from him.

'Ava! You're alive! What's up with your phone?'

'Phone is dud here,' I type back. 'Gonna get a functioning one when I see my dad.'

'What do you mean when you see him?!!' he replies. 'Did you get a better offer at the airport?'

'Not exactly. I'll fill you in later. Just got a couple of mins before tour starts – I'm at Café Britt!!!!'

'That's my girl! Do you want me to let your mum know that you arrived safe?'

I feel a prick of guilt. I hadn't even thought of contacting her – it seemed like I would be heaping salt on the wound – but now Ollie has offered I can see that would be the considerate thing to do.

'Yes, please – you're a gem. Just tell her that all is well.'

'Will do. Hope you learn something new. Give my love to Santiago.'

My eyes start so far from their sockets they practically bounce off the computer screen. How does he know about Santiago? Am I the only person unaware of his legend?

67

'Or Joaquin or Diego or Francisco or whoever it is you've hooked up with,' he adds.

I breathe a sigh of relief. He's just being cheeky.

'Actually his name is Wilbeth.' I write back. ''Do you suspect he may have been bullied as a child?'

'Everyone ready?' I hear a voice addressing a crowd.

'GOTTA GO!' I speed-type before signing off.

It's amazing what a boost it is to exchange a few lines with a friend. I almost feel that Ollie is with me as I follow the other guests out onto the front lawn for the welcome speech.

The tour is truly outstanding. Three actors take the roles of plantation workers with plenty of slapstick in-house bickering. One of them looks like a twenty-something Rowan Atkinson, cue references to Mr Bean and just how apt that is, considering his profession.

His colleague tells us that Costa Rica only produces the arabica strain, which has less caffeine, a sweeter taste and commands a higher price. 'We're no fools,' he quips as he goes on to explain that the best coffee is grown high up in the mountains where it is colder, creating harder beans that can stay longer in the oven and thus develop a better slow-roasted taste.

For the first time I hear the coffee bean being referred to as a cherry – and it is indeed a red berry before the skin is peeled away (by a machine). We follow our guides' welly-boot-clad feet to the next section as they demonstrate that, having dried in the sun, the beans form a layer called parchment.

'Can you eat them at this stage?' a punter enquires.

'Of course,' he nods before deadpanning, 'but it's not good for you.'

'It acts as a laxative if you're not used to it,' Mr Bean advises.

Of the crop, which is harvested just once a year, 80 per cent is rejected and goes to form fertiliser, leaving only 20 per cent to be roasted.

Throughout the tour the Tico guides refer to the coffee bean as the 'golden bean' or the *grano de oro* and this sets my mind whirring, running potential café names with gold in the title. The Golden Cup. No, sounds like a football trophy. Goldbucks? Like it, but no. What about Gold Bean & Silver Leaf as a reference to the tea? Too complicated? I edit myself. I know, I've got it: The Pot of Gold! I love it! We'd have a logo of a curvy coffee pot with the words spelt out in steam. Or is that a bit genie of the lamp? Whatever! The name is the thing.

Mentally I'm spraying everything gold, but physically I'm walking into the roasting room where the beans are rotated inside a drum heated to two hundred degrees Celsius. As they turn, the beans swell and expand and the green colour gives way to

69

a light brown. Then, after seven or eight minutes, a 'pop' indicates the beans are entering the second stage. From then on the Master Roaster checks the beans every few seconds for the perfect colour, size, surface texture and smokiness for either light, dark or espresso coffee. As soon as the appropriate result is achieved they are sent swiftly into a cooling chamber to halt the process. The 'cupping room' is where the flavour is approved and once the highest standards have been met, the coffee is immediately packaged to protect it from oxygen, sunlight and water, all of which can ruin the taste of the beans. Fascinating!

We now move through to a small theatre for a demonstration of the cupping process. Over the next thirty minutes, I learn that it takes two thousand hand-picked cherries to make a pound of coffee, that the people of Finland actually drink more coffee than the Ticos and, through a panto-like stage production, that the drink was initially presented to the Pope as the devil's brew but he liked it so much he gave it his blessing!

This tour has revived me in every possible way.

It's amazing. Even though I am in Costa Rica and ostensibly under my dad's care, it's still Ollie who is showing me a good time.

7

Wilbeth must have a lead foot and a bump-resistant bottom because he manages to drop me off at departures in San José *and* pick me up at arrivals in Tamarindo.

But while he was tearing along in the minibus I was soaring above him in a plane so dinky its floral design was actually hand-painted in gunky acrylics and instead of an air steward the pilot just turned round in his seat and gave us our safety briefing and scheduled time of arrival. I suppose it's natural in a plane so small for weight to be a concern but I didn't expect that after my suitcase was weighed at the check-in desk that they'd actually ask *me* to get on the scales. I literally had to step up on to the metal platform and watch the digital figures whirr. Worse still, I had to pay an excess fee! And they say it's fashion magazines that give women a complex about their curves! I couldn't believe that if I was five pounds lighter I would be a richer woman right now.

Fortunately the view is worth every colón. (That's the currency in Costa Rica. Hard not to think of colonic irrigation, I know.)

From above, I can see the city of San José is made up of a patchwork of corrugated iron roofs in rust-red, gunmetal grey and the green of oxidised copper, lending a misleading shantytown aspect to the aerial perspective. This quickly gives way to an abundance of strokable greenery, fields with combed grooves like corn rows, others which look like square ponds of stagnant algae, trees with bushy afro foliage and a Fuzzy Felt coastline touching hems with the luxurious teal sea. Whatever happens with my father, this sight is a tonic.

We come in to a little light rain but it stops abruptly as we de-plane. Wow. It is considerably hotter here than San José. Poor Wilbeth looks even more in need of a cold flannel to the brow. I wouldn't mind one myself. Even the short walk to the car park has me wondering if they make people-sized cooler bags.

'Is this my father's car?' I ask as Wilbeth loads my case into the boot of a sleek, silver Mercedes with mirrored windows.

He grunts a yes and for a moment I kid myself that there's still a chance Dad may be within, but no, the door opens and the squooshy leather seat is all for me. New-car smell always makes me feel slightly sick but I don't want to open the windows and risk messing with the air con so I'm compelled to snag open the corner of my Café Britt coffee pouch and create a improvised pot-pourri. If I close my eyes and inhale, I could be back in Bath sharing a latte with Ollie. But then my ears start popping which definitely never used to happen in Caffè Nero. Bar the landing strip, everywhere around Tamarindo seems to be on a curvy incline.

As we take a turn so steep we appear to be proceeding on our hind wheels, Wilbeth announces, 'He is your father's house.'

I hate to correct his English when my Spanish doesn't exist but really what he should be saying is, 'He is your father's *mansion*.'

The modern, multi-level, balcony-swathed, wood-and-chrome construction is upstaged only by the view – wildly vivacious vegetation tapering down to a raggedy coastline and seamless, shimmering Pacific. For that reason it's no surprise that the façade is dominated by windows – some floor to ceiling, some slanted skylights, others porthole-style peepholes. In the oval window closest to the main entrance there's a man's face framed so perfectly it could be a family portrait. Not that there's anyone that dark and attractive in our family.

I take full advantage of the fact that, though his eyes are following the passage of the car, he can't see me. Leaning closer, my nose smudges the smoked glass. Wow! He really is stunning – crisp white shirt highlighting the warmth of his glazed-clay skin tones, luxuriant black hair falling in shiny waves around his face. If this man were a gift from my father to redeem himself for his two airport no-shows, he'd be well in the clear. But something about the pride and poise of his stance tells me he's no plaything.

'Santiago . . .' I breathe, chilled by my surety that this is the man my father spoke of with such admiration.

He looks so immaculate. I'm glad that I changed before the flight – I too am in white, though I've gone head-to-toe with a cotton halter-neck and linen gauchos whereas, as he walks past a larger rectangle window, I see his legs are clad in dark denim jeans.

Wilbeth turns off the engine. 'This is here.'

Oblivious to the fact that Wilbeth is making his way around the car to perform his chauffeurly duties, I open my own door and plunge directly down into a gritty rain-swilled pothole. Maybe my dad is getting a little Costa Rican after all – spending millions on a property and not allotting a bean to tarmac the driveway. Amazingly my trousers are spared a smirching as I broke my fall with the palms of my hands, which, as I now check for cuts, look like they've been pasted with a layer of peanut-encrusted chocolate. I try to dust them off on each other but this only serves to spread the mud and grit, now coating my fingers.

'I have cleaning!' Wilbeth hurries over with a cloth so freshly laundered that my instinct is to wipe my hands before I touch it. Great. Now I have two distinctive handprints on the back of my trousers, making me look like I've been groped by a painter mid-canvas smear.

'Little Red!' I'm distracted from my predicament as my dad appears on the front portico treating me to a reminder of my long-forgotten childhood nickname. (He used to call me Little Red Riding Hood on account of my vibrant hair colour – now revived thanks to L'Oréal.) I scuttle towards him deciding to let bygones be bygones. So he didn't meet me at the airport twice! – because of him I'm getting my very own coffee shop, and that at least deserves a hug.

As he clutches me to his silk-shirted chest there seems more vitality to his embrace than I previously recall. I'm used to a perfunctory body bounce but this time he holds me a little tighter, a little longer.

I look beyond his shoulder for Madame Kiki and her pet monkey but instead see the man who deserves his own heart-shaped window, now positioned on the checkered marble floor of the lobby like a pawn in a chess game.

'Ava, I want you to meet Santiago.' My father leads me to him with something approaching awe.

I was utterly intent on finding Santiago nondescript to spite my father but now that there are only two diagonal chess moves between us, I can barely disguise my lust.

Taller than your average Tico, and even more alluring up close, he has eyes that welcome you into a dark and twinkling cave, a mouth you want to whisper secrets to you and skin that would leave traces of gold dust on your fingertips if you touched it.

'Hi.' I opt for the shortest greeting, hoping one solitary syllable won't give me away.

'*Buenas noches*,' he replies, not quite mirroring my swoon – while my eyes shoot moonbeams in his direction, his cloud with suspicion, so much so that when my dad announces, 'This is my daughter, Ava,' I half expect him to request a birth certificate and sampling of DNA.

When my dad adds, 'your new boss!' and slaps him heartily on the back, I thrill inwardly – 'He's going to be working for me?' – giddy at my good fortune, whereas Santiago baulks outwardly: 'I'm going to be working for her?'

'No, no,' my dad laughs. 'The other way round. You're the boss, Santiago!'

'*What?*'

Now it's my turn to baulk. He can't possibly mean this – after all he's promised me! I feel like I've been punched in the stomach.

'Come on, let's go through to the lounge,' he chivvies, attempting to jolly away the clanger.

76

'Wait a second.' I dig my heels in. 'No offence, Santiago.' I flick a glance at the matinée idol turned interloper. 'Dad, you said the coffee shop was all mine.'

'Well, yes, that's right, but then I realised it's not like you know anything about coffee production in Costa Rica.' He gives me a pally grimace. 'You wouldn't even know what time of year they harvest their coffee, let alone all the nutrients the soil needs—'

'Zinc, potassium and magnesium.' I snap back, triumphant. 'And they harvest November to January.'

'Oh yes,' he nods. 'You've just been on that Café Brit coffee tour, haven't you?'

I smart at his dismissal. Did he have to make me sound such a tourist in front of Santiago?

'But what of cupping?' Dad continues in earnest, clearly having been bamboozled with impressive-sounding terminology from Santiago.

'You mean the art of tasting and comparing coffee samples?' I reply. Good ole Ollie with the tour, I'd be way out of my depth now without that.

'Well, all right but would you know how to do it?'

'Pour five ounces of hot water over two table-spoons of coffee. When it's cooled a tad I'd use a silver plated soup spoon to break the crust, inhale deeply then slurp, as noisily as possible, savouring the flavours before I spit it out.' I clip back. 'But

77

that's not the point!' I blast him, dismissing any further quiz questions. 'We're not running a processing plant, we're running a coffee shop.'

'Be reasonable, Ava – Santiago is obviously far more familiar with the market in Costa Rica. Besides, how's your Spanish?'

He's got me there.

I puff and pout. 'So he does all the business and I'm basically in charge of the tea towels and the aprons, is that it?'

'Actually, Kiki has a real eye for the fashion side of things . . .'

I want to find a nice big pothole to throw myself down and then shovel dirt in over my head but instead I snip, 'Where is my new stepmother anyway?' eager to move off the subject of the coffee shop before I get relegated to apprentice washer-upper. I obviously need to confront my father about this when we're alone.

'She was getting her nails done—' he waves vaguely up the stairs.

'Here I am!' a voice chimes out from the body of a woman draped in a coral pashmina descending the staircase with her arms aloft, though I'm not sure whether they're wide and wafting in welcome or if she's merely trying to dry her varnish.

'You must be Ava!'

She's a smart one, make no mistake. And a young one. I realise now that my dad managed to gloss over the issue of her age and though I hardly expected her to be in her greying sixties, I was expecting the beginnings of a little crêpe-ing around the eyes. This woman has such a conspicuous absence of laughter lines you'd think she worked in a morgue. Her kinked blonde bob puts me in mind of Charlize Theron and when, leaning to kiss my cheek, her pashmina slips away, it reveals a slinky cocktail dress and a figure that is correspondingly modelesque. Put all this together and I still come up with an estimated age that falls short of my own. Oh, Daddy, you didn't . . .

'What are you all doing loitering in the lobby? Let's go through to the sitting room!' Kiki commands with a confidence beyond her years and what I now recognise as a Home Counties accent. (I can't wait to tell Ollie, who had predicted a hybrid Hawaiian-Japanese twang based solely on her name. In fact, it's officially Karen, having evolved into Kiki following her endless renditions of '*Don't Go Breaking My Heart*' circa 1976.)

This she tells me as we follow Dad and his thieving right-hand man Santiago into the lounge. I'm just about to pass through the doorway ahead of her when she snickers, 'Looks like someone's been having some fun!' It's only then I recall my mud-printed bum, but before I can even blush she's wrapped her pashmina around my waist and given it a stylish side-knot. Again I can't fathom her

79

motive – saving my face or the surface of the ivory sofa? I feel wrong-footed at every turn and as the cocktails are dispensed I'm torn between exasperation at my father, resentment at Santiago and not wanting to behave like a sulky, stroppy mare in front of Kiki since she's being so unexpectedly nice. Thus far.

'So I believe a little toast is in order!' She continues to head up proceedings. 'Here's to the partnership that's going to create the hottest coffee shop in Costa Rica!'

Dad and Kiki chink enthusiastically whereas Santiago and I barely twitch our glasses.

'You know, when I was young my dad used to try to teach me business jargon and I got all the bulls and the bears of the Stock Exchange, but whenever he'd talk about partnerships I always thought he was saying parsnips!' Kiki tinkles, displaying all the confidence of a person who thinks everything they say has value and interest.

I'm tempted to run with the vegetable theme and make some joke about carats but fear I won't be able to make it fly so keep shtum. Santiago is more silent still. He seems to be focusing on emitting proprietorial vibes – look at him sitting in the biggest, grandest chair as if to imply the rest of us are merely house guests. There's something so dauntingly stoic about him, I really don't know where to begin in terms of tackling him as an opponent. A masonry chisel would seem like my best bet right now.

By the second glass of rum-based concoction my tongue is loosened and I decide to be magnanimous and announce, 'Speaking of toasts – I'd like to take this opportunity to offer belated congratulations on your wedding!' adding a rather less generous-spirited, 'Welcome to the family,' as a particular snipe at Santiago.

'Oh it's such a shame you couldn't have been there on the day!' Kiki laments. 'It was just heavenly – we wanted to have the ceremony on the beach here in Tamarindo but all the turtles had come in to nest so we went down the coast to Islita and found this idyllic private villa.' She takes a sip of drink and then frantically clicks her fingers. 'Oh! Oh! We should make Ava that cocktail we had, what was the name of that fruit-juice mixer?' She directs this question to Santiago.

'Guanábana.'

'I don't know why I find that such a tongue-twister!' she tuts herself. 'I need to think half-guava, half-banana. Not that it tastes of either . . . Wasn't that your grandmother's recipe?'

Santiago nods.

'Bless her for coming all the way from Tortuguero! She really made our day.'

I can't believe it – some random old lady was shipped in for the celebrations but I wasn't even considered? I don't know where to look. I'm actually more embarrassed than incensed right now. I haven't felt this way since I was sent to a neighbour's last minute one Christmas because my mum was having a wobble and I had to sit by and watch everyone else open their presents pretending it was okay that I didn't have any. Mind you, back then I had my work cut out trying to deflect the pitying looks whereas it doesn't seem to occur to anyone in this room that I might be feeling left out.

Kiki is detailing the exact dimensions and flutter-factor of the confetti when her mobile phone bleeps. 'That'll be dinner!' She turns to me. 'We thought we'd have it early as you're probably still a little travel-weary. Shall we go on through?'

Santiago gets to his feet. 'If you'll excuse me, I have some business calls to make.'

'You're not dining with us?' My dad looks puppy-dog dejected.

'Not tonight.' He bows out without even a cursory nod in my direction.

I feel a strange mix of relief and annoyance as he leaves. I had braced myself for an entire evening of narrowed eyes and battling for my father's ear, but now my opponent has unexpectedly opted out. Probably off to draw up some tricksy legal document so that later, when my father is tipsy and susceptible, he can get him to sign away his life. Already I suspect he got his good looks via some deal with the devil. Before he even met me he managed to devalue my potential contribution to the coffee shop. Doesn't he realise it's Kiki's role to change the will and turn her new husband against his family? Yet here she is being so obliging . . .

'Your father said you liked blackberries so I had the cook stuff the chicken with them!'

I can't quite believe it – she must have actually asked my father to name a food I enjoyed and, stranger still, he actually came up with a valid response. *I do exist!*

As I take my seat at the banquet-size dining table, I trace the origin of his suggestion back to when we went fruit-picking one summer and my dad was tickled to watch my six-year-old self trying to eat a blackberry one juicy mini-bobble at a time. The fascination was short-lived for me but apparently it lives on in his mind.

'Wine?'

I probably shouldn't but I do. I like the comforting haze the booze is providing. It makes me feel like conflict can wait. For now I'm going to concentrate on spying on my dad and his new wife. At least that's how it feels as I watch every inter-action trying to suss out their relationship. She definitely talks more than him, which I didn't think was possible – I recall his self-promoting yarns going on for days but he seems happy to let her chirrup away. Maybe he's getting old, I think, and look at him more closely. No maybe about it, he *is* getting old. Since I last saw him his salt-and-pepper locks have become entirely salt, almost to a sci-fi silver-whiteness. Luckily for him he still has a bountiful head of hair – what he lacks in youthful colour he's making up for in volume. You'd think in this heat he'd keep it closely cropped, but apparently he prefers to wear a three-inch-thick hair hat at all times.

Kiki definitely seems very assured of his love, speaking as though they've been married for twenty years as opposed to a matter of days. Does that suggest a rock-solid bond or merely pre-sumption on her behalf? I certainly have never been that confident in any of my relationships. There was one guy I was so keen on people said I positively lit up in his presence, but then I found out he was 'illuminating' a different woman every night. At least my dad seems to have come round to the idea of being monogamous – despite countless femmes following his split from my mother, he never saw fit to marry any of them. (Ollie used to joke that he was like the United Nations when it came to women, working his way through repre-sentatives from Albania to Zanzibar.) So what is it about Kiki that tripped his switch? She definitely seems sweet and hospitable and upbeat, with a Pilates-perfect body, but when you have as much money as my dad that's probably not hard to come by.

Watching them banter affectionately, I decide to chalk it up to chemistry. It sounds more romantic than a midlife crisis.

Very little is made of their age difference in conversation, though at one point Kiki does say she's decided to refer to my dad as 'my first husband', as a little jibe at being his *second* wife. I say she shouldn't begrudge him his head start since he had so very many years to while away before they met. Fortunately they take this slight in the spirit in which it was intended and finally – *finally!* – she reveals her age.

The good news is that she is in fact older than me. Although I don't know how good this is when she doesn't look it.

Thirty-eight. She's thirty-eight to his fifty-nine. Twenty-one years apart. I blame Hollywood.

People say, what's the big deal? You love who you love! Let me just say this: if I did the same in reverse I would currently be dating a boy of nine.

As we return to the lounge for a freshly brewed pot of my Britt beans, I decide that, overall, the strangest element to this scenario is not the age gap or the chicken stuffed with blackberries or the way Kiki rotates her coffee cup so she can evenly distribute peach gloss on every inch of the ceramic lip, but the fact that I don't entirely despise her.

8

I may have spoken too soon.

Within an hour of waking I want to muffle Kiki into eternal silence with my pillow. I think her intention when she pogoed into my room and bounced on my bed while I was still drowsy and trying to make sense of a cut-short dream, was to lend a girly slumber-party vibe to proceedings. And if she was my new step*sister* she might have been able to get away with it, but it just didn't seem appropriate to her status as step*mother*.

'So this friend of mine has just set up an Internet dating agency in San José and she asked all her married friends to take the compatibility quiz to test the system and it was just so embarrassing because Dean and I scored ninety out of one hundred and people who'd been married for ten years were getting sixties and seventies and I was like, you shouldn't feel bad because we're still relatively new and so the sex is still really hot!'

Somebody shoot me. Or better yet, her.

'Personally I'd settle for a sixty after ten years of marriage,' I mumble.

On and on she goes about how harmonious and smitten they are.

'Dean said that generally he finds everyone annoying in some aspect but he likes everything about me!'

Her chime seems almost boastful and I suspect that Kiki needs witnesses to feel officially in love.

Whereas last night I was starting to believe in their suitability, now that she's ramming it down my throat methinks she doth attest too much.

Or am I just bitter?

Chances are, she's harmless. And she seems to make my dad happy – although whether he deserves it or not is a different matter. In this life it almost seems you get what you expect rather than what you deserve. If you think, like my mother, that you've been abandoned by your one true love and you're going to be alone for the rest of life, then you're right! If, like my father, you think you're entitled to increasingly younger models, you'll prove yourself right too. No one ever said self-fulfilling prophecies were fair.

'I think I'm going to jump in the shower,' I finally break her flow.

'Okay, well, there's fresh coffee on – of course – so come down to breakfast whenever you're ready.'

I get fully spruced and dressed suspecting that Santiago may be already clobbering my dad with legalese over the croissants. Or rather black beans and rice, as Costa Rican tradition decrees.

'At first I didn't like *gallo pinto* for breakfast,' Kiki confesses. 'But then you start to crave it, it's weird.'

I take a tentative forkful. Not quite my usual Coco Pops, though the spice-dusted rice does actually closely resemble them.

'So is Dad still sleeping?' I ask.

'Oh no, Santiago called him into town for an early meeting.'

The bugger! I knew it. I'm really going to have to step up my game here or I'm going to get stomped on.

'Do you know if the meeting was regarding the coffee shop?' I try not to let the tension show in my voice.

'It's always regarding the coffee shop with Santiago, it's all he can think of lately.'

'Really?'

Kiki nods. 'Ever since Dean expressed an interest he's been bombarding him with plans and concepts and financial forecasts.'

'Do you know if Dad ever explained to him that it was supposed to be my project?' Steady as she blows.

Kiki looks a little thrown. 'Well. Not exactly.'

I raise an eyebrow.

She looks awkward. 'I think you were very much the *inspiration* behind it but—'

'Can we go now?' I get to my feet.

'Go where?'

'To the meeting. You said they were in town, right? Is that far from here?'

I have to get to my father before anything is set in stone. I've put my life on hold for this – I refuse to be relegated to the bottom of the food chain.

As we ride in Kiki's pink 4×4 she continues to chatter away but I'm only half-listening as I try to formulate an effective strategy for dealing with Santiago. And my father for that matter – the concept of blood being thicker than water obviously won't wash here.

I can't help but feel betrayed, not to mention a little gullible. When I was offered the coffee shop project it felt like such a vote of confidence whereas now I realise it was nothing more than bait. It's such a downer to be demoted before I've even started. And by my own father. I shake my head. How can I possibly work as Santiago's subordinate? It's just too humiliating and frustrating to consider. If I'm not going to have any say in how the place is designed and run then I may as well just go home and offer my services to Caffè Nero. In fact, now I come to think of it, there's a rainforest-themed café in the

Podium shopping centre. Who needs the real thing when you can have bug-free photo-wallpaper?

But no sooner am I thinking of leaving, than Kiki welcomes me to Tamarindo.

As I take in my surroundings, my heart does yet another bellyflop – the name Tamarindo has such a pretty, leafy-grove ring to it, I was picturing shady boulevards of tamarind trees, popping their pods and bursting with flame-coloured blooms, but instead my overriding first impression is of mud and mini-malls. As we slow beside one arcade I see pashminas and sequinned tunics and thousand-beaded necklaces that wouldn't look out of place at the Royal Crescent Hotel, yet the people on the streets outside are bare-chested and bare-footed, stumbling over various humps and troughs. Worse yet, as the road veers up hill, all the rainwater has run back down collecting in a muddy lake that would require knee-deep wading to traverse. I've never seen a town of such mixed messages – the shops say look how chic and gentrified we are, the roads say get your ox cart we're going to market.

'See this roundabout?' Kiki asks, as we reach the end of the main drag. 'This is the town centre.'

'The roundabout is the centre of town?'

She nods. 'That bar gets a bit rough of an evening.' She points to a shack with security caging and tattered red and yellow paintwork. 'You probably won't want to make that your local hangout. But this café here does the best mahimahi wraps, all tangy and juicy with slithers of courgette and avocado.'

'Nice lampshades,' I note the sixties-style inter-locking paper twists that remind me of retro swimming hats.

'They sell them in the shop a few doors down,' she says before moving my gaze on to a restaurant opening directly on to the beach. 'Home to the rudest waitress in the whole of Guanacaste.'

'Really?' Good to know – no doubt I would have taken personal affront had I not known her reputation. My eyes switch to the gift shop across the way.

'That's the place to go for out-of-date guidebooks and flavoured cigarette papers,' she winks.

Continuing on we pass a slick new real-estate office and an Internet café, then a skuzzy hippie offering hair-braiding and a restaurant selling fried pigskin. I take a breath and inhale a mix of salty ocean, tropical fruit and marijuana. And then I spy the man responsible for all three – a mango-sucking surfer dude.

As he clocks my gawping he shakes his jaw-length ringlets indulging me with a slo-mo movie moment. There's no denying he is stop-you-in-your-tracks stunning, a full-grown cherub with a body of carved mahogany. As even the car engine purrs in appreciation, two more guys join him, wedging their surfboards in the sand to create the perfect

Abercrombie & Fitch ad campaign. I can't believe how styled they look. When I come out of the sea my eyes are all pink and my hair has the texture of drowned raffia matting. Maybe if I got myself a shell necklace, I'd feel more the part? Sensing Kiki's eyes upon me I feel I should say something to justify my staring. 'You don't get a lot of surfers in Bath!' is the best I can come up with.

'Oh my god! I have to show you one of their hang-outs,' she says and wrenches the steering wheel round.

'But—' I go to protest, wondering if she could be in cahoots with Santiago, deliberately delaying the showdown?

She places her hand over my anxiously studied watch, insisting, 'We'll just be five minutes!' then makes like a submarine through the giant orange puddle at the bottom of the hill and hauls us up a street with potholes like plunge pools and, of course, ever ritzier shopping arcades. As we wait for a couple of cars to pass, I note that many units are still available and I'm about to ask Kiki if this is perhaps where they're thinking of placing the coffee shop when she surges forward and pulls into the driveway of a hostel named Botella de Leche.

'Bottle of Milk,' she translates, making sense of the black-and-white cowprint splotched on the exterior walls. And interior. And the beanbag covers sagging in the TV room and the knobs on the kitchen stove. The moo motif is taken to the extreme with the secondary accommodation being a converted cattle trailer, divided into five units each containing three beds rentable at $10 per person per night. With unlimited use of the inflatable kiddy paddling pool thrown in!

As Kiki chats to a couple of sedated surfers sunk low into an outdoor sofa I peer inside and discover that one wave-rider's bedroom is another man's tin can. No windows. No sink. No room to even tie a sarong. If the 'room' was at full capacity you'd literally have to file in one-by-one – first person enters, climbs into bed, gives the signal for the second to follow suit, then the third. I can't even imagine how claustrophobic it must be when the door closes.

'They have to have an air-con unit or they'd die,' the Argentinian owner breezes.

'Do you live here?' I ask wondering how someone could stay so glamorous under these conditions.

She emits an 'Are you kidding?' scoff. 'I just come by in the day to make sure everyone is happy.' It's only then that I notice even her dog has Friesian-style splodges and a cowbell around its neck.

As I edge back to the car to let Kiki know I'm ready to leave I conclude that it's a good thing that surfers aren't materialistic. And in turn marvel that Kiki doesn't seem at all self-conscious that her wedding ring could probably buy the entire place, or fund a year's surf vacation.

'Don't you get nervous wearing such a big rock in a country where mugging seems to be a national sport?' I nod towards the glitterball on her left hand.

'Well, I've cut back on my other jewellery outside the home but I'm not going to *not* wear my wedding ring. I mean, if someone wants to come along and cut off my hand so they can get hold of it, well, then that's their problem.'

My brow contorts at her bizarre logic. In my book having a stump at the end of my arm would be very much *my* problem, and just to make sure I don't invite such a fate I discreetly remove my bracelet, even though it is just £6 worth from Claire's Accessories.

It surprises me how blasé Kiki is about the darker elements of her neighbourhood. Just when I have her pegged as a spoilt princess she gets all streetwise on me. Or is she what my mum would call a Pollyanna? She knows there are so-called bad people in the world but is fairly certain that if she ran into them, they'd be nice as pie to her. Tamarindo has me equally perplexed – the beach may look like the stereotypical shot of paradise with its sheer sand, frothy surf and gangly palm trees but there's something unsettling about the overall atmosphere. I wonder if one of the other *playas* – Langosta, Flamingo, etc. – might be a better bet for our coffee shop?

Of course even Bath has dodgy elements, it all depends on where you go. One minute you're tittering at the wit of Oscar Wilde at the Theatre Royal and the next you're subjected to some geezer in a leather jacket cursing at his kids outside McDonald's.

All the same, I have a definite urge to be safely ensconced in my dad's office with my back to the window pretending I'm back in jolly old England.

'Is it much further?' I reveal my impatience.

'Nearly there,' Kiki points ahead. 'Just the other side of the Diria Hotel.'

'Oh god, that's not a great reputation for a hotel to have!' I squirm.

For a second she looks confused and then laughs. 'Not diarrhoea, Diria – D-i-r-i-a. It's actually the poshest one in Tamarindo, though I must confess the rooms do have a strange odour,' she winces. 'That's where I stayed when I first arrived. Your father and I had our first date at the Terrace restaurant.'

I don't really want to encourage further detail but I feel I should at least ask how they met.

'My company was looking for a Costa Rican business partner,' she explains, 'We had meetings with several estate agents out here and your father impressed us the most. But instead of agreeing to the merger he head-hunted me!'

Doesn't she mean bed-hunted?

'So you're the one that ended up with a partner,' I joke.

'That's right!' she laughs, parking up and pausing a moment as she switches off the ignition. 'I don't know what I did to deserve to be this happy!'

I'm finding it tactless to the point of being impolite for her to gloat like this, but apparently she's oblivious to just how wretched I'm feeling.

Two seconds later I'm smiling for real – Dad's office is a cube of ice-cold bliss.

'Hi, Carla!' Kiki greets the receptionist. 'Is Dean around?'

'Actually he just popped out.'

Of course he did. Why on earth would he make himself available to the daughter he hasn't seen in years on her first day in town?

'Did he say how long he'd be?'

'Just half an hour or so.' She takes in my wilting form. 'You must be Ava – can I get you some water?'

I open my mouth to reply but another woman's voice beats me to it: 'Kiki, it's in!'

A doll-sized Tico girl has snuck in behind us and is excitedly tugging at Kiki's sleeve.

'Fantastic! I'll be right there!' She turns back to me. 'I've ordered a surprise something for Dean, do you mind if I—'

'Go ahead, take your time. I'm just glad to be in the cool.' I smile at the receptionist as she hands me a glass of water and take up her offer to flump on the sofa and leaf through one of the property guides.

Gosh. You know you're dealing with a rich clientele when the homes come with maids' quarters, wine cellars and 'exterior lounges'. One property also offers surfboard and ATV storage.

'What's ATV?' I ask Carla.

'It stands for all-terrain vehicle – you know, a quad bike?'

'Oh right!' I go back to my reading, surprised to see that one particular four-storey, five-bedroom, quarter-acre lot with a swimming pool and ocean views is going for about £300,000. In Bath that would currently buy you a two-bedroom *flat* in a Georgian town house in the centre of town. Despite the huge disparity in size and facilities, I know which I'd prefer.

Mind you, I quite like the look of this 'casa' with a pool and valley views ten minutes from the beach for £200,000. Oooh, and look at this lot amid a twenty-seven-acre reserve. And this oceanfront unit crying out to become a boutique hotel! Or what about my very own hectare of teak plantation for just £14,000?

I take a calming sip of water. I'm getting a bit all fluttery-excited at the prospects here. Maybe I misjudged the vibe. The figures certainly seem to add up. As I thumb on through the brochure skipping the golf resort community – I've never been a big

97

fan of skull-cracking little white balls – Carla gives a discreet cough.

'Um, Ava, I hate to take advantage but while you're here would you mind if I just nipped out and grabbed a coffee?'

Ha! A potential customer!

'Of course not,' I smile. 'Where do you get yours from, if you don't mind me asking?'

'There's a new place a couple of doors up – Caféteria Nari – they do the most delicious Irish cream mocha. Can I get you something?'

'No, that's okay, I'll probably pop along for a look when you get back.'

'Okay, won't be a mo.'

As soon as she's gone I get up and walk around the office imagining this to be the future location for the coffee shop, wondering how I could transform the boxy blandness into something distinctive and inviting. And then I wonder some more – with all this new construction, just how long would it take to build something from scratch? Imagine designing your very own coffee emporium. How impressed would Ollie be by that? It's then I realise I've been left alone with a functioning phone – I can call him! But before I've even got past the country code there's a 'Yoo-hoo!' at the door and in pokes a friendly male face. 'Dean around?'

'He's due back in about twenty minutes. Can I take a message?'

'You're English!'

'That's what you want me to tell him?' I tcase. 'I suspect he already knows that.'

'Funny,' he gives a playful grimace. 'Where are you from?'

'Bath,' I smile. 'What about you?'

'Nottingham,' he replies.

Turns out his name is Richard and he runs the Green Turtle Gift Shop up the street. I waste no time asking his USP. He tells me they have two – the first being air conditioning.

'I see people in other shops picking out postcards and photo albums just to fan themselves. I want people to handle the goods cos they want to actually buy them!'

'How novel,' I smile.

'But the main thing is that 10 per cent of our profits go to PRETOMA – a national project to save the marine turtles.'

'I keep hearing about the turtles. What exactly is the deal with that?'

'Well, a couple of weeks ago you could have seen for yourself – they were nesting along the beach here.'

'And you can actually walk among them?' I'm amazed.

'You can if you're with a guide,' he affirms. 'Of course now if you want to do that you'd have to head over to Tortuguero.'

99

Ah yes, Tortuguero. I can just see Santiago's granny hosting my visit, while grinding ox dung into my *gallo pinto*.

'I actually have a friend who lives on the Caribbean coast,' Richard continues. 'I'd be happy to hook you up if you're interested.'

'Oh no, I don't want to be any trouble, besides I'm not exactly on holiday.'

'Well, it doesn't hurt to ask and you might want to grab the opportunity while you can – all four species that nest here in Costa Rica are listed as endangered and scientists predict that the leatherback turtles will be extinct within ten years.'

I'm aghast. 'What's going wrong?' I ask.

'Let me count the ways . . .' he muses. 'The worst hazard is actually fishermen's lines – more turtles die through accidental capture in nets than from all the other threats: contaminated waters, beachfront developments depriving turtles of safe nesting areas, poachers killing them for their shells and meat and stealing their eggs—'

I hold up a finger. 'Can you help me get something straight?' I request. Something has been bothering me ever since I perused a certain café menu in San José . . . 'It's illegal to steal turtle's eggs and that's the only way to come by them, but it's not illegal for restaurants to sell them to eat?'

'Welcome to Costa Rica!' Richard smirks. 'Actually, it gets even more bizarre than that: in

100

Ostional, the smallest sea turtles – the olive ridleys – are protected by an organisation which is partially funded by the sale of turtle eggs.'

'*What?*' I splutter.

'It's true. For the first thirty-six hours of their arrival the organisation let their members – and we're talking a headcount of 240 – harvest eggs for up to fifteen hours. After that it is their responsibility to protect the nests.'

Richard lets me sit awhile with my bafflement before explaining the reasoning behind this – something to do with 'first wave' eggs commonly rotting and thus contaminating later healthy eggs.

'It's what they call "sustainable" – exploiting natural resources without destroying the ecological balance.'

I look at him a little too blankly.

'Excellent!' he claps his hands together. 'Now that I've got you entirely perplexed, I must be leaving! Just tell Dean that I stopped by, would you?'

'Can I ask you one more thing?' I jump to his side.

'Fire away.'

How to phrase this . . .? 'Um, is it my imagination or is there . . .' I can't say it.

'Yes?' He looks bemused.

I try again. 'I just feel, this town . . .'

'Are you perhaps referring to our "seedy" element,' he says oh-so-politely?'

101

I laugh.

'It's actually a lot better than it was. Having said that, even now if you walk down the main drag at night, you'll probably be offered drugs at least a couple of times.'

'Really? The dealers are that direct?'

'Well, they'd probably say something like, "Have you got everything you want?"'

'Well, it's a good thing you told me that or I could have been there all day with my Father Christmas list.'

As Richard laughs, I enquire, 'So is it like this all down the coast – a little bit run-down, a little bit dodgy?'

'Not at all. While you're here you should try and get down to Islita, that's another world.' He looks rapturous.

'Yeah, my dad got married there,' I mutter, trying to stifle my resentment.

'What a coincidence – Dean married there too, within the last few weeks in fact.'

'I know, Dean is my dad.'

Richard looks stunned. 'I'm sorry, I don't remember seeing you at the wedding – how rude of me!'

'Not at all,' I appease him. 'I wasn't there so it's not like you could ignore me.'

'Oh it's such a shame you couldn't make it,' he shakes his head. 'It was just heavenly.'

'So I hear.'

As I wave him off I realise that this will be my cross to bear – every wretched soul I meet will taunt me further about the missed wedding and the idyll that is Islita. All while I'm stuck here in tawdry Tamarindo.

I twist around on the sofa and gaze out on to the street. A man steps into view and mouths the words, 'Got everything you want?'

I blink back at him and shake my head. I don't think he can help me. What I want most right now is a father who keeps his promises.

And while we're at it, what the hell is keeping Kiki?

9

'Any dramas in my absence?' Carla bustles back into the office, conspicuously peppier for her alcohol-infused caffeine fix.

Just a couple of drug deals and an assault with a surfboard, I think to myself.

'Just Richard from The Green Turtle looking for my dad,' is what I say out loud.

'Oh Richard's a sweetie, isn't he?' she coos.

'Yes he is,' I confirm.

'I had the biggest crush on him until I found out he's married.'

Married? Well that puts paid to any first dates at Diarrhoea Hotel.

'Anyway, back to work!' Carla settles behind her desk and tends to the ringing phone. 'Hello? Yes. Yes, let me just check his schedule. He's due back in Manuel Antonio later this week. No, he works from home there, do you have the number? That's right. Okay, will do.' She sets down the phone and scribbles a message on a Post-it note then sits back in her chair and puffs, 'We just get busier every day!'

'I don't mean to be nosy, but did you say my father had a home in Manuel Antonio?'

'Oh yes! Your father has properties dotted all across Costa Rica.'

'Really?'

'He doesn't live in all of them – I mean, he must have a dozen condos here in Tamarindo that haven't even been built yet and a villa in Golfito that's really a long-term investment – that area probably won't get hot until about 2020. But he's smart, it'll happen.'

'So in terms of actual homes . . .?' I fish.

'Well, he's just sold the one in San José and is looking for something in Escazu—'

'Es-cuze me?'

'It's on the outskirts of the city, they say it's Costa Rica's OC in terms of ex-pat residents.'

'Ohhh,' I nod, studying the floor for a second before I ask, 'I don't mean to be rude, but why would anyone want to live in San José?'

'The weather for one thing, it's far less hot and humid.'

'Good point,' I concede, already converted.

'The restaurants, the culture,' Carla continues. 'Do you like the symphony?'

'I don't know, I've never been.'

'Oh you just have to go to the Teatro Nacional

105

while you're here, you'd think you were in Covent Garden – the building is so ornate and everyone is dressed so beautifully . . .'

I'm intrigued. I guess there's a side of San José I haven't seen. Mind you, what's a pickpocket without a pocket to pick?

The phone goes again. Before she answers I quickly tell her I'm popping out to have a look around the town.

'Okay. Don't be long, your dad should be back any minute.'

I give her a thumbs up, think, 'Yeah, yeah,' and exit.

My mind is buzzing with all the new information. I'm back to wondering if another location might be better and Dad having properties scattered hither and thither certainly widens our options. Before I arrived I wanted to get cracking straight away but now I can see the benefit of doing a little recce and research before we commit – I'm still not sure I could spend the next couple of months here in Tamarindo. But then two more head-turningly sexy surfers scuff by – this pair with dreadlocked ponytails and woven wristbands – shortly followed by two surfer girls with big smiles on their faces. And who can blame them? There's got to be five guys for every girl here. Hmmm. Maybe I shouldn't have dismissed Ollie's suggestion of a holiday romance so emphatically?

On the way to suss out the coffee-shop competition I go to stick my nose in the Diria Hotel but I'm shooed away by a security guard because I don't have the requisite fluorescent wristband identifying me as a hotel guest. I tell him I just want to pick up a leaflet from reception and he watches me all the way.

The lobby is open air looking out over the pool, which in turn looks out over a grassy garden sloping down to the beach. I sidestep assorted honey-mooners, more surfers and a pair of the biggest boobs I ever did see, parading around in a bikini that itself will be in need of a holiday after the exhaustion of trying to keep its owner contained. For such an up-and-coming neighbourhood I'm surprised there's not a swankier resort-style option. But then I remember that the Four Seasons isn't so very far from here. (I imagine their guests expect to have the animals parade before them in the lounge area rather than muddy their feet in the rainforest. Perhaps they even have them put on a cabaret – howler monkey singers, resplendent quetzal show-birds, a crocodile doing a magic act with an unsuspecting frog. 'Watch as I make him dis-appear,' I hear the croc growl.)

Ah, here we are: the cafeteria. And not a pot of Tetley or plate of chips in sight.

To me, Café Nari looks more like a Thorntons in

its bijoux size and design – all very European with marble floors and brass-trimmed fixtures but zero local flavour, despite the fact that the shelves are stocked with pouches of Café Britt coffee.

I pick up a menu and peruse. Five dollars for an iced latte? That seems a bit steep. I look around at the people supping on mint mochas and amaretto cappuccinos and decide to go for something equally fancy to justify the price, then make full use of my cup being 'to go' and head on to the next.

Again more decor disappointment: the lighting on the pastries is far too harsh and fluorescent – a pineapple Danish might not have concerns about cellulite or enlarged pores, but it can still benefit from a soft-glow bulb. Again the chairs look tinny and uncomfortable. Where are the sink-into sofas? Mind you, in this heat they'd have to be wrung out every night, whereas I suppose these can just be wiped down.

It dismays me to think that either of these places could just as easily be in Bath. And then it dawns on me that is actually good news for me. Or should I say us. Having been flying solo on my coffee-shop project for so long, it's going to take me a while to get used to having business partners. Or worse yet, bosses. Especially one who makes me feel like I'm battling the dark side every time I look at him.

I look at my watch. Nearly 1 p.m. Surely everyone will have returned by now? Not that I'm too miffed about the delay it's given me a chance to get the lie of the land. Before I was just fuming at the injustice, now I feel primed. I step back onto the street and begin striding back towards the office. The time has come to confront my father.

Thank god he's alone!

I take a deep breath to quell my trepidation and fire up my resolve.

'Dad?'

'Ava!' He looks up from his desk as if he's surprised to see me. As if he'd forgotten that I was even in the country. Excellent start.

'I wanted to talk to you about the coffee shop, and the question of who's in charge.' I waste no time on small talk.

'Is Kiki with you?' He looks around me and beyond to the street outside. Anything, apparently, rather than look me in the eye.

'She went, um, shopping,' I tell him, muttering under my breath, 'Quite some time ago.'

'Oh well, I'm sure she'll turn up in time for lunch. Why don't you take a seat?'

I do so and prepare for as adult a conversation as I can muster when inside I feel like having a Terrible Twos-style tantrum.

'Soooo. How did you sleep last night? It's so peaceful up on the hill, isn't it? We had a wonderful sunrise this morning but obviously I was delighted

109

you were sleeping in after your long journey—'

'Dad!' I stop his wittering. It would be all too easy to find other subjects to chat on (just think of how much has gone unsaid between us over the years) but I fear that if I don't stand up for myself now I'll get assigned a truly dud role and the day-to-day resentment will eat me alive. 'The café?' I get him back on track. 'We really need to talk about this.'

'Well, I mean . . . Ava, it's complicated,' he sighs, already exasperated.

'No it's not.' I keep it calm. 'You promised that the coffee shop would be my project. I just want you to honour that promise.' I give my best assertiveness-training smile.

'Santiago is a very talented young man—' he begins, managing to sound both magnanimous and insulting at the same time.

'More talented than me?' I cut in.

'Well . . .' he flounders.

'You don't know, do you? Because you haven't given me a chance to show what I can do.'

Dad looks weary and says in a small voice, 'I have to go with what I know.'

He doesn't even hear the irony that he knows Santiago better than his own daughter.

'Santiago has worked diligently for me for five years,' he continues. 'He's exceeded every expectation I've had and this promotion is way overdue.'

110

'*And at my expense!*' I want to scream! He just doesn't get it!

'Look, I'll admit that it is because of you that the coffee shop idea came to the fore—'

'Exactly!' I pipe.

'But it turns out Santiago had been working on a similar idea—'

'Oh of course he had,' I say, certain he stayed up half the night coming up with a well-worn plan. I decide to try a different tack: 'So he's really that good, is he?'

'Yes, he is.' My dad stands strong, albeit with a wobbly look on his face.

'So why bring me here?'

Dad looks thrown. 'What?'

'I mean it. I don't understand why you wanted me here. You don't need me at all.'

'I need you here more than you know,' he says, sounding disarmingly sincere.

Yet all I can do is scoff: 'What's that supposed to mean?'

I can't trust anything he says. I have to go the cynical route to protect myself – oh my god, he's not dying, is he?

'It's complicated . . .' is all he offers me.

'Is that your stock get-out clause for everything?' This is really winding me up. 'Saying something is complicated does not grant you immunity from talking about it! If it's complicated then break it

111

down into manageable pieces. That's what you always told me to do with my homework.'

He concedes a smile. 'Hoist by my own petard!'

I sigh. 'You're not ill, are you?' I need to know just how mean I can be.

'No, I'm not ill. I'm not as young as I once was but all things considered—'

'What then?'

He seems to be searching for the right words and for a moment I wonder if he might tell me that he's desperate to make up for all the neglected years between us, that he's had some kind of epiphany and is on a mission to be a better dad, but ultimately his words are these: 'I'm not at liberty to discuss this matter at present.'

My eyebrows rise scornfully. 'So now you're a government agent!'

'It's just . . . Look. Your being here is very important to me. And to Kiki.'

'It's also having quite an impact on Santiago!' I chip.

'I didn't mean to set you up as rivals,' Dad looks apologetic. 'I'm sure you'll adjust just fine—'

'Dad.' I stop him again. 'Do you really think I'm going to give up that easily? You've never rolled over on any business deal. I do have some of your genes, even if they are not visible to the naked eye.'

'Ava,' he reaches for my hand, which tenses at his

112

touch. 'I admire your tenacity and your enthusiasm for the café but—'

But. The tiniest word and often the most crushing.

'But?' I dare him to make me feel any more undermined.

'Oop! Here you two are!' It's Carla. By the look of her, she's had another cup of Irish cream, this time with just a dash of coffee. 'Not interrupting, am I?' she asks, sensing the tension as she wavers by the door.

We both stare back at her saying nothing.

'I bumped into Kiki,' she offers, eyes flicking between us. 'She's gone ahead to get the table for lunch.' I can see all she wants to do is to get to the safety of her own desk but she seems paralysed. 'Did you see we've got our very own Burger King here in Tamarindo?' she says finally.

'That's where we're having lunch?' I'm incredulous.

'Oh no!' she hoots. 'I was just—'

'All right, Carla,' Dad shushes her then gets to his feet. 'If Phil rings about the property registry for Jaco tell him we'll check on the liens and encumbrances this week. And if you could let the *catastro* know which lot of maps we need for tomorrow's pickup . . .'

'Will do. Oh and I promised the Samara guy you'd give him the quickest call?' Carla looks pleadingly.

113

For a second I'm mildly impressed – my dad is in demand and in charge! But then I remember his most recent business decision . . .

'Shall we go?' He motions for me to follow him.

I give Carla an attempt at a smile and step back into the liquid heat. Neither my dad nor I speak as we make our way up the hill, just that little bit closer to the sun. I can't tell if he's wishing I'd never come, smarting from our conversation or simply wondering what he's going to have for lunch. I'd like to think he's having a crisis of conscience but I doubt it. Me, I'm wondering if I should just call the whole thing off as a bad job. They say the definition of insanity is doing the same thing over and over but expecting different results. And here I am again, hoping that this time my dad will make me feel like I matter. Why can't I get it? *It's never going to happen.* I have to let that go, and I have to stop thinking about what he can do for me and go back to doing what's best for myself.

Seeing as he seems so inflexible on this matter I'm toying with the idea of playing along with his decision – but only for a few weeks – so I can add a little international flavour to my CV so the whole thing hasn't been a complete waste of time – but then, as we enter the courtyard restaurant, I see Santiago sitting at the head of the table and my knee-jerk reaction is, *'Oh no you don't!'*

I've fought with my dad before and it's a

thankless task but you, mister? I'm not going to roll over for you.

I stride up and take the seat directly opposite him. This is a man I want to face head on.

10

A Hawaiian pizza isn't exactly embracing the local cuisine but it's going to be hard enough for me to keep my cool without negotiating some mystery dish and accidentally biting down on a chilli that needs a fire extinguisher as a chaser.

Kiki is chattering away about the fabulous new stock her favourite home-furnishing store has imported, and I'm beginning to think she's intent on stretching this topic out through the entire meal when she excuses herself to go to the loo, and Santiago speaks for the first time: 'So has your father explained that we've narrowed down the search to two premises?'

I look at my dad, annoyed that we're starting the conversation with me at a disadvantage. Again.

'Not yet.' Dad looks distracted.

'No time like the present!' I insist, eyeing him fixedly.

'Well,' he coughs. 'It's basically down to one

116

brand new property in the mall across the street – if we buy now we can choose every fixture and fitting at no extra cost. Plus it's set alongside twelve other businesses including a bank and a pharmacy so our through traffic will be diverse and regular.'

'And property number two?'

'An already-existing café. Needs a lot of updating but has more character and is right on the beach. The area around it is less developed but it's getting busier all the time.'

'Well, I know where my vote lies,' I clip.

'You don't need to see the venues before you decide?' Santiago queries.

'Character and the beach is going to win out over one of these soulless mall joints like Café Nari or El Chacha.'

Dad and Santiago exchange a look, as if to say, 'She did just get here last night, didn't she?'

'Well, there is one vital factor I haven't mentioned,' Dad coughs. 'The beach one is in Manuel Antonio.'

'Yet another mark in its favour. I'm sold!' I cheer.

'You've been there?' Santiago looks at me with suspicion.

'No, but it's not Tamarindo,' I shrug. 'That's all I need to know.'

Now that was bitchy of me to slag off Santiago's home town but he needs a reality check. Besides, it doesn't make too much difference where I base myself whereas I'm hoping Santiago won't be so keen to relocate, thus giving me the edge.

'The thing is, on a practical level, it makes more sense to go for the one here in Tamarindo,' my dad reasons. 'I do most of my business here, Kiki's made some nice friends,' he smiles and squeezes her hand as she rejoins the table.

In fear of her going back to talking about curtain tie-backs I jump in. 'Well, it's no problem really. You can just check in on us when you're in Manuel Antonio on business.'

'But I'd miss you if you were based down there!' Kiki pouts.

Oh yeah, like you missed me today once you'd dumped me at the office?

'Don't be silly,' I coddle her. 'It's only a thirty-minute flight and I'm sure you visit the other house all the time!'

'Actually I've never been to that one.' She reaches to squidge her husband's chin. 'You keep saying you'll take me with you but you haven't yet.'

'Well, it's always business twenty-four hours a day when I'm there, I thought you'd get bored.'

'Well, she wouldn't any more 'cos I'd be there!' Oh this is going too well! 'Just think, that way Kiki would have friends in both places, wouldn't that be nice?'

I see Kiki perk up – *she's got a point,* I can see her thinking. Even my dad looks like he's wavering –

118

skew an argument to favour Kiki and you're clearly in business!

I sneak a look at Santiago and the expression on his face chills me. And yet thrills me at the same time – *I'm winning!*

'I think we're getting a bit carried away here.' Santiago tries to rein things back in before we gallop all the way to Manuel Antonio.

'Isn't that what happens when an idea is good?' I smirk. 'You just want to run with it.'

'I'm not saying an outright no to Manuel Antonio, obviously it's a strong contender or it wouldn't have made it down to the last two.'

'We always said we wanted a property on the beach and there's nothing available here,' Kiki explains.

'The fact of the matter is, Tamarindo is the fastest-developing area in Costa Rica whereas Manuel Antonio is more of a steady classic.'

'What if Tamarindo outgrows itself, all the developers come in and it gets too crazy?' I pause. 'I want to say it would lose it's natural charm but—'

'The point is we'd be riding the wave from the beginning,' Santiago digs his heels in. 'We'd have room to grow but we'd also have the market right now.'

'Do you think there's a chance that Manuel Antonio might seem like old news?'

Oh no! I'm losing Kiki.

'I doubt it,' my dad comes out in my corner. 'It's truly beautiful there. And it does have its own national park directly adjacent to the beach.'

I perk up. 'It has its own rainforest?'

My dad nods.

'And here in Guanacaste it's all dry forest, right?'

Both he and Kiki nod.

'And people come to Costa Rica for . . .?'

'I think there's one basic thing we need to be clear on from the start.' Santiago halts my flow. 'Who do we want to sell our coffee to?' Before I can answer he continues: 'Tamarindo is surrounded by million-dollar homes.'

'Money splashed around on property is one thing but really how much can you charge for a cup of coffee?' And then I remember Café Nari and say, 'I take that back.'

'Look at our neighbouring shops here – we can really go for something high-end.'

'But to what end?' I persist. 'It's all very well creating something on a par with Harrods food hall but this is Costa Rica! With the possible exception of Kiki, everyone is going to come in seeped in sweat and iguana droppings. Personally I think we need to aim for a blend of local character, international quality products and a truly unique design, rather than just go all out for swank.'

And frankly I can't believe a native is arguing for the opposite. Is Santiago just playing devil's advocate? Why would a Tico want to price himself above his fellow man? Issues, this guy has issues.

'A unique design is all very well but you're setting yourself up to go out of fashion,' he nitpicks.

'We can evolve with the times,' I argue.

'If you keep changing you lose your identity.'

'Madonna hasn't.'

Santiago looks at me with derision.

I can't believe I used her as an example. Why did I have to go and embarrass myself at such a crucial juncture? I sound like a teenager. I go to move swiftly on but Kiki raves, 'Oh my god, I just love Madonna – can you believe she's writing kids' books now? That woman is a total chameleon.'

'That's what we could call the café!' I blurt, words coming out of my mouth before I've even thought the thought. 'The Chameleon Café!' I pip. 'Then the changes we make would be expected, inte-grated, part of what keeps people coming back!'

'That's good,' my dad nods, suddenly looking at me with a mixture of amazement and 'She gets that from me!' pride. 'Santiago, what do you think?'

'I think that if we were opening a café in Madagascar that would be great.'

'What do you mean?' My heart stops. Oh no . . . Please don't tell me that in a country with over two hundred different species of reptile that no sodding chameleons made it on to the ark?

'As it happens we have a few but it's hardly what we're known for here.'

All is not lost!

'As a concept, it really works,' my dad muses.

'Again we're getting sidetracked,' Santiago huffs as our food is placed before us. 'We need to be clear on our market, that will determine everything, location, design—'

'Surely location comes first, everything else follows from there?' I have no interest in my pizza. My stomach is churning with competitiveness and I'm giddy from the excitement of the ideas in the air.

'What I think we're losing sight of is the fact that Tamarindo is the most sure-fire commercial prospect.'

'Are you just in this for the money?' I ask scornfully.

He looks at me as if to say, 'Are you just in this to piss me off?'

'This is a business venture, Miss Langston.' His coldness belies his Latin roots.

'It's more than that, Mr . . .' Darn! I don't know his last name.

'Umaña Barrientos,' Kiki helps me out.

I can't possibly risk trying to pronounce that so I just leave the 'Mr' hanging and continue: 'This is a chance to create something so much more than a place to purchase or drink coffee – this café can be a haven, an indulgence, a favourite place to chat with friends or find some peace, it can become the highlight of someone's day. If we get the mix right it will become a brand which in turn will create spin-off projects and all the money you could wish for, all with a sense of pride and satisfaction knowing that we have contributed something of quality to the world.'

Was that too much? I'm getting a little giddy from this power play.

Santiago doesn't even attempt a slighting come-back this time. Poor man, he can't possibly realise how much is at stake here. He's certainly underestimating the years of practice I've had trying to win my father's respect and love. Up until now I've failed but this clash is taking on a titan-like significance.

Apparently my resolve is palpable because Kiki suggests we call a truce while we eat, 'Or we're all going to get indigestion!' she laughs, trying to make light of the conflict.

I agree to hold myself in check for the next hour but after that? I know it's inappropriate, unpatriotic even, to come out all guns blazing in a country that has no army but I don't care. *This is war!*

11

'So you've got your Uzi prepped, your tongue barbed and he vanishes again?'

'It's so frustrating,' I wail down the phone to Ollie. 'It's just a lot of bickering so far. I don't feel anything has been resolved.'

'You know, according my Costa Rica research, Ticos are typically all about *"quedar bien"* meaning staying on good terms. It's supposedly against their national nature to criticise and humiliate and refute what someone says in public – trust you to get the one stroppy exception!'

'I know! What happened to the good ole days when all my problems revolved around my father?' I sigh.

'How are you feeling about the old bugger right now?' Ollie enquires.

'Honestly? Frustrated more than anything – when I was firing out ideas over lunch he was actually responding quite positively but that just makes me all the more mad that he won't give me a proper chance to shine.'

'Maybe Santiago has some weird hold over him and his hands are tied.'

'Maybe,' I concede. 'He did say the strangest thing about needing me here "more than you know"! What do you suppose that means?'

'Did you ask?'

'Yes, but he just got even more sketchy.'

'Curious.' I can practically see Ollie stroking his chin.

'At first I thought this whole scenario was about indulging Kiki, and when I got here and she was so eager to befriend me I thought maybe she was short of playmates her age but now I'm not so sure. There seems to be something else going on. I just can't imagine what. There's no legal advantage to having me here, is there?'

'Perhaps it's like in *Pirates of the Caribbean*, you know how they needed the blood of a relative of Bootstrap Bill to lift the curse . . .'

'Well it did cross my mind that he was after a kidney but he says he's in good health.'

'You don't think Kiki's pregnant?' Ollie proposes.

'It's possible but I don't see how that would involve me.'

'He's probably just getting sentimental in his old age,' Ollie decides. 'Wants to make peace with his nearest and dearest.'

'Yes, I expect he's planning a reconciliation with my mother as we speak.' I deadpan.

'God, can you imagine?' Ollie tuts. 'What ever would her reaction be?'

'Anger. Ranting. Too little, too late. Reopening old wounds. *Nasty*,' I shudder imagining her with fresh fuel. *'And he has the audacity to contact me after fifteen years, as if I'm not plagued with enough painful reminders, here he comes flaunting his spiritual enlightenment yada yada yada . . .'*

'Anyway, he's not all bad,' Ollie concludes. 'At least he sorted you a phone so we can keep in touch.'

'Yes, that is a blessing.' I must admit I do like being able to call at my leisure, I just wish there were more air-conditioned places to call from. Right now I'm skulking at the back of the Green Turtle Gift Shop, trying to decide how best to frame my answer to Ollie's question: 'What's this Kiki like, anyway?'

I begin cautiously: 'If I don't like someone who seems nice and friendly and cheerful, does that make me a bad person?'

Ollie chuckles. 'What exactly is it about her that jars with you? Try to be specific.'

I love it when Ollie gets his psychology head on. 'Well, I think it's the sense that she's had everything come easy to her – like she's never suffered, never had to really try, never been disappointed. She's just so darn peppy!'

'Peppy?'

'And happy with her life,' I sigh, finally getting to the crux of the matter.

'So you're jealous?'

'Yes, I suppose I am,' I confess. 'Though clearly not of who she's married to.'

'Well, I don't suppose that helps. She's got the attention of the man who gives you none.'

'I could have sworn that in the old days I used to feel better for talking to you,' I huff, though I know Ollie has a point. 'Anyway, I've got to go now, the man who shows me no attention is showing me the mall property at 4 p.m.'

'You said you're on a camera phone, right? Send me some pics!'

'Will do.' I click the phone shut, give Richard a little thank-you wave for letting me use his 'facilities' and then skulk over to meet Dad.

On the way I ponder: is suffering what gives a person depth and soul? To the contrary, I'd always feared that rejection and loneliness had eaten away at my confidence making me *less* of the person I was meant to be. But maybe an element of sadness or yearning actually makes a personality more multi-dimensional? I've certainly heard it said that we connect over our flaws, not our perfections. Maybe that's why I can't foresee myself being close with Kiki – she has no visible insecurities, doubts or fears. I think of all her gushing this morning and I know she couldn't possibly relate to the pain I've been carrying with me since I split from Nick. Who knew an empty space could weigh so heavy?

It doesn't make any sense to me that the removal of a negative factor in my life could actually make me feel worse but I guess it's the lingering gloom of another failed relationship. What must it feel like to be so sure of your partner, to know wholeheartedly that you've found The One? I long for that feeling of standing on solid ground. For me, when I'm going out with someone, I always feel like one of those circus acts with a board balanced on two cans. Even now that I'm single again, I find myself walking down a street booby-trapped with a hundred ways to stumble. Is someone trying to tell me something?

The mall premises are exactly as I expected them to be – nothing more than a whitewashed rectangle. Which isn't to say a café wouldn't work here. Especially with the Internet facilities Santiago is angling for. But it wouldn't be my dream. And I'm still holding out for that.

The first step towards making this café something I could be passionate about seems to be requesting a viewing of the alternative property. If I can just get everyone to Manuel Antonio, and basically get Santiago off home turf, I think we can really get things moving.

'So, Dad, these places aren't going to hang

around for ever in this market, I think we should make a decision as soon as possible.'

'You're right,' he agrees.

'So can we go to Manuel Antonio tomorrow?'

'*Tomorrow?*' he starts.

'Well, you have to go there this week anyway, right?'

'Well, yes . . .'

'Or I could go on ahead?'

He sighs heavily, having been so recently reminded that my dogged streak comes from him he knows I won't be easily thwarted. 'I suppose Santiago could escort you.'

Is he kidding? There is no way I'm going travelling with the Prince of Darkness. 'Do you think that's wise?' I ask, projecting an image of duelling milk frothers on to Dad's brow.

'Maybe that's not such a good idea,' he concedes. 'I'll see if I can reshuffle my diary.'

'Great! Shall I ask Carla to arrange the flights?' I'm in full hustle mode now.

'And the hotel,' he nods.

'Can't we just stay at your place?'

'There's only two bedrooms. Unless you don't mind sharing with Santiago?' For the first time today there is a playful twinkle in his eye.

'Very funny,' I retort. 'It'll be a dry day in Costa Rica before that happens.'

And right on cue, it starts to rain.

Cocktails that evening are to come with an extra pair of glass-chinkers – Dad has invited his American neighbours Josh and Sindy in a ploy to ease the tension, no doubt.

As instructed, Santiago and I are lounge-bound at 5 p.m., choosing the same precise second to descend the staircase – though what he's doing roaming around upstairs has my brow contorting with suspicion yet again.

He greets me with a clipped nod.

'Evening,' I respond, sounding like a British bobby.

As we make our descent we are out of sync and bob awkwardly as we cling to our respective banisters. All the while my mind races – is this the time to confront Santiago? Should I pull him aside before we reach the lounge? Now the opportunity has presented itself, it feels almost redundant – nothing I can say to him will make him click his fingers and say, 'By golly, you're right – you are the most deserving of boss status, I will step aside immediately!' That ruling has to come from my father. For now I should perhaps be grateful that I'm getting my way with the visit to Manuel Antonio tomorrow – the less I say tonight the better. He's obviously taking a similar tack and our mutual silence affords us the full benefit of two distinct sounds as we reach the bottom step.

The first is unmistakably a groan of sexual pleasure – a two-part harmony no less – coming from the direction of Dad and Kiki's bedroom. (I give the ceiling a look of pure mortification.) The second is the *drrüing* of the doorbell – just a few feet ahead of us.

It seems we have no choice but to put on a united front and welcome Josh and Sindy.

'Allow me,' Santiago steps forward, but just before he grasps the handle he turns back as if he is about to forewarn me about something.

'Yes?' I encourage him.

'Nothing,' he changes his mind and opens the door.

'Oh hiiii!' Sindy launches herself upon him, crushing him in a boob-squishing embrace (and this woman has a lot of boob to squish). 'I have to tell you,' she husks in his ear. 'I tried your grand-mother's recipe for those melon *empanadas* and now I can't get enough of them!'

'Glad they worked out – I'll pass on the compliment,' he brisks, reaching for Josh's hand, ignoring the fact that Sindy's fingers are lingering in his hair, twirling tiny ringlets. 'How are you tonight, sir?'

'Good, good. All the better for meeting Ava, is it?' He brushes past Santiago to greet me.

'Yes it is,' I smile at his bald head. 'Nice to meet you.'

'Well, you're a lot prettier than your pa, aren't you?' he teases, eyes roving lasciviously. 'Are you a natural redhead?'

'Ummm,' I squirm slightly as his hand hooks a strand of my hair.

'Josh, perhaps you'd help me with the drinks?' Santiago hustles him on his way.

'Oooh, are we having your famous Coco Loco, Santiago?' Sindy hurries after him. 'Best mixer and shaker on the Nicoya Peninsula!' she winks at me before turning back to leer at his rear.

Though creeped out, I can't help but smile – it would seem that what Santiago was struggling to convey before he opened the door was that our dinner guests are swingers. Or at the very least outrageous flirts.

'Actually, we're having *vino de coyol* tonight,' he asserts as he navigates the bar.

'Vino de coil? What's that?' Sindy dangles off his every word.

'It an alcoholic beverage that comes from the sap of the coyol palm. It must be cut only during certain phases of the moon.'

Sindy looks utterly rapt.

'After twenty-four hours' fermentation it is classed as *vino dulce*.'

'Sweet wine,' she translates, breathless.

'But now, on day eight and for the next two weeks it's *vino fuerte*.'

132

'*Strong* wine,' she growls. 'Are you trying to get us tipsy?' She reaches out to toy with Santiago's belt loop.

'What happens on day twenty-three?' I ask, trying to spare him, as he did me.

'It turns to vinegar,' he steps away from her to hand me my glass.

'So then you really would be pickled!' I jest.

His mouth concedes a smile – the first I have elicited – and for a second you'd think we were on the same team. But then in flurries Kiki, followed by my flush-cheeked father and the dynamic changes again.

At the dinner table I am positioned with Santiago on my right and Josh on my left, much to my annoyance as his leg repeatedly presses against mine forcing me to edge towards Santiago who in turn is edging away from Sindy, giving us the look of Siamese twins by dessert.

The good news is that Josh's long-winded anecdotes set off my father allowing me to zone out and brainstorm some more café ideas while I eat. I've already worked on the basic design concept for Manuel Antonio, now I want to get on with sketching some logos and seating plans, so when we retire for coffee and Josh pats the sofa cushion next to him, I take it as my cue to excuse myself.

'You're going to bed?' he slurs, making a play for

my hand. 'Don't we get a goodnight kiss?' He attempts to tug me on to his lap.

'No kissing on the first date!' I tinkle, wriggling from his grasp. 'It was nice to meet you, Sindy!' I turn my attention to his wife.

'Hmmm?' She's in another world, gawping at Santiago with misty eyes, chewing on her mulberry-stained lips – a perfect match for the booze rash on her neck.

'Do you want to take a coffee up with you?' Kiki offers, ready to pour me a cup.

'No, not tonight, but thank you,' I give her a courtesy kiss on the cheek then blow one at my father with a little wave. ''Night, Dad.'

''Night, Little Red.'

I pause for a second and then, almost shyly, look back at Santiago. He looks directly at me, and for once his eyes show no guile. We nod, no words required.

I'm distracted as I walk to my room, pondering if I may have misjudged Santiago, only to trip on a ruck of carpet at the door giving myself a fright and a thunk on the head. 'Ouch!' I cry out, leaning on the door frame as I wince in pain.

It's just the slap I need. I have to stay focused: think only of the café. Café good. Men bad.

I turned down Kiki's coffee so I could be assured of a good night's sleep but what proves more effective than caffeine at keeping me awake is trying to create an artful line drawing of a chameleon. What I really need is a pictorial reference so once I hear Josh and Sindy make their all-too-loud farewells and the front door lock, shortly followed by the extinguishing of all lights, I scoot down to the study and hit Google on my dad's computer.

It's ironic I should pick a lizard when I am so repulsed by reptiles but I just love the concept of a chameleon. In my search I learn that their changing colour is more than a camouflage tactic, it also acts as a means of conveying emotions and communicating with their mates. Suddenly our human range of going white with terror or shock and red from blushing or anger seems rather limited.

When I read that chameleons' tongues are a metre long I wonder if I could spell the word café with it, or would that be too weird?

Scrolling down the page I notice something called a 'Chameleon Mug', also described as a 'Morph Mug' – pour any hot beverage into it and the design changes, thanks to the miracle that is thermochromatic ink! Oh wow! There's even a rainforest design – dark flora transforms into colourful fauna in the form of scarlet macaws, red-eyed frogs and hummingbirds! They even offer custom designs so we could brand them with our logo and then maybe even sell them to our customers who in turn would help us with a bit of advertising when their friends pop round to view their holiday snaps.

'Watch what the mug does!'

'Oh that's so cool, I want one!'

'Well, you have to go to the Chameleon Café in Manuel Antonio to get one.'

'Will do!'

No doubt Santiago would find this tacky on principle but I think the right gimmick could really work.

Prior to this I was thinking of mugs with white exteriors so they'd all look uniform on the shelf and then as you are served you would see the interior is a different colour. I always used to admire the mismatched cup-and-saucer combos at the Aroma cafés in London – lovely colours: mauves and tangerines and buttercups and turquoises. I suppose I ought to check on the competition, I don't want to get all overexcited about an idea that has occurred to someone else first . . .

Now this is promising: according to Fodor's online guide, only Café Milagro offers freshly roasted coffee. Their drinks menu sounds yummy, especially the Mono Loco – chocolate + banana + espresso. (Not to be confused with Santiago's Coco Loco which is apparently a shot of the local firewater sweetened with coconut juice.) I'd be concerned about trying to compete with Café Milagro but the good news is that it's nowhere near the beach.

So what of Manuel Antonio itself? What I need is an indication of the vibe of the place – at first glance it doesn't look so very different to Tamarindo: a stretch of beach, multo greenery and the promise of a natural wonderland. But then I notice the hotels are significantly more stylish. Good sign. I especially like the sound of Si Como No, which translates as 'Yes, why not?' (You can keep your cowprint cattle trailers, when my accommodation has a sense of humour I prefer a private balcony.)

As I peruse the hotel website I am entranced by the poetry in the promise of evening air 'laden with the fragrances of a thousand blossoms and a sky so clear you feel you can scoop a handful of stars in your hand just by reaching out'.

Now they're talking! That's the kind of magic I want to evoke. I scroll down the sidebar deciding what section to read next – Ecological Vision, Area Attractions or Notice Regarding Prostitution! Oh no! Apparently here it's the women who go around asking, *'Have you got everything that you want?'*

I refuse to be deterred. Prostitutes drink coffee too. Perhaps we could have a special hooker discount – instead of offering a Cup of Joe it would be a Cup of Ho.

Oh Lord, I'm getting delirious. I need to sleep.

As I get up from the chair, turn out the desk lamp and start feeling my way along the wall, a creaking from the staircase has me darting behind the protective heftiness of the door.

Oh please don't say they're coming this way! I'm not doing anything wrong but I feel like a cat burglar. Placing my hand over my heart as if to muffle its bongo beat, I strain to identify the figure – definitely a man, definitely not my dad as this fella's physique puts the Tamarindo surfers to shame, something I can attest to seeing as he's wearing only pyjama bottoms. As he steps into the pool of moonlight pouring from the skylight I see his face clearly – it's Santiago.

What is he doing walking around the house half naked? Does he *live* here? Was he coming from his own room earlier tonight? Have I been sleeping under the same roof as him without even realising? My god, I had no idea just how close he'd wormed himself to my father.

I watch him pad barefoot across the marble chessboard of the lobby, heading towards the kitchen. Seeing as he barely touched his lunch or dinner, I guess he must be pretty hungry.

I wait until I hear the kitchen door close, wait a minute or two to make sure he's not coming straight back out with a glass of water and then tiptoe towards the stairs. My foot is on the first step when I sense a presence behind me. I know I should just keep going but my head is already turning – the bongo drums now reaching ceremonial proportions.

My primary thought is 'Don't look at his chest!' and fortunately he has a prop for me to address – a steaming non-coffee beverage.

'Are you a secret tea drinker?' I accuse, as if exposing this fact would put him at a disadvantage.

He too studies his drink but simply says, 'It's not tea.'

I wait for him to tell me what it is and when he says nothing I simply chip, 'Alrighty then,' and take a second step.

'It's *horchata*.' He extends the milky concoction for my inspection.

I take a step back and inhale.

'Ground rice and cinnamon,' he tells my flaring nostrils. 'Would you like to try one?'

I don't know if it's the vulnerability of his bare skin but Santiago seems softer in manner, as well as to the eye, when half-naked. (By day his clothing seems so crisp, it makes me want to salute him.)

'Maybe another time,' I defer oh-so-politely.

For a second we just stand there and then he nods towards the landing. 'Well, I'm . . .'

'Yes, me too.'

Unlike our discombobulated descent, this time we match each other pace for pace.

Once in my room I sit on the edge of my bed, again in a daze, too tired to focus now, still clutching my assorted printouts and chameleon sketches. As I set them aside and turn out the light it occurs to me that I have just seen a different colour to Santiago.

And then I proceed to have obscenely erotic dreams about my enigmatic nemesis ensnaring me with his metre-long tongue . . .

12

They say the best way to avoid feeling intimidated by an individual or a group of people is to imagine them naked. What nonsense. Ever since I saw Santiago's bare torso I haven't been able to look him in the eye. I'm supposed to be stern and inscrutable not blushing and flustered in his presence. This morning at breakfast I nearly jumped out of my skin when I absently reached for the jam and found his hand on the jar ahead of mine. I swear he knows what's going on, as if the mere fact that he featured in my dreams means he's privy to their intimate details.

Afraid he'll exploit this weakness, I'm more curt than ever and bide my time by saying I want to see the second option before we debate the café proposal any further. What with packing, the transfer to the airport and a flight that allows no voices to be heard over the burr of the engine, there's actually very little opportunity for chitchatting until we arrive in Manuel Antonio, where Kiki is first to speak.

'This is unbelievably beautiful!' she gushes as we pass infinite blooming foliage and tantalising sneak-peeks of cliff-stacked coastlines en route to our hotel.

Santiago wants no part of her raptures. 'Are the palm trees purple? Do the birds fly backwards? Does the ocean taste of sugar not salt?'

No, but if he's looking for direct comparison to Tamarindo I'd say the topography does seem more dramatic and lush, the vibe is classier and the hotels don't have names that put you in mind of lavatorial disorders. We're staying at La Mariposa – Spanish for butterfly, isn't that nice? Apparently there's even a butterfly farm just a few paces down the road for those who want to admire the real thing.

'Can we go?' Kiki requests, looking no more than three years old.

For once Dad doesn't leap to please her. 'I've always felt that butterflies are essentially bugs with bright-coloured wings.'

Kiki looks crestfallen.

'But with you, my angel, it will be like stepping into a whirlwind of living confetti,' he quickly makes amends.

I smile to myself – she really does have him remarkably well trained. Perhaps if I hang around her enough I'll pick up a little technique? It certainly never used to make any impact on him when my crest fell. I remember when he told me that he and Mum were getting a divorce – I was as shocked as if I'd been slapped. I must have looked devastated but he didn't quickly change his mind in a bid to turn that frown upside down. Sometimes I think I let him off too easily – I didn't have the strop befitting my teenage years or even cry because Mum was already a wreck and I knew that one of us had to be strong. So I started asking the questions:

'Who gets the TV? Will Mum have to move to a smaller house? Will I still get my own bedroom? If she sells her wedding ring does she have to give half the money to him? How exactly are they going to divide up the dog?'

I was trying to focus on the practical to avoid the emotional but Dad read me as materialistic-slash-mercenary. To that end, the deal we finally struck involved him promising that every visit he'd take me to pick out a new album at Our Price and the fridge would be permanently stocked with pistachio ice cream. He kept his word the first couple of times. But never again. I suppose he thought he was off the hook when he moved abroad but really it was my fault – I should have got his promise in writing.

We turn off the main road and tilt up a steep driveway. Above us, the hotel squats angular and white, with broad jutting balconies edged with black wrought iron, draped with languorous vines and pale lilac petals like nature's party streamers.

It seemed a tad extravagant to be checking in to a hotel when dad has a property up the road but now we're here I'm glad I didn't offer to sleep on the sofa at his villa, this place is really quite something.

Twenty-nine vertiginous steps lead up to reception leaving me panting and throbbing of temple and yet I manage to stumble onward, lured out onto a sublime terrace of elegant arches, potted ferns and pristine tables set with white linen and yellow posies. I walk to the edge of the alfresco restaurant and my vision plunges into the aquamarine of the swimming pool two storeys below. I can't help but covet the alignment of sunloungers beneath a leafy pergola – maybe later I'll get the chance to siesta in the shade? Over to my right and one tier higher I see a second pool, this one in the shape of a grand piano, with a swim-up bar and an infinity edge that spills all the way down to the ocean via the most vivacious greenery. Wow. This is the kind of view that alerts your inner gospel singer and makes you want to raise your arms and praise be!

'Isn't it gorgeous!' Kiki raves, wrapping her arms around me from behind and resting her chin on my shoulder. 'I'm *so* excited!'

Unable to curb my joy, I squeeze her back, grateful for the unexpected ally she has turned out to be in terms of championing Manuel Antonio. Not that this location strikes me as a hard sell any more. I almost feel sorry for Santiago. But not quite. Last night he may have exhibited traces of humanity but since we arrived here he's been nothing but brusque.

'Do you want to settle in first or go straight to the coffee shop?' Dad addresses the three of us.

'Coffee shop,' Santiago and I chorus.

'I wouldn't mind taking a shower first,' Kiki goes the other way, leaning in to whisper an addendum to my dad. His eyes instantly light up.

'Quite right, it is a bit sticky,' he coughs. 'Shall we meet back here in a hour?'

I'm impatient to get on but if my father associates Manuel Antonio with daytime sex then I can only see that aiding my cause.

I wait for Santiago to stride on his way and then quickly tug my father back two paces. 'Dad, do you have the particulars for the property?'

'Hmm?' his mind is clearly on other things.

'I just want to have a quick read before we head on down there.'

'It's only a very basic outline,' he says, locating the sheet in his briefcase.

'That's fine, I just wanted to get an idea.' I wave him on his way.

My room can wait, it's the coffee shop I want to see.

As soon as the coast is clear, I dart over to reception and surreptitiously slide the page across the counter. 'Do you know this place?'

'*Si, si*. I know the owner, Ivan. He is friend of mine. You are going to buy?'

'Well not me, my father. Maybe. Is it far from here?'

'No, no, just down on the beach. We have a shuttle that leaves every hour.' He points to the schedule on the wall.

I can't wait forty minutes until the next so I ask if it's walkable.

'Sure. You turn left at the hotel gate, take the hill down, you come to a fork . . .'

'Fork, yes?'

My mind is racing. I'm barely taking in his directions in my eagerness to get there. Something I regret when I'm twenty minutes into the trek with still no beach in sight. I must have taken the wrong prong of the fork. I have no idea where I'm going and the sun is *scalding*. At least in Tamarindo there was the odd cloud to act as a lampshade; this is bald lightbulb glare.

'Mad dogs and Englishmen!' I mutter to myself as I continue twanging my calf muscles on the downward slide, trying desperately not to lose my footing on a path that seems entirely made up of tumbling rocks and scuttling crabs with tomato-red shells.

I come to a halt beside a hi-tech hideaway, wishing I could nip in and stick my head under their designer kitchen tap with extendable hose feature. Where's my rucksack with the built-in water supply when I need it? Getting sunstroke was so not my plan – all I wanted was a quick heads-up. It's not like I was cheating because everyone but Kiki has already seen this property. But now my body temperature is reaching boiling point and I'm getting less fragrant with every passing second. Meanwhile Santiago is probably stepping from the shower, spraying himself with some sports deodorant – again I flash to his gleaming torso – and about to enjoy a long cool drink with his feet up. To think I could be lying on that shady sunlounger with an iced guanábana!

Half an hour into my trek, I'm forced to admit defeat – I'm actually going to have to turn back now because that hill I've just killed myself scuffing down is hardly going to be ascended in a single bound. What a complete waste of time and perspiration.

' "Sure you can walk!" ' I snort at the receptionist's false hope as I begin the upward climb. What failed to mention is that it would take an hour and you should bring your own paramedic.

I have to stop at least ten times on the way back up, nearly in tears from the strain. There's a reason they keep the treadmills and the saunas separate at the gym.

I make it up the driveway with minutes to spare, but the prospect of the twenty-nine steps defeats me. I just can't do it. I pray for a new arrival so I can ask them to pass a message up to reception for me, then collapse on to the edge of a flower bed and wait for the pounding in my chest/skull/eyeballs to subside.

'Oh my god, Ava! Are you all right?' Kiki surprises me, materialising out of nowhere.

'I'm fine – you?' I try to sound casual but she's not buying it.

'Quick, have some water.' She produces a fresh bottle, then watches as I glug it down, gasping as I take the last gulp. 'Thank you!' I rasp.

'Were you out exploring?' She notices my dirt-shrouded shoes.

'Just thought I'd go for a little stroll,' I shrug, eager to underplay my plight. 'You?'

'Actually I had a bit of time to kill so I went to the gift shop on the corner there.' She points down the driveway.

I can't believe it – she managed to have sex and go shopping and she's still ahead of schedule!

'Why don't I go and get the others, no need for you to go up only to come down again.' She turns to leave then hedges back with an afterthought, 'You know, I just bought a bandanna, do you want to maybe borrow it to tie back your hair?'

I start to decline her kind offer until she suggests

148

I take a peek at my reflection in the window of the airport shuttle – I look like I've been fuzzed up with a bristle brush then doused with chip fat around the hairline.

'I'll buy you a new one when we return,' I sheepishly accept the patterned hanky then watch her sprint up the stairs, veteran of a million step classes.

I'm starting to feel guilty about even thinking bad things about her before we met. Her peppiness may be irritating but her kindness is indisputable.

Two minutes later my dad hurries down looking concerned. 'Oh my god, you look terrible.'

'I'm fine!' I grimace, mopping the salty river flowing from my upper lip – turns out the struggle to secure the bandanna only served to frazzle me more.

Meanwhile Santiago taps down the steps, hands casually in his pockets, as effortlessly elegant as Gene Kelly.

Round one to him.

The taxi has no air conditioning so I stick my head out of the window like a dog to get the maximum breeze as we weave down the curvy, verdant road passing an assortment of hotels and restaurants. By the time we pull over and park, I have my breath back and my facial shine has been air-blotted. I'm on the verge of feeling good when I see Santiago take a leather-bound notebook –

damn! All my notes and printouts are back at the hotel. I have a sudden panic as if I've arrived under-prepared for a vital exam but then check myself – everything I need to know is poised and ready for access in my head. I can do this.

'We can cut through here.' Santiago leads the way through a scrappy thicket and minutes later we're on the seashore. I am in awe.

The beach at Tamarindo seemed almost non-descript to me – long and narrow with no outstanding features, except perhaps the waves. This expanse of sand is vast and given form and character by the curve of the bay and the boulder humps wedged both ashore and mid-ocean. By the looks of the layer upon layer of frothy-frilled surf you can wade way out and still only be knee-deep. I love that – there's something so safe and appealing about knowing you're not going to get swallowed up the second you dip in a toe.

I take a deep saline breath, dazzled at every turn. This really is nothing short of magnificent. Even if there had been a beach contender in Tamarindo, there would be no comparison.

'How could you even consider a box in a mall over this?' I question my dad.

'Wait until you see the place,' he says, issuing a caution.

I roll my eyes. How bad can it be?

Oh. Gosh. Suddenly we are standing in front of a

knackered old shack. The first word that springs to my mind is skanky. The second is unhygienic.

Dad motions for us to sit at one of the stone tables set over to the side in the sand.

'What do you want to drink?'

I request something in a brand-name can with a straw and no ice. Something tells me this is not the local hangout for health inspectors.

'So, what do you think now?' Santiago challenges me to gush over this unlovely establishment.

'Location, location, location!' is my emphatic response.

'And what of the café itself?' he goads me.

I hold his gaze but take the 'if you can't say anything nice, don't say anything at all' tack, leaving the optimism to Kiki. 'It's definitely got potential,' she decides. 'This whole outdoor area can really be jazzed up.'

'We'd have to expand the indoor seating,' I volunteer. Especially since there currently is none.

'I never really saw this as an interior option,' my dad frowns, returning with our drinks. 'I think we have to go with alfresco and proud.'

'No air conditioning?' After my recent brush with sunstroke I'm appalled.

'You get used to it.'

'No, Dad.' I give him a pleading look. I don't want to expose my Achilles heel and leave it to the vultures to feed on, but this is a deal-breaker for me.

'Very few of the restaurants and bars around here have air con,' Dad expands. 'It's all terraces and patios and poolside dining.'

'So much the better for us!' I take a stance. 'What a wonderful haven we'll offer when people want to get out of the sun.'

'Trees,' says Santiago.

'What?'

'Trees are what people use to get out of the sun.' He points upward. 'See how they offer this thing called shade.'

'It's not enough,' I can't help but whimper.

'Not enough for who?' he snips. 'Are you suggesting we install an air-conditioning system just so you can keep your cool?'

'Well, unless you expect me to be serving coffee from the ice-cream freezer, then yes!'

Jeez! What happened to the soft-spoken man who offered to make a nice cup of *horchata* last night? When it comes to getting his own way, it would seem all niceties go out the window.

'Okay, you two, simmer down,' Dad urges. 'The fact is, we simply don't have it in the budget to put in air con. Not least because that would also mean putting in walls. This place is way over the price of the premises in Tamarindo because it's on the beach. It's not business savvy to throw any more money at it than we have to. Especially when we've got an alternative lined up with all mod cons and it's

152

just a question of installing the equipment, printing up the menus and saying, "Can I take your order?"' Dad scans his surroundings. 'Now I'm looking more closely, I think even getting this place half decent is going to push us dangerously over budget.'

'Not if we keep it alfresco,' Santiago insists.

'Ava?'

I thought I'd do anything to get my way but I won't sweat twenty gallons an hour just to prove a point. I shake my head.

'I don't think you should give up on this place.' I hear Santiago's voice and for a moment I think he's actually encouraging me to hang in there, but it's my dad he's addressing. 'I've got some really great ideas for the refit and design. I've done some sketches to show how it might look.'

He opens his notebook and fans out assorted illustrations and diagrams.

I expect my dad to be fatally impressed but instead he snaps, 'I wish you'd make up your bloody mind, Santiago! First you're raving about Manuel Antonio, then Ava arrives and you switch to Tamarindo, now you're back to Manuel Antonio again!'

My stomach lurches as I realise that I have been well and truly played. Suddenly I get it – if Santiago stays in Tamarindo he will always be the employee, but if he runs the business here in Manuel Antonio, and no doubt moves into my father's house, he gets

153

to play lord of the manor. He must have been so delighted when I slated Tamarindo. And then more thrilled still when I started to sweat. Knowing how uncomfortable I am in the heat, he has played the entire thing to his advantage. And to think I was all chuffed that I had Kiki on my side, when all along he had me on his!

I hang my head, hating the feeling of being had. Of course the easiest way to get back at him would be to back my father on Tamarindo but even contemplating that has me writhing with resistance. How can I return to that unease when I've experienced this boundless beauty? Yes, this venue is run-down with no doubt all manner of terrifying things hiding behind the fridge, but the spot is prime, set well away from all the other restaurants and bars clustered in town. The potential is just too alluring . . .

'Do you mind if I take a few moments to think?' I get to my feet.

'Go right ahead.'

I excuse myself, moving back into the sun but heading to the breeziest place I know – the water's edge.

The sea water slips over my now-bare feet. I want to keep walking until my knees then my hips then my shoulders are enveloped. Is there any way I can make this fly? I can so envision this place as the Chameleon Café – imagine the trees entwined with fairy lights, pulsating different colours after dark. It could be so heavenly.

I take another step deeper into the water, letting the waves race through my fingers. Talk about a Brew With A View! Ollie would love this place.

'You're not going to do a Reggie Perrin, are you?'

'What?' I turn to find my dad beside me.

'Ava,' he sighs, putting a protective arm around my shoulder. 'If you're having second thoughts . . .'

'What if I used my money?' I blurt, out of the blue.

My dad's arm drops.

'What if I paid for the interior aspect, the air conditioning, all that stuff that would take us over budget?'

'Are you serious?'

'Absolutely.' I nod eagerly. 'You buy the property. I sort the air con and then Santiago and I split the management – you give him the exterior, me the interior. Then we'll see who does the best business.'

'You want to run two rival coffee shops under one roof?'

'Well, no one else would know we're separate. They'd just see outdoors and indoors, and that way we cater to every type of clientele – the sun-worshippers and those about to keel over and die from the heat.'

'We could be all things to all coffee drinkers!' Dad warms to the idea. 'So Santiago would have the authentic beach bar and yours would be the chic little—'

'No,' I jump in, not wanting him to go too far down the wrong track. 'I still want mine to have local character. I think they should be blendable, not some jarring juxtaposition.'

'Right, you're right. We don't want to start any gang warfare,' my father chuckles. 'The Tin Mugs versus the Silver Spoons.'

I smile back at him. 'So I'll run my side,' I clarify. 'Santiago will run his and—'

He holds up a finger. 'On condition that you recoup the cost of the air conditioning from the profits – I don't want you being out of pocket on my account.'

'Well—'

'I wouldn't feel right about it, Ava. You'll need that money for when you get your own place back in Bath.'

'I'm not so sure that's ever going to happen,' I'm still despondent on that topic.

'Nevertheless, that's my non-negotiable condition,' he asserts.

'Okay,' I concede, feeling I'm actually getting a pretty good deal after all. 'But you still need to decide who is the overall boss.'

'I guess that would be me,' he grins.

My hands go to my hips. 'I'm talking in terms of the day-to-day running. I mean, are you going to relocate here? Because I really think it should be someone on site. And not Kiki.' I hurry out the last three words. 'You are her priority. I think it needs to be one of us sad, loveless individuals.'

'Is that really how you see yourself?' Dad looks shocked.

'It's okay,' I swat away his concern. 'I'm happy to put all my energy into the coffee shop.'

'When was the last time you had a boyfriend?'

'Daaad!' I squirm, uncomfortable discussing my personal life with him. 'That is not the issue right now.'

'There are a couple of very eligible estate agents in town, if you like I could—'

'Don't even think about it,' I growl.

'Well, all right, but remember all work and no play—'

'Will make you a very rich man!' I jab his lapel.

He shakes his head, studies his feet for a good minute and then looks up at me. 'Okay. So here's what we're going to do: you've got one month from today until I decide who's done the best job – that includes two weeks of setting-up time and two weeks open for business. How does that sound?'

Oh my god! He's gone for it!

'It sounds like a plan,' I cheer, turning back to the café eager to tell Santiago that I will be getting my air-con unit after all. Oh and by the way, he's no longer the boss.

'You'll let Santiago come in and cool off from time to time, won't you?' Dad stumbles after me.

I go to tell him, 'Sure, when hell freezes over!' but then I realise that if that happens he'll hardly be needing my facilities.

13

Turns out arguing over the location for the café was just the beginning. Now we've established that Manuel Antonio is the place, it has opened up a whole new can of worms. Or condensed milk, depending on what you ordered.

Tres leches. The name alone makes me nauseous. I can't believe Santiago wants it featured on the menu.

'You said you wanted traditional,' he contends.

'I just don't think it would look good if I was retching every time I had to serve a portion,' I explain, though I'm not putting a firm ban on it just yet – I have to pick my battles.

Speaking of which, I'd say the term 'bun fight' was made for today. To look at us you'd think we were arguing over life-and-death issues but for the past hour we've been raging about cakes. Dad felt that seeing as we were the ones with the supposed expertise, we should be the ones to 'duke it out', at least over the aspects we were going to share.

'I'm just saying I don't think we should overwhelm people with choice, it leads to too much dithering,' I insist. 'My opinion is that we should stick to three delicious options.'

'Three?' Santiago scoffs. 'The majority of our customers are going to be from America, they invented the word choice. They won't be happy.'

'Well we could change it – maybe each day we'd have three different items, that would keep people coming back.'

'The people who live here maybe, but what about the tourist who comes back on the second day because they so enjoyed the tamarind cake and we tell them they need to wait until next Tuesday if they want a second slice?'

I hate it when he has a point. 'Well, what if we had a selection of basics – no more than five – and then every day we offered a new special.'

'Well, that's fine if we can find a cooperative baker.'

'Not everyone lives to invent obstacles,' I needle. 'I'm sure we'll find someone to rise to the challenge.'

'Oh, that's good – a baker rising to the challenge!' Kiki titters. She went out to get a smoothie and now sits down, snugly in my personal space.

'I'm just trying to get the point across that if we are going to make full use of the name being the

Chameleon Café we're going to have to embrace change.'

'Well, it's funny you should say that,' Kiki says, taking my hand.

Uh-oh.

'The thing is,' she begins. 'Santiago is adamant that he wants the place to be called Café Coffee—'

'It's very equal opportunities,' he insists. 'Your word for coffee and my word for coffee.'

'I get that!' I groan. 'But—'

Kiki holds up a finger. 'I'm not saying we're changing to that. The thing is, Dean feels it's not really fair for him to favour one name over the other when you are both equal partners.'

'What are you trying to tell us?' Santiago is now equally trepidatious.

'Dean decided it would be best if I came up with a name.'

Oh no. Santiago and I look instantly stricken.

'Do you want to hear it?' Kiki is fit to burst.

I force a nod in the affirmative.

'Café Tropicana!' she squeals, clapping her hands together. 'Don't you just love it?'

'Isn't it a bit Wham?' I voice my concern.

'Well, that's the beauty of it! Who doesn't love that song?'

'Aren't you worried that people will expect the drinks to be free?' I know I've lost Santiago at this point.

'Don't be silly, they're only free at Club Tropicana, this is the café!'

'Oh yes.' I grimace. I am so thoroughly dismayed. Café Tropicana? It sounds so garish, so tacky, so over-processed – everything about Costa Rica is *pura vida* – 'the pure life' – as the national slogan decrees. This is just so wrong.

'It's not going to be in neon, is it? The name?'

'Oh my god, wouldn't that be great – can you get orange neon?'

Santiago's head is now in his hands.

'I know! There's so much to think about – total redesign – but I know you can do it.' She rumples his silky hair with vigour. 'Anyway, I'm going to leave you guys to thrash things out for the next hour and then Dean is taking Santiago for a beer and you and I are going to the butterfly farm!'

'What?'

'Dean's idea. I know he promised to go but he convinced me that you'd enjoy it so much more and, besides, we thought you two might need a break from each other by then.'

Suddenly we don't seem such sworn enemies any more – funny how a shared loathing can bond even the least compatible types.

Santiago and I watch until Kiki is out of ear-shot and then I venture, 'What do you think of the name?'

'I hate it.' Santiago is emphatic.

'Me too,' I sigh

Finally something we agree on.

'You know, I quite liked the idea of all the branded sackcloth and the sandy neutrals you wanted to go for,' I admit.

'And I can see that the lights in the trees might have worked at night,' he shrugs. 'But I think your seventies disco floor may have been a step too far.'

I laugh. I can't believe I actually said that out loud – it was the chameleon theme taken to extremes: a cubed perspex floor with lights that changed colour as you did the hustle across it to place your order. That's the problem with brainstorming with an enemy. They can hold your stupid ideas against you.

'Café Tropicana.' I repeat the name, slumping a little more. 'If we'd have known that our stubbornness was going to lead to this . . .'

'So Kiki just comes up with the name and leaves us to do the rest – is that her contribution?' Santiago sits back in his chair, thoroughly peeved.

'I think she's going to sort the uniforms,' I reply, mentally playing the 'Club Tropicana' video in my head – as I recall George and Andrew were styled as pilots, with Pepsi and Shirlie as their flight attendants. 'I've got a horrible feeling she's going to have us in navy suits and caps with gold piping,' I groan. Remind me to make sure my mum never visits – that would be the end of her.

163

'Ava, you've lost me,' Santiago frowns.

'Don't worry about it,' I tell him.

'So we're back to square one with the design.' He scrumples up several pages and projects them into the bin.

We both stare at our respective blank sheets.

'Tropicana . . .' I muse out loud. 'Tropical . . .'

'Tropic of Cancer, tropic of Capricorn,' Santiago freewheels.

'I'm a Cancer, you know. My star sign.' I blush as soon as the words are out of my mouth. Like he cares.

Santiago frowns. 'I'm Capricorn – 22 December.'

'That's weird.' For a moment I feel like we're being too personal, like we've been set up on some celestial date, and it's making me squirm. 'You know, I might pop along to the Internet café, see if I can rustle up some tropical rainforest themes.'

'You want inspiration? Manuel Antonio National Park is ten minutes' walk from here – it's got mangrove swamps and gumbo-limbo trees – What's that face for?'

I look uncomfortable. 'I had a bit of a bad experience last time I was in a rainforest.'

He looks me over. 'I don't see any jaguar bite marks.'

'*There are jaguars?*' I shrill.

'Occasionally. More in Tortuguero where my grandmother lives.'

I'm silent for a moment then I confess. 'Actually it was an ant.'

'An ant?' He is incredulous.

'I don't want to talk about it,' I mumble into my chin.

In the end I stay put and we settle on green as our overall colour scheme, with contrasting orange detailing and logo to please Kiki.

'I'll integrate the exterior with the interior by using lots of big potted plants, stained-wood chairs, green-glazed floor tiles, maybe even a hammock slung in the front window.'

'You want a hammock on the inside?'

'Well, you're having sofas on the outside!' I retort.

'Just one in the sheltered area.'

'Well, I only want one hammock.'

For a moment our eyes bulge at each other and then we realise this is not one of our greater issues. And didn't it feel better when we were on the same page? Yes, but it's not something we seem able to sustain – tension returns as we debate whether the menu should be in colones or dollars:

'I agree that one would be cleaner,' Santiago concedes, 'but dollars says you are catering exclusively to a tourist market.'

'I get that but if we have both people are going to waste their time trying to work out the better deal based on the current exchange rate.'

'Well, let them,' Santiago shrugs. 'I think they should have the option to pay in either.'

'I suppose we could have a digital board with all the prices keyed in?'

'And how much of the budget is that going to eat up? Besides that will hardly fit with your rustic notions.' His derision is like a slap.

'I was just throwing ideas out there—'

'A little editing doesn't go amiss.' He taps his head.

I purse my lips. 'I'm just saying that two currencies is going to make a lot of extra banking work.'

'We've both got accounting backgrounds, I think we can handle it.'

'You—?' I begin.

'Yes,' he says, feeling no need to share his credentials with me. 'Now. Prices.'

It's clear that Santiago is happier when we stick strictly to business.

'Well, I was thinking about that – we don't want to exclude the locals, maybe we could have a resident discount or some kind of membership card – a free coffee every ten stamps? One of those loyalty programmes. Or maybe each week we could let them try the new flavour or blend for free.'

'You're big on free. You know the aim is to make a profit?'

'Well I wasn't planning on making a loss.' I find myself getting defensive again.

'Who's to say they won't come in just for the free tasting and then go elsewhere for their regular coffee?'

'That won't happen because the delicious new blend won't be available anywhere else,' I chirrup. 'We'll hook 'em by the taste buds and they'll keep coming back.'

'You are an optimist, aren't you?' The way Santiago delivers the word you'd think it was a slur.

In response I conjure my sweetest smile and say, 'I'm planning on working alongside you for a month, I must be.'

We continue to thrash out the business plan, estimating projected income and debating the expenses for our overlapping concerns – definitely far too extravagant to buy two granita machines but we will need a pretty fancy till if we want to code our sales in order to monitor our individual profits. That thought rams home how seriously in competition we are so that by the time Dad and Kiki arrive we've reached a new level of frazzled, talking over each other and using ever more exaggerated hand gestures.

'One at a time,' Dad tries to referee. 'Now I have a question about staffing – how many extra pairs of hands do you think you'll need?'

Santiago and I eye each other. Neither of us wanting to admit we'd need any help.

'Frankly right now the pair of you are far too volatile to deal directly with the customers so I suggest you—'

'I could manage with one.' I cut my dad off.

'Santiago?'

'One,' he confirms.

'Okay, I'll place the ad, I'll leave the interviewing to you guys.'

'Actually, it probably makes sense for me to oversee the hiring.' Santiago says, amending Dad's decision.

'Excuse me –' I'm instantly annoyed by his presumptive tone – 'why you?'

'Well, there's a good chance I may know their family and there is the language to consider.'

'Yes there is – we need to hire English speakers, 90 per cent of the tourists are from America, don't you know?' I fire his own statistic back at him.

'Have you ever interviewed anyone for a job before?' he queries.

'An interview is just a conversation,' I reply. 'The important thing is to be a good judge of character.'

'And you think you are?'

'Oh yeah, I know when someone can't be trusted.' My eyes challenge him.

'Are you inferring—'

'Oh please!' I cut him off. 'You know perfectly well—'

'Look!' Dad holds up his hands, silencing us both.

'I don't know what the problem is – you're both getting what you want!'

'Neither of us are getting what we want!' we cry out in exasperated unison.

'Well, then I guess that at least is fair,' Dad shrugs.

The pair of us are spent. Arguing must surely burn up more calories than normal conversation. All Santiago can do now is flash his carbon eyes and growl, 'I'll be in the bar.'

'I'll be in the butterfly farm!' doesn't have the same ring but I say it anyway.

14

One butterfly creating air-ribbons around you is undeniably enchanting. Several hundred is freaky.

Kiki and I have entered a kind of mesh big top and there are so many shimmery items flickering above our heads you'd think someone had just called midnight on New Year's Eve. I can't help but recoil like Tippi Hedren in *The Birds*, convinced they are forming a psychedelic twister around my head, but after a few minutes I realise that my eyes are not in danger of being pecked out, just dazzled by the iridescent hues.

'These are exquisite!' I marvel at the azure lustre of the blue morphos. 'It's as if they've dipped their wings in the South Pacific.'

'Reminds me of my wedding day,' Kiki whispers, holding her breath as a ruby-spotted swallowtail settles on a leaf beside her.

'You had butterflies as part of the ceremony?' I

ask, mentally placing them in the role usually assigned to white doves.

'On the inside,' she says, patting her stomach. 'I was so nervous while I was getting ready I thought I might pass out but when I saw Dean waiting for me at the altar the nerves turned to excitement,' she smiles in reverie. 'I felt like the luckiest girl in the world and every step I took closer to him gave me more of a high. Even now, I still get a little thrill when he walks into the room.' Then she tilts her head to one side. 'What about you? Got any flutterings for any particular fellas?'

'Not lately.' I mumble, turning away to inspect a brown specimen whose pattern looks like wood shavings inset with shiny black beads. I have no intention of discussing my lacklustre love life with a newly-wed, or anyone else for that matter.

'No beaus back home?' Kiki prompts.

'Nope.'

'So what's the story?' She's comes to a halt directly in front of me. 'A fox like you—'

'No story,' I cut her off, ducking a lilac low-flyer.

'There's always a story,' she persists.

'Is there?' I remain evasive, walking ahead so she can't see my eyes. This is categorically my least favourite subject. I don't think there's ever been a conversation about men or ex-boyfriends that has left me feeling good about myself. I've learned it's better to say nothing. 'According to the chart, these

171

are nero glasswings,' I continue with my diversionary tactics. 'Don't their wings look like miniature stained-glass windows? And these . . .' I gawp at a confection resembling shot silk. 'It's almost as if they're wearing designer gowns—'

'So what about your last boyfriend? Tell me about him!' Kiki demands.

I heave an enormous sigh to show my reluctance and displeasure before revealing, 'His name was Nick.'

'And how long did you go out with him for?'

'Too long.'

She raises an eyebrow.

'A year.'

She looks reasonably impressed. Enough meat on that bone for her to gnaw at for a while. I kick myself for not saying two weeks.

'So what went wrong?'

I give her a look that says, 'It defies explanation.' But I can tell I'll only whet her appetite further if I don't come up with something.

'It just wasn't meant to be. We weren't on the same wavelength. We wanted different things.' I rifle through the clichés then offer up a smidgeon of truth: 'Ultimately I was putting him as the top priority and so was he.'

'So it was all about him and you got lost along the way?' she clarifies.

'Something like that,' I squirm. I don't want her –

or more importantly my dad – thinking I can be easily distracted from my goals. I'm trying to portray myself as a focused, motivated, ambitious individual! 'He wasn't all bad,' I add. 'But the experience was. I won't be going down that road again anytime soon.'

'But you know the only way to truly get over someone is to be with someone else?' She's right beside me now.

'I've heard that.' I remain non-committal. But to me that's a game of catch-up that's never going to end – you're always going to need another to cancel out the one before. I prefer to use my in-between time to get back to me, to remember what my life was all about before Him – the big distraction, the big diversion, the head-scrambler.

'There are a few candidates here in Manuel Antonio . . .'

Kiki is so not helping.

'Did my dad put you up to this?' I turn to face her.

'Not at all!' she gasps, almost offended. 'Although I don't know what is so wrong with him wanting to see you as happy as he is.'

That's lovebirds for you – they want to share the mush.

Kiki takes my hand. 'I used to be like you, all cynical about men, but when you find the right one . . .' She looks imploringly at me. 'It cancels out all the bad stuff.'

'Have you actually had any bad stuff?' I ask, unable to eradicate all traces of annoyance from my tone.

'Yes.' She looks put out.

'Really?' Why don't I believe her? 'Do you like talking about it?'

She shakes her head.

'Then why do you want me to?'

'I'm just trying to help!' she bleats.

'To be perfectly candid, Kiki, the only man I would consider right now is The One. I just couldn't go through the motions for a maybe. He would have to be everything I ever wanted, stood right in front of me, no obstacles, no drama, no wedding ring to prise from his finger . . .' I walk on, following the path of a petite flame-scorched cloak, adding, 'Same taste in music/takeaway/coffee mugs, the works.'

'You want it all?'

'Or nothing at all.' I smile. I simply can't stand the pain of another failure.

'Well then, I think we'd better get some specifics!'

I'd forgotten I was dealing with an estate agent – someone geared to meeting very specific client needs.

'Let's start with the music/takeaway/coffee-mug options.' She invites me to sit on the edge of a flower bed with her.

Rather like the butterflies I am a captive audience, so I decide there can be no harm in indulging her for

174

the moment. 'Black Eyed Peas/orange chicken/big white bowl.'

'Ice cream?' she grins.

'Pistachio,' I smile. This isn't so bad.

'Movie?'

'*Lost in Translation.*'

'Oh my god, I know this guy who's just like Bill Murray!'

I put my hand on her forearm to calm her. 'Bill Murray himself, maybe. *Like* Bill Murray, no.'

'Okay, well, who's the fantasy pin-up, then?'

'Matthew McConaughey,' I mmm his name.

'Stubbly or clean-shaven?'

'I like him both ways.'

'I meant men in general.'

'Stubbly.'

'Candlelit dinners or picnics on the beach?'

'Candlelit—' Suddenly I get a chill. 'You're not going to put me on your friend's Internet dating site, are you?'

'No, I'm using my own personal system,' she says, tapping her head. 'Family-orientated or independent?'

'Independent.' I don't want my boyfriend to be suggesting we spend more time with my mother.

'Work or play?'

'Play.' I don't want a workaholic like my dad.

'Casual or attentive?'

'Attentive.' I'm beginning to think I could save us

both a lot of time and just say, 'The opposite of my dad.' Though of course Kiki has a very different experience of him to me.

She grills me for a further five minutes then strums her lips as she says, 'There is someone . . . He's ticking a lot of boxes.'

I get an uneasy feeling as if I am stepping into a trap.

'Is he local?' I ask, wondering if I should be checking the bushes for beaus – is this whole thing a set-up?

'No, he's currently working in Brazil . . .'

How exotic! It appears us Brits are making a mass exodus to the Americas.

'. . . but he is planning a visit fairly soon,' she adds.

I gulp back my anxiety to ask: 'How do you know him?'

'We were at Bournemouth Uni together – I was studying Tourism, he was Sports Psychology but the bar was shared ground.'

Well, at least the age is about right, quite a relief considering who's doing the fixing.

'Is he an ex?' I decide to mirror her bold line of questioning.

She smiles. 'No. He did offer but he's not my type.'

'But you're his. Which probably means—'

'Oh no,' she dismisses my concern. 'He'd definitely find you attractive. Definitely.'

176

I get a millisecond's kick from her confidence and then the nerves set in – it sounds like she actually means this.

'I know he already has Tamarindo scheduled on his trip,' Kiki is gathering momentum. 'I'm going to insist he comes along to Manuel Antonio!'

'Oh no, don't bring him out of his way.'

'Oh you'll be worth it!' she smiles knowingly.

'No I won't!' I cry, feeling the pressure mounting.

'Oh come on, it's the least I can do in return for all your hard work with the café.'

It's only now it dawns on me that it was Kiki not Santiago I was expecting to be battling every step of the way – wasn't the café supposed to be for her?

'Well, I was superkeen initially but then Santiago explained the day-to-day running and it seems like an awful lot of little chores – putting fresh beans in the coffee grinder, refilling the chocolate and cinnamon shakers, stacking napkins and stirrers, emptying the ice machine, taking out the rubbish . . . And then there's even more of my least favourite thing . . .'

'What's that?'

'Cleaning,' she grimaces. 'Cleaning espresso machines, coffee filters, tables, cups, spoons, windows, work surfaces, cake trays, light fixtures, dusting air vents, sweeping floors, hosing out the bins.' Her nose wrinkles.

'You know, it's weird, I don't mind that stuff. Windows are my personal favourite.'

'Glass is the worst!' Kiki protests, then makes herself jump as she turns to face a display case full of beetles.

After the delicate silken wings of the butterflies, it's all the more repugnant to behold their waxy black shells and polished pincers.

'Look at the size of them,' I gawp, wondering what I'm even doing in a country that breeds such horrors.

'I know!' Kiki coos. 'You see this one?' She points to the most grotesque. 'We had one of them in the house the other day, I had to get Santiago to handle it.'

How appropriate – one of his own kind. This seems an opportune moment to ask a question that's been playing on my mind since last night's half-naked staircase incident. 'How long has Santiago been living at the house?'

'Well, he was there when I arrived but I think he moved in with Dean about six months before that.'

'Do you know why?'

'I think it began as a practical solution – they were working night and day on a multimillion-dollar condo deal and Santiago's place was way out of town . . . Ultimately I think Dean liked the company.'

'Gosh. And you don't mind?'

She shrugs. 'Hardly know he's there. He's a very

178

private man. Sometimes he comes to dinner when we have other guests but not so much otherwise. I like him but he really only talks about work, and when Dean's home I like him to be able to switch off and relax, you know?'

I nod, feeling a pang of jealousy at the concept of 'home'. That seems such a long-forgotten sensation to me. My rented pad in Bath was nice enough and sometimes when I came in from the cold with a takeaway and had my favourite TV show to watch I'd feel like there was nowhere else on earth I'd rather be, but *home*? Since my parents divorced and my mother downsized that concept is gone.

'Are your parents still together?' I'm suddenly curious about Kiki's background.

She shakes her head, her peppiness noticeably subsiding. Interesting. Maybe she has suffered a little after all. It's never easy, divorce, however civilised the arrangement.

'Do you see much of them?'

'Not really,' she says in a small voice.

'Well, I suppose it's a tad far to drop by for coffee.' I try to be nice.

'Actually my dad is only two hours away in Miami.' She looks wistful.

'He works there?'

She nods. 'He's a manager at one of the hotels on South Beach. His second wife is American so . . .' she trails off.

179

'Well, maybe when he retires they'll be able to pop over a bit more often.' I try to jolly her up.

'I wouldn't count on it,' she says, almost sourly.

Kiki obviously has some kind of issue with her dad. (Don't we all?) Could this partly explain why she's gone the father-figure route with my pop? I want to ask more questions but the topic seems to be making her as uncomfortable as relationship talk did with me.

'Ready to go?' Kiki gets to her feet, eager to move on.

Fortunately I know how to bring back her pep.

'So, this sexy uni pal of yours . . .' I set her off.

On the way back to the hotel she links her arm in mine and chatters busily about how Mr Ryan Sheen is going to sweep me off my feet.

It's then I realise that the real reason she's lost interest in the café is because she has a new project in her life – me!

15

When Dad and Kiki return to Tamarindo the next day, it makes sense for Santiago and I to move into Dad's villa, even if it does smack of keeping your friends close and your enemies closer. It's bizarre to think we'll be sleeping either side of an insubstantial wall, painted aubergine on my side and pecan on his. (After the spacious, stark whites of the Mariposa, it takes a bit of getting used to every room having its own moodily rich hue. It's definitely cosier, or at least it would be in less spiky company.)

In order to make this arrangement bearable, we adopt the same businesslike approach to our living arrangements as we have been doing for the café – before we've even unpacked we've worked out a schedule for use of the kitchen and the bathroom so we won't overlap: I will shower first at 8 a.m. and drink my coffee while Santiago performs his ablutions at 8.15. While he is supping his java I will be doing my hair and make-up, then we'll drive in together, hopefully with the radio on to spare us the compulsion to bicker. We'll shop for groceries together but pay for and prepare our food separately. We will alternate the use of the main living area. Basically everything is designed to give us as much independence as possible, despite the fact that we are essentially running a three-legged race.

Several days into the arrangement I find the biggest strain to be the lack of feedback – I am so used to airing my quandaries and opinions around Ollie whereas with Santiago I have to hold myself in check, repeatedly going to speak and then censoring myself. With no one else to hold up a tile sample to, I am forced to go with my gut every time. Which is fine, I certainly had enough practice pre-Ollie, but it would be more fun to share the process. I did try to consult Santiago about a drawer-handle design (I couldn't resist the little spoon handles) but it backfired on me later when he decided that the carte blanche he gave me on that entitled him to order his choice of espresso machine. I felt these were hardly comparable items but hopefully his decision to buy a four-group model over the two-group I'd selected will mean less elbowing during rush hour.

Today is day six of the rebuilding process which has proved to be an ongoing nightmare. Now the electrician is here everyone is afraid of tangling with

182

his wires and much as I want the plumber to complete his role so we can have running water, he seems to have visions of toasters in bathtubs at every turn. What with the two construction guys flailing around with skirting boards, doors, countertops et al, there's too many bodies and too much timber in too small a space. I'm next to useless at supervising because a) I don't understand the technicalities of what anyone is doing, b) the humidity is so sickening all I really care about is installing the air-con unit and c) there's only so far mime and hastily drawn diagrams can get you – I repeatedly have to ask for Santiago's help translating the workman's words which just adds to my general frustration and, of course, his irritation. Every time he settles into a project I seem to be tapping him on the shoulder with an apologetic, 'Sorry to bother you but . . .'

'Are you even *trying* to learn the language?' he huffs at one point.

'Well, with the ten minutes I have free each day to study I just can't understand why I'm not fluent yet,' I smart. I do so hate to feel a burden.

Worse still, while I'm shanghaied by drilling and buzz-sawing and banging and mess, Santiago is making far too impressive progress with his landscaping – having cleared all the debris and trippable roots from his sandy enclave, he's laid a perimeter of rocks to designate his seating area and dug deep

183

trenches to lower in some additional shrubbery to create the illusion of booth-like privacy. I make a note that his bushes could obscure the ocean view from clients sat further back, only to see him personally trim down the hedges. We only have seven more days to pull this whole thing together yet already he appears to be ten minutes of furniture-positioning away from completion.

'Señorita Langston?'

'Yes?' I turn to address the foreman.

'There is a problem.'

'Of course there is,' I feel like saying. This happens practically every hour. I can now add '*Hay un problema*' to my list of Spanish phrases.

The good – or should I say miraculous? – news is that by the end of the day the air con is installed. I can't tell you how happy this makes me. I'd been feeling overwhelmed and overheated and finally I can think straight. I celebrate with a call to Ollie.

'Finally I hear from you!' he cheers.

'Well, it's just been too hot and noisy and busy to call until now!' I explain as I lie flat on my back on the unfinished floor, glad for the opportunity to straighten my spine.

'Noisy and busy I'll buy,' Ollie replies. 'But *too hot* to phone?'

'You have to experience it for yourself to understand,' I insist. 'It's been like working in a greenhouse but instead of mingling with fragrant

184

blooms and automatic misters I've been dodging five shirtless men and random splashes of sweat.'

'That's gross!' Ollie ewws.

'Yes it is. Or rather *was*!' I smile euphorically. 'Now it's lovely and cool and all is well with the world.'

'Have they started to hammer quieter too?' Ollie enquires.

'Actually they've all gone home for the night. Santiago and I typically stay for a couple of hours after they've departed, assessing the progress, tidying up and working out our respective game plans for the next day.'

'And then what – you hit the bars?'

I go cross-eyed at the mere thought. 'Honestly, I'm so wiped out by the end of the day I'm lucky if I can get my clothes off before I collapse into bed. Twice I've woken up still covered in sawdust and carpentry glue. I don't know the last time I ate a proper dinner. I'm practically a human enchilada these days.'

'So this isn't really much in the way of a holiday?'

'It's nothing in the way of a holiday,' I confirm. 'It's weird because we're on the beach so we see all these people lazing around relaxing and going for swims and maybe taking a nap and here we are thrashing around, going like the clappers – I don't know how those makeover shows turn things around in a day, there's just so much to do.'

185

'Are you wishing you'd taken the box in the mall now?'

'No way. Never,' I confirm though my aching muscles and throbbing feet beg to differ. 'Any word on Mum?' I ask as I notice a splinter in my thumb.

'Yes actually, she rang last night to get an update on you.'

'How come she didn't call me direct?' I frown.

'Oh you know her, she's got some mental block about making overseas phone calls – seems to think it would cost her the equivalent of a year's supply of Walkers shortbread or something. Besides, I think she's worried she'd call you and you'd be with your dad . . .'

'It's a fair point. Though he is in a different town now. Anyway, I'll give her a ring in a day or two,' I tell him.

'No rush,' he replies. 'I told her that you'd most likely had a fatal fall in the jungle and were providing a new source of nutrients for the epiphytes.'

'The what?' I laugh out loud.

'You know – plants that grow on trees like ferns and mosses and orchids . . .'

'You never cease to amaze me, Ollie – where did that nugget come from?'

'A little book I'm reading as research for my upcoming trip to Costa Rica,' he breezes.

'For real?' I squeal, scrabbling upright.

'Yes but don't get too excited, I'm having trouble

getting my time off approved – we've had three new renovation projects come in since the Thermae Spa opened.'

'Well, not to put you off but it's no good you coming for at least three weeks – I'm going to be totally tied up till Judgement Day.' I get a twang of nerves just thinking about it. Am I really going to have everything ready in time? Look at the state of this place and we open in a week and then there's all the pressure of outselling Santiago—

'And after that?' Ollie breaks my flow of angst. 'After your dad makes the decision . . .'

'Well, if I win then you can take Santiago's place and work alongside me—'

'*Work?*' Ollie baulks.

'Free cakes and ocean swims on your breaks . . .' I negotiate.

'Oh, okay. And if you lose?'

My stomach dips but I go for bravado: 'We'll go *mono loco*, baby.'

'Crazy monkey?' Ollie translates.

'That's right, smartypants,' I commend him. 'For starters we're checking into La Mariposa – it turns out they've got *three* pools and I didn't get to try one.'

'Poor baby.'

'I know!' It feels good to have some sympathy, even if it is of the teasing variety. I've been so moronically tired of late, just hearing Ollie's voice is rejuvenating. It would be such fun to have him here. Aside from a couple of soda runs I've barely explored the town. Not that there's a whole lot here – all the market stalls repeat themselves after the third trader – hand-carved knick-knacks, screen-printed sarongs and Imperial Beer T-shirts ad infinitum. I did actually buy a hat with an embroidered hummingbird logo for $3 to spare my scalp from the scalding sun and my co-workers the sight of my toil-mangled locks, but other than that it's just been a lot of cans of ginger ale – for some reason it's as ubiquitous as Coke here. And known as 'gin', which amuses me every time.

Ollie brings me up to speed on work and some ridiculous bout of office politics, which I can certainly relate to and yet even though I am struggling with Santiago, I know my prize is far greater. If Ollie bites his tongue he gets to keep his job. If I keep my cool with – and my distance from – Santiago, I might just get a café to call my own. I've never worked for myself before but it's proving to be a great incentive to give my all. Do what you love, career consultants advise. And they're right. But as with everything there is a price to be paid. I certainly know I'm racking up a fair few osteopath bills as I go. Watching Santiago get to his feet and wince as he stretches, I suspect I may not be alone.

'Is he there now?' Ollie asks after Santiago.

'Yes, but he's outside, he can't hear us.' I walk to

the furthest point from the door, just to be sure.

'So he's still being an arse, I take it?' Ollies enquires.

'Yup,' I confirm, adding, 'As am I, to be fair.'

'Like begets like,' Ollie muses. 'Can I go back to bed now?'

My brow furrows. 'What time is it there?'

'3.16 a.m.'

'*Nooooooo!* I'm so sorry!' I have become my father!

'It's fine, I'm just glad to hear from you,' Olllie assures me. 'Now why don't you go and get yourself something nice to eat? I rather like the sound of the *sopa de mondongo* I've been reading about.'

I frown. 'Haven't seen that one on the menu, what is it?'

'Tripe soup.'

'Oh nice.' My mouth twists in revulsion.

'Night, Ava,' he yawns.

'Night, Ollie,' I smile.

The reality is, I don't eat until the morning when Santiago suggests we stop off at Café Milagro to get breakfast.

'Eat in or to go?' he queries.

I'm surprised he'd even consider sharing a table with me. Or is this a delay tactic because he knows he's further ahead than me? 'To go,' I reply.

It seems odd to buy coffee and croissants en route to a café but at this point our cupboards are not just bare, they are non-existent. The fitters are due today, however. Though they're going to have to work around the construction guys who are still working on sealing all possible gaps where hot air might seep in.

'Oh my god!' I can't help but exclaim at the sight of twenty or so chunks of tree-trunk dumped plum in the middle of Santiago's patch. 'Do we have to build the cupboards ourselves?'

Santiago dismisses my concern. 'Those are for me.'

I frown as he starts to inspect his delivery. Tree-stump stools? Rustic but none too comfortable. I make a mental note to ensure my seat cushions are extra soft and accommodating. Soon I'll be attracting numb bums as well as fevered brows, I smile to myself.

Today turns out to be a good day – just as my interior is starting to take shape (structurally at least), Santiago appears to trash his area. Apparently nature's creation is not to his liking – he's hired a guy to carve the stools into some specific design. Curious, I pretend to clean the glass frontage of my unit so I can see what they are up to without obviously gawping. First there's a chainsaw then a chisel. When they sit down on the sand to start on the real detail work, both men position their backs to me, blocking their work. I humph and climb the ladder beside the cabinets ostensibly

190

checking on them but actually trying for a better vantage point. Still no joy. I wonder what they are planning? I wonder if they get extra points for having created furniture from scratch? He will have certainly saved on his budget there – my tables and chairs weren't cheap, but they are plain. Should I have gone for something fancier? I remember Dad taking me to the Rainforest Café in London once and they had bar stools that gave you the rear and legs of a giraffe or a hippo as you sat on them. I wonder if they have a similar goal? I don't see any paint or rope for tails but that could come later . . .

'Shit!' On my way down the ladder I inadvertently send three sample plates flying, bringing Santiago rushing in.

'I'm fine,' I announce, feeling instantly foolish because, of course, his greater concern lies with the broken items.

He stoops and picks up a chunk of china.

'I did it on purpose!' I brazen. 'I'm working on a mosaic table top.'

'Really?' he sounds unconvinced.

'Mm-hmm.' I nod, overdoing my bravado by stomping a larger chunk to smithereens. 'I'm just going to rough out the design on the floor here first . . .'

'Well, I'll let you get on with it,' he says as he retreats back to his carving. 'Good luck.'

Good luck indeed! I huff to myself before

realising I'm going to need it. How exactly am I supposed to transform this chaos of splinters into a work of art? I'll need a pretty thick layer of putty or cement or whatever it is to embed them in or I'll have an uneven surface that'll invite drink spillage. But what of cement spillage – how do I stop it splurging over the edge of the table – do I need a metal ring to contain it? I grab a handful of pieces and look over at the last remaining construction guy.

'Um . . .?' I raise my eyebrows hopefully.

He looks back at me then hangs his head, as if in shame.

I take a step closer so I can better read his face.

'I am so sorry,' he apologises, head still down.

I can't quite work him out – is he lamenting the loss of the plates?

'It's okay,' I tell him. 'No big deal.'

'Really? You are not angry?' He looks up at me like an eager child. It's then I notice that the floor tiling has fallen short of the front wall by a good inch. 'I measured, so careful, but . . .'

I crouch beside him. Oh dear. This isn't good. It's like a gutter waiting to be filled with crumbs.

'I can level with cement?' he offers.

My eyes brighten. He just said the magic word. 'Show me!' I encourage him.

Wasting no time, he sloops in the first scoop. Gently I press my handful of pieces in place.

He looks delighted. 'I like!'

'Me too!' I enthuse, scurrying to gather up the rest of the broken china.

Together we work on the fancy border with jigsaw-like precision and concentration. We're three-quarters done when I realise it's way past his going-home time.

'Luis, you can go now. I'll finish up.'

He protests but I insist. 'This was a good mistake!' I tell him as he gathers up his tools.

He smiles proudly and waves, 'I am an artist!' as he leaves.

'Yes, you are!' I laugh, caring nothing for my sore knees and arched back and scrunched-up fingers. This is the most fun I've had so far.

When I'm done I sit up on my haunches and take a moment to admire our handiwork. I feel all the better for having added a personal touch. Apparently sometimes a little competition can bring out the best in you. I peek up over the sill to check on Santiago. But both he and his saw-wielding friend are nowhere to be seen. I walk outside to check his car is still there – yes, he must have just gone for supplies or sustenance. I kneel down to take a closer look at his carving. It's a simple rainforest scene but the sensuality of the lines takes my breath away. This is incredibly skilled work – I run my fingers over the texture of the leaves and tree bark – suddenly my broken-china-in-cement

193

project seems a little lame. This is true crafts-manship.

Getting up on my feet too fast, I feel a little dizzy. Then my head starts to thump. It's been a long day. *Another* long day. I go into the back bathroom to wash my hands and face and wonder if it's worth all the effort. Am I ultimately decorating this café for Santiago's benefit? I want to put heart and soul into this project but it's hard when just a few weeks from now it could all be taken away from me. More pressing is the fact that we have only seven days until we open. Seven days to turn this into a fully functional café. With staff. We start interviewing tomorrow. Tomorrow is also the day we stock the stockroom and we haven't even put the shelves up yet – something Luis had been scheduled for instead of getting arty with me. I rub my brow anxiously. I promised Santiago I would make sure it was done today. I'd do it myself only I'd be in even more trouble when everything collapsed in on itself. Must remember to store the cleaning products as near to the floor as possible to reduce the risk of damage should they leak or spill. And I really should do up the shelf labels tonight . . .

When I emerge from the bathroom I see Santiago kneeling beside my mosaic border. His hands are gently tracing the pieces – the little triangles and raggedy squares and hand-painted flourishes. I feel a compliment brewing so I cough lightly to let my presence be known. He looks up at me with a smirk. 'I see your floor tiles fell a little short?'

I swallow back my disappointment. There's no point pretending this was all part of my grand plan, I need to save that lie for my father. Instead I simply shrug. 'Ready to go?'

Suddenly I need to be home, in my room with the door firmly shut and the duvet over my head.

'How are the shelves?' he asks, stopping me in my tracks.

'Luis is going to do them first thing tomorrow,' I breeze, trying to sound like everything is going according to plan.

'We're paying him for another day?' Santiago complains.

'Half a day,' I decide on the spot. 'And it's coming out of my budget.'

'Okay,' he concedes. 'But you know the first delivery is due at 9.00 a.m.?'

I give a casual nod but inside I'm fretting – not least because I've scheduled the first interviewee for 9.30 a.m. Busy day tomorrow. Busy, busy day.

16

The next morning I set the alarm for 6 a.m. and book a taxi to bring me to the café early so I can ensure that Luis gets the shelving secure before Santiago arrives. We cut it close but everything is in place when the coffee-bean delivery van reverses up to the door.

I check everything off against the order sheet and inspect for any tears or damage (just like my good book told me) while Santiago helps the driver unload. Dad has insisted that Santiago and I consolidate our purchases for economy's sake. I did raise the objection that it's going to be that much harder for Dad to judge the success of our individual concerns if we're working from the same stock but he said, 'It's not what you've got, it's what you do with it that interests me. Besides, the quality has to be standard throughout.'

I could see that the café as an overall concept needed consistency but we were still arguing over the cakes, so much so that Santiago has scheduled a tasting at a local bakery in between the day's intermittent stock delivery and the interviewing.

'Consider it lunch,' he shrugged when I complained that we were already too overbooked. 'Here's interviewee number one now – Mercedes Alvarez. Hmm, looks promising.' Santiago hurries ahead to greet her.

I can't help but scowl after him – Mercedes is a voluptuous siren disguised as a waitress. That's all I need, Costa Rica's answer to Salma Hayek batting her eyelashes at him and telling him that it would be an honour to work for someone so famously industrious who also happens to be so handsome – something along the lines of 'you have vision/you are a vision!'

Give me a break!

Santiago plays off her words with great modesty but I can see his chest puff up nevertheless.

'What about coffee?' I butt in. 'Got any strong feelings about that?'

'I don't know if I should say this,' she acts all coy, 'but I prefer tea!'

'You don't have to drink coffee to work here,' Santiago reasons.

'No, but it helps,' I complete the slogan.

Over the next three and half hours I feel I'm as much getting a crash course in the local culture as meeting potential employees. Santiago has a tactic whereby he likes to veer away from the traditional interview questions so that the candidates' answers aren't so rehearsed and we can get a better idea of their personality. In that vain I learn that the Paris Hiltons of Costa Rica (i.e. the pampered offspring of the rich) are known as *fresas* (strawberries) and the equivalent of white trash are labelled *comehuevos*, literally 'egg-eaters'.

I already knew that Ticos had an impressive literacy rate but was impressed to learn that Costa Rica has a higher percentage of female politicians than either Britain or the US. It's all the more shocking, therefore, to learn that up until the 1990s a rapist of an underage girl could not be prosecuted if he offered to marry the victim. I don't even hear interviewee number three because I'm still reeling from this grisly, but thankfully now outdated, law.

On a lighter note, I derive much amusement when Santiago asks each candidate to reveal their nickname. Apparently what might seem politically incorrect in other cultures is just friendly joshing here so they happily introduce themselves as *Sapito* (aka Little Toad – thanks to his boggly eyes), *Gordo* (which translates as fatty even though his tummy is perfectly adorable) and *Cejas* as in eyebrows. And very Colin Farrell they were too. (Shame they belonged to a girl.)

'Is that everyone?' I ask, hoping they don't go

away calling me anything worse than Gringo or *Roja Grande* (aka Big Red)!

Santiago consults his notes. 'Well, I'm guessing our 10.30 a.m. appointment got a better offer so, yes, that's everyone. Do you want to decide now or take some time to deliberate?'

I look at my watch. It's nearly 1pm. 'Why don't we let things sit awhile while we do the cake-tasting?'

He nods his approval. 'Let's go.'

I must say I really do love cake. My complaint with most coffee-shop fare is that it's either too dry or too dense. I like a bit of moist fluffiness wherever possible, but I'm coming to the bakery with an open mind as I know these samples will be no Parisienne fancies.

We're welcomed by a petite lady, barely bigger than a cake decoration herself. I can't help but wonder if she moonlights as the bride on wedding cakes as she bids us sit down. Or better yet, perhaps she's discovered some kind of cake mix that actually makes you shrink instead of bulge.

'Please try,' she unveils her selection of goodies.

'Well, these I recognise,' I point to the plate of croissants.

'We call them *cangrejos* – crabs,' Santiago tells me.

'Brilliant!' I laugh. 'Mmm.' The pastry flakes on to my chin. Just the way I like it.

'*Cachos.*' She points to a similar pastry this time in a tube stuffed with cream.

199

'Horns,' Santiago again gives me the translation.

'I'm a definite yes on both of those, I can tell you that now,' I enthuse.

'*Alfajores.*' The lady pushes a plate forward that wouldn't look out of place at the Mad Hatter's Tea Party – round biscuits sandwiched together with jam and dusted with sugar.

I take a bite. The biscuit has a crumbly shortbread taste. My mum would love these ones.

'*Churros.*' Now I'm contemplating a six-inch-long deep-fried dougnut stick.

'I've heard of these . . .' I take a little nibble, aware that fairly soon I'll be feeling sick.

'*Orejas.*'

'That means ears,' Santiago shrugs as he too cuts into the sugar-sprinkled dinner-plate-size pastry. 'Perfection. They are all excellent,' he compliments the baker lady.

After a few sips of water we try some darling little coconut tarts, meringues which I dismiss as too easily shattered, a dry cake I fail to see the appeal of and a sweetcorn tamale made with sour cream and sugar that I don't like the idea of, but love the taste.

I lean back in my chair and expel a breath. Wow. That's a lot of doughy sugar.

'And now for my speciality!'

'I don't think I can eat another thing!' I protest.

'You must,' Santiago hisses. 'She will be deeply offended if you refuse.'

Oh yes. Tico protocol. 'Yum! I can't wait,' I call out as she opens the fridge and produces two small pottery dishes.

My throat clogs at the mere sight of the contents.

'*Tres leches!*' she announces proudly. 'Best in Manuel Antonio.'

I bite my lip and anxiously rub my spoon praying for some kind of genie to appear and make my dessert vanish in a puff of smoke.

'It's really cakes I was interested—'

Santiago coughs, urging me to shut up and bite the bullet. He's already nearly finished his sample.

'Looks delicious!' I try again, telling myself it could be worse, it could be a live witchetty grub.

'Señora – may we see those?' Santiago points to a tray of mystery items layered with bright blue icing on the shelf behind her.

'*Si, si.*'

As she turns away he switches the dishes and quickly shovels down my untouched portion.

I am open-mouthed with surprise and gratitude. Did he really do that for me? Or was he just afraid I'd throw up over her nice tablecloth and thus ruin our negotiations? Frankly I don't care to know his motivation, the fact that he spared me is just too fabulous for words.

When she turns away again, this time to work on some calculations, I rest my hand on Santiago's forearm and quickly mouth Thank you!

He gives me a gracious nod back.

Gosh. Saved by Santiago! Who'd have thought it? He tells me what he thinks the order should be and I barely contend it – I'm still too grateful – though I do stand firm on the *queque seco*. We can easily save money by serving retired washing-up sponges if people like their cake that dry and tasteless.

This I tell him when we're out of earshot of the bonsai baker and on our way back to the café.

'But overall you are content?'

'Absolutely. Very impressed.' I pause, not wanting to sound too gushy. 'And thanks again for—'

He holds up his hand. 'I was afraid you would . . .' he makes a spewing motion with his hand.

'Yes. Well. It was a possibility,' I confess. 'Anyway, it's good to know that beneath your curmudgeonly exterior, a little kindness lurks.'

He stops and faces me. 'What was that?'

I blink back at him. 'A compliment, sort of.'

'*Curmudgeon?*' he repeats with a growl. 'What exactly is a curmudgeon?'

'Well, um . . .' What have I started? 'I think the dictionary definition is a bad-tempered or stubborn person.'

I wait for the eruptive protestation.

'Oh.' He shrugs. 'I'll have to remember that. You want to walk back along the beach?'

'The scenic route?'

He nods.

'Okay!' I agree, shrugging off my flip-flops, feeling I just had a narrow escape.

'Please,' he requests I hand them to him.

I hesitate – is he going to punish my verbal abuse by yanking off the beading?

He beckons for them again. 'So you are free!' he smiles.

'Oh. Thank you.' There I go again with the gratitude. He must be after something.

'So, we should decide on who to employ,' he says as we follow the wavering line of the surf.

Oh here we go. I brace myself.

'For the female, my vote is for Mercedes,' Santiago asserts, oh-so-predictably.

'You also have to give a reason,' I challenge. 'Something to do with coffee, preferably,' I mutter under my breath.

'She has a great nose.'

'Ah yes, her sense of smell must have heightened when her eyesight diminished.'

Santiago stops in his tracks. 'Are you saying that she only found me attractive because she couldn't see me properly?'

'Then you admit she fancies you!' Gotcha! I do a little dance of triumph. 'Look, I just don't think we should encourage that kind of distraction in the workplace. Besides which her glasses are going to steam up every time she froths the milk or steps from the air-con to the outside world. Over the course of the week we'll lose minutes of valuable work time with her cleaning off her lenses.'

Santiago gives me the look of incredulity I deserve then snootily informs me, 'I would never mix romance with business.'

'Really?' The word is out before I can stop it. Worse yet, it actually has a forlorn ring to it.

Santiago tilts his head to one side. 'Would you?'

I shake my head as I look down at my feet. 'Of course not. It's just asking for trouble.'

Santiago nods then continues. 'I suppose you favour Rosa.'

'With good reason,' I enthuse, getting back on track. 'She's funny, she's smart, former teacher, she can add up *and* help me with the language.'

'She's seventy.'

'So?'

Santiago rolls his eyes.

'Actually I want Milena,' I tell him.

'The teenager?' he scoffs.

'You missed her in action, she's amazing, truly.'

'Where was I?'

'You stepped out to approve the hanging of the basket chairs.'

(Though I'm loath to admit it, Santiago's area just keeps getting better – he now has two wicker nests suspended from the tree for individuals to snug into and spin as they sip their drink of choice.)

'Oh yes. But her appearance . . .' he tuts.

'It's okay, she'll have a uniform,' I say, though I must confess I too was ready to dismiss her as soon as she walked in the door, she was dressed so tawdrily and chewing gum at double speed. Even in Kiki's selection of white cotton shorts teamed with an emerald green T-shirt I wondered if she could look presentable enough, but then her first sentence stopped my judgment in its tracks.

'I have to leave the café where I am,' she conspired. 'They use a blade grinder for the beans.'

'And that's a problem because . . .'

She smiled as if I was merely testing her knowledge as opposed to being genuinely in the dark. 'Because the beans are moving freely within the grinder, the cut is random – you have chunks and tiny pieces and powder, all mixed together and that means every brew has a different taste – I can't work like that!'

'Noooo . . .' I sympathised.

She leaned closer. 'Sometimes, the friction of the blades creates so much heat the beans start to cook while they are still being ground.'

'That's sinful,' I confirmed.

'I see you have a burr grinder,' she eyed the equipment lasciviously.

'Would you like to try it out, see if it meets your standards?'

'That was her cup of coffee?' Santiago remembers a particularly delicious brew.

205

I nod. 'And her granitas were easily the best. And she reckons she could get us a discount with the paper-cup supplier.'

'Okay, she's hired!'

'Really?' I clap my hands together. 'You're sure about Mercedes?'

'Now I think of it, she would attract too many lecherous men,' he shrugs. 'Sexual harassment could be bad for business.'

I can't tell if he's joking, but if he isn't I'm a little offended. Doesn't he think *I* could attract any lechy guys? Is my bottom not pinchable? Would I not elicit a saucy *piropos*? That's something that Ollie tells me is a form of flirting gone awry – back in the day when Ticos took a nightly *paseo* around the park, the single men would walk in one direction, the single women in another and it fell to the men to come up with a quippy little verse to impress the object of their desire. However, these have since declined into semi-insulting one-liners such as 'So much meat and me on a diet!'

Mind you, there are still some cute ones – 'I wish I was cross-eyed so I could see you twice!' And who could resist 'For you I could go out and find a job!'

Speaking of which . . .

'To the male employee . . .' Santiago starts heading inland. I'm reluctant to follow – I'd love to keep walking along the beach, it feels so nice.

'Well, I think it's obvious who we should choose,' I call over to him.

Santiago rolls his eyes. 'Javier, I presume.'

'Of course,' I say, hurrying to catch him up.

'And the fact that he was the tallest and most handsome plays no part in your reasoning?'

'The guy is a black belt,' I scold, as if that explains my favouritism.

'Well, that's going to come in handy if there's no knife around to cut the cakes.'

'You said yourself we need some security. I'd feel safer if he was here. On the days you're not around, of course,' I jump in, fearing Santiago will think I'm doubting his fierce masculinity.

'I liked Benito.'

'He seemed a little serious.'

'Conscientious,' he corrects. 'We don't want someone who's fooling around all the time.'

'But we do want someone who knows how to smile – a little customer service goes a long way.'

Santiago holds his chin in his hand and skews his mouth to the side.

'What?'

'I'm just trying to think who had the best smile. Maybe we should contact the local dentist and see if he can recommend someone . . .'

I give him a playful wallop as we step into the shade of the trees. Lately, our banter seems to have taken on a more playful air. Which is strange considering the pressure is mounting daily.

'Excuse me?' There's a timid face awaiting us in the doorway.

'Is there still time for me to arrive?'

'Wilbeth!' I cheer, recognising Dad's chauffeur.

'You have a memory!' His face lights up.

'Yes I do,' I grin. 'And you have quite a smile. Are you here about the job?'

He nods shyly.

'Come in, take a seat.' I cheer.

I'm already sold on him so I leave the questioning to Santiago. His greatest concern seems to be the potential drop in his pay.

'You know you won't earn nearly as much as you did as a driver,' he cautions.

'It's okay. I am never in love with driving.'

'So why did you do it for so long?' Santiago probes.

'The air conditioning.'

I laugh out loud. 'That's what has brought you here?'

'That, and a girl,' he says shyly.

Surprisingly Santiago's face softens. 'She lives in Manuel Antonio?'

He nods.

'Well, I don't think we're the type to stand in the way of true love, do you, Ava?' Santiago has a wink in his eye as he addresses me.

Apparently neither of us wants to see the other fixed up, but we're both more than happy to help Wilbeth on his way.

Feeling all very cupid-meets-Sir Alan Sugar, I lean forward to shake his hand and whoop, 'You're hired!'

17

I couldn't sleep last night for going over and over and over every last detail in my head. About three times I scrabbled to my feet and wrote myself an outsize reminder of the additional things I had to do before we flipped the door sign to OPEN for the very first time.

After two weeks remodelling, stocking and prepping, today is the day.

Up until now the physical work has been so absorbing and exhausting I've just been concentrating on getting each project ticked off the list, but yesterday we started to look more to the future – having familiarised Milena and Wilbeth with the facilities and the prospective drinks menu, we sent them out to distribute promotional leaflets and discount coupons to every visitor, resident and monkey they passed on the street and the beach. Meanwhile, Santiago and I went to meet with our local banker to go through the updated figures now that all our start-up costs are on the table. Once again we looked at our sales forecast, which is basically the following formula:

Market size × growth rate × market-share target (percentage of market we hope to capture) × average sale × average number of visits

Because it is undecided who will be running the coffee shop two weeks from now, we keep our longer-range forecasts a secret from each other – only Dad will be privy to those. Of course both our figures are just guesswork. It's hard to contemplate just how wrong we could be. Apparently the wisest thing to do with a conservative forecast is to cut it by 25 per cent – better to have a pleasant surprise than deal with the alternative.

It certainly helps that both Santiago and I have a financial background. The figures themselves I can handle, it's knowing that mine will be compared to his that freaks me out. Having said that, Dad has made it clear that the profits are only a part of his judging criteria. In a phone call a couple of days ago he revealed that we were being 'watched' throughout the process. I cast my mind back to see if I could recall any glints of sun off paparazzo lenses but then I realised it's a lot more basic than that – everyone knows everyone here and everyone talks.

Well, in a way I'm glad I didn't know, what's done is done. The real test will be the day-to-day running of the place. I'm fairly certain I can offer chirpier customer service than Santiago, though lately he does seem to be mellowing. I'd almost say we were working well together but that's not really something to be encouraged when you are in direct competition. I try to keep in mind my initial duping over the location selection to raise my hackles as well as my game, while keeping in mind that I don't want to inflict any of our tension on the customers.

'Ready?' Santiago taps on my door.

I jump to my feet, grabbing my assorted notes and props, only to drop them all at his feet as I step outside.

'Nervous?' he asks, helping me reassemble my kit.

I go to dismiss his enquiry as nonsense—'Who me?' – but as I look up I see a warm sheen to his dark eyes. I wish I could trust him. I wonder if things might have been different if we hadn't met in such combative circumstances? He's so sweet with Wilbeth and even the gum-chewing Milena thinks he's cool, though she's made it clear she prefers more rough-and-ready types – Santiago is too sophisticated for her palate.

'I'm excited,' I tell him as I get back to my feet. 'You?'

'Terrified!' he grins so I can't tell if he's joking or not. 'Let's go.'

On the journey in we say nothing, but it's not like the early days when we were quietly seething at each other, casting sideways glances of disdain. This time we are silent through concentration and anticipation.

I feel like I'm seeing the café for the first time as we step from the car. The exterior looks amazing – and has been a great ad to passers-by over the last few days. I take in the exquisitely carved wood, the white sand underfoot, the tropical foliage, the low hedge divisions, the hanging-basket chairs now with plump orange cushions . . . Santiago completes the look by tying what looks like a workman's tool belt around the girth of the main tree to act as the outdoor accoutrements unit, tucking various napkins and spoons and cake forks into the pouches.

Meanwhile, I pay the window cleaner who has just given a professional finish to the glass frontage and open the door, making straight for the air-con unit. As it sets to work, I look around at the interior I have created from what was a dingy shack – the glazed green tiling of the floor with its mosaic border and potted plants, the inviting, enveloping sofas, the groovy elliptical tables, the hammock slung in the front window, the local artwork displayed in the central panel of the right-hand wall, the polished counter and the old-fashioned cake display unit soon to be filled with freshly baked goodies. I unwrap the flowers we stopped for en route and set the biggest blooms on the counter before arranging a smaller vase beside the stirrers and cinnamon shaker on the side dresser.

After so much anxiety, I feel a genuine thrill. I can't wait for Dad to see this. I wonder what time he'll arrive? I tried to phone him last night but got his voicemail and no return call. He probably wants to surprise us – sneak in during the lunchtime rush. If there is a rush. What if no one comes? That's not going to happen, I assure myself. After all, I've made Wilbeth promise to invite his ladyfriend for a complimentary beverage and Milena has said her brothers will definitely come by later so that's four bodies at least.

'Kiki knows we changed the sign, right?' Santiago hurries in, suddenly gripped with concern.

'Yes, I told her a week ago that neon was problematic because of all the messy wiring. Your wood carving is beautiful, she's going to love it.'

What is going on? Shouldn't we be spitting at each other?

'So, the coffee is brewing, the bottled drinks are chilling, Milena is on her way with the cakes, Wilbeth with the milk and cream, the money is in the till, the place looks . . .' He pauses to study it for a second, '. . . resplendent,' he concludes. 'So I think we should have a toast!' Santiago produces a bottle of champagne and two glasses out of a cool bag.

214

My jaw drops. 'Oh my god!' I laugh out loud. '*Wow!*' I'm lost for words. This is way too civilised! I actually feel a tear brewing. After all our hard work, it's finally happening – we're open for business!

'Here's to the Café Tropicana!' he presents me with a glass. 'May the best barista win!'

'You want Milena to run the place?' I tease.

He smiles as he shakes his head. 'It's you or me, *chica!*' – and with that we both give an enthusiastic chink, so vigorous in fact that both glasses smash, spilling golden bubbles and glass shards all over the floor.

'Here I am – *Yow!*' Naturally Milena chooses that precise moment to arrive – *barefoot*.

'Shit!' I exclaim reaching for the kitchen roll.

'Don't anyone move!' Santiago barks, getting busy with the dustpan and brush.

'Blood!' Wilbeth whimpers as he walks in, instantly pale at the sight of Milena's spurting foot. 'I need to sit downward.' Which he does, but not soundly enough and promptly falls back, knocking over the vase of flowers and drenching the stack napkins and sugar sachets on the dresser.

'Are you open?' Our first customer is at the door. We look up, perturbed – frozen in our farcical poses.

Suddenly I get some presence of mind: 'Would you like to take a moment to peruse the menu?' I bound across the assorted bodies to distract his eye and guide him to the seat with the best view, away from the blood and glass and sogginess. 'You're our first customer so this one is on the house!' I smile, winningly.

'And what is the house blend?' He looks up from the list.

Darn it! I knew there was something nagging at me that was incomplete! Over the past week Santiago and I have been snagging every spare moment to work on a unique blend. Unable to agree on one we decided we'd have one each – mine would be known as the Greenhouse Blend and his would be the Sandpit Blend, reflecting our respective environments. Only the detail of the actual mix of coffees seems to have slipped both our minds.

'Let me just check on that and I'll get right back to you.'

'Don't worry.' He holds up his hand. 'I haven't got long, I'll have a cappuccino.'

'Coming right up!' I chirrup, turning on my heel and returning to the counter, only to discover that, in his eagerness to get here, Wilbeth forgot to collect the milk.

It's like that for the rest of the day. Every time something goes awry I scan the room to see if my father is looking. But there's no sign of him. During a lull I try his mobile but again there's no reply. Has he forgotten that it's our Big Day? Up until now I

216

was relieved he wasn't here to see all the chaos but now I'm starting to get offended. As far as I'm concerned, this is the equivalent of my graduation day – graduating from ten years of jobs I didn't give two hoots about to a wonderful new career. With his own money invested, you'd think he'd care enough to show up. I sigh grouchily. My head is throbbing, my feet are aching, my finger is blistering from a rush steamed-milk job and my heart is heavy. I didn't think I'd feel like this today. Now I wish I hadn't put Ollie off until after Judgement Day. I could really use a friend about now.

I look out at Santiago, unfazed by beginnings of a downpour. Oh my god – his chalkboard menu, it's all going to streak and run and those beautifully swirled letters of his are going to be lost for ever. I rap on the window and point animatedly to the board. He frowns back at me and goes back to chatting to his last customer. Oh god! I'm going to have to get it in myself! I go hurtling out and try to grab it from its position by the tree, only to find it is strapped into place. The rain is dripping into my eyes so I can hardly see but I'm determined to wrestle it free.

'Ava! What are you doing?' Santiago calls over.

'I don't want it to run!' I yell back, still struggling to salvage what I can. With one final yank I liberate it, only to splosh back into a puddle. As I feel my bottom absorbing water I'm taken back to the day I first arrived and fell down a pothole. Santiago looms above me.

'You know it's protected.'

'What?'

'It's not chalk, it's paint. And it has a waterproof coating.'

I look down and see that the board is pristine. It's just me that's a complete mess. My breathing starts to come quicker and I realise to my horror that I'm about to burst into tears. What kind of unprofessional girl would that make me look? I lurch to my feet and struggle to reposition the board, snapping, 'I can do it!' when Santiago offers to take over. After five minutes' futile manoeuvres I finally have to bow out, running inside and busily buzzing around the sofas and chairs as if I'm searching for something, trying to dodge the tears through movement and distraction. But the feeling is too powerful. I sniff and cough and bluster and try to fight it as I wave off my final indoor customer, but when Santiago appears by my side and softly enquires, 'Ava, are you okay?' the tears come chugging to the fore.

'I-I—' I try to speak but my words catch in my throat.

'I know you were just trying to help. That was really nice of you.'

I throw up my hands as if to say, 'Fat lot of good I did!' but he simply soothes, 'It's okay,' before adding, 'Why don't we go home?'

218

'Bu-bu—' I try to protest that I haven't finished all my chores.

'We'll come in half an hour earlier tomorrow.'

I blink at him with a pair of inflamed pink eyes.

'Have you eaten today?'

I shake my head.

'Tonight I will cook for you,' he asserts.

I feel faint with gratitude.

On the car journey on the way back to the villa, we are again mute, save my occasional quavery intake of breath. It amazes me how many different types of silence there are.

'Cry if you want to,' he encourages as we fastened our seat belts.

And so I do and it feels almost nice to do it without anyone trying to fix the situation.

Not all the tears sliding down my face are sad tears, I think there is some relief and amazement in there too – wanting something so badly for so long and then getting it, it can be a little overwhelming.

When we pull into the driveway of the villa I want to apologise for my waterworks but then I realise I don't need to. Instead I decide to share the disappointment about Dad not showing up, wondering if Santiago might feel that way himself.

'With Dean there is always a reason, always a plan,' he tells me as we enter the living area. 'I have learned that if I wait a day or two before I react, all becomes clear and it is all for the best.'

He excuses himself for five minutes, leaving me to ponder those words. When he returns he announces the bath is ready for me and I am to soak in it until he tells me that dinner is ready.

I could honestly kiss him.

18

'Is it okay if I come to the table like this?' I point to my towel turban.

'Of course, in fact I think we should all wear hats,' he says, pulling the giant red oven glove on to his head.

'You look like a cockerel!' I laugh delightedly as he places a steaming dish of *sopa de pejibaye* in front of me. As he runs through the ingredients – puréed palm fruit (tastes like a cross between chestnut and potato), chopped onion and garlic, diced sweet peppers and chicken stock – I inhale the distinct aromas, drop my napkin on my lap and prepare to dig in.

'Don't eat that!' a voice yelps, halting my spoon.

I look up and find my dad's frantic face inches from my own. Oh my god, was Santiago going to poison me?

'You can't eat it,' he expands. 'Because you're coming to dinner with me!'

'Daaad!' I complain. 'Do you want to tone down the drama?'

'Well, it's a big deal – opening day at the café and Kiki's friend Ryan is in town. We want you to meet him!'

I look longingly at my hot and hearty soup. Funny how an hour ago I was crushed that Dad was a no-show and now that he's here I just seem peeved.

And then it all comes back to me – Ryan is the guy Kiki wanted to fix me up with. Oh not tonight, of all nights! I look at Santiago and feel a pang. I know he categorically won't mix business with romance so maybe I'm being saved from myself – the way I was feeling and the way the soup is smelling, I could have easily started to get ideas . . . And that would have been the beginning of the end – how many times do I have to go down this road before I learn my lesson? You don't have to sleep with every man who is nice to you, Ava! Think of Ollie. Think of how much better that relationship is as a friendship. That is how it should be with Santiago.

'Come on,' Dad chivvies. 'You've got five minutes to get ready.'

Not that I have any choice in the matter tonight.

'You couldn't have called to give us a bit of notice?' I complain from the bedroom as I reluctantly discard my dressing gown in favour of a jade sundress and silver flip-flops.

'You know me, I love my surprises!'

Dishing them out, yes. I wonder how receptive he'd be if he were on the receiving end?

As we roll down the hill, Dad brings Santiago up to speed on various Tamarindo business ventures and I close my eyes in dread of what's to come. Even if Ryan is everything Kiki promised, it's going to be excruciating meeting him with three additional pairs of eyes upon us.

Fortunately the restaurant is so unique that I temporarily forget my plight. We've just pulled up alongside a genuine US cargo plane, a Fairchild C123, with an extremely controversial past.

'During the Reagan administration of the mid-eighties,' my father begins, sounding every inch the tour guide, 'the American government – and Oliver North in particular – set up a bizarre network of arms sales to Iran designed to win the release of US hostages held in the Lebanon and raise money to fund the Nicaraguan counter-revolutionary guerrilla fighters.'

Instantly I feel like I'm in a history lecture at school and I can't help but zone out, focusing instead on the juxtaposition of the dusty camouflage of the cockpit and the emerald-green glow of the neon sign spelling out the restaurant name – EL AVION. As we step up into the hub I hear my dad speak of the Cuban-allied Sandinista government, the CIA, a secret airstrip in north-west Costa Rica and a lorra lorra corruption mushrooming into one of the biggest scandals in American political history aka 'the Iran-Contra Affair'.

He looks at me for some kind of 'Ohhh, the Iran-Contra Affair' recognition but I can offer none. On he continues regardless, mentioning something about a sister plane being shot down and how this one, 'nicknamed Ollie's Folly', was subsequently abandoned at San José airport until the year 2000 when some local entrepreneurs bought it for $3,000 and had it shipped here to this very cliff.

I may not be entirely clear on its political pedigree but I absolutely get its authenticity. The owners have left everything as-was (the peely paint, the military stencilling, the exposed mechanical workings) and then added a makeshift bar, tucked bottles of booze behind the metal ribbing, installed tall bar tables and neon tubing just to make the experience extra-surreal. Of all the themed bars in all the world, this has to rank among the most intriguing.

Better yet, the back of the plane opens out into a large alfresco dining terrace with a second bar, a musical trio and an all-too-significant duo.

Deciding to take the bull by the horns I march straight up to Kiki and boldly shake the hand of the man standing beside her.

'You must be Ryan!' I say in what I hope is an *it's okay, don't feel obliged to fancy me* way.

'Actually this is the waiter,' Kiki corrects me. 'Ryan's at the bar.'

'Oh! Sorry!' I fluster, feeling embarrassingly overeager.

'Menu?'

'Yes, yes, thank you, Ernesto,' I say, reading his name-tag in a bid to make amends.

As we take our seats at the table, Kiki heralds Ryan's approach with high-octane approval: 'Here he comes now!' she toots.

You'd think a plane itself was flying through the restaurant the way every diner is monitoring his advance.

'Hottie at ten o'clock,' I hear the girl on the next table nudge her friend. Even the guys seem covetous, possibly because he looks like a living, breathing action figure, so GI retro in his beige fatigues I'd almost suspect the restaurant hired him to increase the ambience. His hair is desert–storm-tousled, his sleeves rolled to the elbow revealing strong, defined forearms and his shirt has unbuttoned itself in a roguishly casual manner. Put him in a sand dune, a rainforest or in the seat opposite me and he blends beautifully.

'This is Santiago,' Kiki introduces him to the man to my right.

'San Diego,' he nods as he shakes his hand.

'And Ava.'

'Aunt Ava,' he repeats, adding his own twist.

For a second I wonder if he's got a hearing defect or is just a tad dumb but then he explains, 'I've got a terrible memory, these little tricks will help me get your names right next time!'

'Ohhh,' I chuckle.

'It's all the knocks to his head over the years.' Kiki makes a faux aside, tapping her own skull and mouthing, 'Extreme sports' to explain his addiction of choice.

'I've certainly swum too deep and climbed too high,' he acknowledges.

'And now you want to stay on dry land with the ATV tours?' I make a neat segue.

'That's right,' he grins, swigging his beer direct from the bottle. 'We must have taken every tour in Tamarindo . . .' He exchanges a long-suffering look with Kiki. 'Now I'm ready to see what Manuel Antonio has to offer.'

'Maybe you should take Ava on one?' my dad blunders.

'Oh no-no-no!' I swat away his suggestion.

'That's a great idea – you can come with us tomorrow,' Ryan asserts, all too easily persuaded.

'Oh no, I have to work,' I insist. 'We only opened today, I couldn't possibly—'

'Don't worry about the café,' Kiki chips in. 'We'll do one of the sunrise sessions and if for any reason we get held up Dean will cover your morning shift, won't you, darling?'

'Happy to.'

'Well then, that's sorted,' Ryan cheers.

I don't want to get into an argument with someone I just met – I already did that with Santiago – but I feel I must protest a little more. Not least at the prospect of getting up even earlier than I already have to.

'To be honest, Ryan, it's not really my thing. I've never been on a motorbike in my life. I can't even drive a car.'

'All the more reason to go – I need to see how a novice fares on this terrain. Kiki's such an old hand, it would be great to get feedback from a first-timer.' He looks winningly at me.

'Well . . .' I waver, looking around the table.

My gaze settles on Santiago. 'Will you come too?' I ask, feeling it's only polite to include him after so rudely abandoning his soup.

He simply shakes his head. No one tries to persuade him otherwise. I wonder what it must be like to have people take your 'no' as non-negotiable. As my eyes linger upon him, Ryan asks me to pass the bread.

I pass the basket over to him but instead of taking it from me he deliberates over which roll to choose, allowing just enough time for the basket to catch light over the candle.

'Oh my god!' Before I can even think what to do Santiago has drenched the wicker fire with the contents of the water jug. Everyone scuttles their chairs back to avoid the splash, applauding Santiago's quick reflex, while all I can do is watch in a daze as the water seeps to the outer edges of the tablecloth.

I knew this was a bad idea. Today as a concept has been a bad idea. Frankly I think I made a better first impression with the waiter. But then Ryan leans in, giving me the full benefit of his mist-blue eyes and husks, 'You know some people get a spark when they meet, we got full-blown flames!'

'I think we should move tables,' Kiki gets to her feet, giving Ryan a slight clip to the ear.

I'd suspect he was making a one-off quip to make me feel better were it not for the fact that he's now taken the seat next to me, bumping Santiago along one.

'So, Ava, how are you finding it living in Costa Rica?'

'Ava, can I get you another drink?'

'I hear you make the world's best hot chocolate, would you make one for me?'

He's attentive to the point of making my toes scrunch up. I try to address and include our fellow diners in my responses but he repeatedly corrals the conversation back to the two of us. I'm just not used to this level of attentiveness. My relationship with Santiago – aka 'the man in my life' for the past two weeks – has had a very different feel. Tonight was probably as personal as things have got, what with me crying and him offering words of comfort. Prior to that it's been business-related banter. Not that I minded, considering what an abrasive start we got off to, I considered the fact that we could communicate without coming to blows as something of a triumph. But now I am reminded of just how stomach-churningly surly he can be – apparently my father's presence brings out the dark warrior in him – as with each course I watch him getting progressively more withdrawn and it makes me realise I could never be with someone so moody and antisocial. Who needs the drama?

At one point he asks Ryan, somewhat territorially, how long he intends to stay in Manuel Antonio. 'Until I stop having fun,' he replies. 'That's my general philosophy in life.' In that moment the two men couldn't look any more opposite. Now Ryan may be too wild and adventurous for me to consider as a realistic prospect (one too many bungee-jumping anecdotes for my taste) but he's doing a great job of reminding me of the qualities I do want in a man – fun, positive, easygoing, with a predilection for pistachio icecream, I smile to myself as he orders his dessert.

'Ready to go?' The second the bill is paid, Santiago is on his feet.

'What's the rush?' Dad is still savouring his liqueur.

'Well, I know Ava has an extra-early start . . .' He tries to play off his hustling as consideration for me yet I hear it as a dig, as if my priority is to go gallivanting while he diligently minds the shop. As it happens, no one pays him any attention and Dad insists on another round of drinks.

'So, Ryan, what else have you got planned for tomorrow?' Dad enquires as he puffs life into his cigar.

'Well, I thought I'd probably do a spot of sport fishing in the afternoon—'

'What's the difference between regular fishing and sport fishing?' I ask, wondering if it involves stopwatches and on-deck sprinting.

'Sport fishing is when you release your catch back into the sea.'

'Ohhh,' I gurgle appreciatively. 'That's really cool, so nothing gets hurt.'

'That's right.'

'No, it's not,' Santiago grizzles.

All eyes turn to him.

'The fish are usually too weak to live after the struggle and even if they do they're never returned to the exact spot where they were caught, so many times you are separating a mother from her babies who will, as a consequence, die.'

There's a silence while we all feel bad.

Finally Ryan speaks. 'Do you eat fish, Santiago?'

'Yes,' he admits.

'Huh.' Ryan nods knowingly before deftly changing the subject to ask about my favourite local attractions.

As I respond, I sense Santiago willing Ryan to come back in his next life as a red snapper, preferably with a big hook through his lip. Not that I know for sure where Santiago stands on this subject – he could just as easily be a sport-fishing aficionado himself, simply using this info to bait Ryan, pardon the pun.

One thing I do know is that I may have had the worst day but Santiago's having the worst night. I wonder if it's peeving him that I'm making new friends? I'm sure he'd rather I stayed lonely so that homesickness ultimately drove me back to England. Add the fact that he's been toppled from the Boy Wonder pedestal – it's Ryan my dad is slapping on the shoulder for a change – and it's not surprising he wants the day to end.

Personally I'm prolonging the night to put off the morning. Ryan may like me now but how's a self-confessed speed-freak going to feel about my trundling along at 2 mph, screaming every time I have to rev the engine? Less Evel Knievel, more Ava Ain't-Able.

Back at the villa I set my alarm for 5 a.m. allowing myself a good hour to get ready. I may not be going to wow anyone with my wheelies but I can peer out from my helmet visor with a pair of prettily made-up peepers.

As I reach over to turn out my light I hear Santiago pad by my door, no doubt on the way to the kitchen to fix himself a *horchata*. I call out 'Goodnight!' to him but in reply I get silence.

And not the good kind this time.

19

'Morning!' Ryan catches me mid-yawn – the type that gives you a triple chin and makes your eyes water. Though I'm sure he doesn't want to be playing 'count the cavities' first thing, I can't help but offer them up for inspection.

'Sorry!' I mutter, wiping my eyes, marvelling at how offensively perky he is. I could have sworn he knocked back just as much booze as the rest of us last night – I guess that hazelnut tan hides a multitude of sins.

'Ready to make like Tarzan?' he enquires.

I frown out loud: 'Did Tarzan ride quad bikes?'

'No, no,' he laughs. 'We thought a canopy tour would be the best way to kick-start the day.'

'I think I'll stick to coffee, thanks.'

I'm no fool – I saw the canopy tour display when I arrived at the airport: a giant blow-up photo of the rainforest with a harnessed mannequin zip-lining from treetop to treetop. Actually make that a harnessed *dummy* – I mean, who'd be fool enough to try that?

'Oh come on, Ava,' Ryan wheedles. 'You can't come to Costa Rica and not give it a go, it's the sexiest thing.'

'You guys ready to rock?' Kiki sticks her head out of the car window.

'I'm having a bit of trouble persuading your step-daughter here to dangle from a cable two hundred feet in the air.'

Like that'll help.

'There won't be any persuading her, it runs in the family,' Kiki calls back.

'What does?' I ask, feeling slighted. I know she can't be referring to my stubborn streak because my dad bends to her every whim. And she can't be inferring we're cowards because Costa Rica is not for the faint-hearted. What then?

'They're just not sporty people, Ryan,' Kiki asserts.

Even though she's winking at me I feel a bristle of insult. It's true of course, but that's not the point. Does she think I can't handle it? I mean, I don't choose to spend my time bypassing birds' nests at 100 mph but if I wanted to I'm sure I could manage just fine.

'They always start with a couple of low runs,' Ryan continues his recruitment drive, 'and if you don't like it you can stop after that. No harm done.'

'Why do you want me to go so badly?' I challenge him.

'Because it's always more fun to go with someone experiencing it for the first time.' He leans closer. 'And I want to see what your face does when you're truly thrilled.'

A shudder of lust zip-lines through my body. As my eyes flick to his, Kiki leans on the horn. Jeez, I'm guessing she's not an early morning person.

'Why don't I just meet you at the ATV place?' I suggest.

Ryan stands strong. 'All or nothing!'

'Oh god, all right!' I'm not awake enough to resist.

I was hoping to have forty winks in the car but of course the road is too bumpy to rest my head against the window. I'd get concussion if I did. I try leaning back on the seat but it's like trying to take a nap with someone physically shaking you.

'We're here!' Ryan announces as we pull up outside a forest-nestled café. 'Beer?'

I check my watch. 'Thanks but I never drink before 8 a.m.'

He orders two bottles of Imperial, passes one to Kiki and they chink and neck it in one go.

'God, if you two need Dutch courage . . .' I fret.

'It's just tradition!' Kiki slams down her bottle on the side. 'You're probably better off having your wits about you.'

Is she deliberately trying to freak me out? What happened to the Kiki who gently swathed me in pashminas and bandannas? I guess Ryan brings out her blokey side.

'Transport's here,' she announces, striding ahead and springing into the back pit of the battered pickup truck. I require both a push from Ryan and a pull from the Canopy Tour guide to get me on board, and then stumble trying to find a seat amid the coils of rope and clanking hardware.

As we rattle up the hill I feel like an immigrant workman setting off for a hard day's toil. Is this really what people do for fun on holiday?

'This is shorter than the one we did in Tamarindo, right?' Kiki asks Ryan.

'Yeah, but longer than Coco Beach.'

'How does it compare to Chipperfield's?' I try to join in.

They look at me blankly.

'You know – the flying trapeze? The circus?'

'It's really not the same thing,' Kiki snubs me.

'Yeah, there's no safety nets here,' Ryan chuckles.

My stomach sours, making me feel like I've been brought to this remote location to be bumped off at a great height, leaving no contender for my dad's inheritance. If I'm even in his will these days. No doubt Santiago is a major feature.

I feel a little sad that he has reverted back to being a contentious grump. Having seen the more

236

companionable side of him it seems so unnecessary for him to be like that. And it makes me uneasy, knowing how ambitious he is and wondering what lengths he might be going to in my absence to put himself at an advantage at the café – I picture him deviously loosening the handles on my mugs, booby-trapping the till and ordering the world's biggest vat of *tres leches*. What with his behavioural switcheroo last night and now with Kiki choosing the role of rival over gal-pal, I suddenly feel very alone.

After a ten-minute trek through the forest we arrive at the first platform, where we're given an all-too-brief instructional, along with our equipment.

'Helmet.'

I strap mine on, wondering what the hell I'm letting myself in for.

'Harness.'

I step into the lattice of canvas straps. 'It's like some kind of S&M baby bouncer!' I comment. 'Did you have those as a child?' I ask the others. 'You know where you get hung from a door frame and bounce up and down on your tippy-toes, kind of like a prelude to walking?'

Ryan shakes his head. 'We were too poor, my mum just tied a bunch of rubber bands together and strung me up from a light fitting.'

I burst out laughing, relieved to feel that maybe I'm not entirely without an ally after all.

'Glove.'

I accept what looks like a cross between a baseball catcher's mitt and a leather falconry glove.

'What's this for?'

'Braking.'

'How so?' I'm confused.

'You'll see when you're up.' He nods for me to climb on to the wooden platform where the cable begins its race through the foliage.

'You want to go first?' the guide asks me.

'*No!*' I shriek. 'Er, no.' I try for a calmer approach. 'I'd like to see someone do it first, thank you.'

'I'll go!' Kiki volunteers.

As she steps forward the guide hoists her upward by the clip attached to her waist and snaps her on to the pulley device so she's now dangling from the cable.

'One hand here.' He places Kiki's left hand on the straps of the harness. 'The other – the one with the glove – you place over the cable, behind the pulley. To brake you just gently pull down – don't squeeze – and this will slow you down.'

Okay. Slow sounds good.

'But you don't want to do this too much or too soon or you will fall short of the next platform and you will have to pull yourself the rest of the way.'

'Oh no! How do you do that?' I panic.

'You have to twist yourself around so that your back is to the platform you're aiming for, then you release your left hand and place it over the leather mitt and then tug and tug and tug . . .'

I'm feeling a bit faint. 'Oh god, I just know I'm going to forget the rules and end up electrocuting myself,' I mutter.

'There's no power running through these cables,' Ryan tuts. 'These are trees, not telegraph poles.'

'So why can't I touch it with my bare hand?'

'Because you'd most likely slice it off.'

'Oh. Thanks. I feel so much better now.'

'If you want to wait here until we're done we'll probably only be an hour,' Kiki gives a saccharine smile.

Since when did Cupid try to keep people apart?

'No, no,' I grit back, declining her offer to bail. 'I hear they have excellent hospital facilities here in Costa Rica, I'll be fine.'

'You're a very brave girl,' Ryan says, tweaking my cheek.

'Nothing to be brave about,' Kiki argues. 'This is a breeze!' And with that she takes off, skimming along the wire to the next platform. No wonder men love her – she's so confident, so game, so free. Compared to her, I feel like a scrunched-up ball of restriction.

'You want to go in the middle?' Ryan offers.

I nod, now unable to speak. The guide beckons me forth. He's an older man with a kind, weather-pummelled face that invites trust. 'It's my first time,' I tell him.

'I know,' he smiles back. 'I'm going to need you to jump up,' he says, indicating that I'm a little too short for easy-access hooking.

I try a little hop to no avail. Suddenly Ryan's arms are around me, easily raising me into position.

'Thank you,' I fluster as I'm hooked up, disturbingly aware that the harness straps are now digging in deep, causing my bottom to squidge out in an unpleasant manner. I feel like I'm being weighed on some antiquated scales and as the ropes creak I fear I may have to pay excess bummage once again.

'Knees up, cross your ankles, tilt your head to the side so it doesn't hit the cable . . . Ready?'

'NO! Sorry! Wait a moment.' I can't believe I'm about to be launched into oblivion.

'This one is very low, very slow, no danger.'

'Okay.'

'I'll be right behind you!' are the last words I hear as I whirr along the wire. 'Knees up, head tilt, don't squeeze – oh damn!' I come to a halt several metres before the platform. I'm about to start twisting round so I can pull myself in when I feel a hand clamp around my ankle.

I look down and see the guide on the forest floor, now pulling me along by my leg. 'You do it next time!' he smiles.

Were we really that low? This isn't so bad. I almost enjoy the next one. It's really quite soothing – nice breeze, nice green blur. Nice Action Man checking on my well-being.

'Are you all right to continue?' Ryan asks. 'After this we pass the point of no return.'

'No problem,' I chime, pointedly at Kiki. 'This is fun.'

'Attagirl, I knew you'd like it. Let me show you how the insane people do this.'

Ryan takes first position but instead of easing himself off the platform in a sitting position, he takes a flying leap and streaks through the air at an alarming pace, bouncing maniacally as he goes.

'I'm not doing that,' I tell the guide.

'You are wise,' he colludes with me. 'This one is fast.'

'Mind if I go next?' Kiki steps over me. Despite having a bottom Jennifer Aniston would envy, she apparently has no intention of bringing up the rear.

'Go ahead,' I tell her.

Kiki opts for similar suicide-styling to Ryan. I wonder if my dad has seen this side to her? No doubt he'd find it sexy, seeing her being so fast and fearless.

Me? I'm taking it slow.

AAAARRRRGGHHHHH! Even with the most timid of starts I scoot off with such velocity you'd think I'd been sprung from a catapult. Shocked at my ever increasing speed, I inadvertently squeeze the mitt so that my right hand locks on to the wire while the rest of my body continues its forward propulsion, yanking my arm taut and wrenching at the socket. AARRRGGHHH again! Dizzy with agony I release the mitt hand and continue on, only to find myself slowing as the cable starts climbing upward. Bugger. I've fallen too short again. I do the twist and tug myself along as best I can until the others can reach out for me, then go to crumple on the wooden platform, only to find the sturdy beams have been replaced with a spindly metal grid. As I move, it moves, motivating me to grab for the tree trunk only to have my hand smacked away by Ryan.

'Poisonous ants all over it,' he explains.

I reel back, relying on the harness to keep me attached. It's then I make the fatal mistake of looking down between the mesh squares. I can't believe how teeteringly high we are. I never thought I was afraid of heights but now I have good reason to be. This isn't a theme-park ride. This is real life. And real ants. For the first time it hits me how ludicrous and perilous this activity is. There's not even a million-pound reality-TV prize awaiting me if I complete the course.

Worse still, there's another three platforms to go.

'Next one is faster,' the guide advises. 'And longer.'

I look at the drop and then look at him, trying to

employ my dental-chair strategy, i.e. when I'm lying there having my mouth excavated I spirit myself away to another land. Mind over matter.

'Your hands are shaking,' he notes.

'Isn't this great?' Kiki gushes. 'Total adrenalin buzz!'

'Ava?' Ryan looks concerned.

I'm feeling quite dazed and the strain in my arm is agonising. This isn't chivvy-yourself-up fear. This is too much for me. I'm paralysed by the knowledge that there is no turning back. The only way home, and back to my beloved coffee shop and what now seem like mild inconsequential tiffs with an easygoing fellow named Santiago, is along the cable. There's nothing else for it, I have to block out everything else – don't think, just do.

Tears glaze my eyes as I step forward.

'Do you wanna taxi?' Ryan offers.

I look at him. 'I think Superman is all that can save me now.'

'Taxi is when you go in tandem,' he explains.

Suddenly there is hope. 'Will it hold two of us?' I query.

'She'll be fine,' Kiki steps between us and grips my shoulders, 'You can do it, Ava.'

I look her straight in the eye and say, 'I'm not being a wuss, Kiki. I know my limits and I really can't.'

'Oh come—'

'Kiki,' Ryan shushes her.

'I think she should go taxi,' the guide advises. 'The next one after this is noble, she will be fine then.'

'Noble?'

'Gentle, respectful, no crazy, just glide.'

Music to my ears.

As Ryan and I are interlinked I glance back at Kiki, who definitely seems to be pouting.

'I knew this was a bad idea,' I hear her muttering under her breath.

'It was *your* idea in the first place,' I rally back, indignant. I can't believe how unsympathetic she's being and make a mental note to only ever serve her stale cake and scalding beverages.

'I didn't think you would actually do it,' she snaps, exposing herself.

Oh so that's it? She changed the schedule in the hope that I'd drop out and she'd have Ryan all to herself. Or at the very least keep him away from me. But why, when it was her idea to matchmake us in the first place? It doesn't make any sense. She's happily married. Ryan's single. I'm single. Where's the crime? If anything we're only doing what we're told.

I don't get the chance to take this thinking any further because we're off – belting along, whistling through the trees, wind rushing at our skin, and though we're racing twice as fast I get a thrill of exhilaration because this time I have no fears about controlling the speed or negotiating the landing, I am free! I cry out in joy, a big 'Woooo-hooo!' release in celebration of the fact that my terror has turned to triumph.

'That was fantastic,' I gasp as we hit our next platform. 'Oh my god!' I look back at the miles we've just traversed. *'What a rush!'*

'There's the face I wanted to see!' Ryan takes my head in his hands and gives me a powerful kiss. Followed by a more feathery-light brush stroke.

'Look out!' Kiki comes skidding into view, seemingly using me as a target. 'Oop!' she yelps as her boots make contact with my shins. I can feel the bruises burgeoning as I stumble backwards. No shorts for me for the next two weeks. Hold on! *Did that gorgeous man just kiss me?!* I blink, trying to relive the last few minutes of my life – everything happened so fast: the ride, the kiss, the wipeout . . .

'Let's you and me do a taxi!' Kiki hurriedly wraps herself around Ryan, edging him into position before I can catch his eye and see where he's at.

'What for?' he questions her.

'For kicks!' she challenges.

Ryan looks back at me. 'Are you going to be all right now?'

Suddenly it's as though I can see far deeper into his eyes. Kiki can do what she likes, but we've crossed over and I feel a quiet, instinctive

245

confidence that there's more to come. No rush. 'Noble, right?' I check with the guide who nods assurance.

'I'll be fine,' I tell him.

I'm not fighting over a man. At least not at treetop height with Batgirl as my opponent.

The pair of them take flight and then I have my second-best ride of the tour. This one really is gentle and elegant and pure pleasure – for the first time I take in my surroundings and breathe in the air as I burr along the wire.

On the last one I scutter and jerk a bit, still not quite having mastered the braking system, but I make it on to the platform without having to strain my arm with any backward tugging. I can't quite believe it but it's over and I survived!

'Wow.' I marvel as I get back on solid ground. '*Now* I need a beer!'

'So, you liked it?' Ryan beams at me.

'It was amazing. I'm glad I did it. I'm never doing it again.'

'Never?' Ryan looks playful.

'*Never*,' I insist.

At least this seems to make Kiki happy.

20

'So, are you ready for the ATV tour?' Ryan claps his hands together.

'Oh my god!' My knees buckle. I'd forgotten about that. 'Is there no recovery period allowed?' I wail.

'You're the one who's in the big rush to get to work!'

That's true. At least it was. Funny how that compulsion has waned. It's actually a pleasant release to do something different, albeit life-threatening.

'We are running a bit late,' Kiki checks her watch. 'Maybe we *should* take you back now?' she suggests, ever-accommodating when it comes to trying to make me disappear. I guess jealousy is not a logical emotion. But has she really got anything to be jealous about?

I look at Ryan and ask myself, Is it the rush of the zip-lining that's got me so giddy or the man himself and his spontaneous sky-high kisses? I get an excited flutter just thinking about his lips on mine. Is there anything more delicious than being found attractive? Anything more instantly gratifying than seeing an intrigued, alert brightness in a man's eyes and knowing it's there because of you? Perhaps it's the initial zing that Kiki is coveting, rather than Ryan himself? She's turned down his offers in the past so she can't really feel she's missing out. But what do I feel? I suppose the number one word right now is *tempted*.

I try to remind myself of the personal perils of any hint of a relationship but desire overrides caution – coffee may be addictive but love is the drug so, for the next hour at least, work can wait.

As we transfer to the bikes, the magnitude of regaining my capacity to have a man-thrill sinks in. For the past six months I haven't got further than 'He's all right' or 'Maybe I could at a push' and I was beginning to seriously doubt my ability to ever again engage the forces of attraction. Yes, there was the initial piquing of my interest when I first laid eyes on Santiago but that was squelched in a trice. Admittedly there have been a few intriguing moments since then – I suppose if you spend an extended time with someone eligible of the opposite sex the occasional warming is inevitable – and it is possible that the soup scenario has somehow primed me for this moment, but what I'd forgotten is that sometimes you don't have a choice, that a chance glance can be all the trigger you need to get you back in the water. And potentially in way over your head, of course.

I'm actually glad that Kiki's here. Despite the fact that she's being an obstructive cow, I don't think I could cope with the intensity of being alone with Ryan right now. And I'm glad we've got an activity to attend to, as opposed to focusing solely on each other, say over moonlit cocktails. As it is, my attention is ricocheting every which way – between Ryan and Kiki and the new younger guide and then off to the coffee shop wondering if Santiago is blending a little Cyanide Steamer for my return, then pinging back to the bike itself.

'Oh no,' I say as I'm introduced to my hefty steed.

'What?' Ryan looks up from assessing his mud-dusted machine.

'It's got gears. Five of them.'

'That's the norm,' he shrugs.

'Not for me. I told you I've never driven anything more than a bumper car.'

'Oh.' He pauses. 'Well, it's just on the left handle here, it's not like you've got a gearstick.'

'But I don't know anything about when to shift up or down,' I explain, panic rising.

'You just instinctively feel it.'

'I have no instincts in this area,' I object, ever more anxious. This is too much for me. I can't bluff this. I hate being so sure of my limitations, but I am.

For a second Ryan looks perplexed.

'I'm sorry, I hate to be a pain.' Have I blown it so soon? My novice status was a novelty on the canopy tour but now I'm just a burden, I can feel it.

'Let's have a test run,' the guide says, inviting me to follow him around the field.

'Go on,' Ryan encourages. 'See how it feels.'

What I feel is horribly self-conscious as I putter along behind him, heart fretting and hyperventilating, sweat absorbing into the padding of the helmet. There is no way I could conceive of going full throttle on this, it's so much more menacing and so much more metal than I imagined.

'Turn here!' the guide instructs.

I mishandle the handles and carve an awkward, jerking curve.

'Now faster!'

Gingerly I twist the grip on the right-hand bar and surge forward, igniting the fire within my bike's belly.

'Now stop!'

I reach for the brake lever but my fingers slip and I pull back again on the accelerator, ramming into the back of the guide with a snarling crack.

'Oh god, sorry-sorry!' I babble, mortified. Even without looking I know that Kiki wants to reverse over my head, again and again. She must think I'm making a meal of this but I am truly embarrassed.

'Look, maybe I could just go at the back of the line so I'm not holding you guys up?' I suggest when we return to the others, me with my tail between my wheels.

'No, no,' the guide protests.' 'The most inexperienced rides behind me.'

Kiki is getting impatient. Again.

'Never mind, I'll wait here,' I say, feeling a complete failure. 'You guys go on, it's no big deal.'

I might fancy Ryan but the chasm of difference between us is becoming all too apparent, all too soon.

'Well, I guess that's that,' Kiki says, wowing us with her insight.

The guide offers a solution. 'Of course you could just ride with your boyfriend?'

Kiki's engine revs in protestation but Ryan's eyes light up and he doesn't even bother to correct the guide. 'What a dunce, of course!' he cheers. 'But what do we do with the other bike?'

'We just leave it here, it's cool.'

'Isn't that a waste?' Kiki sulks, though I doubt very much she's paid owt as it is.

'If you don't use it, you don't have to pay for it,' the guide announces.

'Hah! You'd actually be saving us money!' Ryan laughs. 'Excellent work, Ava Langston, I like your style – step aboard.' He pats the seat behind him. What little there is of it.

I really have to ram myself into his back just to fit on, and still the rear half of me is spilling over on to the hot metal bike itself.

'You have to hold on tight,' the guide insists.

I place my arms around Ryan's torso and lean my head on his back, grateful that the engine's rumble and snort is drowning out my inner squeals. I can't quite believe that last night I was counting this man's chest hairs and now I can feel them through his shirt.

Within minutes of setting off I am thanking the heavens for my caution – there is no way I could have handled this route solo. Even Ryan turns back and tells me, 'You made the right decision. This is wild.'

At one point we tear through a hearts-of-palm plantation. The trees squat low in the earth and their leaves – offering a thousand paper-cut possibilities – are at face level. Ryan breaks a passage through as they thwack-swipe at his helmet leaving me to marvel at the pretty patterns the sun makes filtering through their green blades. The next minute we're out in the open, whirring down a road waving to locals then bumping down a dirt track, only connecting to the earth long enough to bounce us along another couple of metres. As we approach a series of giant muddy puddles, our guide motions for us to raise our feet in the air – as the orange liquid passes through the bike it spurts out like

252

extra-strong tea straight from the urn and he doesn't want us scalding our ankles.

I can't believe how far removed this is from my life in Bath. Ollie won't believe I actually volunteered myself for this level of discomfort and danger. I become even more incredulous as the guide cheerily tots up the number of deaths on his watch. It puts me in mind of circus people who accept the occasional fatal fall from the high wire as an inevitable statistic. But then he tempers this with a soothing nature amble.

Instructing us to leave our bikes under the shade of the trees, he hands each of us a walking stick (finagled from the undergrowth) and invites us to weave up a woodland hill. En route he shows us a flower that turns red when you hold a lit cigarette up to it, the 'no-taste' tree whose wood is used to make lollipop sticks and – most amazingly to me – a cashew-nut tree. At first I think he is pointing to an apple tree as it is decorated with small waxy-red fruit but then I notice the kidney-shaped shell sticking out like a stalk from its base and I realise that is encasing the nut. Just one per fruit. No wonder cashews are so pricey! A whole tree's worth would barely fill a bag!

A few paces on he stoops and invites us to squish a berry and sniff its juice – zingy citronella! – then he reaches up and plucks a starfruit from a high branch. My eyes widen further – all the things I've seen in the exotic food aisle at Waitrose are available and pickable right here! I suddenly feel utterly in awe of nature and all its hidden – or rather ignored on my part – treasures. It makes me realise how unconnected I am to my surroundings. Though one aspect I am definitely ultra-aware of is Ryan. Even when he is stood behind me I feel all my nerve endings standing to attention. It's as if we are quietly biding our time until our next chance to speak.

He takes my hand as we edge down to a clearing with a beautiful waterfall as a centrepiece. Kiki responds by stripping down to her silver bikini and submerging herself in the cool clean water, floating on her back to show off her upright boobs and flat stomach.

'So, what's it like having Kiki as a stepmother?' Ryan enquires as he unlaces his boots on the adjacent rocks.

'I just can't believe my dad is married to someone with a belly-button ring!' I sidestep his question.

The fact is, until Ryan used the word 'stepmother' I simply wasn't registering Kiki as my father's wife today. Her whole vibe has been very single-female-competing-over-available-man. Not pretty in itself, but when I think of my dad . . . I quickly deflect a pang of concern deciding that his relationship karma is none of my business. It's certainly too late for me to offer any advice now. If he'd invited me out prior to the wedding maybe I could have made a casual observation that she may have a few 'issues' regarding male attention . . . Not that she seems to play up in front of Santiago. But then he's wired differently to normal human beings – definitely not as easy to read as Ryan. Nor as hands-on:

'Care to join me for a dip?' he asks, offering me an open palm as he gets to his now bare feet.

'I didn't bring my costume, I didn't realise . . .' I flounder.

'Well, what have you got on underneath?'

I peer down my shirt having very little recollection of this morning's dressing. My bra would be okay, it's dark, but my knickers are white. I shudder at the prospect of how that would look when wet.

'You could at least dip in your feet,' Ryan suggests. 'Here, let me help you.'

He rolls up my trousers to the knee, removes my terracotta-spattered socks and trainers and then immerses my feet in the exhilaratingly refreshing water. I feel like a cross between Cinderella and Mary Magdalene.

'What about you? Aren't you swimming?' I ask as he wades knee-deep beside me.

'I'm fine right here,' he smiles, again reaching for my feet, now massaging them between dexterous fingers. I want to surrender to the moment but instead my eyes flit to Kiki who has swivelled herself round so she can check on us while still showcasing her physique, which isn't going entirely to waste as the guide is more than entranced by the metallic contours of her bikini. Maybe she's just an exhibitionist full stop. I suppose her Jungle Jane routine during the Canopy Tour could just as easily have been for the benefit of the guides as for Ryan, whose hands are currently rounding my heels.

'You have such pretty feet,' Ryan marvels as he steals up my shins.

I imagine him keeping going – the further his hands climb the deeper I lower myself into the water until the pair of us are submerged and entwined and dipping in and out of cool water and warm air.

'Ava?' The guide has crouched beside me with a large leaf in his hand. 'May I give you a tattoo?'

I nod, intrigued. Frankly I'd say yes to anything right now.

He duly scrunches and kneads the stem until it emits a burgundy ointment. 'Henna,' he tells me as he fingerpaints a butterfly on my upper arm. The image takes me right back to the butterfly farm and the wishes I shared with Kiki. Could they really be granted this easily? I mean, is that all it takes, asking for what you want? I look at my tattoo and then back at Ryan feeling almost dizzy. I've lived my life always wanting more, always feeling mildly deprived of what I really desired. I never expected to know what it would feel like to have everything I wanted in one moment.

An encouraging voice within me whispers, 'You're getting warmer . . .' But then I feel a chill and look up to find Kiki blocking my sun.

'Ready to go?' she asks, dripping icy splashes beside us.

Slowly I return to reality. But not all the way. Something tells me that my fantasy is not too out of reach. It could be simply a case of losing the chaperone . . .

21

As I approach the coffee shop I feel a strange twinge of guilt, as if I've been on an illicit date and now I'm creeping back home, hoping my husband won't notice my giveaway glow. But when I walk in the door, Santiago is nowhere to be seen.

'Where's the boss?' I ask Wilbeth. 'Well not *the* boss but the *other* boss?' I correct myself.

'In your rear,' he points behind me.

As I turn, I come nose to nose with Santiago. 'Oops,' I stumble backwards, thrown by his proximity.

'You're late,' he growls. 'Is this likely to become a habit?'

Aggravated by his instantly snotty attitude, I mentally pop my bubblegum in his face and shrug, 'I don't know, I haven't decided yet.'

'How professional,' he sneers. 'Day two and you're already slacking.'

'Look, you know exactly where I was – it's not like

I'm going to go zip-lining every morning before work, it was a one-off,' I reason. To think I was going to start gushing about his beautiful, resourceful country.

Santiago's eyes narrow at me as he snipes: 'I guess the café just isn't as important to you as it is to me.' He goes to walk on but I stop him. Sensing a scene brewing, Wilbeth scuttles to safety behind the counter.

'What's that supposed to mean?' I scowl, hand still on his chest. I'm not letting him get away with his dismissive ways of old.

'This place is clearly just something to amuse you until something – *or someone* – more interesting comes along.'

'*How can you say that?*' I despair. 'You know perfectly well I've been dreaming of opening my own coffee shop for—'

'We all have dreams, Ava,' he cuts in. 'But not all of us have fathers to fund them.'

'Oh my god – are you kidding me with the nepotism stuff?' I reel. 'Prior to this trip I hadn't seen my father in three years. He didn't even invite me to his wedding. But you – YOU!' My voice quavers as it rises. 'You're like the son he never had! If anyone's getting parental favours—'

I have to stop myself, one more word and my tears will spill. Instead I barge roughly past him, jab at the till, pull out a bunch of notes and announce that I'm going to the bank to get some change. I need some air. Even if it is hot and moist.

Isn't it always the way – you have some fun, maybe a little flirtation and boom! You have to be brought smack back down to earth. So much for my theory that Santiago was mellowing. The guy who would run a bath and make me soup and carry my shoes and eat a bowl of *tres leches* to spare me was apparently a fleeting aberration. I suppose it's no coincidence that he's getting back to his grizzly self now my dad – aka Judge Langston – is back in town. Well, if he thinks I'm going to lower myself to his level of petty bickering he's mistaken – I had my share of mud-slinging on the ATV ride. For the rest of the day I'm not speaking a word to Santiago. Nothing he can say or do will rile me. I'm just going to crank up the a/c and freeze him out.

'Oh thank goodness you're back!' At least Milena is pleased to see me. 'We're all out of notes, we've had to give the customers great bucketfuls of change.' She looks expectantly at me. 'You went to the bank, right?'

I give her a rueful look as I hold up a swag bag of coins.

'You got *more* coins?'

'Don't ask,' I tell her. 'I'm having a weird day.'

'Well, mine just got better.' Her eyes light up as

she looks past me. I turn and see Ryan jutting his head in the door.

'Hey, Ava,' he calls over. 'I meant to ask: what time do you finish tonight?'

I flush pink as Milena turns green. 'Around seven,' I reply.

'Cool!' he says, exiting with a wink.

My mouth continues to gape – have I got a date?

Milena seems to think so. 'You lucky goat!' she blurts.

'Cow,' I correct her.

'Who was that?' she demands, still looking gaga in his direction.

'Ryan,' I tell her. 'Friend of Kiki's.'

'Has he got any friends?'

'He's too old for you,' I tut.

'No such thing,' she grins. 'Ask Kiki!'

I chuckle to myself as she skips out the door. I still can't believe it – a stupendously handsome man just asked me out. In public. I have witnesses! Better yet, tonight we'll get to do something I'm good at – eating! At least I presume we're having dinner. Of course we could be rappelling down some cliff face but I'm optimistic that at some stage there will be food involved.

'Ava. *Ava?*' It's Santiago, barking at me again.

'What?' I snap, forgetting my earlier oath to icy serenity.

261

'Is there a particular reason you're pouring hot chocolate in the till?'

I look down and see that I have indeed neatly filled the empty compartments with steaming brown fluid.

No smart comebacks this time. Just a shifty little sensation that maybe he's right – maybe my mind isn't on the job. Maybe I have found something – or someone – more interesting.

Or better yet, and most galling of all to Santiago, maybe I'm about to have my tamarind cake and eat it too!

As I clean out the till my mind races – I mean, it doesn't have to be one or the other, does it? I swore I'd stay focused this time, choose work over romance, but guys like Ryan Sheen don't zip-line along every day. Isn't it possible that I could put 100 per cent into work and 100 per cent into play? Ryan could be my fun reward at the end of long day . . . Couldn't that actually work in my favour?

Until now Ryan seemed too far-fetched an option – in all my dream lover fantasies I've never pictured myself with a khaki-clad action man, it would hardly have fitted with my life in Bath. I mean, what would someone like Ryan do there? Scuba-dive in the Roman baths? Hang-glide down the High Street? It just wouldn't fly. But while my life is here, for however long that lasts, it could actually work – by day we do extreme sports and espresso shots respectively and then by night we come together and relax. I sigh as I recall how good it felt to have my arms around him on the bike, the embrace I received when I landed on the zip-line platform, and as for that kiss . . . my fingers toy with my bottom lip.

'Can I get cappuccino with no caffeine, no dairy and no chocolate powder?'

'So basically you want a glass of hot water?' I tease the customer in front of me. 'Just kidding,' I quickly add as her face contorts in confusion.

In between my daily chores I get flashes of baby-bouncers slung from fifty-foot trees and ATVs with kiddy-carriage sidecars. Women get ridiculed for thinking so far ahead before a relationship has even begun but these test-visualisations are just like checking over a car, seeing if it's got the mileage to get you where you want to go.

At 6.15 p.m. I put Milena on double-duty so I can scoot to the bathroom and do my make-up.

At 6.45 p.m. I'm pretending to reorder the tea box display. (I can't trust myself with anything potentially scalding or breakable.)

At 7 p.m. I have to turn away when Santiago passes because I don't want him to see the demented glee on my face. *Any minute now . . .*

At 7.20 p.m. I'm starting to feel a little foolish. He didn't actually say, 'I'll pick you up at 7 p.m.' But it was implied, *wasn't it*?

At 7.30 p.m. Santiago asks if I need a ride back to the villa. I'm surprised he's even offering but then again how would it look to my dad if he refused to drive me?

'Er no. You go. I can always get a cab if—' I falter. I don't really want to say 'If I get stood up' out loud. 'If necessary,' I complete my sentence, a little tartly.

Once Santiago is gone I walk over to the hammock, instantly regretting choosing this seating arrangement as there is simply no elegant way to clamber out when Ryan gets here. If he gets here. It's amazing how much you can want something when you're not sure if you're going to get it. Earlier I was all blasé because he was so done-deal keen, but now I think of how every head turned in the restaurant last night and Milena's reaction today and I think how many more people he would have encountered since he left me this morning . . . He's not shy. I get the impression he talks to everyone. Maybe he got a better offer?

'Ava?'

I turn round full of hope but already I know it's not his voice. It's Santiago.

'Did you forget something?' I ask.

'No. I just—' He squirms slightly. 'If you're waiting for Ryan . . .'

Oh god. This looks bad.

'. . . he's in the bar across the street.'

'Oh.' I heave a sigh of relief. 'Okay. Well, I'm just

264

finishing up a few things here,' I lie, quite blatantly considering I'm lolling in a hammock.

'Okay, well, have a good night.'

'You too.' I give him a polite nod.

Well, that was oddly considerate, putting me out of my misery. Or is he trying to put me in it? Suddenly I know why Santiago wanted me to locate Ryan – because he's with another girl.

I scramble up, quickly deal with the locks then thrash along the cut-through to the main strip. I see him straight away, sitting on the terrace at the Marlin restaurant animatedly involved with a bobbing head of blonde spirals. As I watch him he calls over the waitress and orders two more beers. Unbelievable! He's not giving me a second thought! I turn to stalk away and get knocked for six by a longboard.

'Sorry!' 'Sorry!' 'No, I'm sorry!' A barrage of apologies follows. The surfer is more concerned with my battered side, me with his potentially dented board. Road rage is a whole different kettle of fish here.

'Are you causing trouble again?' I look up and find Ryan grinning back at me. Stood beside him is the spiral-haired blond – complete with goatee. Yet another surfer who missed their calling as a L'Oréal spokesmodel.

'This is Flare,' Ryan introduces his fellow beer-supper.

'As in style or emergency signal?' I ask as I shake his nut-brown hand.

'Well, I spell it the emergency-signal way but the meaning I'm going for is pure skill on the waves, you get me?'

'Yes I do!' I want to pip – *you're a man!* Which means Ryan is still available. If a little late.

'So, did you finish early?' he asks.

'No. Bang on 7 p.m. as predicted.'

'I thought you said 8 p.m.,' he frowns.

'No. Definitely 7 p.m.,' I confirm.

'Well, aren't I the lucky guy?' He looks at his watch. 'I just got an extra twenty minutes of your time.'

Following a weird gangsta hug-off with Flare and Dare (as the dude with the board calls himself), Ryan summons a taxi.

'You hungry?' he asks me.

'Most definitely.' I assert as I slide beside him on the back seat.

'Excellent. Me too.' He gives the driver a card, presumably featuring the address of our destination. I wait for him to tell me where we're headed but even when I ask outright he remains mysterious.

'It's somewhere very exclusive,' he says, putting me on pause as he makes a quick call. 'This is Ryan Sheen. Yes. We'll be there in five. Great.'

'Tell me more!' I shuffle closer.

'Well, it has a feature I know you'll particularly enjoy.'

'And what's that?' I ask, wide-eyed with anticipation.

'Air conditioning . . .'

'Get out of here!' I gasp, delighted. I am beyond impressed. I thought Café Tropicana was the only place in town that offered blessed relief.

'So what's it called?' I probe for more information.

'What's it called?' he repeats before smirking, 'It's called Room Service.'

At which point we pull into the Mariposa car park and I twig what's going on – I am being lured to his room!

Fantastic!

'Like I say, it's a very exclusive venue – just one table.' He winks at me as he reaches in his pocket. 'And one key.'

I follow him up two tiers of the black metal grid staircase, along the tiled walkway that overlooks the pool and around to his private terrace. Through the window I see a waiter standing dutifully beside a beautifully prepared dinner table. I can't believe he's gone to all this trouble for me – who knew someone so rugged could be so smooth?

Ryan slides back the patio door and we enter the delicious chill of the room.

'Good evening, Ms Langston, Mr Sheen.' The

waiter pulls back the chairs and allows us to take a seat.

Up until now, room service to me meant an outsize BLT sandwich on some wheelie trolley in front on the TV. (And then snaffling the diddy bottle of ketchup as a keepsake.) Ryan has taken things to a whole other level. I can't believe we're actually being waited on. I don't quite know how to behave to warrant such indulgence. My fingers fidget nervously in my lap as the waiter pours the wine.

'To us,' Ryan makes the toast.

'And to the success of our businesses,' I manage to de-romanticise the moment in six words. Well, it's hard to be slushy when you know the waiter is listening to every word.

'Bread?'

'Thank you,' I say, wondering for the hundredth time why we clog our system with dough before a fancy meal.

As I attempt to daintily spread butter on my olive roll I notice two things: first that my face is excessively hot, second that every other word wafting from the stereo is amour. I can't believe how self-conscious I feel – almost as if I'm being upstaged by the setting. How can I compete with this romance? I wish someone would hand me a script so I'd know what I'm supposed to talk about in this rose-scented candlelight.

'So, how was the rest of your day?' I attempt to deflect the attention on to Ryan as the waiter serves our cognac-splashed lobster bisque.

'Well. I have to say your father has been a huge help hooking me up with all the right people,' he begins. 'What could have taken me weeks to suss out feels like it's already shaping up into a viable prospect.'

'So you might actually base yourself in Manuel Antonio?'

'It's looking that way. I mean, you can't beat the scenery here,' he says, looking me up and down.

I blush, and try and hoik the conversation back on track. 'So, how would it work?'

'Well, initially I'd start small, take the tours myself and then build up a quality staff – I'd definitely like to get Flare on board.'

'On board – good pun!'

'What?' he frowns.

'Surfer, board . . .'

'Gotcha! Yeah, he's a good dude. He says he knows some cool Ticos, we need at least one local to ease the hostility of an outsider coming in and taking jobs they could do. Like the deal you've got going with Santiago.'

'Well, he's a bit more than a token—'

'Yeah, your dad seems impressed, bringing him to dinner and everything!'

269

For a second I'm thrown. It almost sounds like Ryan sees Santiago as some kind of servant. Maybe because Kiki has told him that he lived with them in Tamarindo he's got the wrong impression. Suddenly I want to change the subject.

'So, Kiki tells me that you're into the Black Eyed Peas.'

'Oh yeah, they're great.' He reaches for his wine.

'Have you got a favourite song?' I ask, feeling like a teenager on a date at the mall.

He ponders for a moment and then laughs out loud. 'Do you know, I can't think cos I've got this one song on rotation in my head – ever since the waiter said your name tonight . . .'

I sigh – this wouldn't be the first time someone has broken into 'Ave Maria' around me, even though the pronunication is quite different. But then I remember the waiter addressed me using my surname.

'Is there a band called Langston?' I query.

'A singer – Grant Langston – he's this alternative country guy, I caught one of his shows in Memphis.' He laughs again. 'His lyrics are so hilarious. Listen, I'll play you a little sample . . .'

He gets up and removes the endless amour CD from the stereo and inserts his own, announcing: 'This one's called "Three Dollar Whore".'

I listen along hoping that the waiter is missing the subtleties.

my booty is what you are after
i guess you struck out at the bar
you're looking so pretty and talking so dirty
and outside my door in your car

i suppose i should just stop complaining
sometimes fast food does the trick
so i will relax and rest well in the fact
that i have a happy meal dick.

'Isn't that a hoot?' he chortles.

I smile weakly. It's actually a jaunty tune with lots of twanging guitars and rain-on-a-tin-roof drumming and yet the context seems all wrong. Throw down a little sawdust and peanut shells and we could talk . . .

As Grant continues to serenade us, now with a song called 'Divorce Number One', the waiter announces that he's done for the night. Our yellowfin tuna main course is served (grilled on a chipotle pepper sauce) and our desserts are set covered on the side, to be eaten at our leisure. If we need anything else we're to call him.

As he slides the door closed, I heave a sigh of relief. And then realise I'm still feeling just as tense. Clearly I haven't drunk enough wine.

'Attagirl,' Ryan says, encouraging my enthusiastic gulp. 'Plenty more where that came from.'

We chit-chat some more, Ryan marvelling at

Grant Langston's ability to use 'Sunday school' and the word 'shit' in the same sentence, me wondering out loud if he owns any cowboy boots. He does, he even has them with him – a pair of extra-battered, dusty-matt Marlboro Man jobs. He models them for me as we allow our main course to digest. Amazing. He could be wearing MC Hammer trousers and a weightlifter's leotard and still look good.

I'm finally starting to loosen up but what causes my shoulders to slump in utter submission is the iced passion-fruit mousse cake.

'Oh wow,' I swoon at its tangy fluffiness. 'I've got to have this regularly. For the rest of my life.'

'You really like it that much?' he leans in, seductively.

I match his move and lower my voice. 'I really, really-AAIIGGHH!' An almighty splat on the patio door has me screaming out loud. We look up and see a giant frog slime-suctioned to the glass.

'Where the hell did he propel himself from?' Ryan gasps.

Grossed out but fascinated, we edge over for a closer inspection, me grabbing at Ryan's sleeve as if the frog might somehow be able to push through the glass and squelch on to me.

'My heart is going like the clappers, feel it!'

Ryan places his hand on my chest, half on the material of my top, half on my skin. 'I can feel it,' he breathes, as his fingers weave beneath the embroidered yoke and find their way to my breast. 'It feels good,' he burrs, seconds before kissing me ravenously, his fervour sweetened by traces of the dessert.

In one swoop he's scooped me into his arms and is striding towards the bed. I want to laugh out loud – do people really do this kind of thing? Am I about to discover how the other half have sex?!

'This is some restaurant – comes with its own bed!' I josh as he stands over me undoing his buttons then flaring back his shirt to reveal a pair of furry pecs with a twist of fuzz descending to his navel. I get to see just how much further down that goes as he unzips his trousers. 'Very lenient dress code too . . .'

I barely get the words out before he is upon me. Everything happens so fast I don't even remember his underpants coming off but when my hand strays down his back I realise there's no elasticated waistband to let me know I've gone too far. Nothing is off-limits. Everything is writhing. Especially my hips in a bid to at least keep the lower half of my clothing on for a respectable five minutes or so. I mean, I'm all for passion and the heat of the moment but I'm actually feeling more ravaged than ravished, and I really would have liked the chance to have shaved my legs . . . As he grinds into me and again ruffles up my skirt I get the strangest sensation of being watched. Then I

273

remember the frog – are his global-rotation eyes still upon us? I strain away from Ryan's mouth and progress my kisses to his shoulder so that I can glance over at the window, only to inadvertently karate-kick his groin as I see Kiki staring in at us.

'Jesus!' Ryan howls. 'You nearly got my—'

'Ryan, stop.' I push him away from me, hissing. 'Kiki's out there.'

'What?'

As I grapple for the sheet, I point over to where she remains – apparently paralysed with embarrassment on the patio.

Ryan's head drops as if this is some tiresome inconvenience as opposed to a gross invasion of privacy and sighs heavily as he pads, stark naked, over to the glass door. Sliding it back he asks, 'What is it?'

Her cheeks flush deeper pink as she blusters: 'I just came to see what kind of evening you had . . . But I see you're still having it.' Her lips purse.

'Let's talk tomorrow, shall we?'

She nods dumbly, inadvertently taking in his nether regions. 'Call me when you're up.' Mortification flashes across her face. '*Awake!* Call me when you're awake.'

'Will do.'

By the time Ryan turns back to me I'm fully clothed and on my feet.

'Ava! What are you doing?' He rushes back to my side.

'I'm going home.'

'Are you crazy? You're not going to be put off by a little thing like—'

'My stepmother watching our naked bodies entwine?' I suggest. 'I'm afraid I'm done for the night.'

'But—'

'I can't, Ryan. I'm sorry.' I hate to let Kiki win but I have to get out of here. This scenario is too, too weird.

'Ava.' His voice softens as he takes my hands. 'Don't go.' He gently kisses first my knuckles then my neck, causing my eyes to flicker closed for a second. But then I'm haunted by an image of her face, now with a strange, almost proprietorial expression . . .

'I really can't do this, it's too freaky,' I shudder, releasing my hands.

'All I have to do is draw the curtains,' he pleads, blocking my path.

I shake my head and tell him emphatically, 'Not tonight, Mr Sheen.'

22

By the next morning, I'm wondering if I over-reacted. I mean, it wasn't Ryan's fault that Kiki came over all voyeuristic. And just because he's unfazed by his own nudity doesn't mean that they have a history in the bedroom. I mean, he was perfectly willing to get naked in front of me and we only met the day before. As for Kiki, I decide her problem is that she's experiencing a belated bout of what should have been *pre-wedding* cold feet. They rushed to the altar and now she's having a delayed reaction. And who can blame her? There's Ryan all young and virile (at least until I karate-kicked him in the groin) and she's naturally questioning the wisdom of shacking up with an OAP. None of which is my problem, so I decide that as soon as I've had my coffee I'll call Ryan and set up some kind of rematch for tonight. My body experiences a strange sensation in response to that proposition. Well, okay, so the physical aspect wasn't exactly a sensual serenade but I'm sure if we slowed things down a bit – took the noble route! – things could be pretty mind-blowing. Which reminds me – I need to shave my legs.

Bleary-eyed I stumble into the bathroom, only to jump back with my hands clamped over my eyes. I've just seen my second naked man in less than twelve hours.

'I didn't realise you were here,' Santiago emerges, now shrouded in a robe.

'Why wouldn't I be?' I challenge him without making eye contact. 'I do live here.'

'I didn't hear you get in last night.'

'Oh, did I miss curfew?' I snap, still mad at him for yesterday.

'Look—' he begins.

'I'm sorry, I haven't got time to chat,' I step past him into the bathroom. 'I don't want to be late for work.'

When we do arrive, ten minutes early, there's already a man sitting supping a caramel macchiato on the patio.

Santiago looks as confused as me as he tries the door. It's open. We walk inside and find my father standing at the counter in an apron.

'Dad, what are you doing here?'

'Well, someone's got to keep things ticking over while you guys are gone,' he says busying himself with the sugar crystals.

'Gone?' Santiago and I exchange a look. 'Where are we going?'

'Tortuguero. I know you wanted time off to visit your grandmother,' he addresses Santiago. 'And then Richard from the Green Turtle Gift Shop called to say he'd spoken to his friend about getting Ava to see the turtles nesting and, well, I wouldn't want her travelling unescorted, so bingo! Off you go!' Dad throws up his hands with a cheer.

Both Santiago and I remain stony-faced and motionless.

'I thought you'd be pleased,' Dad says, looking confused. 'You don't have to worry about the café, I've seen your cleaning and brewing schedules, everything else I could possibly want to know is written in your training manual – good job by the way, Ava – so it should run like clockwork.'

'It's just the timing,' I explain, referring both to Ryan and the fact that there are only eleven more days till Judgement Day and I still have some new ideas I want to try out. 'Thanks for the thought, though.'

'It's more than a thought, Ava, it's all booked.'

'*What?*' I snort, indignant. 'It can't be – you didn't even ask us!'

'Well, Kiki said it would be more fun as a surprise.'

Ohhhh. I see what's going on. Despite having matchmade me and Ryan she now wants to scupper any further interplay (especially of the naked variety) by sending me to the other side of the country. Well, I'm not playing along this time.

'I can't go, Dad, I'm sorry.'

'But this is your last chance to see the turtles, their nesting season ends this week.'

'Really?' I sigh, conflicted. I would have liked to have seen that but however adamant my father is, I refuse to play into Kiki's manipulative hands. Unless . . . I get a sudden, rather impish thought: *What if I asked Ryan to come too?* He's game for anything and it would certainly quash my concern that I'm not adventurous enough for him – how fabulous a thank you for dinner would this be? Not to mention the bonding potential of sharing something neither of us have experienced before. All the better to peeve Kiki. And to protect my dad. Not that I really think that she'd make a move on Ryan while I was gone – my instincts tell me this is less about her having him and more about me not. Not that that makes a jot of sense on paper, but women know women.

'Where would we be staying?' I gather more info.

'Well, I presumed Santiago would be staying with his grandmother in the village?'

He nods.

'And Kiki has booked a room for you at the Mawamba Lodge.'

So the accommodation is all sorted. All I need to do is check I can nab Ryan a flight and extend the invitation.

'Could you just give me five minutes, Dad? I think I might be able to swing it after all . . .'

'Help yourself.'

I get my phone out the second I'm out the door and call Nature Air – plenty of seats. Okay. Now the big one: Ryan. I get overeager palpitations as I dial his number and do a little jig as I wait for him to pick up.

'Hello?'

'Ryan, it's Ava.' I'm breathless.

'Heyyyyy, gorgeous,' he purrs. 'You and I have got some unfinished business to attend to! What are you doing later?'

'I was about to ask you the same thing,' I say, brazenly propositioning him.

'Oh really?' He sounds intrigued and makes uh-huh noises as I tell him the plan.

'So I get to share a room with you *and* see turtles nesting? I think that might be the best offer I've had all year!'

I twirl around in sheer delight, unable to believe my luck. This way everyone's happy, except Kiki. Just the way I like it. I'm definitely experiencing some finely tuned hostility towards my stepmother. She's clearly so used to having everything her own way, this will do her good.

'I'll call you back just as soon as I've nailed the logistics.'

'Okay, but we're not going to be leaving within the next hour, are we?'

'I'm not sure. Would that be a problem?'

'Well, I'm actually out on a boat right now, going for a quick snorkel. I'll be back on dry land around noon.'

'I'm sure that'll be fine. In the meantime I'll leave the details on your voicemail.'

'Great. I can't wait to pick up where we left off . . .' he growls.

Oh my Lord! I've done it now! I pogo back to the coffee shop and tell my dad that I am up for Tortuguero after all.

'What made you change your mind?'

'It's those turtles, Dad,' I only half lie. 'I've just got to see those turtles.'

For now I'm keeping shtum about Ryan coming along. I'm not telling Dad because I know he'll tell Kiki and I'm not telling Santiago because, well, it's none of his business. When he shows up at the airport I'm just going to act all casual and say, 'Oh didn't I mention that Mr Sheen is coming?'

For now I'm just concentrating on packing.

'So I gather it's rainier on the Caribbean side?' I call out to Santiago who's doing the same thing in his own room.

He must be psyched about seeing his granny because his mood has changed markedly since Dad announced the trip and now he deigns not only to reply but also to be quite helpful.

'You'll need your waterproof jacket and several changes of clothes – even though we're only going for one night you'll get repeatedly soaked so you'll need a dry alternative to put on. Well, dryish, it's so clammy that even the things in your suitcase will get moist.'

'Moist?' My nose shrivels in revulsion.

'For the turtle tour you need dark clothing, black preferably. And pack walking shoes. You don't want the bugs getting between your toes.'

I march over to his door frame. 'You don't have a pair of socks I could borrow, do you? You know, so I can tuck my trouser legs in?'

He studies me for a moment. I'm aware that I'm behaving differently too – something about knowing Ryan will be there is making me almost cocky. Besides I want to practise curbing my bitchy side before Ryan joins us.

'Sure,' he concedes, throwing an oatmeal ribbed pair at me.

I return to the room and add my umbrella and mosquito spray to my bag.

'Should I pack a torch?' I call out one more time.

'The guide will have one,' Santiago calls back. 'In fact, you're not allowed to take your own – he will

282

use a red light because that doesn't disturb the turtles.'

Again I do a little dance – this is going to be soooo amazing. As I check my drawers for any last-minute essentials I spot the underwear Ollie gave me as part of my going-away present. Should I? Gingerly I edge the violet tissue paper towards me. Not classic jungle undies, but it looks all very *FHM* fantasy trekker juxtaposed next to my hiking gear. Oh why not? If I'm going to get soaked through to the skin with rats'-tail hair, at least my T-shirt will be clinging to something pretty.

'Ready?' Santiago is now in my doorway.

I go to heave my bag on to my shoulder but he swipes it from my grasp. 'I've got it,' he says, marching ahead to the car.

For a moment I feel guilty. He's being courteous at a time when he could really be sticking it to me. Then I realise that, like me, he's decided to set aside our differences to get through this trip with minimum angst – we may still be in dispute over who is the favoured 'child' but apparently we have a few adult traits between us too.

'So, is your granny excited about your visit?' I try to maintain the air of civility as we head to the airport.

He gives me a playful smirk. 'She'll be doing her Happy Granny dance as we speak.'

'What's she like?'

283

'You'll see.'

'Oh no, I won't intrude. You do your thing and I'll . . .' I trail off at his raised eyebrow. 'What?'

'You don't know anything about where we're going, do you?'

'No, but I'm sure I'll find my way around.'

He smiles to himself.

'Or is it not that kind of place?'

'Not really. You'll see.'

I give a carefree shrug. I'm going with Tarzan and a Tico, I couldn't be in better hands, so why worry?

Discreetly I lower my eyes to the mobile phone in my lap. Still no word back from Ryan. I've already left two messages for him, I don't want to keep bugging him but I can't help feeling a little antsy. Why hasn't he responded? I guess he presumes it's all arranged. Some men don't feel the need to reconfirm. I tut at myself – this is so me – whenever I've got something really wonderful to look forward to, all I can think of is all the things that can go wrong, usually starting with my hair. But bad hair is a given on the Caribbean coast so at least I can cross that off my list. Okay, breathe. I've got to stop fretting and start savouring. These next twenty-four hours are going to be pretty special.

'Anything wrong?' Santiago asks as I once again get to my feet and pace anxiously, scrutinising every face that appears in the departure lounge, even though Ryan would stand head and shoulders above the diminutive locals.

Where is he?

'Ava?' Santiago persists.

'I've just got to make a quick call . . .' I tuck myself around the corner out of sight and scrunch my eyes in misery as his phone once again goes to voicemail.

'Ryan, it's Ava. The flight leaves in fifteen minutes but there's another one in an hour so if you miss this—' I take a breath. 'Just call me and let me know what's going on.' I leave the number again just to be extra-extra sure.

I can't understand it. He sounded so game. Did Kiki get to him? I imagine him kidnapped, bound and gagged in her closet. Hmm, I wonder if Dad can shed any light on proceedings?

'Hi, yes we're boarding in a few minutes. I just remembered something I had to tell Ryan, you haven't seen him, have you? No. Okay. No, it's not important. Is Kiki with you? She is? No, just tell her thanks for arranging this. Okay. Will do. Bye.'

Well, he's clearly been eaten by a shark.

'Ava, we're going through,' Santiago motions for me to join the queue to board.

'Okay, just one more call!'

Frantically I dial Ollie in the UK, with zero regard for the time difference. 'No time for chit-chat, just listen!' I instruct as I précis my predicament. 'Well?' I squawk once I'm done. 'What should I do – stay or go?'

'Are you serious?'

'Yes, of course! Just tell me what to do!'

'I'm sorry, is this the same Ava who swore "I'll never put my life on hold for a man again!"? Are you seriously telling me you'd miss the once-in-a-lifetime chance to see turtles nesting for a guy? Back home you wouldn't miss your favourite TV show for a date.'

'But he's so sexy! You should have seen him swinging through the treetops – he's just so gung-ho, so *carnal*!'

'Ohhhhh,' he crows knowingly. 'So this is your loins talking.'

'No it's not. Well, maybe.'

'Look, it's really a no-brainer: these turtles have a time limit, Ryan doesn't – he'll be there when you get back.'

'Unless he's been eaten by a shark.' I venture my theory.

'Well, if he has then there's nothing much to stay for, is there? You can't shag scattered body parts.'

'Ollie!'

'Ava. Be rational. You're only going to miss him for one night. He's into you. He'll be into you when you get back. And nothing your psycho stepmom does can change that.'

'I'm not so sure,' I mutter.

'Have a little faith. And remember – absence makes the heart grow fonder. Besides, what kind of sap would you look like if you backed out now?' He adopts a girlish whine, *'Oh I didn't go cos you weren't there to hold my hand!'* He's Jungle Jim, he doesn't want some simpering limpet for a girlfriend.'

'You're right,' I sigh. 'I just don't understand why he hasn't called.'

'Men don't call. It's just one of life's miserable truths. Get used to it.'

'Ava!' Santiago calls over from the final security post. 'We're waiting for you!'

'Bugger, I've got to go!'

'Break an egg!' cheers Ollie.

'What?'

'Like break a leg but this time it's – oh never mind, just go!'

The line clicks dead.

'Sorry!' I bluster as I hurry towards the departure gate.

'Your bag?'

'What?'

'They need to check your bag.' Santiago motions for me to relinquish it to the security guard.

Despite the impatient look on the face of the pilot, the guard methodically removes every item. Toilet bag. Proper shoes. Santiago's socks. Ah. My Agent Provocateur undies. Out of the corner of my eye I see Santiago's mouth twist in a smirk. I just know he's thinking, 'One glimpse of me naked in the shower and the lingerie turns X-rated.'

'It's not what you think,' I mutter self-consciously.

The guard looks apologetically at Santiago. 'Sorry if I ruined the surprise!'

'You didn't! They're not—' I begin a protest but what's the point? I can't tell Santiago that the corsetry ribbons were intended for the man who has stood me up or I'll look even more ridiculous. Instead I say nothing, preferring to preserve my energy for an hour-long blush.

Though my eyes remain averted for the duration of the flight, I can tell that Santiago is looking at me in a whole new light. When we land he takes me to one side and says, 'What I said yesterday about the nepotism, I was out of line.'

I want to believe that his apology is sincere, that he's waving a white flag but I'm afraid that if I look closely I'll find the flag is actually a pair of his boxer shorts.

Apparently that lingerie really does work.

23

This is my first airport to hotel transfer via boat. The muddy waterways are unmarked save for the occasional stilted shack or pair of ponies chomping at the grassy banks, yet I get the feeling these are the local equivalent of roads. ('You want to take a right at the fifty-seventh crabwood tree, mate!')

As we course down the main artery, we pass assorted offshoots, threading deeper into the tumble and tangle of foliage. Every possible leaf-style appears to be represented here – palms, ferns, winding vines like feather boas, outsize leaves known as 'poor man's umbrellas' – and as we forge on, the greenery starts to crowd so close to the river's edge the trees appear to be growing directly up out of the water itself.

I don't know quite what I was expecting but I wasn't prepared for the scale of this place – canals of caramel latte and burgeoning vegetation ad infinitum. I stepped aboard the boat with a group of fellow tourists and by simple virtue of the scenery and the remoteness of our location we have all morphed into bold adventurers. Initially there was chatting and pointing, now we all sit in serene silence. The peace is divine. It occurs to me that my urgency to be with Ryan has subsided, almost like it never existed.

I'm deep in a meditative trance when Santiago calls to the driver in Spanish and he immediately cuts the engine and steers towards the bank.

'Can you see?' Santiago points to the treetops.

'What am I looking for?'

'A three-toed sloth. Try these,' he offers me his binoculars.

My jaw drops as I locate the comical fellow – his tiny head is round yet weasel-like, his limbs are gangly, his bottom saggy and his fur a swishy shag.

'You know he only comes down from his tree to, er, use the bathroom once a week?' Santiago informs me, slightly embarrassed by the indelicacy of the information.

'So they really are as lazy as people say.' I note.

'Not so much lazy as slow-moving. And that in itself is a protection against hawks and eagles who spot prey from their movement.'

'Really?' I muse. There we go making judgements when if we just took the time to look at the underlying motivations we would get a whole different take on the situation – our scorn might even switch to admiration.

'You would like to see some more wildlife before we go to the hotel?' the driver enquires of his passengers.

The scramble for cameras is all the answer he needs and he swerves left down one of the smaller waterways then creeps along, eyes scanning for creatures.

I feel like this is the Costa Rican equivalent to punting and go to drape my hand in the river but hesitate, asking Santiago, 'Are there crocs in the water here?'

He nods an affirmative.

'Ones that eat you?' I gulp.

'Me? No. They don't like the taste of the locals. But international visitors . . .' he twinkles at me.

I give him a playful thwack. Santiago's noticeably more relaxed in this environment – something about being home, no doubt. But then again so am I, and I've never been here before.

I watch him bantering with the driver and can't help but find him appealing once more. When he's grumpy and competitive there is no one more aggravating, but when he's chilled he's a delight. I don't want to forgive him so easily for being such an arse when I came in late from zip-lining with Ryan, and yet unruly nature is so disarming, it's hard to hold a grudge here.

'*Caimáns*, do you see?' Santiago nods to the twigs threaded over the water's surface.

'I don't even know what a *caimán* is,' I confess. Am I looking for a bird?

'It's Spanish for alligator.'

'*What?*' Has he summoned them up just to torment me?

'These are just the baby ones,' he quickly assures me. 'See.'

Again the camouflaging is highly effective but eventually my eyes distinguish the live foot-long stick from the others. She's so dainty, she's almost pretty.

'How big do they grow?' I ask him.

'Little more than three-and-a-half feet. You want to see a full-grown crocodile—'

'No I don't!' I protest.

'They can grow up to sixteen feet long. There's this great place for spotting them on the drive from San José to Manuel Antonio . . .'

'That's okay,' I tell him.

Santiago laughs.

'It's all right for you!' I pout. 'You grew up around all this, the most a person has to put up with in England is wasps buzzing around your ice cream in the summer and the odd daddy-long-legs in your bathroom!'

'Do you miss England?' he asks, taking me by surprise. I think this is the first personal question he's asked me.

'I miss my friends,' I say. 'But other than that, we've been so busy, I haven't been thinking about too much else. I mean, my mother, obviously . . .' I trail off. The truth is, it's been a relief to have a break from her guilt-tripping and mind-tainting moaning. I really don't know what it's going to take for her to get a cheery perspective on life. Would the sight of a Jesus Christ lizard do it, I wonder? They get their name because they can actually walk on water. That's a mini-miracle right there. Maybe I shouldn't give up on her just yet . . .

'We're here,' the driver announces as we pull up to a jetty ominously hung with dozens of oilskin ponchos and row upon muddy row of wellington boots. The sky is such a wishy-washy grey now it's hard to imagine it conjuring the legendary rains but everyone insists there's a storm a-coming. Their tone suggests one of biblical proportions and yet there's a distinct absence of ark-like vessels to hand – all the boats moored at the dock look far too easily filled with water and sunk, if you ask me.

'So, I guess you'll be going to see your granny now?' I ask as Santiago helps me disembark.

'I'll wait to see you settled in first.'

'No need,' I say, a little too dismissively. 'I'll find my own way from here.'

Chatting on the boat was one thing but now that my bag is back in my hand, along with the infamous undies, I find I am unable to look Santiago in the eye.

'Will you join us for dinner?' he enquires.

'Nooo, you make the most of your time with your grandmother. A meal is included with my booking so I'll just—' I wave in the direction of the alfresco dining room.

He looks a little offended. 'If you're sure?'

'Yup, sure.' I tell him.

'Okay, well, I'll see you later for the turtles.'

'You're coming too?' I start.

'I have no choice,' he smiles. 'I'm your guide.'

Huh? 'But I thought Richard arranged—'

'He did but Jimmy is sick. I'm the replacement.'

'When did you find that out?' I frown, bewildered.

'On the boat,' he shrugs. 'Tortuguero has a population of six hundred. Everyone knows everyone.'

'Oh.'

'I'll meet you in reception at 10 p.m.'

'Fine, 10 p.m.,' I repeat trying to make it sound as un-date-like as possible. 'Anything I should remember to bring?'

'Actually there's two things *not* to bring – no cameras and no perfume.'

'No perfume?' Do I look like an Avon lady?

'Turtles are very sensitive to smell. Even having alcohol on your breath can deter them from nesting, so keep away from the cocktails!'

294

'Are you serious?' I blink at him.

'I'm serious.'

Wow. I'm getting nervous now, I don't want to do anything to upset the ecosystem.

'Okay, well, see you later,' I make another attempt at breeziness.

'You'll be okay by yourself?' Santiago still seems reluctant to leave.

'Yes, me and my fancy underwear will be fine!' I want to snap. 'Get your mind out of the gutter and go see your granny!'

Instead, I purposefully heave my bag on my shoulder and follow the path through a games room complete with pool table, past reception and down a raised wooden walkway to Room 14. I don't know if there's anything that feels more wasteful than spending the night alone in a gorgeous hotel suite but I'm certainly not going to invite Santiago to stay with me just because – My train of thought is halted as I open the door.

I don't know quite what I was expecting, but it wasn't this. The room looks like an abridged version of the shack Snow White shared with the seven dwarfs, only here there are just three beds, each of them barely qualifying as a single. I don't mean to be ungrateful but I've seen fancier garden sheds. The walls are panels of unfinished wood, the wardrobe nothing more than a couple of peg-hooks last seen in a kindergarten cloakroom. Which brings me to the colour: every detail – the hooks, the bookshelf, the bed frames – is painted canary yellow. Worst of all, there is no air con, just a basic ceiling fan. I tug at the beaded cord until it warms up from lackadaisical rotation to whirling dervish and stand directly below it.

One night. That's all I have to get through. It's then I realise with dismay that I'm starving and dinner isn't served for another two hours. Something tells me there is no room service, though I do remember spying some tea and biscuits in the games room.

When I step outside I see that the sky has already begun to change, turning the vista a moody monochrome. Ominous clouds are stealing in like shadowy figures about to claim a victim. I get a disturbing sense of foreboding as if I am about to be swept up in a twister. Suddenly I wish I had taken Santiago up on his offer, I bet Granny is spoiling him with cake and reinforced walls. I'll be amazed if my room doesn't collapse at the first splosh of rain, or at the very least shrink.

Helping myself to three mini-packs of biscuits and a camomile tea I decide that it's actually more pleasant to sit outside now the air is cooling and make my way to what looks like a bandstand slung with a hammock overlooking the river. As the rain begins to smatter the surrounding earth, I lower myself in, managing to balance my tea and biscuits as I do so. I see other guests scurrying back to their rooms, giving me a quizzical look. What? I want to say. I'm alone and there's no TV here, I've got to get my entertainment where I can.

Okay then, show me! I challenge the heavens. They respond by crackling into action – charcoal phantoms loom and magnify, the wind gathers force agitating the neighbouring trees, causing them to bow then throw back their branches in frenzied dance.

Spears of searing white lightning ignite a rumbling bass of thunder resonating within my chest. I barely remember to breathe as heaving torrent after torrent of water is unleashed until I can no longer distinguish the raindrops from the air – everything around me looks liquid! The more it pours and the brighter it flashes, the more electrified I feel. I have never known drama on this scale. Yet still I remain miraculously dry and protected.

Initially I wish Ollie could be here sharing in the magnificence but, funnily enough, not Ryan – for some reason I don't feel he's a good fit for this place. And then it occurs to me that I'm perfectly content that it's just me. Everyone always talks about sharing the moment but sometimes, it would seem, it's all the more precious for being your very own.

As a further barrage of rain is released I laugh out loud! *Are you kidding me?* And then, quite unexpectedly, it subsides. When I look at my watch I'm surprised to see it's nearly time for dinner.

One imaginative buffet and several international conversations later, I still have two hours before my rendezvous with Santiago so I mooch around the gift shop and buy a mud mask from Arenal, the ever-erupting volcano up north. Apparently you can dine not far from its base while watching its red-hot molten lava flow. I settle for putting some of its terracotta paste on my face. Ten minutes, it says. I dutifully lie like a corpse on my small person's bed. And promptly fall asleep.

The next thing I know, there's knocking at the door.

'Ava?'

For a second I think it's Ryan, mostly because I've just been dreaming about him (line dancing with a dozen women who all look like Kiki), but then I see the time – 10.15 p.m.! Shit! It's Santiago. I sit upright in a panic and go to respond but find my face paralysed. What the –?

It's only when I rush to the bathroom that I remember the mask.

Again with the knocking.

'Just a minute!' I say breaking free of its taut constraints and sending orange powder across the tiles.

Frantically I splash my face with water. Scoopful after scoopful until every last dusty, cloying particle

298

is gone. There! I look up and see with alarm that my face is stained bright orange. I look like Paris Hilton in a Little Mermaid wig. Nooooo!

I run back to the door. 'I'm actually going to be two minutes – is that okay?'

'I'll wait in the bar.'

'Thanks!' I bleat.

Goddammit!

I go back to the sink and scrub with the corner of a towel and then work my toner in vigorous circles, all to no avail. I can't understand it – I only left the mask on an hour and forty minutes too long!

I do the best cover-up job I can then remind myself that the flashlight Santiago will be using has a red beam and presumably that's for seeing the way as opposed to studying my complexion. So I'll be fine.

Nevertheless, as I approach Santiago at the bar I can't help but shuffle awkwardly, keeping my chin tucked down and letting my hair fall over my face.

'Ava, if you're still embarrassed about the under-wear—' he begins.

'No, no,' I assure him. 'I've got a whole new reason to cringe now, thank you very much.'

'And what would that be?' he enquires.

'My face,' I reply. (I've never been one of those people that can keep their big mouth shut.)

'It's not that bad,' he teases.

I roll my eyes and confess: 'It's orange. I left a face mask on too long . . .'

'Let me see.' He draws back my hair like a theatre curtain and studies me for a second. 'It suits you.'

'It does not.'

'No really, the orange goes with your hair.'

I bat him away but he takes a firm grip on my hand. 'Come with me, I want to show you something.'

'Something other than the turtles?'

'It's on the way.'

He leads me down the path.

'Now I know you have an aversion to the rain-forest—'

I immediately freeze.

'I promise you'll be fine,' he coaxes me onward. 'Just watch where you tread.'

Easier said than done – how can I watch what I can't see? It is pitch-pitch black, his flashlight is switched off and there is a distinct absence of street lamps casting a comforting glow. Mind you, I guess my face has that aspect covered.

'Wh-what are we doing here?' I ask as we burrow deeper into the forest. 'I thought the turtles were on the beach.'

'They are but I thought I'd give you a scenic night walk as a bonus.'

'Great!' I feign enthusiasm but all I can imagine is the infra-red version of what I'm walking through with all the beasties highlighted and no doubt leaning in to nibble on my ear and— Suddenly there's a scuffle in the bushes.

'What was that?' I virtually leap into Santiago's arms, utterly freaked out. 'It sounded big.'

'Could be a dog. Or an armadillo.' Santiago is still. I think I can hear his heart beating.

'An armadillo, really?' I squeak, oddly impressed before my fear returns. 'They don't bite, do they?'

'Anything that has teeth can bite,' Santiago retorts. 'You bite, don't you?'

'Well . . .'

He takes two paces and then stops again.

'What are you doing?' I hiss, nervously latching on to his shoulder.

'Look around you.'

'It's black, I can't see a thing.'

'Look,' he repeats.

For a second I think I see the phosphorescent aftermath of a flashlight, as if glimpsing other trekkers dotted throughout the forest. But then I realise these are not shafts of light but dozens of tiny moonbeams doing Morse code.

'What is it?' I breathe as my eyes play dot-to-dot with the silver-white lights.

'Lightning bugs,' he tells me. 'Or as you call them, fireflies.'

'They're beautiful,' I sigh, entranced. 'Straight from the wand of a Disney fairy godmother!'

Our faces are so close now as he whispers, 'We have a story that we tell about the firefly. We say that he always felt self-conscious because he knew he was not as attractive as the other insects – the patterned butterfly, the shimmering dragonfly . . . He couldn't see how a thing so ugly could attract a mate until one day a wise elder told him that he was beautiful on the inside and all he needed to do to show the world was to shine!'

My face illuminates with delight. 'That's so sweet!' I say as I watch all the fireflies busily displaying their inner beauty.

'Don't worry about your skin,' Santiago gently touches my jaw. 'You always shine.'

And with that he walks on.

For a moment I stand stunned. Aside from the fact that there are scary beasties all around me and I'm with the wrong guy, that felt strangely romantic.

I try to convince myself it's all part of his one-night seduction but instead I connect back to the quiet sympathy of the evening he cooked for me, before my dad burst in and whisked us off to El Avion to meet Ryan.

Ah yes, that guy I was desperate to bring along here with me. I doubt I would have seen the fireflies if I'd been with him – something tells me he would be too busy thrashing through the forest with a big stick to have noticed the dainty, dancing lights.

24

Even by day the sand on Tortuguero beach is a dark mink; by night it's like tramping upon muddy pepper. I look out at the black water, chased with crests of white and wonder, are you out there, turtles? Are you on your way in to nest? With clouds muffling the light of the moon and stars, the mood seems almost eerie and I feel as if I am trespassing on another world.

'How many can we expect to see?' I whisper to Santiago as he edges us forward.

'Well, last year they had a record count of three thousand nests,' he tells me.

'In how long?' I can't quite recall the length of the nesting season.

'In one night,' he replies.

I want to gasp, *'What?'* but settle for a less disruptive widening of my eyes.

As we walk on I concentrate on my footing, looking down at my shoes teamed with Santiago's socks when suddenly I feel his hand upon me, slowing me, settling me. We have arrived.

My heart starts to thump. Even though I know I have nothing to fear in terms of getting bitten or ambushed, I am nervous, unsure somehow that I deserve to be here. I feel like I need to ask the head turtle for permission to observe before I can relax.

'Do you see?'

I squint, trying to adjust my eyes to the darkness. 'Look for the movement.'

I am breathing heavily. I can hear a swishing-dragging sound but I can't see what is making it. Santiago eases me close to him, positions my head and then shines the red beam of the torch. I see her! Ploughing a furrow through the sand, like an exhausted shipwreck survivor elbowing ashore, she gets sufficiently far from the tide and then begins using her hind flippers to scoop out a hole.

Santiago's lips are beside my ear. 'That is where she will lay her eggs.'

I nod in response, transfixed. Now I notice others around her – having seen one, I seem to be able to differentiate their form from the shadows. I smile, remembering as a child picking up a tortoise, amazed by the toughness of its shell, the soft wrinkles around its neck, the little bald head, the scaly toes. Now the scale has shifted – these have got to be three feet long, making me feel pixie-sized. And they aren't even the biggest – giant leatherbacks grow up to six feet long, weighing up to a thousand pounds. That's like the weight of all of the Black Eyed Peas plus Ryan and his country-crooner pal Grant Langston combined. I wonder what Mr Sheen is doing right now? Whatever it is, I can't help but feel he's missing out. What I am witnessing is both humbling and exhilarating – turtles truly do look ancient beings, befitting their legacy of having walked the earth with the dinosaurs. The one nearest me has a pattern on her face that resembles crazy paving – grey patches with white 'cement' around black, almost seal-like eyes, a small pinched nose, a bulging chin with markings and grooves like a well-worn chopping board, a shell of thick lead roofing. Yet from all this weathered cragginess comes a pristine, smooth white egg.

And then another and another. A hundred on average per 'clutch'.

In just a few months a hatchling will wriggle free and make its pilgrimage back to the sea. I tell Santiago that I want to come back and be one of the volunteers who shepherds and protects them during their most vulnerable phase, asking, 'Wouldn't it be easier to just pick them up and carry them to the water's edge?'

Santiago shakes his head. 'You can't do that because the females will one day return to this beach to lay their eggs and the maiden voyage from nest to sea is what imprints them.'

'Aaahhh!' I nod.

It seems unfathomable to me that anyone could knowingly harm these gentle giants. It would be like mugging an elderly person with a walker. The curious thing is that many of today's guides are former poachers. Santiago says he has an older male friend who has no shame in admitting his former 'profession' – before they became a protected species it was no different to the locals than fishing.

'The green turtles are most under threat as they're killed for their meat,' he goes on to explain. 'The leatherbacks eat jellyfish and the hawksbills eat sea sponges and both are toxic to humans but the greens feed on seagrass and that's what makes them taste so good.'

I can't help but feel a little queasy – yet another day where vegetarianism seems the only civilised way to go. Even karmically it's got to make sense.

For the next forty minutes we say nothing, just exchange the occasional look of wonder and delight, crouched so close that our breathing becomes synchronised. Earlier today it seemed unthinkable to leave the café so soon after opening, not to mention prise myself away from Ryan. And the thought of travelling anywhere with Santiago in such a strop . . . Yet look at us now – sharing an experience that is destined to be for ever a part of me.

As I think back on my recent days in Costa Rica it

occurs to me that the outdoor adventures I had with Ryan, the Canopy Tour and ATV ride, were all about speed and sinew-twanging whooping whereas with Santiago and the fireflies and the turtles, the emphasis has been on being still and quiet. It's ironic that the man who initially made me cry 'This is war!' is now offering me such peace.

I could stay here all night watching the turtles perform their egg-laying relay but the sky is starting to spit and Santiago is indicating it is time for us leave.

'Thank you' seems inadequate but I say it anyway as we amble hotel-ward.

'I really am so grateful,' I tell him, marvelling: 'That was something else.'

He goes to speak but his words remain on his lips as his eyes divert skywards, 'Here it comes,' he cautions.

We quicken our pace, hurrying to the sheltered walkway, by which point the rain is pounding down, dancing with clogs on the corrugated iron.

'That was a close call!' I laugh as I unlock the door to my room. Suddenly my garden shed seems cosy and welcoming and I wouldn't change a thing. I turn to face Santiago. 'I can get us tea and biscuits, if you like?'

'No, I'm fine. I should be going.'

'You can't walk back in this!' I exclaim. His journey would be one long carwash of a sluicing.

'I'm used to it,' he shrugs. 'I kind of like it.'

'But!' I puff. 'There's no need – you can stay here: look, there's three beds. We can even have a whole spare one between us for decency!' I laugh.

He shakes his head.

'I'm not going to pounce,' I assure him. 'I know that underwear looks like it has an agenda but I promise you I don't.'

For a second he looks directly into my eyes and suddenly a seduction scene with him seems like the most appealing thing in the world. No fancy frilly accessories required, just those eyes . . .

'Don't go,' I say in a small voice.

Now that we've reclaimed this truce, this closeness, I don't want it to end.

'Does the storm makes you nervous?' he enquires.

'I'm not nervous,' I tell him. 'But if you got washed downstream never to be seen again I wouldn't feel like I'd won the café fair and square!'

This makes him smile. 'Okay,' he concedes. 'But I have to get up early. I have many chores for my grandmother—'

'That's fine!' I feel triumphant, even though I know nothing can or will happen – we've both got too much at stake.

'Sooo . . .' Suddenly I don't know what to do with my guest – there is no TV to flick through or minibar to offer him a nightcap. I guess we should just go to bed.

'Shall I use the bathroom first or . . .?'

'You go,' he replies.

'Okay. I'm just going to have a quick shower,' I say, wishing we at least had some music to ease the silence – it seems so much more loaded knowing we are both about to disrobe and get horizontal. I wonder if there will be much talking after this or if it will start to feel stilted?

As I set the shower running, it occurs to me that our communication style has been akin to tuning a radio – initially our opposing agendas and preconceived notions created static and interference, but gradually gradually working side by side offered us fleeting glimpses of clarity and harmony, to the point where we were actually starting to sing along. But then Ryan showed up and we lost the signal. A few scratchy, patchy bits later and we're back in tune again. I wonder how long our accord will last this time?

Entranced by the illusion that it is raining inside and out, I stay too long beneath the teeming warm water and when I emerge, Santiago is fast asleep. Still in his clothes and boots, half propped up on the bed nearest the door.

I stand in contemplation, wondering how I can make him more comfortable, wishing there was enough room on the pint-sized bed for me to lie beside him. It must be the turtles making me senti-

309

mental, I decide. In conspiracy with the fireflies. And the rain – there's something so intimate about huddling together against the elements. When the sun is shining the world is a wide-open invitation but when the weather is bad it shrinks like woollens and you and your companion find yourselves all the more tightly-knit. Or is that just wishful thinking on my part? He didn't seem keen on staying. Maybe he worried it would seem disrespectful to his granny? Maybe he wanted to but felt it was inappropriate because of Ryan. Not that he knows the details of that situation, but he knows Indiana Jones and I had a pretty late night.

For a moment, I considering waking him but for what? He's made it clear that he has no intention of making a move and much as I'd love for us to whisper secrets and stories till dawn, I shouldn't be getting any more involved. I have the coffee shop to think of: Santiago is still the enemy in that context. Imagine how messy it would make things if we got physically intimate – right now I feel like even one kiss could cause a fatal avalanche of emotion. He's done me a favour by falling asleep. That way I can stay immune to his charms.

But then he turns and snuggles down into the pillow, tugging my heart into the crook of his chest. If I keep looking at him I'm going to do something I'll regret. Instead I take a breath, creak across the room to the furthest bed, turn out the light and heave an elongated sigh as I slip between the covers.

Once I'm finally settled I hear him murmur, '*Buenas noches*, Ava,' releasing a thousand Latino butterflies into my heart.

25

Before I open my eyes I know that he's gone. I lie
still, aware of my chest rising and falling, relieved
that nothing happened between us last night so
there can be no morning-after awkwardness. Yet I
also have a tinge of regret. Being here is like a step
out of time. I don't know when we'll have the chance
to be so neutral and unguarded again. Today we
return to our battleground in Manuel Antonio. And
to Ryan. In theory, anyway. I still haven't heard
from him. Not that my phone has any signal here.
It's funny but I simply don't care. All that insane
urgency I felt at the airport has evaporated. It's
almost as though he doesn't even exist any more.
Nothing outside of Tortuguero exists.

As I sit upright, I gaze wistfully at Santiago's bed
and notice a piece of paper on the pillow.

'*Come for brunch*,' it says, beside a scrappy little
map etched in pencil.

I smile to myself. Suddenly I want nothing more

than to meet his granny. I'm so glad he still wants me to, pleased I haven't spoilt anything by insisting he stay the night. I feel a little embarrassed that I even offered, now. Oh well, I'm a foreigner, hopefully he'll make allowances.

As I open my case and discover that all the clothing I have brought with me is indeed moist, I recall Ollie's last educational email telling me that home is so sacred to Ticos that they welcome only their most intimate of friends. In fact, an invitation is typically a gesture of friendship and rarely followed through on, so much so that Nicaraguans joke: 'A Tico is quick to invite you to his home – but it's tough to make him give you the address.'

Seeing as I have been honoured with a *map*, I feel I should don Sunday best and yet the best I can do with what I packed is to add a pair of dangly silver earrings to pretty up my white vest and khakis. Next I worry about turning up empty-handed. Perhaps I'll be able to purchase a little something en route? Whatever, I really need to stop shilly-shallying around and get moving!

Right! According to the sketch I need to begin by walking parallel to the beach, burrow through some bushes and then I'll hit Tortuguero high street. It turns out to be the *only* street – or rather well-worn grassy pathway – lined with various home-sweet-shacks, a couple of surprisingly large gift shops and a tempting bakery where I purchase a 'pan bon'

313

fruitcake attracted by its heavy glaze and gingery aroma, happy now to have a little package in my hand. You can tell this is the Caribbean coast – many skins are darker, accents are more laid-back-lyrical and the even the school is painted in carnival colours. I pause beside it to study Santiago's etchings and work out that the cute lemon bungalow across the way must be Granny Raffaella's place.

'Knock knock?' I go for the traditional British holler only to recall that *'Upe!'* is the expected alert when entering a Tico house.

'Ava! Your timing is perfect!' Santiago greets me with a flourish. 'Please allow me to introduce Señora Raffaella!'

I step inside and look around the dark yet cosy room, searching for a second figure, finding none. Santiago indicates I should lower my gaze and there she is – right beside him, so mini, she barely comes up to his ribs.

'It's very kind of you to invite me into your home,' I tell her.

'From the package in your hand, I would say I made a wise decision!' she twinkles as she accepts the cake.

Whereas Santiago's height clearly does not sprout from her side of the family, they certainly share a sparky nature. The two of them banter playfully as they finish setting the table, all too soon involving me.

314

'Rice and beans?' she chirrups, hovering with a large pan.

'Yum!' I enthuse just as Santiago snorts, 'She hates gallo pinto!'

'No I don't!' I protest huffily, instantly resenting the fact that we sound like warring siblings.

'She'll like mine,' Granny Raffaella winks at me as she gaily spoons a grainy mountain upon my plate.

And I do! Apparently it's the coconut milk they use on the Caribbean coast that makes all the difference. (Though of course I would have eaten it all and asked for seconds just to prove Santiago wrong.) As I keenly balance the nodules on my fork, Raffaella places a small dish of leafy paste before me – some kind of spicy accoutrement? I'm willing to give it a go and reach for a spoonful.

'No!' she corrects me. 'This is for your face.'

'My face?' I frown, confused.

'To take away the orange.'

'Oh!' I flush, turning myself scarlet. I'd got ready so quickly this morning I hadn't properly studied the aftermath of the face mask. 'Th-thank you.'

'She's got a remedy for everything,' Santiago confides, part admiringly, part eye-rollingly. He takes a sip of coffee then ventures, 'You know, I couldn't help but notice last night that you had a little trouble sleeping . . .'

Only because you were lying so temptingly close to me! I want to reply. Hold on! I thought he was

315

out for the count – if he was asleep, how would he know I was tossing and turning?

'I guess sometimes I find it hard to nod off,' I shrug, a little flustered. 'When I think too much about the coffee shop . . .'

'Here,' Raffaella reaches to the sideboard behind her then offers me a handful of leaves to be boiled in water. 'This will have you asleep like that!' She snaps her tiny brown fingers.

'What about waking up?' I gulp, tentatively fondling the foliage. 'I mean, *will I*?'

'Of course!' she laughs, before deadpanning: 'Eventually.'

Once I have savoured the juiciest most golden pineapple I ever had the pleasure to dribble down my chin, she leads me out to the garden and introduces me to an assortment of plants, including the dainty '5 o'clock' leaf that curls up at 5 p.m. each night and unfurls dead on 5 a.m. Virtually every other herb or bud seems to possess some miracle property, all of which she is happy to pluck and pass to me. I feel like I'm consulting some kind of gardener/drug-dealer hybrid.

'It's a good thing you don't have asthma,' Santiago watches us from the doorway. 'She'd have you eating a live beetle.'

'*What?*' I spin around. 'Why?'

'It opens up the airways of the lungs,' she informs me.

316

'Riiight.' I play along.

'The most bizarre of all Costa Rican cures is for earache,' Santiago continues. 'A lactating mother must squirt breast milk in your ear!'

'I've heard everything now!' I quip, wanting to ask Granny Raffaella if she's got anything for bad taste in men but I don't want her taking that the wrong way and presuming I mean Santiago.

For the next hour or so we sit on the sofa and chat about nature and old wives tales and I tell her of the dock leaves we use to soothe nettle rash, wispy dandelion clocks blown upon to tell the time and buttercups held under our chins to determine if we like butter. I also laugh more than I have done since I arrived in Costa Rica. I never met either of my grannies but how delightful it would have been to have one who chuckles so often and so infectiously. She certainly brings out the lighter side to Santiago. Until, that is, she produces the inevitable photo album charting his youth. Though he is squirming I can't help but swoon all the more – it's hard not to warm towards someone when you see them with scuffed knees age six holding up a 'blue jeans' frog (glossy red with indigo legs) or age ten convulsed with giggles from being tickled by their now departed granddad.

'In his teenage years . . .'

As Raffaella threatens to compound Santiago's

317

embarrassment he jumps up and announces, 'No time for that – we've got a flight to catch.'

'No flights,' Granny Raffaella asserts, blithely turning the page.

'What?' Santiago goes to the window and hangs his head. 'I'll be back in a minute, I'm just going to see if we can get a ride with Jimmy as far as San José.'

'I thought he was sick?' I frown.

'He's feeling much better today,' Santiago mutters as he walks out the door.

'What's going on?' I turn back to Granny Raffaella.

'Weather,' Granny Raffaella shrugs. 'You're not in any hurry to get back, are you?'

I don't know if she's asking me or telling me. Either way she's right.

There's not many places you visit that, no sooner have you arrived, you know you that leaving will be a wrench. That's how I feel now. A sort of homesickness before I'm even out the door.

While Santiago is gone, Raffaella insists I try a cup of what looks like frogspawn and we continue the pictoral reminiscing – was that a stab of jealousy I experienced when she pointed out Santiago's first girlfriend?

I'm almost sorry when he returns because it is also the time to leave. As I stoop to hug Raffaella goodbye, my head lingers on her small shoulder

318

perhaps a little longer than etiquette decrees.

'You will return!' she predicts, seemingly sensing my reluctance to part.

'I hope so,' I smile as I accept a bundle of assorted leaves and linctuses from my dinky personal pharmacist. 'I'll probably need a cure for all this!' I tease as I wave farewell.

I would never have thought it was possible to get used to potholed roads – the dips and dents come so unexpectedly, but the dusty tracks awaiting us after the sodden river transfer almost seem to have their own bumpity-bumpity rhythm. I judder and shudder like I'm in a space shuttle simulator but instead of grimacing and cursing the lack of Tarmac, all my attention is on the passing fields and the hundreds of bony-hipped cattle a-grazing. These are extraordinary looking beasts – big dark doe-eyes, slim, elegant faces, long hare-like ears drooping downward, beautiful off-white fur taut across their gauntness. Santiago tells me they are a species that originated in India and well suited to the tropical climate here. They certainly couldn't look any more different to the hefty Fresians back home. The contrast makes me feel very 'abroad'. And then I see two young barefoot children riding a water buffalo beside a stream. It's the kind of image I only ever expected to see in a travel photography exhibition, never in real life. This, teamed with my recent experience with Raffaella, not to mention last night's turtles, reminds me how lucky I am to be here. What sights! What emotions! It hadn't even occurred to me that I was bogged down in Bath, or even if it did, it never dawned on me that there might be an alternative. Back then, if you had told me that a cluster of roadside cattle would hold me rapt, I would have thought you were crazy.

An hour or so along, we stretch our legs beside a banana plantation. It's amazing to see the fruit in its pre-stickered state and I feel like a kid on a field trip as Santiago explains how the huge bunches of bananas are run from the tree to the sorting/packing division by a pulley system operated by human runners. I'm just thinking how quaint this is when Santiago reveals that the men doing the running, though in their twenties and thirties, have the buckled spines of seventy-year-olds from propelling their weighty fare. Add to that the stories of banana workers poisoned by the pesticides and I think that Erin Brockovich has found her new cause. This situation truly needs highlighting and resolving. I make a mental note to make this a project for me and Ollie to work on when he comes out. He's great at arguing causes and doesn't lose his cool like I do.

A few minutes on, Santiago points to a plot of box-like houses. 'See the one set three back, the one with the blue curtains?'

I nod.

'That's my parents' house.'

My jaw drops. 'They work here? On the plantation?'

'Mmm-hmm.'

'This is where you grew up?'

'*Sí.*'

'How did you—' I stop myself for fear of offending him.

'Escape?' He predicts my choice of words. 'Education. A lot of extra reading. Wanting something else . . .'

'Gosh.' I'm humbled. He's really worked so hard to get to where he is today. No wonder he thought I had it easy with a dad who, when my café option fell through in Bath, summoned a replacement with a finger-click. I feel guilty when I think of how much time me and my friends back home waste coveting those who have more than us, moaning, 'it's all right for them' as if we're so deprived. Right now I feel totally indulged. Even a little ashamed.

As we near San José, Santiago calls ahead to the airline to check our flight possibilities.

'They don't think there's going to be any let-up in the fog for at least a couple more hours,' he grimaces. 'We might be better off hiring a car—'

'Or . . .'

'Yes?'

'Well, if we did have a few hours spare, I'd love to see the Teatro Nacional – Carla raved about it.' I hold my breath, feeling like a child asking for an extravagant treat.

But Santiago seems pleased that I'm taking an interest in the city's pride and joy and says he'll see if there are any tickets available for tonight's Orquesta Sinfónica Nacional.

This is such a contrast to my first wobbly day in San José. Three weeks ago I felt anxious and at odds, intent on keeping myself to myself, now I want to get involved. I know I am still an outsider but with Santiago by my side I'm an outsider with privileges. We do get tickets for the concert and what's more Santiago arranges for us to borrow a cocktail dress and a suit from his friends Joaquin and Carmen so we can look the part.

'Wow!' we gasp in unison as we step from their bathroom and bedroom respectively.

Santiago looks more striking than ever in a black suit with a white shirt and pewter-sheen tie. I can't help but reach out and smooth his shoulder fabric admiringly. In turn he makes me do a spin in Carmen's low-cut net dress with flared skirt and ruched waist. I've tied my hair up in a *Breakfast at Tiffany's* topknot bun to show off the faux-diamond drop earrings, which Santiago lightly jangles and he whisks up a stray wisp of my hair.

'And to think, a few hours ago we were in a swamp!' I laugh.

Santiago smiles and then extends his arm to me. 'Shall we?'

I know it's taboo and that nothing can or should happen until the winner of the café is announced – ten days and counting! – but as I place my hand on the crook of his jacket sleeve and head for the door, I decide to let myself believe that – for the next couple of hours at least – Santiago is my date.

26

Carla was right – the Teatro Nacional could easily be a transplant from Covent Garden with its ornately pronged cast-iron gates guarding a sculpted sand-stone façade and prized collection marble statues and elaborate frescoes, circa 1897.

'There's one particularly impressive room you have to see.' Santiago leads me up a staircase lined with the kind of paintings I expect to feature clouds and cherubs but instead depict straw-hatted planta-tion workers. 'This building was funded by coffee merchants,' he explains, as he steps aside so I can marvel at the grand salon.

Though the walls are an elegant duck-egg blue and the carpets a serene minty-sage, they are completely overpowered by baroque gilding – I have never seen more twiddly gold bits in my life. If you told me that this was the palace of the Prince and Princess of Costa Rica, I'd believe you.

Just standing in a room of such ostentatious

glamour has me feeling as though my gauzy knee-length dress has bloomed into a ballgown of shot satin and Santiago's suit appears to grow tails and a wing-collared shirt before my very eyes.

'We should probably take our seats . . .' Santiago guides me back down to the auditorium.

This is my first classical concert. The sheer grown-up-ness of it all makes me feel even more childlike. I watch with wide-eyed wonder as the orchestra files on – the strings, the wind section, the brass and percussion – gotta love those giant cymbals. Judging by the applause, the conductor seems to have the kudos of a lead singer, without making a sound.

There is a moment of expectation and stillness and then the first note – a misty strain of violin followed by a distant horn, the toot of a flute . . . Gradually the instruments awaken to Strauss's Blue Danube waltz, building momentum, surging and spiralling until I feel an entire ballroom of aristo-crats are spinning in my head. I can almost hear the swish of fabric as the ladies dip and turn, see the blur of the twinkling chandeliers as I too am swept along in the arms of some dashing fellow with tassled epaulettes.

It is nigh on impossible to keep my head from keeping time and I notice few in my row have full control over their feet as they tap jauntily along. This really is a full-body experience. Whereas most modern music tends to hit me in the hips, this is higher – making me almost light-headed. I recognise certain refrains from TV ads and occasional brushes with classical radio but nothing compares to the warmth and depth of being just a few feet from the instruments themselves – I feel completely enveloped by the dancing notes and with no lyrics to direct my thoughts, my mind runs wild . . .

I sneak a sideways glance at Santiago as they move on to Tchaikovsky's *Swan Lake* – it is as though all my feelings for him have been transformed into one audio experience: the initial curiosity, the twittery nerves, the threatening crash of cymbals just as we clashed, the lilting sway as we learned to work side by side, the enchantment of these past two days together, the yearning to know if he feels the same way . . . The conductor's wand appears to be attached to my heartstrings – tugging and jabbing and flicking to the point where I feel he might actually yank out my most vital organ altogether.

Yet all the while Santiago maintains a composed nobility. I try to match the dignity of his profile but I feel so brimming over it's all I can do to stay in my seat.

How come day-to-day life never feels this poignant or dramatic? Or rather it does – all the time! – but we suppress it, so bogged down with getting to work on time and negotiating the trolley at Sainsbury's that our hearts rarely get to take flight like this.

This is music worthy of so much more – music of fireflies and thunderstorms and forbidden kisses . . .

Santiago turns to me and mouths, 'Well?'

'It's wonderful,' I whisper back.

And then I smile to myself – always whispering, he and I . . . First at the turtles, now here. Whispering because we can't say what we want out loud?

With the climactic conclusion of 'Pomp and Circumstance' I finally understand all the raucous behaviour at Last Night of the Proms. The music is so powerfully rousing I feel positively punch-drunk. The musicians themselves must get such a high contributing to this majesty. It's almost enough to make me want to take up the tuba! Come the dizzying finale everyone is on their feet applauding and shouting 'Bravo!' and I can't help but turn and embrace Santiago.

'Thank you so much for making this happen!' I squeeze him tightly.

I feel his body relent momentarily as he hugs me to my core but then just as quickly he retreats. How have I managed to get a crush on the one cool-blooded Latino?

I take a deep breath and look at my shoes – well, Carmen's shoes – as I attempt to squish all my emotions back inside, but it's like trying to pack a duvet into a pizza box.

'It's okay,' I tell myself. 'If I can't let it all out now, I'll store it to use later.'

And yet . . . Filing out on to the street, seeing the illuminated faces of the other audience members, I can't help but wonder if I'm missing the point – I suspect the idea might be to live with this stuff on the outside.

With the fog still squatting stubbornly in the sky, we decide to hire a car and drive back to Manuel Antonio. Santiago knows the curves of the road and with little night-time traffic he says we can probably make it in three hours. Again I'm not in any hurry – there's something so intimate about night-driving, I'm loving the feeling that we're travelling in our own mobile cocoon.

As he drives, various opuses continue to swirl in my head. Who would have thought that I would enjoy my first symphony in Costa Rica? Who would have thought that I could be feeling what I'm feeling now for Santiago? Any ill will seems to be water under the bridge. Which is ironic as we have just pulled up short of one.

'Follow me,' he walks me to the centre. 'What can you see down there?' he shines his flashlight down to the river bed.

'Mud, water, bumpy logs.'

He smiles. 'Those bumpy logs? They're crocodiles.'

'What?' As Santiago lobs a fallen apple their way I

328

watch a dozen or so of them snap and swish and clamp their trap-like jaws. They are enormous. For a good five minutes I gawp at these corrugated brutes, figuring they could probably fit about three of me inside them and then use my hair to floss with.

As we return to the safety of the car I can't help but wonder if this is Santiago giving me an unconscious warning. As much as tonight has been conducive to romantic flights of fantasy, there is something holding me back from broaching the subject with him. And I suspect there's more to it than competition over the café. He really is the hardest man to read, ebbing and flowing more frequently than the tide. I think of Ryan, a more straightforward proposition altogether. But is he worthy of a concerto? I mean to ponder this further but the twists in the road all too soon rock me to sleep.

Every now and again I open my eyes to see that we are still climbing some steep, foliage-heavy road. When the car finally slows, I expect to find us in the villa driveway but instead we're at a fork in the road.

'Everything okay?' I ask.

'You need to get to bed, right?'

'No, I'm fine – I've been kipping!' I stifle a yawn and sit forward to try and identify the road. 'Did you want to check on the café?'

'Yes,' he smiles at my prediction. 'Is that cool?'

'Definitely! The hot chocolates are on me!'

Santiago grins appreciatively and curves to the right. And to think I was dreading returning – as we unlock the door and steal inside it feels like we are coming home. To our creation. I go to flick the light switch but he stops me.

'Let's keep it on the down-low, shall we?' He suggests as he hands me a candle.

'Okay,' I whisper, loving the secretive vibe. 'Take a seat, I'll be right over with the drinks.'

He heads straight for the hammock and lolls limbs splayed, patently exhausted, as I prepare the drinks to perfection – hot but not too hot to drink, with a frill of cream on top.

'There you go.' I hand him his mug. 'Thanks for doing all the driving.'

'My pleasure. Thank you for the company,' he says, sidling over so I can sit beside him.

'It worked out well, didn't it?' I settle into the crocheted cradle. 'I liked your granny.'

'She liked you too.'

'Did she really?' My mouth gapes.

Santiago laughs. 'Why do you find that so hard to believe?'

'I don't know.' I shrug. 'I guess I didn't think I made great first impressions with people named Barrientos,' I expand, still struggling with the pronunciation.

'That's not true!' he chuckles.

I raise an eyebrow.

'You made a great first impression with me. But then you started talking . . .'

'What?!' I gasp, switching around to bat him.

'Careful, you'll spill the drinks!' he cautions, looking at me so warmly I can't help but forgive him his impudence.

As we fall into a companionable silence watching the sea tiptoe ashore and then scurry back, I recall when I first saw Santiago's face framed in the downstairs window of my dad's house in Tamarindo, remembering how handsome I thought he was and how infuriating he became the second he opened his mouth. So I guess we're even.

'What exactly did my dad tell you about me before I arrived?' I wonder out loud.

I wait for a reply but none is forthcoming. 'San—' I quickly press mute – he's out for the count, bless him, baby zzzzzs wafting all around his head.

I lean across to remove the mug from his hand but he's got a firm grip and as I attempt to prise it from him, I inadvertently lever him on to me. Now what? I can't sit like this – a mug in each hand and a man in my lap!

'Um . . .' If I lean forward to put the mugs on the floor I'll upturn us both. I wonder if can make the table to my left? I stretch as far as I can without disturbing him but it's not far enough. There's nothing else for it, I drain both mugs and then set them to the side of me. Now where to rest my hands?

I place one on his back, nothing wrong with that. I let the other fall by my side. But within seconds it's oh-so-gently stroking his hair – so shiny and soft I feel my besottedness burgeoning. Despite the long day and lateness of the hour I suddenly feel zingingly awake, so excited to be able to finally touch him. But then it filters through to my brain that his eyes will not be flickering open any time soon. There will be no kisses tonight. But it doesn't matter. I can relax in the knowledge that when I wake up, he will be right there.

'*Sueños dulces*, Santiago,' I whisper as I let my eyes close. Sweet dreams . . .

27

I experience everything all at once – the fuzzy mouth, muzzy head, disorientation, squinty eyes and startlement that my dad, Kiki and Ryan are all staring at me. And Santiago.

Entwined. In broad daylight.

'I think someone needs an espresso!' Dad chortles.

'Did you lose the house keys?' Kiki wants to know.

'Did you get my messages?' asks an anxious Ryan.

I shake my head to everything but the offer of an espresso. 'My phone wasn't working in Tortuguero,' I tell Ryan as Santiago announces that he's going to dive in the ocean in lieu of taking a morning shower. It's so easy for men.

'But, since you've been back?' Ryan is still staring at me.

I can only half form a shrug – it hadn't even occurred to me to check.

'Dead battery,' is the best I can muster.

My dad hands me my coffee. I knock it back in one and then explain that I need to go back to the house to change. 'If someone could give me a ride . . .'

'Happy to!' Ryan offers me his arm.

'Allow me.' Dad steps in front of him.

'It's no problem, sir, I'd be glad to take her.' Ryan elbows his way back to the premier position.

'As would I.' Dad stands strong.

They face each other off until my dad intones, 'You wouldn't begrudge a father a little time with his daughter, would you?'

Ryan takes a step back.

Hmmm, there's something fishy going on here.

Once we're in the car, I wait for my father to offer an explanation but instead he makes casual enquiries about my trip to Tortuguero. I tell him it was amazing, unforgettable. Another world.

'And Santiago?'

I'm loath to let him see that I've come round to his way of thinking but quietly concede, 'He's a very special man.'

He really is. I'm just not sure exactly how that relates to me personally at the moment but I certainly have new-found respect and affection for him.

Dad nods sagely, then adds, 'I didn't realise that you'd invited Ryan . . .'

I try to deflect my embarrassment by looking out

of the window and mumbling, 'It was just a whim!'

'Apparently one of the snorkellers got into peril and his boat was diverted—'

'Whatever,' I cut him short. I'm still feeling very Zen, very untouchable. I don't want to think of what might have been. Or what might *not* have been, had he come.

For a moment there's no talking, just the sound of the car suspension being abused. Then Dad gives a cautious cough.

'Of course it's really none of my business what you do . . .'

Why would it be, you're just my father, I think to myself.

'. . . but I have to say I'm not 100 per cent sure about this Ryan chap, there's something a little shifty about him.'

'Shifty?' I chuckle. 'How so?'

'Well, he seems extremely taken with you—'

'Oh well then, there must be something seriously wrong with him.'

'No, no, that's not what I'm saying!'

'What then?' I huff. Why is coming back after a trip always such a downer? 'What shifty behaviour have you observed?'

Dad's brow furrows like a detective on duty. 'All yesterday he was asking questions about the things you like . . .'

Uh-oh, I see a lot of blackberries in my future.

'. . . and he seems very eager to get you alone tonight. Overly eager.'

'Go on.' I feel a twinge of nerves. I don't know if I'm ready to go one-on-one with him so soon after being with Santiago. Even though nothing happened between me and my co-worker, it doesn't seem right somehow.

'Well, I was suggesting dinner for the four of us at Barba Roja and he said he was hoping he might steal you away by himself.'

'Really? And what did Kiki have to say about that?' I ask, remembering that the trip to Tortuguero was originally designed by her to keep us apart.

'She seemed all for it,' Dad shrugs. 'Said we shouldn't stand in the way of true love.'

'She said that?' I gawp. Gosh. Ryan must have given her a serious talking to while I was gone. Or maybe she's just regained her senses, courtesy of an expensive gift from my father.

'The thing is, he wants to take you to the Makanda.'

'Anda . . . ?' I don't get the significance.

'Well, it's a very exclusive resort. The restaurant is extremely romantic – all the tables are set for two.' He gives me a look of undue significance.

'What exactly are you getting at?'

'I think Ryan's going to propose!' Dad blurts.

'WHAT?!' It's a good thing my dad is driving because I would have us upside-down in a ditch

right now. 'Have you lost your mind? We may have shared a few life-threatening adventures but I've spent a total of . . .' I do a speedy tot-up '. . . twelve hours with him!'

'Well, I knew I was going to marry Kiki the moment I laid eyes on her,' Dad pouts.

I quickly review my first meeting with Ryan: I suppose I was pretty struck by him, but wow to vow is quite a leap. Maybe I'd be more smitten if we hadn't broken the flirtation – the trip to Tortuguero seems to have de-tingled me. And yet apparently absence has made his heart go into warp drive. *Hold on! Hold on!* This is just Crazy Dad speculation! Frankly he must have employed a trampoline to jump to this kind of conclusion. I can't believe I'm buying into his insanity.

'Honestly, Dad, this is all very flattering but a little far-fetched.'

'All I know is that I overheard him and Kiki talking about Punta Islita – you know that's where we got married?'

'Yeees.' I roll my eyes. Not that place again.

'It sounded like they were making some pretty specific arrangements.'

'Well, it's not like he can go and marry me without me noticing, I do have a say in this!'

'And what are you going to say?' Dad's eyes beseech me.

'When?'

337

'When he proposes!' he hisses.

Jeez, I've never seen my dad so het up. This is fun.

'Tell me again why you don't like him?' I bait him further.

'So you're considering it!' he accuses, aghast.

'Dad, you're too young for this level of senility. I wish you could try and be clearer about what you so dislike about Ryan.'

'I just get the feeling he's not quite what he seems.'

'And what if someone had said that to you about Kiki?'

'What?'

'What if I'd met Kiki and said, "Don't marry her, Dad. She's a wrong 'un through and through."'

'Well . . .' he stumbles.

I raise an expectant eyebrow as he pulls into the driveway.

He switches off the engine, spends a good minute in contemplation and then mutters, 'I suppose I'll keep my opinions to myself then.'

I smile to myself as I step from the car.

It's a wonderful thing having a uniform – I can spend the time that I would have typically spent choosing an outfit on calling Ollie.

'So what do you make of all that?' I ask once I've brought him up to speed.

'Two nights and you've switched allegiances? What were you drinking?'

'Well, I did try this really weird concoction called *chan*, looks like frogspawn—'

'Let me get this straight,' Ollie huffs. 'You're done with Action Man Ryan and now see yourself and Santiago as a pair of Starbucks-crossed lovers?'

'Well . . .' I begin. I can see how this could come off a little fickle seeing as the last time we spoke I was actually considering forgoing my trip to Tortuguero to stay behind and get it on with Ryan. I never did get the chance to share with Ollie the sweet moments with Santiago, mostly because I felt I had to halt any brewing infatuation in the name of professionalism and general sanity. 'Ryan certainly has his appeal,' I explain. 'It just felt like something more with Santiago . . .' I'm sounding airy-fairy, even to myself.

Again Ollie sighs, wasting no time getting to the crux of the matter: 'You have no idea how Santiago feels about you but Ryan is back to being a sure thing.'

'Yes.' Sure thing to the nth degree if my dad's right about the proposal.

'I hate to sound like a risk analyst here but I need to point out that going for Santiago could be potentially ruinous at this juncture.'

My heart sinks.

'You know how he double-bluffed you over

Manuel Antonio being his number-one location choice for the coffee shop?'

'Ye-es.' I don't know if I like where this is going.

'Well, I'm not saying that he's toying with you but please keep in mind that he wants that coffee shop even more than you do.'

'How do you know that?'

'Because Costa Rica is his home, his life. You have other options.' He pauses. 'Look, I don't want to sound racist but from what I've been reading even Ticos themselves admit they're not the most scrupulous people when it comes to business.'

'Are you saying it's ingrained?'

'It is what it is. And he's Latin so there's going to be a element of charm involved . . .'

A fight breaks out within me – part of me is taking these truths on board, the other half is clinging to how I felt with Santiago on the beach and at the banana plantation and in the hammock . . . Could it all be part of a smokescreen to distract me? Is that why I can't sense what he's feeling, because he's deliberately hiding the less-than-savoury truth? Could he really be that ruthess? I've certainly been fooled by men before – so eager to perceive myself as the object of their affections that I see only what I want to see. I don't want to believe it but I can't rule out the possibility that I am being played again.

'The thing is, you've only got, what, a week until

340

your dad announces the winner?' Ollie jolts me back to the present moment.

'Eight days.'

'So do you think you could keep your knickers on till then?'

'Ollie!' I protest.

'I'm serious. Passion is all very well but this is your future we're debating. Best-case scenario: your feelings are a mirror image of each other's and you live happily ever after. Worst-case scenario: he screws you emotionally and financially. It's just not a worthwhile risk. Not until after the winner is announced.'

As ever, Ollie makes perfect logical sense. 'You're right. It just felt so—'

'Of course it did,' he cuts me off. 'You were at the symphony, for god's sake. Why do you think Richard Gere took Julia Roberts to the opera – it's all about stirring up the emotions.'

'But that was my idea!'

'That's not the point. Try a little dose of day-to-day before you start getting notions.'

'All right,' I sulk.

'And remember, he had you alone in a hotel room and he didn't try anything.'

'No, but maybe he was just being respectful . . .' I *so* sound like I'm fooling myself.

'Trust me, everyone looks like an angel with a halo of fireflies around their head.'

I look out the window. My dad is checking his watch, I should really hustle but I feel to even things up I should give Ollie the chance to be equally damning of Ryan. I'm surprised when he goes the other way.

'Well, you've got to at least have dinner with him.'

'You don't think Dad could be right about the proposal?' I fret.

'Well, anything is possible!'

'Noooo!' I could have sworn he was going to dismiss that out of hand.

'There are men out there who lose their minds over a redhead. He could be one of them.'

'Oh, Ollie!' I despair.

'Tell you what, I have a question for you,' he says, turning the tables.

'Yes?'

'Are you certain that you couldn't like the one who likes you back?'

I'm about to slump down on my bed overwhelmed by introspection when Dad calls, 'Ava, are you ready?'

'I've gotta go.'

'Okay. Just be careful about what you bite into tonight! And by that I mean food items that could have engagement rings buried within,' he clarifies before signing off.

On the way back to the café I wonder if I too have

342

certain traits ingrained in me – has my mother trained me to consider every man I spend five minutes alone with a potential husband? Is this 'Love the one you're with!' gone wild? Is it possible I'll say yes as a knee-jerk reaction, irrespective of my true feelings?

Mrs Ryan Sheen. Ava Sheen. Even considering my new name makes me nauseous. On the upside, I least I could pronounce that . . .

28

Throughout the day, I'm given to poignant reflections and wistful sighing – this time yesterday we were rummaging through Joaquin and Carmen's wardrobe, this time the day before we were ogling three-toed sloths – but already the vibe between me and Santiago has changed. I notice I'm the only one who's saying things like, 'Doesn't Wilbeth's new haircut remind you of the crested caracara we saw?' and, 'I wonder if we should start serving *chan*!' He's already moved on. Back to work.

Even after I'm done for the night I risk leaving Ryan dangling at our Mariposa meeting point by lingering on, hoping for a chance to be alone with Santiago so we can have a quiet moment to reconnect. But when I step outside and ask Wilbeth where he is, he tells me he's already gone.

I roll my eyes at my own silly expectations. What do I want from the man? Him to say, 'Don't dine with Ryan, let me cook you a fresh batch of *sopa de pejibaye*! Oh and by the way I don't mind if you win the café and I lose everything, I want all my girl's wishes to come true!'

I eye the dress I brought to change into. No great outfit dilemmas there, I really only have one posh frock with me and tonight would seem to be the night to bring it out. I step into the loo and step out in coral – plunging V-neck bodice with a swishy chiffon skirt. Gold earrings, gold shoes and a gold clutch bag with a trigger in the snap-frame that actually switches on a little light when you open it, illuminating the satin lining so you can see the contents – saw it on TV and couldn't resist. Of course this is great in a dark bar or club but out here with all the al fresco dining, I'll probably just end up with a bag full of bugs.

'Well, don't you look a tangerine dream!' Ryan greets me with a kiss.

'It's coral,' I mutter as I tuck myself on to the bar stool beside him at the Mariposa pool bar.

'Can I get you an aperitif or do you want to get going?'

I'm back on my feet in a trice. 'No, let's just get it over with.'

'Pardon?'

Did I just say that out loud? 'You know, the getting there, the ordering of the food – I'm starving!' I bluster.

Nerves are already getting the better of me. I know realistically there can be no proposal imminent, but the fact that I've even had that thought has me jittering all over the shop.

'It's just down the road here, are you happy to walk?'

I consider the very path that got me dusty and hyperventilating on my first day in Manuel Antonio and emit an unconvincing, 'Sure!' adding a self-preservation clause of, 'We can always get a taxi back. Right?'

'Yes we can. We'll probably need one later.'

What does he mean by that? Is he foreseeing an excess of booze? Me in a swoon from the proposal? Or just a pair of overly burdened bellies? My brain rattles with bothersome anticipation as we scuffle down the hill and instead of concentrating on where I'm walking, I subject him to a relentless twitter of small talk.

'So I wanted to explain about missing the flight,' he finally jumps in. 'You know how keen—'

'Eeeeekkkk!' I screech out loud as a bat does a hair-skimming fly-by. 'Oh my god, I think it touched my ear!'

As if encouraged by my reaction, a duo do a formation swoop and I spin round in a scrunch-faced fluster until Ryan grabs my hands and soothes, 'Ava, it's just dinner. Relax.'

I inhale at his insistence and then exhale at

length. I suspect he may have clocked my nerves.

'Okay?' he says as my breathing steadies.

I nod my reply, cursing my father for having passed his crazies on to me. The man said it: *It's just dinner . . .* There's nothing to worry about.

'Here we are.' Ryan motions for me to take the first step on to the hotel driveway.

Makanda-by-the-Sea. Couple Central.

It's curious how strangely it sits with me to be considered a couple. I don't so much see my exes as previous relationships, more a series of false starts. I expect to be directed to the novice basement of the hotel whereas no doubt Ryan would go straight to the penthouse. He has such a 'knowing' quality to him, a quiet confidence that he could have any woman he desired. Does that make him a bad person? After all, he just knows what he knows and he does have a point – now that I've calmed down enough to actually look at him, I see that tonight he's looking extra honeyed and strokeable with smooth-shaved skin and his typically tousled hair swept clean away from his face so that not a millimetre of his manly bone-structure is obscured. I don't think I've ever really admired a man's forehead until this moment. His looks so sheeny and strong I can almost feel the sleek skin of his browbone beneath my fingertips.

'I take it that the restaurant is alfresco?' I say as he

directs me away from the main building and down some foliage-shrouded steps.

'Correct.'

'That really is a misnomer here, don't you think? At least, I hear fresco and think "fresh". Al sauna would be more appropriate for these climes.'

My hair wilts a little more as I discover that – as if there weren't enough moisture in the air – we're dining poolside. I don't know why the humidity keeps coming as a surprise to me. I need to make a concerted effort to switch off my inner thermostat and revel instead in the magical scene before me – a damson-draped table for two bathed in reflective aqua-essence light set against a backdrop of woven vines and dainty flowers.

The waiters draw back our chairs with a certain reverence – 'Ah welcome, ye chosen loved ones' – that makes me feel even more of an interloper. Once seated I use my menu as a shield so Ryan can't see me mop my upper lip then, despite such tastebud-activating items as mahimahi in a sorrel-and-starfruit sauce and rack of lamb with a jalapeño glaze, I find my eyes straying to the long, cool pool. It would just be so much more comfortable if we were semi-submerged. I wonder if we might be able to request a shuffle three feet to the right? I mean, swim-up pool bars are all the rage, is there really any reason not to extend that pleasure to eating? It would be so very high fashion to sit there with dress skirts billowing out in the water, him with his shirt wetly contouring his body. I can just picture floating lily pads as place mats and the gentle aroma of chlorine mingling with the jasmine rice. On the downside I suppose there's a risk that unattended napkins would simply float away and the pool would end up looking like a fish tank that hadn't been cleaned in a year.

'Ava?'

'Yes?' I look up at Ryan.

'Everything all right? You seem a little distant.'

'I'm just a little overwhelmed by the choice – everything sounds so delicious.' I stare fixedly at the menu.

'Would you like me to order for you?'

I blink back at him. That has always seemed such an alien concept to me – how can you possibly know my tastes and more to the point what I'm in the mood for? Besides which, are you implying that I am incapable of making my own decisions?

'Yes, that would be lovely,' I hear myself submit. Well, everything does sound good and it saves me having to use a brain that is so thoroughly pre-occupied. 'You will say, "The lady will have the blah-blah," won't you?'

'Of course,' he obliges, ordering me the Costa Rican trout with almond dill pesto and for himself, the Chilean salmon in a mustard balsamic marinade, both with a *mariscos* soup starter. 'I always

349

like to eat fish when I'm at the coast,' he tells me. 'Oh and a bottle of champagne,' he calls after the waiter.

'Something to celebrate?' He scoots back, eyes glow lasciviously. Do the newly-engaged tip better? I wonder.

'Every moment with this woman is a celebration,' Ryan replies.

Oh, he's good. Nice deflection.

'Actually I wanted to make it up to you for missing the trip to Tortuguero,' Ryan adds, after the waiter has gone.

'No need!' I chime, perhaps a little too emphatically. 'Really, it's fine.' I try to soften my response.

'Nevertheless, I was really miffed that I missed the chance to go away with you. I have to confess I was a little bit jealous of Santiago.' He gives me a meaningful look, as though he's fishing for some kind of reassurance. I guess he wants to hear some dismissive remark but I can't supply one. Whatever arguments are pending over the café, that time with Santiago will always be too precious for me to taint with idle slurs.

Ryan continues his prompting. 'He's an attractive guy . . .'

'Do you want me to put in a good word for you?'

He snorts a laugh. 'You're a tough crowd, you know that?'

'Am I?'

He studies me for a second and then nods. 'I do find you somewhat hard to read.'

There's a lot of it about, mate.

'Maybe that is why you find me oh-so-intriguing,' I tease, tilting my head coquettishly.

'Maybe,' he muses.

For a millisecond I feel like I have the upper hand. But one sip of champagne and I blow it by announcing, 'You know, I think people who are easy to read are people who are clear in their own minds and thus sending out unmuddled messages to the world. I'm probably hard to read because you are contemplating a matrix of confusion.'

'What do you have to be so confused about?' He looks perplexed.

You. Santiago. My flick-flacking emotions, I want to say. I mean, really, just how did not one but two males sneak under my skin after such careful abstinence?

'I guess I have a lot of coffee-shop data distracting me right now,' I cop out, taking another sip of bubbly.

Ryan leans closer, invading my half of the table. 'I've got a lot on my mind too,' he confesses, reaching for my hand. 'But I'm pretty clear on one thing.' And with that he leans the extra distance until his lips meet mine, smooching me with a total come-hither kiss.

All I can think is, 'Don't make me have sex with

351

Tarzan!' But then the waiter arrives and Ryan is obliged to lean back to allow our starters to be set before us. (Surely that's a sackable offence here – interrupting a kiss!)

While Ryan tucks in with gusto, I'm still experiencing stun-gun symptoms.

'I thought you were hungry,' he says, nodding for me to get started.

'Mmm,' I murmur, giving my soup a thorough swish-through to check there are no diamond rings chipping at the china base. It's fortunate that he's ordered fish for my main course as I will be able to hunt through every layer on the pretext of checking for bones.

'So how is it?' Ryan seems eager for his selection to be approved.

I raise my spoon to my lips and take my first slurp – no metallic aftertaste, a good sign. I take another but realise almost straight away that I've lost my appetite. There's a good reason men spring proposals upon women – my internal organs appear to have knotted together in some kind of macramé design, no longer interested in the basic function of accommodating food.

I set down my spoon and take another sip of champagne.

'Don't you like it?'

'Just a bit hot,' I excuse my delay tactics. 'But otherwise very tasty.'

'You tasted pretty good yourself.' He chews his lip as he lowers his lids to study my mouth.

There is something fully carnivorous about this man. I suppose Tarzan himself was most likely a vegetarian – he couldn't really eat meat cos the animals were his friends – that would be like me chowing down on Ollie just because I got to the M&S food hall after closing time.

'Ava. You've gone again.' Ryan tries to bring me back into focus.

'Sorry,' I apologise, reaching for a sobering sip of water.

For the duration of the main course I manage to stay with the programme, though I do have a small coronary when he scoots back his chair and drops to his knees – but it turns out he's merely dropped his napkin.

'So listen, I suppose really I should have asked your father first, but I decided it would be more fun as a surprise . . .'

My heart does an emergency stop: *It's begun! The proposal has begun!*

'. . . I've gone ahead and booked the Punta Islita!' he fanfares.

Huh? Hasn't he missed a stage? Isn't there supposed to be a question beginning with 'Will you?'

'I hope you don't think it's too presumptuous?'

353

Before I can answer a categorical *YES*, he continues, 'I mean he liked it enough to get married there so I think he'll approve.'

'What about me?' I want to scream. Why is everyone so intent on pleasing my father?

'I've invited Santiago, obviously.'

Oh my god! What must he be thinking? No wonder he left early.

'Is there anyone else you think should be there?' Ryan queries, oblivious to my vexation.

I can't believe my ears – try my mum and Ollie for starters! What is it with this insane rushing?

'Um. Ryan,' I begin, deciding I am going to have to be firm and direct with him. 'Don't you think this is all a bit too soon?'

'Well, I know he and Kiki were just there a matter of weeks ago but they seemed to like it so much.'

I can't keep it in any longer. 'The way you're talking, this whole thing sounds more about them than us!' I blurt.

He gives me a quizzical look. 'Well, it is your father's birthday we're talking about.'

'What?'

'Next Wednesday. He's going to be sixty. You did know that?'

Oh god! No I didn't. To me next Wednesday was all about announcing the new manager of Café Tropicana. Of course it's his birthday, I should have known better – there never was a proposal. It was all just my dad putting two people together and supplying his own confetti. I can't believe I fell for his theory. I am going to murder him. Twice!

'I've been trying to think of a way to thank him for hooking me up—' He stops then smiles, 'Oh I see, you thought—'

'No, I didn't!' I screech.

'You thought I was taking you to Punta Islita to make up for Tortuguero.'

'No—' I protest. Hold on. That's a lot better than the truth. 'Well, yes . . .' I give a shy faux grimace.

'Oh, Ava, don't you see that's all part of my wicked plan!' he reaches under the table this time, to caress my knee. 'Although Kiki has advised me that we should get separate rooms because she doesn't think your father is quite at the stage where he sees me as son-in-law material!'

'Son-in-law! Hahaha! You're so funny! *As if!* Hahaha.' Take it down a notch, woman! I scold myself, looking wildly around for the waiter – the grilled tropical fruits with a Grand Marnier sauce sound lovely but I need to order a portion of ice cream just to slap on the back of my neck. It's just too darn hot!

In lieu of slathering myself in mint gelato (I've suddenly gone off pistachio) I take myself off to the loo – which is actually a delightful wooden hut with floating candles and exotic flowers. I soothe my

355

frazzled state by staring at the soft flickering flame as I run my wrists under the cold tap. This is good news! I assure myself. I never wanted him to propose in the first place. It was all too ridiculous. Of course it's nice to feel wanted and he does want me, which is nice, but truthfully I just don't have the time for this arch romance. As Ollie reminded me today, I've got a coffee shop to win – he just got the primary enemy wrong. Santiago has already tuned me out, I can feel it. Now the greatest potential distraction is coming in the form of Ryan. It's time to get a grip – I've already let one day slip mooning over Santiago, I can't be doing the same with Ryan tomorrow. Business first. At least for the next eight days. Got that?

I give an assertive nod to my own reflection before I return to the table.

Unfortunately, while I've decided to simmer down, Ryan has become even more amorous in my absence, apparently excited by the fact that we are now just a taxi ride away from his bed.

I hear Ollie's question: 'Can't you be into the one who's into you?' and though some small part of me wants to succumb to the kisses he's plying my neck with as we slide into the car, I fear that it would be more about blocking out the rejection from Santiago than celebrating any kind of electric attraction between us. Besides, if the frog-splat night is anything to go by Ryan is not a slow and caressing kind of lover and I'm not in the mood to be jiggled around.

So when Ryan reaches over to pay the cab driver I halt his hand and say, 'I've got it – I'm going to take this on to the villa.'

'You're not coming up?' He looks scandalised.

'It's been such a romantic night, I just want to savour—'

Before I can complete my sentence his lips are upon mine, doing his darnedest to ignite a sexual spark in me. 'Let's keep the romance going,' he husks in my ear, sliding his hand along my thigh.

'How could you turn him down?' I hear my friend Danielle spluttering. 'I thought you said he was gorgeous?'

'He is,' I'd confirm.

'But you just didn't fancy him?'

The truth is I do feel some kind of primal attraction but it doesn't have the poignancy of what I feel for Santiago, however woefully one-way that may be. (Any reciprocity – imagined or otherwise – only seems to exist when Strauss is playing.) I feel conflicted but the fact is, this is not a one-time shot with Ryan – as urgent as he may consider the situation, I can say no tonight and not have blown things entirely. Yes, he'll be a little miffed now but tomorrow is another day.

So, after years of obliging men for fear of peeving them, I finally take heed of the phrase 'If in doubt, *don't!*' and tell him, oh-so-sweetly, 'No!'

29

The next morning I wake up glad for the second time this week that nothing happened with the guy from the night before. I can face Santiago without feeling sleazy, even if I do catch him looking past me as I emerge from my room to check that I'm not leaving a certain someone in my bed.

He's on his mobile phone for the duration of the journey into work so I don't get to gauge his mood, although the fact that he's chosen to talk to someone else probably speaks volumes. This trend continues for the rest of the week. I guess he's made a decision not to mix business with pleasure too. It certainly makes it easier for me not to moon over him – nothing zaps your fantasies quicker than spending time with the man you're fantasising about, and having him behave like you don't even exist. I tell myself it's a good thing I get this reality check – if I'd been left unattended for a week, I would have started to believe that we had something special, something that could actually be parlayed into a quality relationship.

Instead we sidestep and 'scuse-me' and make all work-related exchanges without eye contact. I realise there is a small child within me that has her arms outstretched and is longing to be picked up and cuddled but, once again, I'm asking the wrong man.

When I do first see my father, he seems so relieved that Ryan didn't propose that I suspect the reason I've remained unengaged all these years is because he willed it to be so. Mind you, when he learned that Ryan had arranged a birthday trip for us all to Punta Islita, he told me that maybe he wasn't so bad after all.

'I was starting to get the impression that he was on the make,' my dad confided on one of his daily snoopings. 'But now I see he gives as well as receives.'

'So just how much giving and receiving is going on?' Ollie asks me on day seven of Mission Let's Take it Slow.

'Not so much,' I admit. 'In a nutshell, I've seen Ryan three nights out of six and two of those were spent with Dad and Kiki.'

'What was he doing on the other three?'

'I don't know, it was me that opted out – we've decided to try to tap the sunrise/early-bird market – you know, the people who want to tour the park

360

before it gets too sweltering, others who are just making their way home after an all-nighter – and that's meant 5.30 a.m. starts.' I yawn at the mere thought of it. I am truly knackered, working seventeen-hour days is taking its toll. It's also a great excuse for keeping Ryan at arm's length.

'I'll be able to give you my full attention once I know which way things are going to go at Café Tropicana,' I told him.

'So no sex.' Ollie cuts to the chase.

'No sex,' I confirm. 'It's weird, he struck me as such a horny little bugger at first but now he seems to accept that his loins are being put on ice. In essence we're just hanging out.'

'And how's that working for you?'

I heave a sigh as I take a moment to give that question due ponder. My mind is so preoccupied with the café announcement scheduled for tomorrow that I've just been blundering on, sparing myself the usual over-analysis of every action.

'Well, you know how in the beginning you just want to devour the person – you're desperate to touch them and they seem to represent the potential fulfilment of all your dreams but as you talk and listen and watch them, those feelings change.'

'With any luck you desire them all the more.' Ollie suggests.

'Yes, I suppose it can happen that way. Or you realise that perhaps you weren't quite as compatible as you hoped. And your heart sinks a little and that affects your libido. That's my theory anyway. Not that this experience is exclusive to Ryan by any means. It's just that usual sense that something is missing . . .'

Typical really – I want the intimacy I felt with Santiago with Ryan, and for Ryan's desire for me to transfer to Santiago.

'I think you'll find that's the human condition – we all hope to fill the void but all solutions are temporary,' Ollie opines. 'I saw Barbra Streisand interviewed on TV saying something about that the other day. She said, "What we resist, persists!" We try in vain to fill that emptiness when the trick is to accept that you're always going to feel like that.'

'How depressing!' I wail.

'Actually, she felt the opposite. Apparently if you accept that feeling as part of life, it sets you free.'

'Really?' I frown. 'I'll bear that in mind but for now I have to go – I actually have a date with Ryan – he's taking me snorkelling . . .'

'In the middle of the day?'

'Dad's given me and Santiago two hours off so he can do his final assessment without us giving him the evil eye.'

'Well, don't write off Ryan just yet,' Ollie advises.

'I won't. I get the feeling that he's going to unleash himself in Punta Islita.'

'Oho! Somebody's going to get some—'

'He's here.'

'Oh. Okay.'

'Bye.'

'*Adiós*.'

To give Ryan credit where it's due, he has introduced me to some fun new experiences. Not that I'm planning on zip-lining or riding ATVs again any time soon, but the snorkelling proves to be absolutely enchanting. In spite of the fact that Kiki has invited herself along. Again. I suppose it's to be expected really – Dad's working, we're more her age, Ryan is one of her best friends . . . I still don't feel entirely comfortable around her but her weird competitiveness seems to have subsided. She even tells me at one point that Ryan and I make a cute couple. It's not true, but I appreciate the good intention behind the lie.

We ride into the blue in a small speedboat, blustered by a welcome breeze, then curve around some rocks and cut the engine. Ryan kits me out with flippers, mask and mouthpiece. At first I want to gag and reject the plastic but Ryan keeps my mind focused by instructing me to breathe noisily in and out to get me used to using only my mouth. He then edges me over to the little silver ladder. With my flippers feeling like clown shoes I misjudge every step and trip and flounder in the most ungainly manner. When I do finally crash into the sea I perform an anxious doggy-paddle until Ryan is beside me, calming me sufficiently to put my face in the water.

Knowing that I will be viewed from every angle I opted for surf shorts and a tankini but Kiki has gone for a teeny pink bikini so that every inadvertent glimpse in her direction feels like an underwater peep show.

At first I try to keep track of the amount of times Ryan looks in her direction but then I can't really blame him, she does look amazing with the translucent glow from the sunlit water chasing over her skin. Besides, as soon as I spy my first school of fish all insecurities are forgotten. I follow them skitting around the rocks spying electric-blue surgeonfish, fluorescent-lemon and black barber-fish and a hundred tiny slips of silver moving as one, switching and dipping and wiggling with flawless synchronisation. Watching them is so mesmerising I lose all sense of time and direction, not to mention track of Ryan and Kiki.

Bobbing my head up to see if I can see them, or even the boat at this point would be a start, I feel a sudden tug on my leg. It's a major relief to see the hand on my ankle belongs to Ryan as opposed to some sunken pirate and yet I'm slightly bewildered as to why he's holding a yellow ball beneath the surface. He points exaggeratedly at it until I click – it's a pufferfish! All puffed up! He motions for me to touch it – I misjudge the distance between us and despite its prongs my finger dents its rubbery exterior.

'Nmmhmygd!' my words distort down the mouthpiece and tubing. This is one of the coolest things I've ever seen. His startled little eyes, his pouty little mouth, his big inflated body! As soon as Ryan releases him he zooms off like a balloon releasing its air. I give a thumbs-up sign to show my approval and then he's off again.

In some ways I like Ryan's independence and the freedom it gives me but it doesn't feel like we're sharing the experience like it did with Santiago and the turtles. Oh Santiago and the bloody turtles! I curse myself for having another unwarranted pang. Just be in the moment! I instruct myself as another shimmering wonder catches my eye.

When I do finally cease my horizontal sightseeing I'm surprised to find Kiki and Ryan back in the boat enjoying a beer and waiting on me.

'Whenever you're ready!' Ryan teases.

I take him at his word, swimming over to the boat then pulling off my heavy flippers and slinging them on board, relishing the sensation of the cool water on my now bare feet and doing a circuit before I finally pull myself on board.

On the way back to the shore I experience a novel sensation – I'm actually shivering in Costa Rica! And it's not just because I'm wet and the sea wind is brisk. Part of it is the realisation that by now Dad will have made his decision as to who he will ordain owner of Café Tropicana. Yes he will probably go over the figures one more time when he gets back to the hotel, maybe spend the evening mulling over the data, reassessing each and every factor, debating our pros and cons with Kiki, but deep down, *he knows*. I feel nauseous at the thought. Not least because I can't see myself getting Kiki's vote.

Santiago probably thinks I'm palling around with her, ingratiating myself, but in reality we barely exchange a word when we're together. It's quite a contrast to how chatty and keen to bond she was initially. Ollie's theory is that she's still embarrassed about her earlier competitive behaviour regarding Ryan – she's realised she was making a fool of herself and consequently feels a little shamed and ill at ease whenever I'm around. In turn Ryan seems to make Santiago particularly uncomfortable – whenever he comes into the café Santiago rams the plates into the dishwasher with undue gusto, talks a little bit louder to whoever he happens to be stood next to and always seems to infer that wherever Ryan has chosen to stand to have a word with me, is entirely in the way and obstructing the flow of customers. I suspect he fears that if I won the café, I would replace him with Ryan. But that's not true. Exposed chest hair near the cakes just wouldn't meet my hygiene standards.

30

'Your back!' Santiago looks startled.

I look at my watch. 'Yup, right on time.' Jeez, anyone would think he'd planned a shark attack and was counting on never seeing me again.

'No, your back. Ava, it's absolutely scorched.'

'What?' I twist around but obviously to no avail.

Santiago holds open the door to the bathroom. I turn on the light and shuffle backwards to check my reflection. Oh my god, I'm puce! Livid, raging rouge. Santiago points down to the backs of my calves.

'I'm afraid it got you there too. Didn't you put any sunscreen on?'

'Yes! But clearly not enough.' Now I come to think of it I do feel a bit taut and tender. I do the scratch test, whisking a nail across the surface of my skin. Absolute agony. I am indeed scorched. 'It's okay, my uniform will cover it.' I go to close the door and get changed but Santiago protests, 'You must treat it now or it will get so much worse.'

'I haven't got time to go back to the house,' I protest.

'Then we will have to do it here.' He sets down the sack of coffee beans he's carrying. 'I'll get some aloe vera.'

'Okay,' I shrug, rotating my shoulder blades – ouch, ouch – then reach back and gasp at the heat radiating from my skin. This is bad. But not entirely so – this is the most Santiago has spoken to me all week and it feels so good to be interacting with him using whole sentences again.

'Oh my god, I thought you were going to the chemist!' I gawp as Santiago returns, not with a green tube but an actual spiky prong from an aloe vera plant.

'It's pure, it's better,' he says motioning for me to move along so he can join me in the bathroom and close the door.

'Oh no, that's okay, I'll manage,' I tell him, suddenly overwhelmed at the prospect of being in a confined space with him. Having been so long ignored, I'm just not prepared for this intensity of attention.

'You won't be able to reach—'

'I'll get Milena to do it.'

'Forget it. Her surfer beau just came in, you'll get no sense from her for the next hour.'

Any more resistance and I'll just seem uptight or ungrateful.

'Should I . . .? I ask, pulling at my top.

'I'll look away.'

I quickly whip it off and then grasp it to my front, making sure that my boobs are thoroughly covered. 'Okay!' I cringe. This is so embarrassing.

I hear some preparatory snapping and scraping and then feel two hands lubricated by a jellylike substance sliding over my back. Even though his touch is featherlight and there is a brief cooling sensation, my back is too sore to find the physical sensation pleasurable. And yet. There's something about knowing that Santiago's hands are gliding over my bare back that has my mind in a swoon.

As I take a breath my eyes gleam with emotion – I have been so longing for some contact with him. I may be tender on the outside but this feels good on the inside.

'You'll need to let it dry for a few minutes before you put your clothes on,' he advises.

I can't turn round. I feel like I'll just fall into him and he won't be able to hug me back cos I'm all burnt and sticky.

'Let me just do your legs while I'm here.'

He drops down and smoothes his palms over my calves. I actually shudder in response. It's not often a man touches the back of your legs. The experience seems new and oh so personal.

369

'I saw a pufferfish today!' I announce, trying to take my mind of the procedure.

'Really? They're crazy, aren't they? You know they contain a toxin that is a thousand times more deadly than cyanide.'

'I touched it!' I freak.

'It's okay. It's mostly in the internal organs. You need a very skilled chef to prepare that fish.'

'People eat them?' I gasp.

'Japanese delicacy. There you are, all done.' He returns to an upright position.

'Thank you,' I quaver.

I hear the door close behind me and sit down on the loo. I've tried so hard to follow Ollie's advice and divert any and all feelings to Ryan, but there's a stubborn part that is still so attached to Santiago. Something as slight as him slathering me with goo gives me hope. But am I fooling myself? He simply did the decent thing, why am I trying to read more into that?

I give my back one last look – oh that's so very attractive. I try to put my bra on but it feels like it's made of cheese-slice wire so I have to go au naturel under my shirt, a fact Ryan picks up on straight away when he comes by to pick me up.

'Heyyy, is that for me?' he leers at my chest.

'No, I burnt my YOUCH!' I spring away from him as his hand rounds my shoulder.

'Ava!' he yelps in return.

'Oh I'm sorry!' I've just spilt espresso all down his beige linen trousers.

I look up for the cloth and Santiago throws it to me with a satisfied smirk, noting, 'You need to work on your aim!' – he can see I missed Ryan's groin by a few centimetres.

'I'm going to have to change now before we—'

'Actually . . .' I interrupt. 'About tonight – my back is really sore and wearing anything at all just aggravates it. I need to lie down, on my front, and let the air get to it.'

'I can do that.'

'What?'

'I can rub a little lotion in.' He goes to reach for me but I squirm away.

'Ryan, this isn't a little flush of pink.' I expose some violent bubbling skin to prove my point.

'Jesus! Woman!' he shrinks back, repulsed.

'It's not contagious,' I assure him.

'No. But, yeah, I get it. You need to just chill.'

'That I do,' I confirm.

'So. What? I'll just see you at the airport tomorrow?'

Now there's a turnaround. 'If I decide to show!' I torment him.

'Hey now don't try and get your own back! Punta Islita is going to be paradise, I promise.'

'I'll be there,' I tell him. Not least because my dad has decided that is where he'll be revealing the name of the new manager of the Café Tropicana. Presumably to put sufficient distance between us and the café so the loser won't be tempted to trash, loot or torch the place in a fit of pique. Actually 'pique' wouldn't come close to how I'd feel if I lost this place. I've never put so much of myself into a property before – my flat in Bath was all hand-me-downs and impulse purchases but with the café everything is on purpose!

Whatever the result, I'm proud of myself. Proud of all I've learned, how hard I've worked, I've even come to love the early mornings and taken to sleeping with the curtains open so I can get the full benefit of the sunrise when I first open my eyes.

To lose this – I swallow down a lump in my throat – I can't even imagine how I might feel.

'You're in pain, aren't you?' Santiago sounds genuinely concerned as he steps beside me.

'I'm okay,' I lie.

'If you're coming home, I could put another layer of aloe on later.'

It's only then I realise he's talking about my back. 'Thank you, that would be great.'

'Are you ready to go now?' he asks.

I take a last look around the café – there is nothing more to be done. Dad has made his judgement and Wilbeth and Milena are fully primed for our two-day leave. I nod and get to my feet, ready to follow Santiago out.

'Hey, your mobile!' I pick it up off the counter and hand it to him. He slips the phone into his bag and his bag into the boot of the car. For the first time this week he doesn't seem to be in any hurry to be speaking to someone else.

As I open the passenger door I can't help but smile at the prospect of a night with Santiago, only to have my face contort to a grimace the second my back touches the seat. I have to spend the whole of the journey tilted forward, like I'm willing myself to be projected through the windscreen.

'I'm sorry you're hurting so much,' Santiago sighs.

'Don't be – you're not the one who burnt me, you're the one who's making it better,' I assure him.

And then I blush, turning my face fuchsia to match my back in anticipation of his hands on my naked skin once again.

When it comes to it, he decides to apply both healing aloe gel and a rich cream to soften and supple so I get double the pleasure/pain.

'Okay, you let that work its magic, I'll get us some dinner.'

He returns less than five minutes later with a glass of wine and a large envelope.

'A little appetiser?' I tease, still flat on my tummy.

'It's actually something I got for you in Tortuguero but forgot to pass on.' He looks a little shy as I prop myself on my elbows so I can open it. 'I was sorting out my case for Islita and—'

'Oh Santiago!' I gaze up at him. 'You adopted a sea turtle for me!'

'Anyone can do it,' he tries to sound matter-of-fact as he tells me that I'll also be getting a quarterly newsletter, but he's not fooling me.

'You've named her Ava,' I breathe.

'I need to check on dinner—' He's out the door before I can say another word.

I prop the certificate on the headboard so I can look at it lying down then read every word out loud – 'Sea Turtle Survival League. A programme of the Caribbean Conservation Corporation. "Together we can ensure a future for our friends of the sea." Scientific name – *Chelonia mydas*, tag number 94211.' I touch the parchment picture – I can't believe there's an actual green turtle out there called Ava! What an amazing gift!

I feel so content in this moment that I expel a luxuriously long breath. And when I breathe in again, it's morning.

I'm now lying on my back with the sheet barely covering me. My first thought is, 'Oh god, I hope I wasn't exposed when Santiago returned to tell me that dinner is served! My second thought is, *Aaagghhhhh!*

The rich cream has acted as a kind of paste, sticking me to the bed sheet and as I sit upright it

374

rips away from my skin like I'm having my back waxed.

'Ava, are you okay?' Santiago is at the door in his pyjama bottoms.

It's a good thing my eyes are welling with tears and thus blurring my vision. I tell him I'm fine, explaining what just occurred. He walks over to the bed and sits beside me, tracing a finger over my back with a whisper-light touch.

'It's blistering,' he sighs. 'Pretty soon that's going to start itching. Try to resist.'

'Resist!' I mutter back as his bare shoulder touches mine. Resist! I tell myself as my chest heaves beneath the sheet and my head feels as if I've just spun round ten times on the spot. All I can think is, if someone walked in now we would so look like a couple – both naked from the waist up and ruffled of hair, sitting in the same corner of bed. I want to freeze time and stay here until I find the courage to tell him how I feel.

But of all the words we could speak, we both choose the same one. The one we know best.

'Coffee?'

31

Taking advantage of the fact that we're up so early, Santiago and I stop off at the café to prepare a birthday platter for my father and manage to deliver it to him while he's still in bed – this may not compete with the extravagance of Ryan's deluxe mini-break to Punta Islita, but we have the element of surprise on our side and there is something of the sense of Christmas morning as we sit at the foot of Dad's bed joining him and Kiki in sipping hot aromatic coffee and flaking pastry between the hotel sheets.

Ryan is mercifully still sleeping in his room and continues his kip just as soon as we board the plane. I can't deny that I'm relieved – with Santiago sat directly behind us, I didn't want to feel like I was putting on a show. Even now the back of my neck feels excruciatingly self-conscious. I want to turn and talk to Santiago but the engine noise is tough competition. Dad tries to share some facts – for example, the tiny town of Islita has a population of just 110, most of whom work for the hotel where we'll be staying – but the elaborate mimes required to convey this information are too exhausting for everyone concerned so we fall silent for the rest of the short flight, leaving me free to ponder my destiny.

There is definitely something about being in a plane that gives you a different perspective – it's so easy to get attached to our earthly roots, it's good from time to time to fly above them and realise that the world spans out for miles and miles in every direction, as opposed to beginning and ending where you stand. For a moment I am spared the feeling that my happiness depends upon my father's decision.

'We're here!' Dad cheers, clearly delighted to be back at what he probably considers his fifth home.

I look out of the window at what could be aptly termed an airfield, with the emphasis on field. There is a landing strip, that is to say an expanse of dusty grass, but other than that there's simply a wooden picnic table and a couple of padded tree-trunk armchairs beneath a raffia shelter. If it weren't for the wall mural and butterfly mosaic I'd suspect they'd just rustled up the 'arrivals lounge' an hour prior.

As we claim our luggage direct from the plane, I

find myself distracted by some movement in the adjacent bushes. I'm still awaiting my armadillo sighting but the foliage appears to be ruffling way above ground level. So I don't think now's the time. I step closer and squint. Whatever species it is, there's more than one. My heart is beginning to pound. What if we are suddenly stampeded or set upon? I know this isn't Africa but there are ocelots and flick-knife-pawed jaguars and I've recently learned that the tapir is in fact akin to a small rhino without armour, growing up to six foot—

'Señorita?' The driver who has been sent to meet us seems to sense my wild imaginings and casually identifies the source of the rustling – other hotel guests.

'Is that what people do for fun around here? Hide in the bushes and watch planes come in to land?'

He laughs as he shakes his head. 'They are observing the howler monkeys in the trees.'

'Really?'

'You want to take five minutes to look before I take you to the hotel?' This time he addresses the group.

Everyone is keen so he leads us down the leafy bank to where the undergrowth mats at the base of the tall cacao trees. We nod respectfully to the other guests, crowding around a large telescope on a tripod. Even before I take my turn to peer down the

378

lens I can clearly see clumps of fuzzy black monkeys high in the canopy. I count at least ten, one of whom is languishing on his side as if waiting for someone to feed him grapes and another who is swinging joyfully from the branch by its extra-long black tail. I look around for someone to share my delight with – Dad is wrapped around Kiki who has her eyes trained skyward, Ryan is checking out the teenage girl in hot pants and Santiago is . . . looking straight at me.

'Isn't this cool?' I gasp, feeling a twang of déja vu as our eyes meet – for a moment it feels like we're back in Tortuguero . . .

'Amazing,' he concurs. 'I could watch them for hours.' He steps closer. 'Do you know there is only one animal louder than the howler monkey?'

I raise an eyebrow.

'The blue whale.'

'Oh my god!'

'They can be heard up to three miles away.'

'Should we be wearing earplugs?'

'They mostly rage in the mornings as a way of checking their distance from other troupes.'

'Ohhh,' I nod.

He nudges me to take my turn on the telescope. My eyes start as I see a heart-shaped leather-black face staring directly at me with shiny jet marbles for eyes. 'What exactly is it that you want?' he seems to be saying. 'Hmmmh?'

379

The magnification is so great I can almost feel the texture of the dark cowl of fur surrounding his petite face. As he continues his jaded stare-out I take in his sunken cheekbones, his small tufty ears and long, pencil-thin fingers. He really does look unlike anything I've ever seen before – chimpanzees I'm familiar with, in terms of seeing their comical faces on TV and in books, but this is something new. It seems incredible to me that not only am I seeing a new creature but I'm hanging out in their natural habitat, no cages or fences between us. I want to revel in the first-time wonder of it all but Kiki beckons us back to the transportation with a brisk, 'We need to go!'

Though the seating is banquette-style (meaning that our knees are rutting against those seated opposite) and the road is rucked to the degree that we period-ically bump off the seats altogether in an impromptu Mexican wave, Ryan sleeps through the entire overview of Islita village. The rest of us jump on and off the bus, ticking off the trademark landmarks – church, football field, bar – and then marvel at what sets Islita apart: the vibrant artwork on the walls of every other house – local scenes depicted in aqua, lagoon-blue, honeyed peaches and candy pinks – even the trees have swirls and stars painted on the trunks and coloured whirly-discs hooked to the branches. And then there's the alarming recurrence of David Hasselhoff. I kid you not. When I see the first $8 \times 10''$ pic of the bushy-bonced *Baywatch* star tacked up in the schoolhouse I think I must be seeing things. Upon spying a second in a villager's home, I know there is something weird going on. Our driver explains that when Mr II visited the resort, he elected to hand out headshots to all the villagers, who dutifully set his picture alongside their family portraits. Santiago's face seems to say 'I love my people and yet . . .'

'Here's the beach!' Kiki scoots forward as we round a corner and encounter a broad stretch of coast sprigged with squat, feathery palm trees. 'You can hire boogie boards and kayaks and there's a big freshwater swimming pool and a restaurant that does great snacks . . .'

'These are the stables,' Dad points beyond a wooden fence to where a trail of Mohawk-maned horses are chowing down. 'I tried to get Kiki to take a ride along the beach with me last time but she wasn't having any of it.' He gives her hand a squeeze as she blanches at the mere thought.

Interesting. So she'll zip-line through the trees and tear up the road on an ATV but she won't hoof it. Apparently she is not entirely without fear after all.

'Had to go with Santiago,' Dad continues. 'Maybe it was for the best – give those guys an open field and they go like the clappers.'

Santiago whistles in accordance. 'Like Pegasus.'

The colour returns to Kiki's face as we ascend the steep driveway and she points out the hotel spa. 'And the reason I'm alerting you to that is because I've booked us all in for treatments this afternoon!' she fanfares.

'I didn't know about this!' Dad coos, delighted.

'It's called a surprise,' she nuzzles him back. 'It's my birthday present to everyone – besides I thought we could all do with an après-journey massage.'

'I might have to skip the deep-tissue element.' I wince at the thought of having my raging sunburn squeezed and kneaded.

'Don't worry, I've got you down for a cucumber after-sun treatment and a rather yummy manicure.'

'Oh! Gosh. That's really considerate,' I concede, looking down at my nails. 'And not a moment too soon.'

'All the guys are going to be having Pina Colada Pedicures!' she adds, chuckling at her own mischief.

Dad looks down at the hairy toes peeking out from his sandals. 'Well, I was going to announce the new boss of the Café Tropicana over our welcome cocktail . . .'

Santiago and I lock eyes for the briefest moment, two hearts suspended mid-air.

'. . . but I think I'll wait until after the spa when we all smell a lot sweeter.'

'Good thinking,' Kiki agrees.

Santiago and I expel a wobbly breath. I'm desperate to know the verdict yet at the same time glad to be putting it off.

'Right – everybody out!' My dad hustles as the shuttle halts at the top of the driveway. 'Wakey-wakey, Ryan!'

He responds with a big lion's roar of a yawn, gives me a clumsy headbutt-cum-kiss and tumbles out of the car.

'Mr and Mrs Langston! What a pleasure to see you again so soon!'

A sylphlike blonde introducing herself as Lauren leads us down the path to the open-air reception. There's something so relaxed and personal about her approach I feel just as welcome as the more regular punters among us and happily accept the key to my *casita* along with a dewy glass of juice. Maybe it helps that for once I'm not the only person present who didn't attend the infamous Punta Islita wedding. I sneak a look at Ryan, wondering if he's as impressed as me. This resort may be five-star calibre but all the furnishings and fixtures look lovingly handcrafted and home-stitched, enhancing the secret hideaway vibe. It's just a shame they don't have more rooms – I pity Santiago having to share with Ryan. How weird to think they will be lying side by side tonight, albeit in separate beds. I'm just grateful Ryan didn't presume to kip in with me. At least not officially, anyway. Sensing a hand about to toy with my rear, I scuttle onward to inspect the view.

As with the Mariposa, the reception leads through to an alfresco dining area, only instead of bright, sophisticated whites the palette here is melted Caramac and dusty straw with brick flooring, barn roofing, earthenware pots and wrought iron chandeliers. Drop down a couple of steps and you're cradled in the inset bar which also serves the pool, stretching along the horizon with only a row of slatted sunloungers to differentiate between its liquid turquoise and the sapphire of the distant sea.

'Maybe we could set up a little franchise right here,' Santiago teases as he joins me on the grassy verge teetering on the edge of this scenic swoop.

'Nice idea!' I sigh. 'But it's so peaceful I don't think I'd even have the strength to lift a coffee cup to my lips let alone serve anyone. I'd just lie here in a stupor all day.'

'Not so great for business but not a bad way to live.'

'Do you think you could make a home somewhere this remote?' I ask.

'If I was with the right person,' he replies.

For a second it seems like everything I need is right here – Santiago, sun, sea . . . But then comes Kiki.

'We're running a little late,' she calls over. 'If you want to quickly drop your bags in the room then head up to the spa . . .?'

I sigh, reluctant to walk away from Santiago. In fact, neither of us moves until Dad chips in, 'You guys?'

'Yes?' we respond in unison.

'After the spa, let's meet here in the bar for our little chat. I'll be the one with the pineapple rings on my toes!' he winks.

'Until then!' Santiago excuses himself with a neat bow.

I can't help but smile as I weave down the hillside, past various discreetly nestled *casitas*, en route to my own. I didn't want to come here but the romance of the place is so potent. Now I wonder if it isn't all beautifully meant to be – I can't think of a more idyllic setting for the grand climax. In my fantasy version Dad makes his announcement and then Santiago gathers me up in his arms and – *but no!* I'm getting ahead of myself. First I have to make it clear to Ryan that as flattering as it was initially to be on the receiving end of his advances, we're done. I wonder if now is the time – Santiago opted to get a drink at the bar rather than go to the room so Ryan would be alone. According to my map, I'm right by the path that leads to his *casita*. Should I take it? I take one step in his direction only to jump three paving slabs back. Another dreaded iguana has

385

scuttled from the undergrowth and is facing me down. Will I ever get used to these scaly eyesores? I take this as a sign and backtrack to my own path – I'll deal with Ryan later.

Ah – here's me.

I unlock the door and step into a suite of rustic, pared-down simplicity – whitewashed walls, terracotta tiles, raffia matting and a rough-hewn four-poster. I want to touch everything – the cream calico drapes that can turn my bed into a cocoon, the smooth white sheets, the velvety petals of the decorative bloom on the pillow.

The bathroom takes me another step closer to nature with a floor-to-ceiling glass wall spanning the outer edge of the tub, designed to showcase a private outdoor rockery sprouting vibrant tropical foliage. It'll be like taking a shower in a bijou garden of Eden, I decide as I run my hand along the slim green fingers of the potted palm positioned this side of the glass.

In lieu of unpacking I take a ginger ale from the minibar and step out on to the terrace. Oh wow. WOW! I wasn't expecting this – my very own plunge-pool jacuzzi and a hammock from which to gaze out across the vista – quite different to my straight shot at the beach back at the café. Here I'm shaded by the papery fronds of the thatched roof, there's a neat green hedge bordering my square of lawn and trees that look like clusters of broccoli florets acting as visual stepping stones down to the sea below.

Aware that I'm about to fall into a trance that could last for days, I hurry back inside, blast myself with a cold shower, slip on a clean camisole and skirt and head up to the spa, only to undo all my cleanliness en route – the humidity is so cloying and the path so steep there's an inbuilt workout to the journey. I was feeling a bit self-indulgent at the prospect of an afternoon at the spa but as I stumble up to the welcome desk moist and panting, I feel I've earned my pampering reward.

'I'm sorry if I'm a bit late –' I puff, dabbing my brow.

'Are you here for the Thousand Strokes Hair Treatment?' the beauty therapist enquires, looking a little daunted by the length of my hair.

'Er, no, I'm the sunburnt girl?' I say, flashing a patch of scarlet as if it's some kind of secret society branding.

She looks down at her booking log. 'Miss Ava?'

'Yes!' I smile.

'Follow me,' she says and bids me enter the first room along a corridor. 'You can undress and put on this robe. I will return in a few minutes.'

'You seem to be missing a wall,' I want to say as I turn round and see that the entire valley of Islita is exposed before me.

I can't quite believe it. Everything else is in place – the towel-snug padded table, the myriad pots and potions, a shower for spritzing, pegs to hang my clothes upon but no fourth wall. Am I really going to get undressed in broad daylight without even a gauzy swathe to add a little mystique to proceedings? Surely anyone could walk by – a tour guide, a coffee picker, a stablehand, a waiter, Santiago . . . My eyes scour the foliage in search of a giveaway glint of binocular glass. Nothing. I remember Dad saying that the hotel owners had bought the surrounding acres so there would be no more building work to spoil the vista so I suppose it's really just the odd voyeuristic frog that I have to worry about. Oh well. May as well give his eyes something to really bulge at – I whip off outers and undies getting a surprising thrill of liberation as the warm air greets my bare skin. I'm part-way into the robe when the therapist returns.

'Shall we begin with the manicure?'

'Oh yes!' I say, relieved that I'm going to have half an hour or so to adjust to the prospect of having a stranger's hands in my nooks and crannies. I do find it curious that such procedures get filed under 'relaxation'. During my one previous massage I flinched every time the towel was folded back yet another pleat – it felt like a total invasion of personal flesh, but then that was a large, all-too attractive man and this is a mere slip of a girl from Poland.

Alexandrina smiles encouragingly as she places my hands in a glazed pottery bowl heaped with orange powder. As she pours in warm water from a large ceramic jug the powder blends like Berocca conjuring a delicious scent of orange blossom. Gently she slurps water over my hands. I feel my shoulders descend and my breathing deepen. The previous spa was clinical, surgical even, with Tupperware-style accessories and metal pans you'd expect to see extracted bullets rattling in, not to mention the noxious smell of acrylic nails twanging my nostrils. Here, the process seems so much more organic, ritualistic even. Once my hands are blotted dry she produces a creamy sweet-smelling dessert rippled with squishes of pink.

'Is white chocolate with strawberries.'

'Oh yum!' Treats too, this is great. Wait a second – she's dipping in a basting brush and pasting it over my hands.

'Oh my god!' I startle at the sensation of the warm goo.

'You like?'

I nod eagerly. Now I understand why Kiki described the manicure as 'yummy'. Next my hands are sheathed in plastic gloves and enfolded in a towel. She places her own palms on top for extra warmth.

Every stage is so soothing, so loving. I choose a polish the colour of strawberry mousse to complement the fragrance and when the last nail is perfected I marvel at my hands as if she's given me a brand new pair.

'Thank you,' I sigh dreamily.

'When you are ready, you can undress and lie on the table.'

'Can I just nip to the bathroom?' One quick wee before I submit.

'Of course.'

I shuffle down the corridor, hands flared out like I've just performed a magic spell, humming to myself: 'I've got pretty hands, I've got— *Owwww*!'

I jump as I feel an all-too-familiar intrusion upon my rear.

'Got anything on under there?' Ryan leers as he paws at my robe.

'Careful! My nails are still drying!' I squirm away from him, fanning my fingers out of his reach.

'So if I was to undo this' – he reaches for the sash – 'you couldn't stop—'

'Ryan!' I yelp, twisting away. So much for serenity, now I feel jostled and manhandled.

'Okay, okay,' he backs off. 'I gotta get myself covered in coconut milk and honey. If you're good I'll let you lick it off later . . .'

I roll my eyes as he lurches back down the corridor. How did I ever find that man attractive?

As I step into the bathroom I make a promise to my reflection that even if Santiago turns me down, there will be no more Ryans. I've had a taste of the *pura vida*, now I only want love in its purest form.

The second treatment escorts me to a new level of contentment. Having chit-chatted through my manicure I now realise as I lie with my face in a cushioned horseshoe that there is a 'sounds of nature' CD playing, somewhat superfluous considering the real deal is just a few feet away.

Oh so tenderly, Alexandrina slides cooling gloop over my scorched skin. She's no Santiago but her touch is so daintily deft it's almost as if the liquid is traversing my body by itself. As the pinched tautness that has vexed me so gradually eases, I experience a flow of relief, followed by the dual sensations of eroticism and innocence, peace and elation, surrender and empowerment.

I don't know exactly what a chakra is but I think mine just aligned.

Suddenly I feel like I have no more inhibitions, no anxiety over the coffee shop and Ryan has become someone from my distant past. It makes me happy to know that I am well and truly done with him. Instead I feel as if I am being cleansed and anointed so I can move gracefully into the next stage of my life.

Santiago. As I think of him my heart swims with bliss and I feel so open. Somehow Alexandrina has summoned my inner glow to the surface and I can't wait for him to see it! All that remains is the pronouncement from the tribal chief and I can finally discover if there is any hope of us being together romantically. At this point I feel nothing but optimism – what universe would create such a magical backdrop for a first kiss if it didn't intend for us to take full advantage?

32

Descending the hill from spa to bar, I gather so much momentum there's practically smoke coming from my heels as I screech the breaks to avoid slamming into Santiago.

'Hi!' I pant as I divert on to the bar stool beside to him. 'Oh wow – you smell gorgeous, what is that?' I lean in and breathe the air around his neck, instantly heady from the clean yet spicy aroma warming on his coppery skin.

'Cinnamon and lemon grass.' His words ruffle my hair.

My longing for him is profound but I check myself – just a matter of minutes until I discover his true identity. My future beau or devious competitor? What's it going to be? My nerves make me silly: 'Smell my hands!' I gleefully proffer them for his inspection.

He inhales then smiles. 'So girls really are made of candy!'

I laugh delightedly.

'What is it, strawberry and . . .?' He raises a quizzical brow.

'White chocolate! Can you believe it? They put it on like a paste.'

Now his fingers are swirling in tiny circles on the back on my hand. Fearing I might slip from the stool in a swoon, I brace my foot against the bar.

'Your skin is so silky,' he sighs as he bumps over my knuckles. 'Ryan is a lucky guy.'

My heart leaps – was that a flirtation? A lament? I know I shouldn't say anything yet but my father has already made his decision, what harm can it do to set Santiago straight on one basic fact?

'You're right,' I begin a little squeakily. 'Ryan is lucky. He's lucky he's still in one piece after all the dumb daredevil stuff he does.' Lowering my voice to a whisper, I add: 'But, you know, he's not lucky with me.'

Santiago's eyes meet mine. 'He's not?'

'Whatever it was,' I wince having to admit there ever was something, 'it's over.'

Telling Ryan is a mere technicality at this point.

'Really?' Santiago's eyes brighten. 'I think maybe we should drink to that!' he beckons the barman.

As Santiago secretively points to an item on the cocktail menu my chest swells with hope. I may only be tiptoeing towards him at this point but at least I feel I'm headed in the right direction. Right now the outcome of the battle for supremacy at the coffee shop seems irrelevant. Yes, I would love to win for both my personal sense of achievement and to have that long-sought-after approval from my father, but with regard to Santiago, I don't want to be boss and underling, I would far rather us be *partners*.

I huddle up to watch the various whiskings, shakings and frothings of the barman but then catch sight of my dad marching purposefully towards us and experience a flare of nerves. There's no more denial or fantasy – seconds from now, if I win I will either receive a congratulatory embrace from Santiago or he'll go on some sullen rampage. If *he* wins he will either be gracious or fire me. It's make-or-break time and I'm praying for the grand prize.

'Little Red Riding Hood.' Santiago sets my drink before me.

'Did you just make that up?' I laugh, surprised at his reference to my dad's old nickname for me.

'No it's legit.' He shows me the catalogue of recipes. 'See – gin, crème de mûre, wild-strawberry liqueur and a splash of orange juice.'

I take a sip, feeling very special. 'Dad, you've got to try this!' I offer as he joins us at the bar.

'No getting the judge drunk!' he chuckles, turning me down. 'I need a clear head to say what I have to say.'

Santiago and I exchange one last look before our expressions switch to grave focus.

'Sooo,' he smiles heartily. 'This was a tough one.'

Oh this is horrible. All the drawn-out nonsense, 'You've both done so well, exceeded my expectations, risen to the challenge blah blah blah.' Just say it! Just say the name!

'Ava.'

'Yes?'

Here we go with the double bluff much beloved of reality TV shows.

'The lure of the air conditioning has proved a resounding success. You are clearly not alone in craving some respite from the humidity. I have had reports of every seat being filled during the midday peak.'

'It's true,' I nod in acknowledgement.

'Santiago.' He turns to my rival. 'Those beautifully carved tree-stump stools, the freshly raked sand, the neatly trimmed hedges – the great outdoors has never looked so groomed!'

'Thank you, sir.'

'Most impressive,' he adds before turning back to me. 'I see that a couple of your furniture choices have not been as resilient as natural wood in terms of spillage.'

Darn! Those strategically placed cushions clearly didn't fool him.

'You're right,' I'm forced to concede. 'I was actually researching some stainproof fabrics just before we left.'

396

'Wise move.' He turns back to Santiago. 'As you are no doubt aware, the outdoor food sales are not as high as the indoor ones.'

'No, sir. I think it's because all the cakes are in view of the inside customers, it puts temptation in their way.'

'And that's a good thing,' my father notes.

'Yes it is,' he admits.

'In your favour, you do seem to have a faster turnaround of customers – I notice that they come up off the beach, sit and have their drink then return to sunbathing et cetera, whereas Ava's customers tend to linger longer in the cool.' He takes a breath. 'As for your choice of staff . . .'

Santiago and I exchange a furtive look. Has he noticed that Wilbeth is equal parts liability to asset? Or that Milena's sassiness borders on cheek? Though we're more than aware of these facts, neither of us could bear to lose either of them.

'I think you've created an excellent working dynamic,' he asserts. 'I was initially hoping for some consistency in terms of the image you're projecting but I think the contrast between the shy, earnest boy and brassy, over-confident girl works well.'

We smile, relieved and gratified. Only to be found fault with again.

'I see that neither of you have come up with a conclusive house blend yet.'

'No,' we admit in unison, free of excuses.

397

I have no idea why this task has proved so elusive, we just can't seem to get the right blend of beans.

'Well, I suppose the winner will have the honour of deciding that,' Dad decides before clearing his throat. 'Ava?' He sounds grave.

Here we go with more back-and-forth compliments and critiquing. I don't know how much more of this I can stand.

'Yes?' My tone is on the verge of testy.

'You've won.'

Silence. Is he for real? My eyes dart around in confusion.

'Did you hear me?' he laughs. 'The coffee shop is yours.'

'I've won?' I look straight at Santiago. He's calmer than I was expecting, as if he's waiting for my reaction. I just can't work out what that is.

'Th-thank you!' I reach to hug my dad, still in shock.

I've pictured this outcome, hoped for it, dreamed of it, yet – apparently – never expected it.

'You earned it,' he tells me, proudly.

I turn back to Santiago, still suspended in mid-air. 'I couldn't have done any of this without you,' I begin, ready to splurge all my suppressed gratitude and accolades upon him.

'Hold on a moment!' Dad senses my intention and halts proceedings. 'I'm not done yet.'

We turn back to my father.

'Santiago, you have done such a fine job, showed an even greater range of talents than I already knew you had.' He pauses for effect then says, 'That's why I'm promoting you to Head of Projects in Tamarindo!'

'*Tamarindo!*' I can't help but blurt.

'Just you wait till you see what I've got lined up! I can show you some of it now online – come on, son!' He slaps his hand on to Santiago's back as he pulls him to his feet.

'There's no rush,' he protests. 'Perhaps you want to celebrate with Ava?'

'I think she needs a moment to let it all sink in.' He tweaks my pale cheek. 'Enjoy your cocktail and the view, we'll see you at dinner!'

I watch in a daze as he hustles Santiago on his way, mentally running after them shouting, 'Wait! Wait! What's going on? You can't leave me!'

But my body remains rooted to the bar stool.

This doesn't make any sense. If I'm the winner then why am I alone? If I'm the winner why do I feel so defeated?

I sit in confusion wondering where all the heavenly poise of the spa has gone.

It takes me a while to figure out that I don't have to accept this situation just because my father has decreed it to be so. We have a choice, Santiago and I! I don't know what he wants but the only way to find out is to ask him. And maybe the step before

399

that is to tell him how I feel. Instantly queasy, I reach for a napkin and ask the barman if I can borrow a pen. I have to write this down, I need it to come out just right . . .

Where do I begin?

I look down at the napkin and there are just two wavery words inked: *Don't go*.

I want you to stay, Santiago. I want us to run the coffee shop together. I want to wake up in the morning smiling because you are beside me. I want to kiss your shoulder as you remain in a white-sheeted slumber and slip into the kitchen and grind our own unique blend of beans. As I am waiting for the coffee to brew, I will lean on the door frame and look out across the wild greenery and down to the ocean and wonder how I got to be so blessed. Then I'll pour your coffee into your favourite cup and place it on a tray with a freshly peeled orange and a tiny square of tamarind cake and I'll carry it in to you and watch as you push your dark hair from your face so that you can let all that love pour from your eyes into mine. This will be our special start-of-the-day ritual.

'Another, Little Red?' The barman interrupts my reverie.

'No thanks!' I say, jumping to my feet, now feeling energised and full of purpose. As I scamper along the path, I imagine the rest of our day unfolding . . . chatting about our schedule on the curvy journey to the café, the warm rapport with the staff and customers, the aroma of the fresh baked cakes, the fly-by kisses, the mid-morning lull, the teatime rush, Santiago dancing with the ladies from the hair salon, me helping Wilbeth with his English, the sense of satisfaction and achievement as we lock up at the end of the day . . .

I open the door to the Internet room. Just two older ladies giggling at some shirtless pictures of the plumber from *Desperate Housewives*. Maybe Dad brought his laptop with him and they're back at his *casita*?

Now in my mind it is nightfall and Santiago and I are making our way home. As he prepares dinner, I light the candles and set the table and arrange the flowers he bestowed upon me that afternoon. The mood is intimate, comfortable, harmonious. We chat and laugh as we eat, then lie out on the patio sofa counting the stars instead of sheep before we sleep.

I knock on my father's door. No reply. Perhaps Santiago's already at my place? Perhaps he's waiting to share the same vision with me? I'm running now, rattling with anticipation. The sooner I am inside my *casita*, the sooner he can knock on the door. I fumble the key in the lock and rush inside. For ten minutes I pace every which way, tweaking an already perfect setting, making sure everything is just so. Getting a little too manic, I decide I need to quieten myself and sit on the sofa and take several deep breaths with my eyes closed, concentrating on willing him here. Willing him to knock on the door . . .

Rat-a-tat.

My eyes spring open – it's him! He's here! Oh my god, here we go! I feel life rushing up to meet me! I take a composing breath and open the door – only to have my face fall twenty storeys: it's Ryan.

'Heyyy, champ!' He wrenches my arms up like I'm a boxer, jiggling them roughly as he makes faux cheering-crowd noises. 'I knew you were a winner!'

Though I'm devastated with disappointment, I decide this isn't such a bad thing – my arm sockets may be reliving the agony of the zip-lining yanking but at least I'll get to purge my world of Ryan before inviting Santiago in. This is the right way to do things. All is well.

'Ryan—' I begin in my sternest tone.

'Just give me two minutes, babe, I need to use your shower – I'm covered in spa crap.'

'Why can't you use yours?' I wonder out loud as he begins shedding his clothes.

'Santiago's in it. I mean, he's a nice guy and all but . . .'

The image of Santiago drizzled in shower-spray, with shiny rivulets aquaplaning over his various contours, distracts me sufficiently to allow Ryan to slip past and get under way in the bathroom.

I wait patiently as, amid the lathering and sudsing, he subjects me to a medley of self-loving tunes – from an inquisitive 'Do Ya Think I'm Sexy?' to an affirmative 'Simply The Best'. Little does he know that when he emerges I'm going to finish with him. I suppose this is what they call a clean break.

'Hey, Ava! Are you going to join me in the shower?' he bellows, informing surrounding wildlife of his intentions.

I open the door and hiss at him to be quiet. I don't even want a leaf-cutter ant to get the wrong impression about us any more.

'Are you peeking?' he says, faux coy.

Who said breaking up is hard to do? This is going to be sooooo easy. If I can just get him to listen for half a second.

'Ryan. Ryan?' I try to get his attention as he towels himself down. Nothing. 'RYAN!!!' I scream.

'No need to shout, babe,' he says, tearing his eyes away from the mirror so he can advance towards me.

'No!' I hold my hands up as he goes to grab me. 'Ryan, stop it!' I swat him away.

'What's the matter with you?' he huffs. 'You said that once the announcement was made you'd start paying me some proper attention . . .'

I take a breath, knowing I have to keep this simple and direct. 'This thing with us, it's over. Done. Finished. *Kaput*.'

He frowns, disbelievingly. Can I really be the first woman to say these words to him? I'm almost tempted to tell him that I'm a lesbian because I think it's probably the only explanation he'd accept for a woman not finding him physically attractive. And yet that's not the problem. He *is* physically attractive. It's just that now I've got to know him, I've become immune to his outward charms.

He steps towards me. 'You can't mean this.' He goes for a smooch.

I put my hand over his mouth like a clamp. 'There will be no more kissing between us.' I recoil. 'You need to find a new girl to play with.'

This time I get him out the door but I suspect he's still not fully processed what's going on because his parting words are: 'You women *love* to play hard to get, dontcha?'

I take a series of deep breaths to defrazzle myself. Why didn't I see what a snatch'n'grab operation he was from the beginning? Not that he was at first but that's probably because he was being coached by Kiki – I remember at the butterfly farm her asking me what I was looking for in a man and he seemed to tick all the boxes that first night. Well, I guess you can only fake it for so long . . .

I look at my watch. Less than an hour until dinner. Maybe I should spend my time making myself look as ravishing as possible for the evening ahead. Ryan said Santiago was in the shower, maybe he's doing the same. Not that it takes him more than a quick sluice and tousle to look divine but chances are he'll be there early for cocktails, so if I hurry we can have our moment before the others arrive. All I have to say is, 'I want us to be partners.' He'll raise a curious eyebrow and I'll say, 'In every sense of the word.' And then he'll lean forward and I'll finally get to kiss that crazily beautiful mouth of his.

Now I truly have butterflies making jerky flicker-book starts and swoops in my stomach.

Ten minutes later I'm steeping drowsily in the bath, reconnecting with my former spa bliss – oh the sensuality of those fragrant caresses . . . And to think, the next hands to touch me could be Santiago's! A sudden rush of lust propels me out of the water, eager to accelerate through my beauti-fications and get to him.

I twist my hair into soft spirals and select all my most shimmery beauty products. I want Santiago to see fireflies twinkling back at him when he looks in my eyes, the crushed-diamond glintings of the sea when his gaze glazes over my skin.

As I slink into my new Grecian goddess dress with the twisted silk straps and step my gold sandals out the door, I think to myself, he can't say no now, the night is too perfect – the air is soft as cashmere, the sky a panoramic swathe of peach and the cicadas are in perfect sync with the man on the marimba.

I'm first at the bar. I take my seat, order my drink and try to bite back an all-too-delirious grin. My feet may be fidgety, my white-chocolate hands a little sticky but my heart is wide open and it feels good.

One by one the others arrive – first my father, then Kiki, then Ryan, who is studiously ignoring me. It's wonderful, I feel entirely immune to him now. Nothing can spoil this moment.

'I'm ravenous,' my father announces as he knocks back his gin aperitif. 'Shall we go through to the table?'

'Shouldn't we wait for Santiago?' I chip, still high on nervous anticipation.

'Oh, he's gone.'

'What?' Someone has just slammed on the brakes.

'Yes, he couldn't wait to get started on the Tamarindo job.' Dad looks strangely proud, as if to say, 'That's my boy, total workaholic!'

Around me a million china plates shatter on the floor but everyone else seems oblivious, getting off their stools and filing through to the dinner table.

'Ava, are you coming?' My father turns back to me.

I can't move. I can barely speak. How could he leave like that? 'I don't feel well,' I mumble.

'You do look a bit strange,' he frowns, concerned.

'Sometimes spa treatments can make you feel a little woozy – all those toxins coming to the surface . . .' Kiki offers.

'Perhaps you should go and lie down for a bit?' Dad soothes.

'But I don't want to miss your birthday dinner,' I protest, feeling guilty at choosing my own pity party over his celebrations.

'Oh phooey to that!' he tuts. 'We've already had a beautiful breakfast together. Just let me know if there's anything we can bring you.'

'Thank you but please don't worry,' I sigh knowing that nothing could possibly make me feel any better right now.

33

I schlep back to my room, feeling stunned and disconnected. Slipping off my shoes at the door, I pad across the tiled floor and flump face down into the bed. I can't believe he's gone.

A pain spears through my chest as I imagine returning to the café without him and for a moment I cease my breathing, just holding myself in a numb limbo, trying to stave off the tears and regrets. I simply can't accept this. I can't face the loss. All too soon the tears begin in earnest, sending sparkling streams of anguish down my face.

When I have cried myself through hysteria back to numbness the phone rings. It's funny how even when you know there's not a chance it could be Him calling to make everything all right, you can't help but hope it. I take a moment to reset my expectations so that when my dad asks how I am, I can answer without any giveaway snuffling and whimpering.

'Hello?' I say, keeping my voice low and steady,

only to gasp out loud as my heart slams like a squash ball against my ribcage – *it's Santiago!*

'I'm sorry to trouble you but no one else is in their room and the spa is closed.'

'The spa?' Have I missed something? What has the spa got to do with our situation?

'I left my mobile in the treatment room. I was wondering if—'

'Of course, I'll get it. I'll go first thing tomorrow.' I'm eager to get all trivial practicalities out of the way so we can scoot on to the good stuff, but his tone remains formal, if not a little forlorn.

'Thank you. I'll arrange to have it picked up from the café.' In the background I hear a voice calling him to board. 'I have to go.'

'Wait!' I screech.

'What is it?' he asks, sounding cautiously hopeful.

How can I condense all I need to say into one sentence? Under such pressure all I can manage is a plaintive, 'Why didn't you say goodbye?'

'*Why?*' He is incredulous, as if to say, '*You know perfectly well why!*' Though of course I don't. I need to hear a reason but all I get is a heavy sigh.

'Santiago?' Is there something he's not saying?

'You did get my note, right?'

'What?'

Again with the official voice in the background.

'That's the last call, I have to go.' He sounds anxious.

'*What note?*' I urge.

'I gave it to Kiki to pass to you, didn't she . . .?'

'NO!' I howl outraged, springing to my feet.

'Ava, I'm holding up the plane. I have to go.'

And with that the line clicks dead. For a second I'm still and then I fly out the door fuelled by hope – written hope. I fly out of the door, curve the path and take the steps to the restaurant three at a time. But as I approach I see the table is empty.

'All gone,' the waiter confirms.

I give him a manic wave and scuttle down to my father's casita, taking the wrong path twice and arriving in a twirl of impatience. I can barely stand the time it takes him to open the door.

'I just need a quick word with Kiki,' I pant, looking hungrily past his shoulder, now just seconds away from being able to revel in Santiago's hand-writing. (My name on the turtle adoption certificate was a good start but a personal message is going to mean so much more . . .)

'She's not here.' He throws me off course. 'I thought she was with you.'

'With me?'

'Checking on how you're feeling . . .'

'Ohhh. Well, I just came from the restaurant.'

'You must have just missed each other. Are you feeling any better?'

'Oh much. MUCH!' I over-enthuse.

'Your eyes . . .' He peers at my puffiness.

'Oh no, I'm fine!' I assure him. 'If I miss her again can you ask her to call me in the room?'

'Certainly,' he says, ever-jaunty. 'Goodnight, Miss Tropicana!'

'Right, same to you,' I mutter distractedly.

I take a few hesitant paces then stop. This place is like a maze, I don't know which path she might take so I decide to wait a while on the corner nearest my dad's door. When she doesn't show up after ten minutes I slowly make my way back to my *casita*, stopping intermittently to cock my ear like some Native American tracker. There are plenty of sounds, but none a match for human footsteps.

I don't know what to think – that she simply forgot about the note before dinner, that she's on her way with it now or that she's deliberately keeping it from me in the hope that I'll reconcile with Ryan. Perhaps it was she who prompted my father's decision to bump Santiago to a new project? Get him out of the picture. But why so fast? Why tonight?

I truly don't know what to make of Kiki any more. I know she is capable of manipulation and I know she has sufficient influence to pull it off but I am still in the dark as to why she'd need to get up to such witchery in the first place. Of course some people just thrive on stirring up other people's business.

Had she been camped out on my terrace I would have asked her outright. And if she'd slipped the

411

note under the door I would have forgiven her, but I return to nothing and no one.

For a second I toy with the idea of checking to see if she is with Ryan but decide that as there's a 99 per cent chance he'll answer the door naked, I'll give it a miss.

I call my dad one more time but he says she's not back yet.

'Probably out polishing the moon,' he sighs dreamily.

I want to say, 'Is that what they're calling it these days?' But I don't. It's simply not polite.

Throughout the night, it seems like every hour I get up and drag back the patio door so I can contemplate the sky in the hope of detecting some shift from darkness to light. Oh morning, why is your approach so sluggish today? Why are you stars still out partying? I yearn for the blackness to soften to mauve then brighten with yellow rays.

I suppose this is how Icelanders feel during their winter. Mind you, I did once read that they actually find it a romantic time, not least because they don't get a fright when they awake to some less-than-gorgeous conquest in the cruel light of day, mainly because there is no light, cruel or otherwise. I wonder if the same could be said of my current situation – in the dark I remain in a state of ignorant anticipation, come daylight I will read Santiago's note and it may not be all I hope, or indeed need to hear. I sigh and return to bed once again, trying to meditate myself to a calm acceptance but my feet seem to be working on some hectic interpretative dance.

When the clock does finally concede to lay its hands on the eight and the twelve, I'm finally ready to sleep, all heady and drugged with fatigue. Note, what note?

Grudgingly I lever myself into an upright position. As I turn on the shower, a certain pessimism rains down on me. Do I really want to read his words? The upshot is that he's gone. He chose to leave early. He knew things were done with Ryan and yet was he such a sore loser he couldn't bear another hour in my presence. These are the facts.

The thing that gets me blow-dried and dressed and out the door is the prospect of having a go at Kiki. Contents be damned – she's withholding something that belongs to me and I need to vent my misery upon someone.

As I approach the restaurant I feel feistier and more indignant with every snap of my flip-flops. There she is, sat beside my dad, forking down her eggs. Nothing like polishing the moon to work up an appetite.

'Can I have my note?' I hold my hand out over her plate with deliberate expectation.

She stops chewing as she looks up at me.

'The one from Santiago,' I prompt, in case she's hoarding a whole filing cabinet of intercepted correspondence.

For a minute she looks thrown and then gasps, 'I can't believe I forgot to give that to you!' smacking her forehead with impressive vigour, yet nowhere near as hard as I would have liked. 'I'll get it for you as soon as I've finished eating.'

'I'd prefer it now.' I stand strong.

'Ava, she's in the middle of breakfast!' my dad reprimands me.

'The food's not going anywhere,' I shrug, unconcerned.

'But it'll go cold!' Again he speaks for her.

Before I can counter, the waiter asks what he can get for me. I do a quick assessment of Kiki's plate and then say, 'Scrambled eggs, bacon and mushrooms, please – there, you've got a hot one coming up!' Still I loom over her.

'Ava—' My dad goes to scold me further but Kiki steps in and soothes, 'It's fine, Dean. It's obviously urgent.'

She gets to her feet and I follow her down the steps, resisting the urge to push her down the last ten or so in case I send the room key flying.

My heart is thumping as much from confronting her as it is at the prospect of finally having the note in my hands. I go to follow her into the *casita*

414

but she shuts the door firmly in my face. Perhaps she hasn't read it yet and is now sufficiently intrigued to steam it open? Or maybe it's stashed in a suspiciously covert place and she doesn't want me to see her rifling through her knicker drawer to get to it?

'No envelope?' I look her straight in the eye as I take the folded slip of paper from her hand.

'I guess he was in a hurry.'

My eyes narrow accusingly but I realise I now have better things to do than argue about stationery. Without another word I turn on my heel and head towards my room. When I know she can't see me, I run. By the time I undo the lock and hurtle over to the bed, I'm shaking. And still clutching the unread note. I take a deep breath and unfold it. As my eyes scan the paper, I am swamped with disappointment. I wanted a page of tightly packed words but there are just two lines. How can that be enough to say everything that needs to be said? I brace myself and then read:

Ava, I just wanted to say congratulations. You deserved to win. Don't forget the turtle eggs hatch in Tortuguero in three months. Maybe I'll see you on the beach. S.

Oh god. Just a handful of words and I'm still going to analyse them to death. It seems as if he's proposing we meet again. Sort of. But it's not like he's in any hurry – three months? See you in ninety days! *Maybe*. Talk about *He's Just Not That Into You*.

I sigh. What did I expect?

Ever since you first walked into my life with your pothole pants and your surly competitiveness, I knew there could be only you. No one froths milk like Ava Langston. Be mine for all eternity.

I mean, really!

As I lean back on the wooden beams of the bed I wonder what it's like for people who aren't disappointed in love. There must be some people who actually get what they crave emotionally. I can't imagine what that must feel like. I just know I hate feeling this disillusioned. It saps all my energy – everything seems too much effort. Existence itself seems a drag. Knowing that I've got to go back to the café, albeit *my* café, seems nothing more than a chore. All the magic has gone now.

As I stare moodily at the wall I run my fingers over my bottom lip, pressing and kneading the soft skin of a mouth that will never be kissed by Santiago. My eyes well with tears. All this time I was waiting for the Day of Judgement, counting down until I could know for sure whether he was for real or not and when that day comes he simply vanishes.

I didn't see that coming. I thought he would either be a baddy and I'd hate him or he'd be who I hoped he was all along and that I could finally give myself permission to love him. I didn't ever think he'd just be gone.

Amid my frustration and confusion I get a sudden urge to call him and ask him exactly what his note meant and how all that we've been through together can mean so little to him, but then I realise that he doesn't have his phone with him, and that I'm in charge of getting it back.

It's pathetic, I know, but even performing a task that relates to him makes me feel like we're still connected in some way, helping me to summon the strength to mountaineer up to the spa.

34

The scent of mango honey is luring me onward, just a dozen or so strides to go when my dad appears before me, emerging from the gift shop.

Without Kiki by his side I don't feel nearly as hostile towards him. Besides, I need a favour.

'Dad, a word?' I draw level with him.

'I'll give you twenty, after that I'll have to charge you,' he joshes.

I'm glad to see he's not holding any grudges about my breakfast behaviour and muster a smile as I draw level.

'The thing is,' I begin awkwardly. 'Ryan seems to think he'll be staying at your villa when we get back to Manuel Antonio . . .'

'Isn't that what you want?' Dad asks.

'No,' I state baldly. 'We've split up. Not that we were ever a fully-fledged item. Despite what some people with confetti in their eyes thought!' I tease.

'Oh Ava, I'm sorry about that. I didn't mean to get your hopes up!'

'Hopes?' I snort. 'Hives maybe. Ryan is one of those people that when you really see them, you really don't know what you saw in them. If you know what I mean.'

'So you want me to break the news to him?' he clarifies.

'If you would.'

'Don't worry about it – I'll get Kiki to have a word. I'm sure he'll understand.'

'Just tell her to bring along her sander. The man has the hide of a rhino.'

'Will do.'

As I watch my dad turn and walk towards the hotel, I experience an unfamiliar pang. I try to put a name to the emotion and come up with grateful. And then fond. And then I sense a touch of neediness, like I need to reach out to him.

They say that a girl can always trace the origin of her troubled love life back to her father and with Santiago gone I feel more raw than ever, like I have nothing left to lose by approaching him. Mum was never able to offer any comfort for my heartache and I never gave my father the opportunity. Could this be our moment?

Goaded onward by the belief that he may have some answers for me, I am forced to acknowledge that the first thing I need to do is be brave enough to ask the questions.

He's at the bar now, opening out his newspaper and placing his order. Look at how charming he is with the staff, remembering all their names and seemingly giving them a boost by his mere presence. I could be accused of staring but what I'm really doing is seeing him anew. Have you ever looked at your father, not with 'that's my dad' eyes but observing him as a man trying to do his best? A man with his own demons to face? In my father's case that could well be his weird taste in women – my mother included. And then there's the daughter who keeps a haughty distance. She has her reasons, of course. But what were his? Did I ever give him the chance to tell me? Did I ever ask why?

'Dad?'

'Yes?' He turns towards me.

Just say it. 'Um . . .'

He tilts his head. 'What was that?' he asks, as if he's missed something. We've always been missing each other.

'Is it okay if I join you for coffee?'

'Of course.' He pats the seat beside him. 'This one's got your name on it.'

As I sit down I feel awkward yet pioneering at the same time. Instead of taking my usual judgemental tack – I'll never forgive you for XYZ! – I think, why did you do XYZ in the first place? Stranger still, as the questions come to my lips I ask them out loud. And even though they cut to the core, he doesn't even flinch. It's almost as though he's been expecting them.

'When you left Mum, did you miss me?'

'Why have I seen you so rarely over the past ten years?'

'Did you want to be a father or was it just expected of you?'

'On special occasions you always sent me money, never anything personally chosen . . .'

Though the first three questions elicit predictable replies – 'Of course I missed you – every day!' 'I've been so busy and with so many miles between us . . .' 'I don't suppose I had particularly strong baby opinions prior but I was delighted when you arrived!' – it's the fourth question that delivers the most unexpected response.

'Why money instead of a gift? Well, I felt it would give you a better sense of the value of things. In life, houses and cars and sofas and washing machines do not land in our laps as a gift. We have to budget for them,' he announces before reminiscing: 'When I was a child I always got money for my birthday and Christmas and it made me really stop and think about what I was going to spend it on. I mean, it's one thing pointing in a shop window and saying, "I want that toy car from Santa!" it's quite another thing to hand over the cash for it yourself. Each

421

year I'd make a list of my top items then trot around the shops and inspect each of them and weigh up the pros and cons of owning them. After an evening's deliberation, I would return to the shops and make my purchase. That process stood me in good stead for adult life and judging by your accounting prowess I'd say it hasn't done you any harm either.'

'So the real gift was intended to be an early sense of autonomy?' I'm dumbfounded.

'Exactly! Besides, who better to know what you really want than you?'

It seems such a convincing argument. Why did I always see it as a cop-out? And who knew that my father was ever a little boy? My grandparents passed away before I was born so I've never really registered either of my parents as being grown-up children.

'Did you spend much time with your father when you were growing up?' I venture, wondering about his own situation.

'Well, obviously I was mostly away at boarding school—'

'You went to boarding school?'

He nods his head.

How can I not know this? Did I never ask? How selfish offspring can be! I'm ashamed to have complained that he took no interest in my life when apparently I never extended the basic courtesy to him. Until now. 'So what was that like?' I ask, pulling my coffee cup a little closer.

He shrugs. 'Not great. I was bullied—'

'You?' I splutter, unable to compute this information. How can such a confident, boisterous individual have ever been cowed by another?

'For such a large man I was a fairly small boy,' he laughs.

'Well, what happened? Was it an older boy?'

'Yes. That's usually the way.' He sounds so casual, so detached. 'Obviously my mother wanted to step in when she found out but she knew it would only make it worse for me if she was seen to be protecting me – mummy's boy and all that – so I was left to deal with it.'

'But that's awful.'

'That's life. It did me a favour.'

'How? How can that possibly have been a good thing?'

'It made me stand on my own two feet, made me self-reliant,' he affirms.

'But!' I puff, confused. Is this his way of making peace with his past? It must have been so scary but he seems genuinely pleased to have had the experience. I certainly hope his home life was happier.

'I bet your parents made a real fuss of you when you came back for the holidays?'

'Not really.'

'Why not?' This is too sad.

'Well, they had their own problems. My mother had worked full-time right up until she married my father and she was finding it claustrophobic being cooped up in the house all day while he was out at work. I came home to a lot of arguing.'

'But what about you?'

'What about me?'

'Well, it sounds like they were very preoccupied with their own situations . . .'

'They were. I learned to amuse myself.' Again with the nonchalance.

'But didn't you want some attention?'

'What for?' he blithely enquires.

He actually means this. He's not being flip. I'm stunned.

'Because all children want attention from their parents . . .' My words come out slowly, almost stilted.

While he takes a sip of coffee I have an epiphany. He didn't think he was doing anything wrong. All these years he's thought that his absence has been making me stronger. His intention was for me to become independent and self-reliant, just like him. He honestly thought that a lack of mollycoddling was the best parenting he could do. I feel almost spacey.

Suddenly I get his thinking – he's turned out all right so why wouldn't it work for me? More to the

424

point, I'll bet he thinks I'm just dandy. I don't suppose I've given him any reason to believe otherwise. And yet . . .

'With me and men,' I begin tentatively, not wanting to frighten him away while he's in this receptive state.

'Yes?'

'I mean, this is a strange question and I know you don't really know the intimate details of my love life – lucky you! – but if you had to come up with some kind of theory, any kind of insight . . .?'

'What do you mean, exactly?' He doesn't seem to be following my tack.

'Well, what do you think I'm doing wrong?' I can't put it any plainer than that.

'You want relationship advice from me?' he hoots.

'Well, it's worked out with Kiki, hasn't it?'

'Yes, I suppose it has – she makes me so happy,' he beams dreamily.

'Why can't I have that?' I blurt.

He gives my question due pause.

'Well, you do give everything to your work, I don't know how much is left over for a man—'

'It's not that,' I assure him. 'Before coming here work was hardly a priority.'

'Hmmm. Well, it's a mystery to me – lovely, talented, feisty girl like you.' He cups my jaw.

'Am I too feisty?' Is that it? I never used to think

of myself that way, not until I arrived in Costa Rica and was immediately sent into battle.

'You just need someone who can give as good as he gets. Someone like Santiago.'

My heart flips.

'But not Santiago himself, obviously,' he quickly adds.

'Why not?' I'm shaking inside as I say the words. Does he know something I don't?

Dad opens his mouth to speak and then falters. 'Well . . .'

'We were actually getting on pretty well towards the end,' I begin, as if convincing my father of our compatibility will somehow make Santiago love me. 'And you should have seen us in Tortuguero—'

'Oh Ava.'

Dad's tone is so poignant as the penny drops for him that my eyes instantly prickle with tears.

'I've actually got to run a little errand for him,' I jump to my feet intending to be on my way before emotion overwhelms me but Dad reaches for my hands, clasping both tightly in his and looking me directly in the eye as he insists, 'He'll come for you, your guy, I promise. You are not destined to be alone.'

I nod, pursing my lips together so no blubbering will accidentally escape me.

'And in the meantime, Ollie's going to visit, isn't he?'

I conjure a natural smile at the mere mention of his name, not least because hearing my Dad speak it proves he does listen when I talk about my life back home after all.

I take a deep breath. 'I haven't packed yet so I ought to—'

'Yes, yes, me too.' Dad gathers up his paper and requests the bill, which I insist on settling.

'Thanks,' I tell him, with all sincerity as I lay down the colourful notes.

'For what?' He looks confused.

I turn and smile at him. 'For being my dad.'

35

'Hi, I wonder if you could help me?' I smile at the woman at the spa welcome desk. 'There was a group of us in yesterday and my friend Santiago thinks he left his cell phone in the treatment room . . .'

She pulls a face as she checks the drawers of her desk. 'I'm sorry, nothing has been handed in.'

'Maybe it slipped behind one of the counters?' I persist. 'Would it be possible to have a quick look?'

'Do you know which room he was in?'

'Well, I know it wasn't number 1 because that was me, Ava Langston.'

'Langston?' She brightens. (I take it my dad left a handsome tip.) 'Ah yes, I have your booking here. Mr Dean in Room 2, Ms Kiki and Mr Ryan in 3 and, here we are, Mr Santiago Room 4.'

Hold on a minute! 'Excuse me, did you say Kiki and Ryan were in Room 3?'

She nods.

'Together?'

'Duet massage.' She gives me a knowing look.

'Kiki and *Ryan*, not Kiki and Dean?'

'Dean is the older man, yes?'

'Yes.' I frown.

'He had the Healing Stone Massage after his pedicure, I know because I gave it to him.'

'Could I just take a peek at that?' I tilt the booking log in my direction. It's all there in black and white – Kiki and Ryan, naked bar a teeny towel, slathered in god knows what. And then I notice that they were only booked in for an hour, whereas the rest of us were held captive, however blissfully, for two. So what did they do for that second hour? I shudder as I recall just how eager Ryan was to get in the shower when he came to my *casita* yesterday afternoon.

And then the far worse implication hits me – my father's brand new wife is cheating on him.

Of course I've found aspects of Kiki's behaviour around Ryan suspect all along but only now is the potential harm of my suspicions fully resonating. But what to do about it? Just minutes ago Dad was raving about how happy she's made him. Would it be kinder to say nothing? Perhaps. And yet I can't bear for him to be made a fool of like this. I need to think clearly, rationally . . .

'Could I possibly make a copy of this?' I ask. 'It's just that I'm compiling a birthday scrapbook for my father and I'd love to include some pages on the spa, we all enjoyed it *so* much.'

'Of course,' she smiles, gathering me up some leaflets and brochures to boot. 'And now the cell phone!'

I'd all but forgotten about what I came in for. On the way to Room 4, the walls lurch and distort around me – I can't believe what went on here yesterday, just a few feet away from everyone else. That grabby-gropey fool and that spoilt princess! The madder I get the more compelled I feel to reveal the infidelity, but I just know it can't be here at Punta Islita – how could I crush my father's romantic dreams in the very place where, just a few weeks ago, he made his wedding vows? I'll have to wait until we get back to Manuel Antonio. Or better yet, mid-air with Ryan and Kiki hooked up to a couple of ejector seats.

'Here!' With a waft of zesty citrus the spa lady produces Santiago's phone. It was indeed playing hide-and-seek amid the wonderland of potions.

I take it from her, beholding it like it is Santiago's last remaining legacy.

'It is okay?' She looks concerned.

'Yes, yes. Thanks for all your help!' I smile earnestly as I hurry on my way.

As I scurry back to the main hotel you'd think I was a medium trying to get a reading from an object the way I'm caressing the phone, smoothing the

430

display, holding it up to my ear as if he might speak to me.

'Hellooo!'

I jump at a man's voice. It takes me a second to realise it's my father calling to me from the reception area. As he beckons me over, I contemplate him with a mixture of pity and envy – he doesn't know the truth yet, he's not hurting yet.

'So listen, I know you've got to get packing but I just wanted to let you know that it's all sorted with Ryan.'

'It is?'

He nods. 'I had a chat with him and he's decided that Manuel Antonio's not for him.'

Oh thank god! There's hope he might just fly away, preferably back to the Amazon and never be heard of again.

Not so fast.

'He's actually going to come back to Tamarindo with us.'

'*What?*' I baulk.

'So you'll have the villa all to yourself,' Dad continues, oblivious as ever.

'But what about you?'

'What do you mean?'

'He's not staying with you, is he?' Please say no.

'Of course, I couldn't have him paying for a hotel when there's six rooms going begging—'

'But you don't even like him!' I protest.

'Oh I'll hardly see him,' he dismisses my concern. 'Besides, he can keep Kiki amused while I'm working late.'

I wince at his innocence, and then experience a new level of revulsion for Ryan – the audacity of the man! The low-down, under-the-same-roof sleaziness of him! And as for Kiki . . .

'Ava, are you all right?'

I look at my father and I think – I can't let this happen! I have to tell him now! But selfishly I don't want to sour our relationship so soon after our breakthrough conversation. They say 'Don't shoot the messenger!' and maybe I wouldn't get a bullet but what are my chances of getting another hand squeeze? Slim to zero. It's then I decide it's Kiki I need to tackle – it's her job to tell my father what is going on, not mine.

'Where is she?' I ask, sounding all too like an assassin requesting the location of her next kill.

'Kiki? She's still packing—'

'You stay here,' I lay a firm hand on him. 'I'll be back shortly.'

Mentally I strap on armour of black leather, check my guns for ammo and bore through the undergrowth with laser-vision eyes. As I pace forward I play back the sequence of events that have led to this moment: first Kiki wants to set me up with her friend Ryan but when he arrives and expresses an interest in me she gets all crazy-competitive so

432

she packs me off to Tortuguero with Santiago. Ha! I'll bet there never was a problem with the fishing boat, just Kiki playing siren on the rocks. So then I come back and he wants to whisk me off for an ultra-romantic dinner and suddenly that's allowed because now I'm the alibi – *How can I possibly be shagging Ryan when your daughter is?* No wonder he accepted my 'Let's take it slow!' line so easily – he was busy with Kiki in the wee small hours. Which also explains why he falls asleep at every available opportunity. After all, I'm safely back at the villa, Dad's in his usual coma-like sleep—. Suddenly I stop short of the door. Was this whole thing pre-arranged? Was the whole reason Kiki was so keen to get me to visit that she wanted to make a show of fixing me up with Ryan when all the while . . .? I give the door a furious rap. When it opens a crack I barge in.

'I know what's going on with you and Ryan,' I spit.

'What?' She blanches but admits nothing.

'I know everything. And I've got proof.' I waste no time laying my evidence on the table. I can't be doing with any fey 'Whatever do you mean?' posturing from her.

'What's that?' She looks down at the sheet of paper.

'The spa booking.' My eyes narrow to poison darts as she stoops to read it. 'How could you do it?' I snarl over her. 'You know how he feels about you.'

Recoiling, Kiki falls heavily against the wall. 'I feel dizzy,' she whimpers.

'Oh here we go.' I roll my eyes, though from the look on her face she does indeed look like she could pass out any minute.

'You have to believe me,' she urges, lips and legs visibly atremble. 'I tried to break it off yesterday at the spa. As soon as we stepped inside the treatment room I realised I couldn't go on – this is where Dean and I married after all!'

'And what a sacred moment that was,' I sneer.

'He wouldn't listen to reason,' she continues. 'He got angry. I was afraid Dean might hear us arguing so I back-pedalled. It's not what I wanted! I've never done anything like this before. It's like I've been possessed!' she wails.

I say nothing.

Sensing her supernatural protestations are falling on deaf ears she asks, 'What are you going to do about this?' and points to the evidence.

'That's up to you.' I remain curt.

'What do you mean?' Her eyes strain as if I am the torturer, she the victim.

I shrug, not buying into her angst. 'Well, either you tell him or I do.'

'You wouldn't!' She looks stricken.

'Of course I would,' I scoff. 'Why wouldn't I?'

'Because I love him!' she wails. 'Because I didn't mean for any of this to happen!'

I emit a testy sigh. 'And why should I believe that?'

'Because it's the *truth*!' she near-screams. 'I never- Oh god!' She lurches forward as if jabbed in the stomach. 'I have to sit down.' Now on the sofa, with her head in her hands, she begins to rock maniacally and then the babbling begins: 'I don't know what came over me. This whole thing- I can't explain—'

'Try.' I dare her, sourly. 'Try the real truth.'

Her eyes flit as she apparently searches within for some feasible explanation. When her mind is done roaming, the hysteria subsides and she begins speaking as if under hypnosis.

'Ever since I first saw Ryan look at you, then fawn over you and touch you . . .' She gives an involuntary spasm. 'It's like it triggered some primal jealousy in me. *And it doesn't make any sense!*' She looks agonised. 'I've never wanted him for myself. I've turned him down time and time again with no regrets.' She takes a breath. 'Maybe that's it – maybe for the first time I could see it wasn't me he was craving over everyone else.' She takes a moment to absorb the thought. 'Not that it excuses what I did.'

'No, it doesn't,' I confirm.

'It's like I've become taken over by this dark alter ego,' she gurgles.

'Oh please.'

'Have you never felt like that?' She looks pleadingly at me. 'Like you are at the mercy of your
emotions? It's all I could think about – winning him
back, getting him to look at me like the goddess he
always told me I was.'

'But my father looks at you like that. Every day.'
I'm confused. 'Isn't that enough?'

'It should be, shouldn't it?' she says, suddenly
wistful. 'Dean is the best thing to ever happen to me.
I can't believe how wonderful he's been. So devoted.
And fun! All my other relationships have been such
a *struggle*, one or the other of us vying for control.
With Dean it's always been so comfortable and . . .
warm. I never knew love could be like that.'

'So then how could Ryan even be a temptation, if
you really felt like that?' It seems absurd – you get
the thing that everyone craves and then go all out to
sabotage it. It's nuts.

Again her eyes roam the room as if she's looking
for a clue. 'I guess deep down I never really felt I
deserved to be loved like that.'

'So you did something to make you utterly un-
deserving?'

She looks up at me with suitably tortured eyes.
'I've hated myself every single day since he got here.
I wanted to stop. But I couldn't.'

For a moment she sits there, shell-shocked, and
then she speaks, this time in a small, resigned voice:

'So now it's all ruined. All the good in my life is gone. What do I have without Dean?'

'Heyyy! It's my two favourite girls!' We look up to see Ryan stood in the doorway.

Before I get the chance to tell him that now is not a good time, Kiki flies at him, thrashing wildly as she uses her fists to vent all her frustrations and remorse on his chest. *Get out! Get out! Get out!* she screeches like a crazed banshee, wrenching up the words 'I HATE YOU!' from her very core.

I'm stunned by her exorcism but Ryan, as ever, is unfazed. While Kiki scuttles hoarse and sobbing into the bathroom, he whistles, 'Wow. I'm not sure whether that was PMT or GBH.'

'Neither,' I tell him, in a death-knell tone. 'It's RYH.'

'RYH? What's that?'

'Ryan, You're History.'

'What?'

'You have to leave.'

'Oh do I?' he swaggers. 'As a matter of fact your father has invited—'

'Consider yourself uninvited,' I cut in. 'I think you've screwed enough Langstons, don't you?'

His eyes dim as he looks at me. Finally I've got through. 'She'll talk him round,' he nods in the direction of the bathroom. 'Beg his forgiveness. Promise a fresh start. But look at you – all alone.'

'Don't worry about it,' I retaliate as I forcibly

shove him out the door. 'I'm the best company I ever had.'

For a moment I lean heavily on the wall, placing my palms flat to the plaster trying to centre myself while my veins feel like they are coursing with triple espresso. So many emotions, I don't know which to tend to first – the euphoria of banishing Ryan, the concern for my father, the nagging, nauseous yearning for Santiago, the mixed feelings I find myself having for Kiki. She does seem genuinely devastated. Sorry in every way it is possible to be sorry. And, now I come to think of it, her eyes did look a little pink when she came in for dinner last night. I didn't really register it at the time because I was so preoccupied with Santiago's departure. I sigh. There's no denying that we all make mistakes, my dad has certainly made similar ones in his time. In fact, now I come to think of it, I would consider Ryan one of my errors of judgement so I suppose Kiki and I have something in common after all. Wouldn't it be the more sisterly thing to do for us girls to band together against the lothario rather than let him have the final say?

Suddenly there's a smash from the bathroom.

'Kiki! Kiki? Open the door!' I rattle the handle frantically.

'It was an accident!' she cries, revealing a floor jagged with glinting spears of glass. 'I just wanted some water but my hands were shaking—'

'Okay, just leave it, come on through to the lounge.' I lead her firmly by her wrist. I can't help but feel a wave of sympathy as I sit beside her. We are both so riddled with regrets right now. I know I would give anything for a second chance with Santiago – to rewind the past weeks, erase Ryan and then play the days again powered by a bolder heart.

If you give a second chance, I wonder, does it improve your chances of getting one?

'What if neither of us said anything to Dean?' I find myself proposing.

She looks up at me, eyes mottled red.

'Ryan has done enough damage to you and me, why let him hurt my father, your husband as well?'

Kiki is breathless. 'Ava, do you mean that?'

I actually do. At this point it seems less a question of morals and more a question of damage limitation. For my dad's sake I'd like to think this situation could be salvaged. There's just one absolute condition:

'You'd have to promise to never see Ryan again.'

'Oh that's easy,' she half laughs.

'Are you sure? It wasn't so easy for the past fortnight.'

'Believe me, I've woken up now. *You've* woken me up. It's over.'

I nod, believing her. Her attack was no act.

'You'd probably better splash some water on your face before—. What?'

439

I turn and follow her now terrified gaze to the door. It's Dad. And there's no mistaking his expression – Ryan has clearly left him the cruellest parting gift.

'I've come for my passport.' He speaks with robotic detachment.

Kiki goes to reach out to him but Dad rejects her. 'Don't. Just don't.'

'But—'

'Kiki.' His temples pulse.

She falls back on to the sofa, paralysed with contrition as he reaches into the drawer, roots for what he needs and heads back out the door. I sprint after him.

'Dad, where are you going?'

He continues to march forth. 'Back to England. To Bath. To your mother.'

'*My mother?*' I scramble alongside him, now he's the one who sounds possessed.

'I have to apologise to her. What Kiki has done to me, I did to her. I have to make it right.' Suddenly he stalls. 'Do you want to come with me?'

'What? Back to Bath?' The words sound so alien. I'm thrown utterly off-kilter. How can everything have gone so pear-shaped so fast – a landslide of misfortune beginning with Santiago's departure.

'Well?' He's impatient for an answer.

I flounder. 'Well, obviously I'm planning on going back eventually, but *right now*?' Then again, is there anything to stay for with no Santiago and no father? As my mind races every which way I try and rein it back to logic. 'I think the best plan is for me to stick here with Café Tropicana and in my spare time I can go online and research potential café venues in Bath and when something appropriate comes up—'

'Like the shop in The Corridor?'

'Like the shop in The Corridor,' I confirm, surprised he remembered the detail.

'Actually, that's available now.'

'How do you know?' I gasp.

'Because I own the lease.'

'What?' I can barely process the information. 'What are you saying?'

He gives me a sly look.

'It was you who outbid me?' I can feel my heartbeat echoing in my chest. It can't be true.

'Yes,' he confirms his subversion. 'So it's yours any time you want it.'

Now it's my turn to feel dizzy. 'Why would you do that?' I mumble. 'Why would you deliberately stand between me and my dream?' I am beyond stunned. Is there one solitary trustworthy soul on this entire planet?

'Don't look at me like that, Ava – I so wanted you to visit and my motives weren't entirely selfish . . .'

As he continues speaking his words distort and warp with the rushing in my head. Even if I could hear him, there's not a thing he could say that would make it all right. All I can think is that none of this madness and mess and heartache would have happened if he hadn't meddled. *None of it.*

'Ava, I've got to go.' He's touching my arm. 'They have a car waiting for me, it's the only one available. If I don't go now . . .'

I don't respond.

'Ava?'

My gaze is blurred. My limbs are weighted down. I feel winded.

'Just go,' is all I can manage.

For a good ten minutes after he's gone I remain motionless, overwhelmed with a feeling of being toyed with and betrayed. I'm too weak to feel angry. I'm too stunned to be able to focus. *He didn't!* He did. *It can't be true!* It is. All the struggle, the arguments, the sunburn, the sweating, the sleazy time with Ryan, the falling in love with Santiago, all for nothing . . . All but the last I can live with – most of it is done now, regrettable yet forgettable. But what kind of father would wish a broken heart on his own daughter?

I try and picture myself in Bath, envisioning how things could have been – a café cosy with chattering customers, Ollie making me laugh as I perform my artful cinnamon dustings, the girls popping by for a Saturday shopping break, a café name I actually wanted, a design entirely of my choosing. Sipping that elusive perfect blend . . . Everything just as I always hoped it would be. But instead I'm here feeling cheated and mangled and, yet again, abandoned.

Eventually Kiki appears by my side. 'Ava. Are you okay?' She squats beside me on the path. 'I brought you a drink.' She hands me one of the two brandy miniatures she's carrying. 'For the nerves.'

I hold mine limply.

'Come on.' She unscrews the top for me. 'After the fourth, things start to feel a lot better.'

I shake my head. Drinking just exacerbates a situation for me. I wish I could drink to forget but with me I drink to make embarrassing phone calls. Even the smell of booze on Kiki's breath makes me want to ring Santiago. My hand goes to his phone. I've been feeling so cut off knowing I can't call him but I realise now, all too depressingly, that if he wanted to speak to me he could, he certainly knows the number.

'Don't you think we should try and get him back?'

For one hopeful moment I think she means Santiago. But then she mentions my father's name.

I shake my head. 'Not really.'

'But he's so upset, Ava. I can't bear to think of him on that long flight back to England, all by himself, torturing himself with thoughts of—' Her voice quavers. 'Don't you think we should stick together? Try and work things out?'

Frankly I'm so numb I just don't care any more. I can't even reply to her questions.

'Ava! Where have you gone!' Kiki clicks her fingers in front of my face.

'Look, Kiki!' I suddenly snap. 'You do what you've got to do. I need to be by myself for a while.'

'But—'

'There are no cars to take you to the airport, Dad left in the only one. Short of you hijacking one of the horses and taking a short cut through the fields, you're not going to get to him in time anyway.'

'That's brilliant!' She leaps to her feet, suddenly energised.

'No, it's not.' I frown.

'Yes it is. I'm going to get him back! I'm going to get my husband back!'

And, despite the fact that I could have sworn Kiki had a major aversion to horses, she does a two-legged gallop in the direction of the stables.

Has the world gone mad?

Suddenly I'm distracted by a scratching in the undergrowth and out lumbers the world's biggest iguana, eyeballing me in a menacing fashion. For once I don't scuttle back afraid. Instead my jaw juts as I give a low grizzle: *'What are you looking at?'*

36

When I find myself getting in the way of other hotel guests dripping back to their rooms from the pool, I decide to relocate to the ledge where Santiago suggested we set up a little franchise. (I may be a zombie but I'm a sentimental zombie.) Did I really read him so wrong? When he asked me if I could ever imagine living somewhere so remote it felt like a proposal to me. Was that interpretation entirely wishful thinking on my part? I stare out at the shimmering blue and the beauty actually smarts.

'Miss Ava?'

'No, I miss Santiago,' I want to reply.

'I'm sorry.' The hotel staffer looks fretful. 'It's bad.'

'What is?' I look around me for a clue. Bad hair? Bad weather? Is there a perilous storm approaching and all hands are required to batten down the hatches?

'Miss Kiki,' he grimaces.

Oh dear. Her drunkenness has obviously been clocked. Perhaps they want me to quietly escort her back to her room.

'Is she?' I throw my arms around to enact the word 'crazy'.

'No,' he looks on the verge of tears now. 'She is broken.'

'She's broken something? It's okay, we'll replace—'

'No-no,' he shakes his head. 'She is broken. She fell.'

I'm on my feet, level with his face. 'Not from a horse?' I speak my fear out loud, heart pounding.

He nods.

Oh god! It's my fault! I put that stupid idea in her drunken skull.

'Where is she?' I panic. 'Is she okay?'

'We want to take her to the hospital. Can we?'

'Yes, yes, of course, I'll come with you!' I hurry after him.

I think these past twenty-four hours may have been the worst of my life. Please tell me that there's nothing worse to come.

'Is she breathing?' I survey Kiki's muddy, bloody head as she is slotted on a stretcher in the back of the shuttle bus. (The one blessing being that the transport has returned and we're not having to give her a fireman's lift to the hospital.)

446

'Breathing, yes. But she is unconscious,' he informs me.

'But she's going to be okay?' I feel so responsible.

'She will be in very good hands at the hospital,' is all he will commit to.

En route I realise how ill-equipped I am for this situation – what if they ask for her next of kin? The only thing I know is that her father is a hotel manager who lives in Miami. What about medical records, blood type, allergies? I don't even know her date of birth.

Her bag is still strapped to her body so I start rifling through in the hope I can find some emergency data. A Filofax! Excellent start. I flick immediately to the address section hoping that someone's name will ring a bell – even if it's a friend in Tamarindo who can point me in the right direction . . . Nothing until I reach D and get a whoosh of hope at the word 'Dad'. I take out my phone and dial directly.

Please answer, please answer . . . I mantra to myself as I inadvertently reach to grip her hand. Riiing, riiing . . .

Someone's picked up! I look to Kiki for some kind of reciprocal 'hoorah' expression but, of course, find none.

'Hello?'

'Mr, um . . .' It's then I realise I don't know her maiden name. 'Um . . . is that Kiki's father?'

'Yes,' he replies cautiously, 'Who is this?'

'Um, well, technically I suppose I'm your step-grandchild!'

'*What?*' he snaps.

I take a breath preparing to expound on our complex connection but realise there's no time for geneology and cut to the chase: 'I'm calling from Costa Rica, I'm here with your daughter. She married my father, Dean Langston . . .?'

'What the hell are you talking about?' His impatience is growing.

This isn't going so well. I need to get back to basics. 'You do have a daughter?'

'Yes.'

'And her name is Kiki?' I take it slow.

'Yes.'

'Are you saying you didn't know she'd got married?' I finally isolate the problem.

'I had no idea.' He sounds lost.

Wow, one person who's even less in the loop than me.

I want to tell him that they had a heavenly ceremony in Punta Islita and drank guanábana champagne cocktails but now is not the time.

'I don't want you to be alarmed but your daughter has had an accident. We're on the way to the hospital and I just wanted to give you the details in case—'

'*What is it, what's wrong with her?*' Now he's coming round to my level of panic.

'She fell off a horse.'

'A *horse*?' He sounds outraged. 'But she hates horses.'

I stop myself saying, 'Apparently the feeling is mutual.' Instead I say, 'Seeing as Miami is relatively close, I wanted to offer you the option of coming over . . .'

I feel a little guilty as I say it, as if he'll know that I'm trying to palm her care off on him, but there is no hesitation. 'I'll be on the next flight,' he tells me. 'Can I reach you on this number when I get there?'

'Yes, and if I could take your mobile number? Thank you. And your name?' I remember to ask in the nick of time.

'Ken. Ken Taylor.'

This is all so awkward – two strangers trying to politely negotiate a crisis situation. I hate to drop the bomb and run but we're already at the hospital.

'I have to go now,' I tell him as I duck out of the back of the shuttle bus, never taking my eyes off Kiki. 'I don't think you can use mobiles inside . . . Mr Taylor?' The line seems to have gone strangely quiet.

'Tell her—' he blurts, the words catching in his throat.

'Yes?'

I can hear him struggling but he can't seem manage anything further.

'It's okay, I'll send her your love,' I assure him. 'Call me when you get here.'

As they rattle Kiki onward I am waylaid with paperwork at the reception desk.

'The patient's name?'

'Kiki Langston,' I reply.

'Your name?'

'Ava Langston.'

'Sisters?'

'Er, yes,' I lie, having some recollection that unless you are a relative they won't let you see the patient and right now I'm all she's got.

As the questions continue I feel like I'm in an improvisational sketch, making up answers as I go along.

'Does she have any allergies?'

'I'll have to check with her dad.'

'You have different fathers?

'Yes. Well, actually . . .' I decide I'd better come clean. 'The thing is, she's married to mine.'

The receptionist looks appalled.

'She's not really my sister, she's my stepmother.' I can see I'm making this worse, giving the nurse flashes of the slapping sister/mother scene in *Chinatown*.

She lays down her pen.

'It's okay,' I assure her. 'Her father is on his way.'

'You mean your husband?'

'No, no, we're not married, I've never even met him.' I sigh, trying to get back on track. 'Look, I can't give you very much information other than she was very emotional and distressed before the fall—'

'Drinking?'

'Yes. Brandy mostly, I think.'

'Okay, well, if you would like to take a seat we'll call you when you can see her.'

'Right.'

I wander to the waiting room wondering, Have I done all that I can? If she really were my sister would I be demanding to remain by her side? Then again I'd probably just be in the way – they could be operating this very second. I feel both queasy and anxious at the thought, as if her life is somehow as much in *my* hands as the doctors.

So what now? I think to myself as I watch various hospital activities going on around me. I can't call my dad because he's mid-air, Ryan is a clear no-go. I wonder if I should try Carla or even Richard at the Green Turtle Gift Shop? As I reopen her Filofax, the page falls beyond the diary and address book, revealing a little scrapbook section. Pasted upon the colourful pages is an assortment of romantic memorabilia – a Tamarindo Diria cocktail napkin, a pressed flower, a note of the date he first said, 'I love you!', a ribbon from a gift box, Post-its from her pillow – every item annotated and relating to Kiki

451

and my father. I feel like a private eye who has just been given tangible evidence of her sincerity – this is not the collection of a mercenary on the make, but the girly-sentimental treasures of someone who can't quite believe her luck that she has met the man of her dreams. I know, because I still carry the ticket stub from the San José symphony like a charm in my pocket.

On the last page is a photo of them in matching bathrobes looking insanely blissful and entwined – the kind of picture that would motivate you to overcome your dread fear of horses and mount a rampaging stallion.

If there had been the slightest inkling that Santiago liked me back, I would have done the same for him. But he didn't.

I don't know how long I sit there lost in thought, periodically distracted by medical odours, but now the nurse is standing before me, saying I can see Kiki.

'Ava?' she blinks at me, looking disorientated.

I smile back as warmly and encouragingly as I can.

'Is Dean here?'

I wince at the hope in her voice. I shake my head. 'I'm sorry.'

Her hand goes to her brow but I quickly guide it back to her side. 'You have a few stitches, it's probably best not to touch them.'

She tries to sit up, flinching at the unexpected pain.

'Bruises,' I tell her. 'But no broken bones.'

'So he's gone?'

I nod.

She slumps back into her pillow as she realises that her plan failed. She didn't get her husband back.

'It's going to be okay,' I tell her, knowing nothing of the sort but wanting to believe it myself. 'Is there someone I can call for you, a friend?'

Her face shows blank despondence.

'Well, um, I hope it's all right, but I called your dad.'

You did what?' she splutters, suddenly animated.

'I called your dad.' I don't know why I'm telling her twice when it went down so badly the first time.

'You actually spoke to him?'

'Yes.' Oh dear, what have I done?

She looks bewildered. 'Wha-what did he . . .' She trails off.

'It was a very brief conversation but the upshot is that he'll be here in a few hours.'

'What do you mean?' Again she looks stricken.

'He's coming to see you.' I state it as plainly as I can.

'Here? He's coming to Costa Rica? Why?'

I look around for a nurse. She seems quite delirious. 'I just thought, I don't know . . . I thought

453

it was what you're supposed to do in this kind of situation – call the parents.'

'Did you call my mum?'

'Well, no. I can if you like, I just thought that even if she tore up to London and got a flight there, she'd then be in the air for the next ten hours worrying, not knowing . . .'

Kiki's brain seems to be busy processing other information.

'Did you tell him I was married?'

'I may have . . .' I cringe, not quick enough to lie.

'What did he say?'

'Not a lot. It was rushed . . .'

'Well, it doesn't matter now, it's over,' she says bleakly.

'We don't know that for sure.' I realise now that to pray for my dad and Kiki to reunite is to wish away the chance of reconciliation for my mother, and how could I deny her a cure for all that bitterness and misery?

'I mean the wedding day is over,' she corrects me. 'The whole issue of Dad giving me away . . .'

I ease on to the edge of her bed. 'You didn't want that?'

Her eyes get a confrontational glint. 'I'm not his to give. He might think I belong to him, that he gets to decide everything I do in my life, but he doesn't.'

454

'So you decided to give yourself away?'

'*My* choice.' She nods, then suddenly looks remorseful. 'I'm so sorry we didn't invite you.'

I shrug. 'It doesn't matter.' It certainly feels like water under the bridge now.

'It was my decision,' she says in a small voice. 'Dean wanted you there, obviously but . . .' She sighs heavily.

'But what?' I'm more curious than angry now.

'It's just this father/daughter thing.' She looks embarrassed. 'I wish it didn't get to me as much as it does but it's like my trigger.'

'How do you mean?'

She sighs, searching for the words to explain. 'You know how when you're single it makes you feel sick or tragically alone to be in the company of couples, especially lovey-dovey touchy-feely ones?'

'Yes,' I nod, only having to cast my mind back to when I first arrived and joined the newly-weds for dinner to find a match for that feeling.

'Well, it's like that,' Kiki confirms. 'If I'm around happy families it just reminds me of what I don't have and I didn't want my special day ruined with . . .' She seems distracted by the expression on my face. 'What?'

'I don't really think that would have been a problem,' I frown. Surely she knows that prior to this trip my dad and I were hardly close.

455

'Look, I know it's irrational and it was a selfish decision but we can't all have the idyllic father-daughter relationship you two have.'

I look around the room to see whom she can possibly be addressing. 'Are you talking to me?' I laugh. 'We may have straightened out a few things since I got here but before that it was terrible. We barely even had a relationship.'

'That's not how he tells it.'

I'm incredulous. How can he possibly spin it so we come out looking like Zoë and Johnny Ball?

'When we first met he told me how independent you were.'

Didn't have a lot of choice, I feel like muttering to myself.

'He said he respected the fact that you'd never asked him for anything, that you'd made your own way in the world. He thinks parents cock things up when they get too involved, and speaking from personal experience I have to agree.' She pauses and then says, '"*If we're always guided by other people's thoughts, what is the point in having our own?*" Are you familiar with that quote?'

'Not until now.' I confess. But it does resonate. It is possible that my dad actually did me a favour with his absence? That instead of wasting years trying to gain his approval I made choices based on what suited me? It would certainly seem that an overly involved parent can be a potential curse. Perhaps the lesson is not in which type of father you get, but how you react to him.

But how exactly are you supposed to react when your father deliberately sabotages your life? I'm still trying to get my head round his Bath café manoeuvres – hardly an example of him standing back and letting me do my own thing. I probe Kiki on the subject but she doesn't seem in on the deal and is eager to get back to rationalising my father's meagre involvement in my life.

'You are both such busy people, after all . . .'

Now I'm getting irritated – it's one thing to get a different perspective on your formative years, another to have a relative stranger telling your life back to you in a way that doesn't ring true.

'I was never too busy to be his daughter,' I contend. 'If he'd have wanted that.'

'He got the feeling that you wanted your space.'

'How convenient for him!' I snap, irritation growing, goodwill dwindling.

'Well, didn't you?'

'No,' I say, though it may or may not be true.

'Well then, why didn't you tell him?'

'How did this get to be about me?' I snap but again her words hit home.

Apparently a father will go about being a dad in the way he thinks is best. It's up to you to let him know if that way is not working for you.

'Have you ever talked to your dad about him

being overly controlling?' I ask Kiki, switching the spotlight to her relationship.

'Of course! We've had so many arguments—'

'I'm not talking about accusations and recriminations,' I explain. 'It seems to me that you get a lot further by asking questions and getting to the root of someone's behaviour as opposed to stockpiling the case for the defence.' I take a moment to sit with my legal metaphor then add, 'It's answers you want really, isn't it?'

Like right now I want to know why my father screwed my Bath deal. And why Santiago left without saying goodbye. And, while we're at it, why he doesn't love me back.

As Kiki and I continue to talk I realise for the first time just how much we have in common – both our parents divorced when we were teenagers, both of us grew up feeling like we got a raw deal with our dads, both of us have made bad choices with men, both of us thought we'd found our dream guys in Costa Rica, though she did get a little further with hers than mine. As we get deeper, it dawns on me that with her dad being so controlling, her way of reclaiming her power was to control *other* men, while for me, I was looking for a man to take the reins so I could lean my head upon his shoulder and not feel so isolated. At least that was true until Santiago. He definitely sparked a competitive edge in me that levelled out into some excellent teamwork. Or so I thought . . .

The nurse comes by to suggest Kiki needs rest but she disagrees. 'I need this conversation more!'

We talk right up until her father arrives.

'I can stay if you like,' I offer as she prepares to receive him. 'Or wait outside. Or tell him to go away. Whatever you prefer.'

'I'll be fine,' she assures me with new-found confidence and a plumped pillow. 'I can do this.'

'It doesn't have to be a battle,' I remind her as I turn to leave.

'I know – I'm going to turn it around by asking about *him*,' she asserts.

'Don't be surprised if he wants to ask how you are first,' I motion to her bandaged bonce.

She smiles. 'It's perfect timing really, if the conversation goes pear-shaped I can blame it on concussion.'

'Okay, well, call me if you need anything, otherwise I'll check back on you tomorrow morning.' I give her a little 'good luck' wave then hand the baton to the sandy-haired man waiting outside.

Whatever issues they may have, it has to be noted that when it came to her hour of need, her father dropped everything and flew to her side.

That's a quality we all want in a dad *and* in a partner, isn't it?

Hmm, obviously something I have to work on because, when I needed them most, the two key men in my life flew away.

37

After a muddled and pensive night's sleep back at the hotel I awake eager to speak to my father. Yesterday I was incensed at him for meddling in my life, but my dreams were peppered with flashes of all the magical things that have happened over the past few weeks – the first cappuccino I prepared for a real paying customer, watching the howler monkeys at play, the pinky-lilac sunsets – and amid the killer ache for Santiago I find myself feeling grateful for having had these experiences. (This is definitely one of those times where getting philosophical seems the speediest route to sanity – everything happens for a reason, *right*?)

I scooch myself into an upright position and take the phone in my hand. It takes me back to my youth to dial a number not knowing if my mother or father will pick up.

'Hellooooo!' Well, the voice is female so I know it's my mother but I barely recognise the tone – she

461

sounds ecstatic. 'Ava, darling, hold on a minute . . .' she coos and I hear some background clattering as she sets down the phone – sounds like heels on the tiled floor. My mother in heels! Well, that's bad news for Kiki. I guess the reunion was a success. It's strange how much of a mismatch my own parents seem now, I can barely imagine them together.

'Here I am!' she puffs. 'Sorry about that. It's all go here today!'

'Well, I won't interrupt, I just wanted a quick word with Dad?'

'He's not here,' she sings.

'Oh, well, when will he be back?'

'He's not coming back. Oh Ava, it was such a shock to see him – he's so *old*!'

'Well, fifteen years will take its toll on anyone,' I reason before starting: 'What do you mean he's not coming back? Where's he gone? What happened?'

She sighs, sounding almost awestruck. 'I just got my life back.'

'*How?*' I gasp.

'I opened the door and there he was and two things hit me – one, how old he is—'

'Yes, I got that.'

'And two, he's just a man!'

I wait for her to continue.

'All these years . . . I thought he was everything, I thought he'd *taken* everything when he left. I was nothing without him. But now I see that was just my

462

heart's trickery. He's just a man. He doesn't hold the key to me. There is no alchemy that only he can provide.'

I can't believe what I'm hearing. And there's more.

'When I saw how old he was, it was like I finally realised just how much time I've wasted. I couldn't see it until today – *I'm old too!* Anyway, I can't talk now because I've got a hair appointment and then Ollie's taking me shopping at Jolly's.'

My jaw drops. That man is a saint. As for the less virtuous elements of society . . .

'I don't suppose you know where Dad's gone?' I jump in before she scoots off to shed her skin.

'Don't know and I don't care,' is her breezy response.

'Okay. Well, have a nice makeover.'

I feel a bit flat as I put down the phone. I should be both delighted and inspired by my mum's news, but frankly I feel a bit left behind in the life-transforming department. I'm still at the stage where I believe that Santiago is my own personal alchemist. I hope it doesn't take me fifteen years to see that that's not true. I obviously need to get back to Café Tropicana, back to having a sense of purpose. But first I need to check on Kiki.

Oh no! I should never have left her unattended – she's awash with tears. I hurry to her bedside shooting a warning look at her father only to find that he's equally dribbly of eye.

'I'll get some tea!' He springs to his feet, turning his face away from me, clearly uncomfortable with having his vulnerability witnessed by a stranger, his manly restraint making the moment all the more poignant.

'Are you okay?' I ask as the door closes behind him.

'I never knew . . .' she sobs, reaching for my hand.

'Never knew what?' I ask, squeezing her back.

'What he'd been through as a child.' Her eyebrows knot together. 'It's just like Dean,' she quavers, wiping her nose. 'His parents were never there for him but rather than perceiving it as a good thing, making him more independent, my father felt rejected and unloved.' She gulps back a further wobble. 'He always swore he would always be there for his child, and he was – he just took it to the point of suffocation.' She looks up at me with pained eyes. 'Why didn't he tell me this before?'

'It probably never even occurred to him.' I say, thinking of my dad's boarding-school scenario and the thirty years it took me to learn of it. 'You know, it really does seem that it's not up to them to tell us, it's up to us to ask.'

'Wow.' Kiki swallows the thought and lets her breathing even out.

'I know.'

464

For a moment we just sit there, marvelling at how topsy-turvy we've had things in our adult years. As much as the man/woman roles needed updating with the sexual revolution, so now do our outdated notions of parent/child responsibilities. After a certain age we're partners, just as much in charge of the relationship as they are.

'Tea!' Ken returns with a little clutch of polystyrene cups and I take this as my cue to let them get back to their heart-to-hearting.

'I'll take mine To Go!' I announce making a little 'cheers' motion as I exit.

Edging down the hospital corridor nursing my hot beverage, I think about how both Kiki and I have given our dads so few points for effort over the years, focusing instead on all the things they *didn't* do. We go on and on about the casual remarks destined to 'scar us for life' when in reality we've probably hurt our fathers in ways we'll never know, because they've never told us.

We expect so much from them and yet I suppose the fact is that some combinations of child and parent work better than others. That's not even good or bad parenting, that's just chemistry.

That said, seeing Kiki and Ken make amends makes me all the more eager to make peace with my father. I don't want to wait until I'm hooked up to a respirator for our reconciliation scene. Mind you, there's not a lot I can do until he deigns to call me from whatever continent he sees fit to grace next. I know he was talking about Romania being the next big thing property-wise. For all I know he could be drowning his sorrows in Transylvania.

When the time comes for me to leave for the airport, my guilt at leaving Kiki is assuaged by the knowledge that she is in good hands – the hospital have given her the all-clear and her dad has offered to go back to Tamarindo with her for a few days to make sure she has someone to keep an eye on her until her head heals, and then hold her hand when Dean finally calls and she learns her fate. All this, not in a controlling way, just a helpful, 'got your back' support.

Though Kiki is concerned about me heading off alone, the reality is that with the solitude comes a kind of relief. I get my first sense of calm in days while sitting by myself on the plane, once again grateful to be lifted high above my earthly troubles. It's all going to be all right, I tell myself. There was a spate of madness, a frenzy of clashing personalities, but now the dust is settling, I'm getting back to me and I can see that I have exactly what I came out here for: the café.

The first thing I do when I arrive back, after I've squeezed Wilbeth and Milena tighter than the espresso compactor, is to advertise for a new member of staff. I sit in the newspaper ad department and mull over the appropriate adjectives . . .

'Self-starter, quick witted, fast-pouring . . . Someone with a good head for figures, preferably bilingual.' Do I need to specify Spanish and English? I suppose I should or I'll end up with someone who speaks Finnish and Urdu. Um . . . 'Someone confident, well groomed . . .' Can you say that about a woman? 'Someone with a strong work ethic who can also make a positive contribution to our welcoming ambiance. Someone who knows when to be chatty and when to be respectfully low-key. Someone honest, patient, compassionate and dignified.' Oh god, it sounds like I'm trying to employ a deity. I need to let them know I do consider flawed human beings as well – 'Wilful curmudgeons also considered.' Best I wrap it up: 'If you both know and love coffee we'd be delighted to hear your ideas on the perfect blend.'

There. Done.

The ad itself is hardly the problem. Filling Santiago's shoes is another matter. There was just something about his presence . . . I try to stop myself getting morose again. He can't have been the man I thought he was or he wouldn't have walked out on me like that. I have to move on.

And yet.

When it comes to changing the things we argued over, I find I don't want to. I like the café just the way it is.

38

The next day I'm busily fixing a wonky table leg when I catch myself smirking at the memory of Santiago's scolding me for turning up late after the ATV tour with Ryan. An hour on I get a sentimental pang recalling how he always repositioned the cakes once I had set them out. This is bizarre – how I can be missing his terse side and controlling foibles as much as his kindness and consideration? I guess the good and the bad are so tightly integrated with him that to love him is to love all of him.

When my phone rings later that afternoon I hope, as I do each time it lights up, that it is him calling me to explain our separation has all been a terrible mistake but it's not. It's the other MIA Man in my life – my father – announcing that he's on his way back to Costa Rica.

'Have you spoken to Kiki?' is the first question from my lips. (Though what I really want to ask is: 'Have you heard from Santiago?')

'Yes,' he confirms. 'In fact, that's something I wanted to ask your advice about.'

'Really?' That's a turn-up for the books.

'She wants me to have dinner with her and her father. I'm in two minds . . .'

'Go.'

'You think?' He sounds unconvinced.

'Definitely. I think you'll find the experience quite edifying.'

'Is that so?' he sounds intrigued. 'If you're sure, then . . .'

'She really is desperately sorry, Dad. I know that for a fact.' I never thought I'd be coming out in the corner of the adulterer, but life is full of surprises.

'Well, I've hardly been a saint in my time,' he concedes. 'And the thought of being without her . . .' He trails off, instantly wretched. 'I suppose it wouldn't hurt to give her one more chance.'

I experience a stab of envy. They're going to work it out, I can feel it.

'So, Dad,' I decide to cut to the chase, no time to wait for The Appropriate Moment.

'Yes.'

'I need to know – why did you sabotage my café plans in Bath?'

There's a short silence before he emits a sheepish, 'I told you the day I left.'

Like that's going to get him off the hook.

'I didn't hear a thing you said that day,' I explain.

470

'I was too stunned to take in anything except the bald fact of what you'd done. Tell me again.'

'Well, first off I didn't see it as sabotage, just a *delay*,' he begins.

'But why? Why go to so much trouble to get me over here?'

'I don't know that it even makes sense now. Obviously I wanted to see you—'

'The real reason, Dad. Let's get to the crux.'

'Basically I knew Kiki had a big issue with her father, so much so she wouldn't even have him at the wedding—'

'Speaking of which,' I cut in, 'I know it was at her insistence that I wasn't invited. She told me.'

'That's right,' my father confirms. 'And as low as I felt for going along with it, you can't have an unhappy bride, there's just no point.'

'Fair enough,' I concede. Put that simply, it actually makes sense.

'Once the wedding was out of the way,' he continues, 'I convinced myself that if she could just meet you and see how good things could be between a father and daughter then she'd have hope that her own relationship could be salvaged.'

'You wanted me there so we could be a role model for her?'

'Well, don't sound so dumbfounded!' he hoots. 'I was willing to try anything at that point – she told me she'd cut him out of her life and that it was for

471

the best, but every day in some way or other it would flare up like a rash. Even in her sleep – she'd have nightmares and wake up screaming at him.'

And to think I thought she had an issue-free life.

'Why didn't you tell me all this in the beginning?' I ask. I might have had a tad more sympathy.

'I couldn't, it would have compromised her privacy. Besides, she wants everyone to think she's got life on a leash. She can't bear people feeling sorry for her.'

I can relate to that. I never wanted people looking at me the way they look at my mother.

'She wouldn't get any therapy,' Dad continues. 'Wouldn't even discuss the possibility. Bringing you over was the only thing I could think of to help.'

'That's the strangest logic and yet, in a really roundabout way, it worked!' I laugh. Sure there had to be infidelity and rearing horses to move things on a stage or two but the end result is that she's now on good terms with her father. At something of a personal cost to mine, however.

'You know you're going to be fine, Dad. It's all going to work out between the two of you.'

'And what about you?' He sounds genuinely interested. 'How's everything going at the café?'

'Everything is going great. I do still have Santiago's phone,' I add, trying to sound light and breezy as I ask, 'Have you heard from him at all? Any idea of where I should send it on to?'

'Actually I haven't managed to get hold of him yet but I'm sure when I'm back in Tamarindo tomorrow—'

'Yes, well, let me know.' I have to change the subject, even talking about Santiago in this abstract way is causing my eyes to mist up. I miss that moody individual so much. 'I really should be getting back to the customers . . .' I submit.

'You know I'm going to make it up to you,' Dad hurries out his words, sounding earnest. 'I'm going to come to Manuel Antonio next week and we'll have some quality time together, just the two of us.'

For once I believe him and say 'I'll look forward to it' with sincerity.

'All right then, Little Red, off you go.'

'All right, Big Grey. I'm off!'

It's a treat to hear my dad laugh at my instigation and I put down the phone with a teary-eyed smile on my face.

Only to find that Wilbeth has just opened another packet of sugar in his usual explosive fashion. 'I'll pay! I'll pay!' he apologises as he crunches the scattered crystals underfoot, grinding them into white powder as he does his all-too-familiar apologetic dance.

Before I can respond Milena has instructed him to wait in the stockroom to allow her to deal with the mess. For someone so feisty, she's surprisingly patient when it comes to Wilbeth. So much so that when I arrive at work the next morning – after one of my most lonesome nights – she takes me to one side and shows me a Division of Labour Chart she's devised to play up both their strengths and minimise their weaknesses.

'He's so much better at stocktaking and end-of-day figures than I am,' she explains. 'I'd like to trade that for his practical chores. This way, he'll never have to open another bag of sugar again!'

I grin at her, impressed at her initiative. 'You're a smart girl, Milena. I wish I could clone you for the new job.'

'Any news on that yet?' Her ever-inquisitive eyebrows raise.

'I'm taking the applications home with me to review tonight.' I pause for a moment. 'Perhaps you'd like to sit in on the interviews with me?'

'Great!' she cheers.

For the rest of the day I feel like I'm going through the motions, amazed that I'm even able to function and oh-so-grateful every time someone is sweet to me because I still feel so fragile – I once heard heartbreak compared to a broken rib because no one can see your injury but it hurts every time you breathe. What keeps me going is Wilbeth and Milena and my beloved customers but all the while I eye the clock – just a few more hours before I can go home and crawl into bed, hug my pillow to my aching chest and put Ollie on speakerphone so we can continue plotting his upcoming visit.

Around 5.30 p.m. I run my hand along my arm surprised to find I actually have goose bumps. Am I finally acclimatising?

'I'm just going to step outside to warm up for a moment,' I tell a suitably surprised Milena.

The light is fading, the sun dipping into the sea and all our outdoor patrons are wending hotelward or transferring to the local bars for early evening cocktails. I sit on one of Santiago's hand-carved stools and lean back on the tree trunk and close my eyes, instantly soothed by the blackness beneath my lids. It feels good to have the balmy air wrap around me. I think tonight when I get back to the villa I might actually open a bottle of wine and sit out on the terrace for a while. But first I need to find the strength to perform my end-of-day chores.

I take an extended breath in and then waver it out. In, and out. In and—. Suddenly a million fireflies appear to be dancing outside of my lids. My eyes spring open to find the branches above me entwined with myriad flickery fairy lights – pulsating pinks and reds, purples, blues and yellows all winking and twinkling to chameleon effect. *Just as I had always fantasised.*

My stomach does a Mr Whippy swirl. I hardly

dare hope it, but could this multicoloured Morse code be spelling out a message from—

'Miss Ava?'

I look over to find Wilbeth sticking his head out the café door. 'There's someone here to see you about the job.'

My heart bungees upward, then begins yammering expectantly. I strain to make out the figure coming towards me – the silhouette is tall enough, the hair aptly wavy – *it is!* It's him! After so many phantom imaginings of Santiago coming through the door, I find his tangible presence overwhelming and my eyes instantly brim with tears. I can feel my body shaking and I want to propel myself into his arms, to feel his navy cotton-clad torso clasped to mine, but I can't bear a second cruel rejection – last time we were together he left me with only the flimsiest of farewells, I need to hear what he has to say before I react.

'Hello, Ava,' he begins, looking equally tentative.

'*Hola!*' I sing back, searching his eyes for some clue as to whether he's here for business or pleasure. Or, best of all, both.

For one fleeting moment I think he's going to swoop me up and embrace me with such vigour I would surely faint! But then he checks himself – his usual bravado is replaced with caution, my longing now pure nerves.

'I saw this.' Santiago hands me a newspaper

cutting that trembles in my hands.

I scan the keywords of the ad I placed – 'We are looking for someone fast-pouring . . . bilingual . . . number savvy . . . well groomed . . . dignified . . .' – and then my eyes start at the penultimate sentence: 'Wilful curmudgeons also considered.' Only now do I realise that I've put everything except 'shiny black hair and goes by the name of Santiago'.

'So curmudgeon is actually a desirable trait?' he teases, biting his lip.

I can't help but snuffle out loud – I hadn't realised the significance of what I had written! Should I be thanking my subconscious for his appearance here tonight?

'Are you serious about working here?' I ask, not quite trusting the veracity of the vision before me.

'Well, that depends on one crucial factor.' His voice lowers.

'What's that?' I croak.

'Ryan,' he says, face darkening.

'What about him?' I feel shifty at the mere thought of him.

'I see he's not here.' He glances around the café. 'And I see this.' He refers again to the job ad. 'But there's something I don't understand: that last night in Punta Islita, you said it was over between the two of you, yet when I came to your *casita*, the door was ajar, I looked in and there he was, *naked*.' His voice sours at the memory, as does my stomach.

'I could see how that could look bad,' I concede with a blush, 'but the reality is that he barged in and stripped on the spot, no invitation. In fact, technically it was *your* fault that he was naked – he said you were in the shower so he needed to use mine.'

Santiago checks his memory and finds a match.

'I promise you, there was nothing going on. And, as for now, Ryan is well and truly banished from this kingdom,' I assert.

Santiago's face brightens. 'That was my hope,' he admits. 'I did try to get an update from your father but as soon as I mentioned Ryan's name he changed the subject.'

'Yes, well, there's a good reason for that,' I puff. 'It turns out that Kiki and Ryan were having an affair.'

'While he was with you?' He looks scandalised, as if to say, *How could any man want more than you?*

'Well, yes,' I reply, 'but rather more importantly while *she* was with my father.'

Santiago shakes his head. 'Those two always had a strange energy between them but I never wanted to believe . . .' He trails off, looking despairing.

'It's okay,' I soothe. 'I really think Dad and Kiki are going to work it out.'

'Really?'

'There's still a chance for a happy ending,' I smile encouragingly. As soon as my words are out, they seem to take on a personal significance and before I know it, I find myself daring to ask, 'So is that why you left so suddenly, because you saw Ryan . . .' I don't want to continue reconjuring that image but I have to know.

He nods slowly, recalling the events from his perspective. 'Before that, at the hotel bar, when you told me that you two were no longer together, I was so optimistic,' he begins. 'I thought our time had finally come. And then your father made the announcement and it was so unexpected, not you winning but me being relocated to Tamarindo – I should have seen it coming but I didn't.'

'Me neither,' I confirm.

'I was in shock. Dean was so keen to show me the new project yet all I wanted was to get back to you and find out if you felt the same way as me, and if you did – *and I prayed you did, Ava,*' he husks, stepping closer, treating me to the gentlest waft of cinnamon, '– for us to work out a way to be together.'

I can't believe how close we were to the clifftop kiss of my dreams! 'Go on,' I prompt, mesmerised.

'Seeing you with Ryan was more than I could stand,' he continues. 'I had to get away – fast! And far . . .' He sighs.

I want to envelop and console him and show him that we can delete that memory and move on, yet after weeks of playing hide-and-seek with our feelings we seem wary of physically reaching for each other.

'So!' He nods again to the newspaper cutting. 'Do you think I might be what you're looking for?'

My face illuminates with hope and adoration as I breathe the words, 'You're exactly what I'm looking for!'

Then, just as I feel I might faint with anticipation, he gathers me up into his arms and melts me with the softest, warmest, hair-rumpling kiss. It's even more tender and charged than I could have dreamed. I feel a rushing as all my suppressed lovings come to the fore, celebrating the fact that they no longer have to deny their own existence. He's here – right here in my arms, kissing me with such seductive intensity that my nerve endings can't help but hallucinate all the pleasures to come.

'Finally!' Milena cheers from the doorway.

We look over and laugh, arms wrapped around and around each other.

'Really!' she tsks indignantly. 'What took you so long?'

Santiago studies me fondly before announcing, 'I guess you could say we were *percolating*!'

'Taking your own sweet time, more like!' she sneers like a cor-blimey Londoner.

'The best coffee is never instant!' he retaliates, happily. 'Sometimes great love requires great patience.'

I sigh deliriously as we wave off Wilbeth and Milena and then settle into the outdoor sofa. Snug to his warm chest, we talk through all the moments of burgeoning desire over the past weeks – from Tamarindo to Tortuguero – and with each reminiscence I feel what had become burdensome anguish lifting – now that we're free to say what we really feel and to intersperse each sentence with lusciously languorous kisses, these are memories to be savoured, part of our history together. Unlike any of my other relationships, there is such a promise of future and security with Santiago – we already have a home and business together and instead of the usual shifting sands beneath my feet, I feel like we have a solid foundation to build upon. Which is ironic considering we're actually on a beach.

'You know, it's terribly remiss of me,' I say, as my hand dips beneath Santiago's shirt collar and along his silken shoulder. 'But I haven't even offered you a coffee since you've been here!'

'Mmmm,' he savours, hand circling my hip, giving me tingles. 'I've been craving one of your caramel lattes all afternoon . . .'

'Really?' I say in a provocatively low voice, looking as if I'm moving in for a sultry kiss, only to jump up and run inside. 'Double or single shot?' I call back to him.

In seconds he's by my side, clearly eager to get back behind the counter. As I set out his cup and reach around him for a spoon I find myself flashing back to the day I so covetously watched the girl with the chocolate shaker at the Bridge, the afternoon that Ollie and I first spoke of owning a café. Just look how far I've come since then!

Our synchronised frothing and stirring gives me a wonderfully warm sense of familiarity. After so much anxiety and urgency, I now feel like we have all the time in the world. I love knowing that we'll be going back to the villa together after this – sharing one bed for the very first time! – and that tomorrow we'll be right back behind this counter, updating our coffee-bean order. The thought of both the routine and the new thrills to come makes me beam euphorically.

In turn, I feel his chest inflating with pleasure as he snuggles up behind me. 'You know, I think we've finally found it . . .' His breath warms my ear.

'What's that?' I ask, turning to face him, now hip to hip.

His espresso-dark eyes shine as he whispers these words: *'The perfect blend.'*

Divas Las Vegas

Belinda Jones

A tale of love, friendship and sequinned underpants . . .

Jamie and Izzy, friends for ever, have a dream: a spangly double wedding in Las Vegas. And at twenty-seven, they decide they've had enough crap boyfriends and they're ready for crap husbands – all they have to do is find them. And where better than Las Vegas itself, where the air is 70% oxygen and 30% confetti?

But as they abandon their increasingly complicated lives in sleepy Devon for the eye-popping brilliance of Las Vegas, their groom-grabbing plan starts to look less than foolproof. And those niggling problems they thought they'd left behind – like Izzy's fiancé and the alarming reappearance of Jamie's first love – just won't go away . . .

'A wise and witty read about the secret desires deep with us'
Marie Claire

'A hilarious riot'
Company

'Great characters . . . hilariously written . . . buy it!'
New Woman

arrow books

I Love Capri

Belinda Jones

**Sundrenched days, moonlit nights and Italian ice cream.
What more could a girl ask for . . .?**

Kim Rees became a translator for the glamourous jet-set lifestyle. So, five years later, how come she's ended up in a basement flat in Cardiff translating German computer games in her dressing gown? Fortunately her mother has a plan to extract her from her marshmallowy rut: a trip to the magical isle of Capri.

At first Kim refuses to wake up and smell the bougainvillea, but as she starts to succumb to the irresistible delights of cocktails on the terrace and millionaire suitors, she's surprised to realise she's changing. And when she meets a man who's tiramisu personified, she finds herself falling in love. But how far will she go to win her Romeo?

arrow books

The Paradise Room

Belinda Jones

When Amber Pepper's jeweller boyfriend Hugh asks her to join him on a business trip to the paradise islands of Tahiti she's not keen – Amber loves big jumpers and rain. She'd rather be pedalling through puddles at home in Oxford than lolling in the gel-blue waters of the South Pacific. However, the prospect of sipping Mai Tais with her long-lost friend Felicity is incentive enough to coax her on the twenty-hour flight.

Within hours of touching down on coral sands the girls venture into a seductive new world of mesmerising music, exotic black pearls and sexy strangers. And for the first time Amber falls head over flip-flops in lust, only to receive an unexpected proposal of marriage.

Will she opt for a barefoot beach wedding or cast caution – and her coconut bra – to the wind? No easy decision for a drizzle-loving gal when it's ninety degrees in the shade . . .

'As essential as your SPF 15'
New Woman

'This is definitely worth cramming in your suitcase'
Cosmopolitan

arrow books